Copyright © 2018 by B.L. Brunnemer

All rights reserved. This book or any portion thereof may not be
reproduced or used in any manner whatsoever without the express
written permission of the publisher except for the use of brief quotations
in a book review.

❀ Created with Vellum

FOUND

B.L BRUNNEMER

1

I made sure to blend in with the crowd of gawkers watching the police work in the alley. It was late, and with winter already upon Chicago not much could get me outside at night. But the news of this latest crime scene sent me running out of my apartment. Something about it didn't sit right with me. The paramedics started bringing the gurney out; it had a black body bag on it. I sighed. I knew there was no point in hoping. If someone had been injured, they would have moved faster. I waited as they made their way over the snow. Thankfully, I had managed to slide close enough to the yellow caution tape to be near the mouth of the alley as they walked by. I took a deep breath. Sulfur. It was a demon kill. I couldn't ignore this; I had to get to work.

I started moving back through the crowd when my skin began to crawl. I kept walking away from the people and down the street. Footsteps crunched in the snow behind me. Someone was following me; probably a mugger. Deciding to get this over with, I crossed the street and took the long way back to my car. If someone was following, then they'd have plenty of time to act. The footsteps continued. I kept my pace even, going so far as to pull my gray wool pea coat closed and hunched my shoulders to make myself look small and vulnerable. The footsteps still followed. I sighed as I walked into a dark alley and slowed my pace. My pulse picked up as someone followed me into the alley.

When we were far enough along to be hidden from view, I turned around. It wasn't a mugger. His dark gray suit and white dress shirt showed off his broad shoulders and chest. His white blonde hair was short on the sides, a little longer on top, but perfectly styled. His piercing golden eyes contrasted with slightly tanned skin. Something about him sent my heart pounding, my skin tingling. I'd never reacted like this to a man in my entire life. It put me on edge. I didn't know who he was, but even from almost ten feet away I could tell that he wasn't human.

"What are you?" I asked. His lips moved into a polite smile.

"I'm the same as you," he said, his voice an odd mix of authority and politeness I'd never heard before.

"Annoyed? PMSing?" I asked dryly. His left eyebrow twitched.

"Gargoyle." His voice was warm. I eyed him cautiously. Besides my parents, I'd never met another gargoyle. He stood with his hands clasped behind his back as he watched me closely.

"I didn't know there were other gargoyles in the city," I said slowly, examining him. He looked amazing in that suit but it was his face that held me. His face was perfection. Straight nose, elfin cheekbones and jawline. Just perfect masculine beauty. He would have women watching him wherever he went. Those piercing eyes met mine.

"There weren't," he said as he slowly stepped closer, his hands still clasped behind his back. "My squad only flew into the city this morning. We were sent here to investigate a rising issue." I swallowed hard. Squad? There were more of them? I tried to wrap my head around the fact there were others out there. The news knocked me off balance. I could hardly believe it. Since my parents died I'd been alone. But now ....

"I thought I was the last," I admitted in a whisper. There were others. He went still, his eyes watching me.

"No, you're not alone," he said gently. "There are others. Not as many as there used to be, but we're still here," he explained as he took another step closer. The scent of old parchment reached me. My body gave a deep, hard throb. What the heck is going on? I looked up in time to see a flare of heat in his eyes. It was only for a split second before his face was blank again.

"Where's your family?" he asked, his voice appraising.

"They're dead," I said absently, trying to understand why I was reacting this way. There was something Mum had said ....

His gaze ran over me before he looked down the alley toward the street. "Perhaps we should have this discussion out of the snow?" he suggested. I nodded.

"Um, sure, there's a café just on the corner," I replied, still a bit dazed. There were others. I wasn't alone.

"My name is Atticus." He held out his perfectly manicured hand.

"Evelyn." I reached out and shook his hand. Heat flashed through me, between my legs and over my body. Atticus grunted in pain. I jerked away and backed up. His golden eyes glowed as they watched me, my core aching, my breasts instantly heavy as I tried to catch my breath.

"It's just pheromones," he said, his voice strained and his face flushed. Was he telling me or reminding himself?

"I know," I bit out, trying to get my body under control. What was it Mum said? Something about gargoyle pheromones? I took several deep breaths and focused on the snow around me. I was in an alley in Chicago, not exactly the sexiest place on the planet. When I was calm enough, I looked at Atticus. The flush had gone from his cheeks and his face was blank as stone. "Coffee?" I suggested as I got my breath back.

"Coffee," he agreed.

We started back down the alley towards the street. The crowd had started to break up, so the sidewalk was packed. Atticus walked beside me, keeping his body between me and the street. His hand hovered over my lower back. The heat coming from him was ... different. Comforting. Why was that? Who was this male? Why did he affect me this way? What do I tell him? How much do I tell him? My parents' warning ran through my mind. Papa had come home bloody one night. Mum and Papa sent me to my room as they spoke in the parlour. Eventually, they called me down. Papa had cleaned up but there were still bruises on his face. He looked into my eyes and said, 'Don't ever trust a gargoyle named Cyrus. If you hear that name, you run. No questions, no dawdling. Do you understand?' I had followed their warnings all my life. But ... he wasn't Cyrus.

When I spotted the café I went to open the door but Atticus was there before I touched the handle. He opened the door for me automatically, as if he'd done it a thousand times. Hesitating only a moment, I moved inside. The blast of heat was nice as I pulled off my coat and headed for a small table away from the other customers. Again he was there, pulling out my chair before I could. Surprised, I sat down, trying not to breathe in his scent. Most men in this century have never been taught how to be gentlemen. It was a nice change. He moved around the table and took the seat across from me.

"I don't even know where to begin," I admitted, still off balance.

"Let's start with what you know," he said. I nodded.

"My parents educated me as much as they could before they died," I began. "I know we're the guardians of this world, that it's our duty to take down demons and any other supernatural beings that break the laws." The waiter came to our table and took our order. As he walked away Atticus met my gaze again.

"That's a solid foundation," he said as he absently un-buttoned his suit jacket. "What ...." He cleared his throat quietly. "What happened to your parents?"

"A demon killed them," I summarized. It wasn't nearly the whole story, but I wasn't about to go into detail. He nodded as if that made sense.

"I'm sorry they were taken from you." His voice was so sincere that I had to look away.

"So am I," I admitted quietly. The waiter came back with our drinks. I was adding sugar to mine when I asked, "What about your parents?"

He stopped stirring sugar into his tea. "They died. When I was ten years old." His voice was slightly rough along the edges. My heart ached for him. Did any gargoyle parent get to see their children turn one hundred?

"I'm sorry," I said softly.

His eyes rose to meet mine. "Thank you." He ran his gaze over my face before going back to his tea. "So... what have you been doing since they passed? Did you go to school?"

What an odd question. "Yes, I went to school. But I don't have a degree from this century if that is what you mean."

The corner of his lips lifted to a half grin. "A degree isn't always necessary these days." Something about the way he grinned made me want to smile back. What was it about him?

"Only if you want to work as a doctor, or a lawyer, or... well, you see what I mean," I countered.

His eyes ran over me, curious. "Did you want to be a doctor?"

"No, I was just using it as an example," I explained.

His eyes surveyed the rest of the café before going back to his tea. "Did ... did you want to?"

"Go to a university?" I smiled. "It would be interesting, though I never seem to have enough time. Not between working and keeping other species in line."

He seemed to understand that. "What kind of music do you enjoy?"

An awkward silence fell as I sipped my coffee. Why was he asking? "Um, you said your squad was sent to do an investigation. Does it have anything to do with that demon kill back there?"

"It does," he said carefully. "What do you know about the situation?"

"I know it's the third in a week; it was the first one where I could get close enough to confirm it was a demon kill. I was going to look into it when I noticed you following me," I explained. His eyes narrowed at me.

"There's no need for you to investigate," he stated. No need? Three people were dead.

"There isn't?" I asked, though his order bothered me. Was his team going to take over? The thought was actually a relief. I had enough on my plate with the store but at the same time ... this was my city, my job. I took a sip of coffee.

"No. Because I've found you things have changed," he

explained as he pulled out his phone and texted someone quickly.

I set my mug down. "What do you mean?"

He slid his phone back into the breast pocket of his suit jacket. "The Elder Council, the heads of our species, has left a standing order that bringing home females overrides any other objective. It's an old order, left over from our retreat from the cities. But it hasn't been retracted," he explained. "Getting you home safely is our job now." I went still. Did he really just say that? It was disturbing on so many levels I didn't even know where to start.

"Let me make sure I understand this," I began slowly. "You are going to ignore the demon kill, not five blocks from where you're sitting, in order to take me with you?"

He finished his sip of tea. "That is correct," he said gently. I couldn't believe this. When did the other gargoyles forget their duty? What made him believe that I would just leave with him?

"What was the order exactly?" I asked, curious.

His lips rose into a grin again. "The exact wording?" I nodded. "I believe it was, 'Bringing all of our females home is now the most important aspect of our survival.'"

"That doesn't sound like an order to me," I told him with a smile.

His grin disappeared. "Believe me, it was."

"But I'm not one of your females," I countered. "No one even knew I existed ten minutes ago."

His eyes were warm when he answered. "True, but you are still a member of our species." Darn, he had me there.

I tried logic. "I think the murdering demon requires more attention than I do. After all, the point of our species is to protect humans from them." He took a slow, deep breath and let it out before answering.

"That is true, though, we can't do that if our species dies out. There are fewer than two hundred of us left," he countered. "Did your parents tell you what happens if we die out?"

"The barriers between Heaven and Hell shatter: The Apocalypse. Basically, everyone dies," I summed up. He nodded, his gaze approving.

"With our numbers so low, we can't protect humans anymore," he explained, "especially without evidence and with a female in the field."

I sat stunned for several heartbeats before I could answer. "I smelled sulfur. And a simple trip to the morgue to examine the other bodies will give you all the evidence you need." I was ignoring the 'female in the field' part for now.

He slowly turned the mug in his hands. "I believe you did. But this order takes precedence." He met my eyes. "Unfortunately, a female's role has changed. They no longer do field work or perform investigations. They stay in our community, under guard, as they work for the survival of our species."

It took almost a full minute for his meaning to sink in. I sat up straighter. "You want to take me back to... have children?" I asked, hoping he just wasn't being clear.

He set his cup down. "These are extreme times. While it's not our normal way, with our species on the verge of extinction, the Elder Council made the difficult decision to pull all females back home and keep them there to ensure their safety."

"I'm sorry, but no," I stated, keeping my voice polite. His face became unreadable. "I'm not going to have someone's child simply because our numbers are low. If I ever have a child, it will be when I choose and with whom I choose."

"That sounds reasonable," a deep voice behind me

stated. I looked over my shoulder to see another male. From his skin tone, I could tell he was born in a desert somewhere. His black hair was long enough to fall into his silver eyes. His chiseled jaw was handsome.

"Zahur," Atticus greeted, his voice growing colder. "How'd you get here so quickly?"

"I was in the Veil in Montana. I've finally found someone to work on that issue," he stated from behind me, his gaze going to Atticus. "It didn't take much to enter the physical world here." He walked around the table and met my eyes. "Do you mind if I join you?"

"Of course not," I said.

"Who did you find?" Atticus asked, his voice oddly neutral. I eyed him. I didn't understand the change.

"A long shot," Zahur admitted, "but the only option we have at the moment."

"Who?" Atticus asked again.

"A teenage Necromancer by the name of Alexis," he admitted.

Atticus narrowed his eyes at him. "Have you lost your senses? A teenager? And a Necro at that?"

"I know, but our allies and resources are running thin at the moment," Zahur pointed out.

"Has she even reached the Veil?" Atticus asked in a patient voice.

"Not yet."

"Zahur." Atticus's voice was stern.

"Then you find someone. Good luck. I've looked everywhere and you damn well know we can't do it," Zahur countered, clearly done with the conversation.

"Why can't you fix whatever this problem is?" I asked, curious.

"We can't interfere if some human throws things out of

balance, only if a supernatural does. It's part of the contracts between Heaven, Hell and Earth," Zahur explained, his voice tired. The waiter came to the table, Zahur ordered coffee.

After the waiter left, he looked me over. "So, you're our latest female," he said. "It's not an easy job."

"I'm not having children just to shore up numbers," I repeated, my voice firm. He raised an eyebrow.

"Interesting," Zahur muttered. "I don't recognize you. What's your family name?"

My pulse picked up. "De Haven," I lied. I didn't know him; I wasn't about to tell anyone my real last name.

Zahur eyed me, his eyes searching. "I've never heard of that name."

"I wasn't raised with the rest of our species," I countered.

"Yes, but Zahur is over two thousand years old," Atticus announced. "He remembers every gargoyle bloodline there was." My shoulders grew tense. I started playing with the locket on my necklace; it helped calm me. I needed to change the subject, get them off this line of questioning.

"So, when should we expect the others?" I asked. "I imagine, since Zahur is here, you've called your squad in." They shared a look.

"I imagine that Ranulf will be here by midnight, he had a lead he was following. He took Falk with him," Zahur offered, his voice telling me that he was aware of what I was doing.

"Then we'll be on our way by one," Atticus announced. "We'll charter a plane and head back." Atticus turned to me. "We'll help you pack." Was he serious? Hadn't he heard a word I said?

"I'm not leaving," I stated quietly. They both grew still. I kept my eyes on Atticus's. "There have been three deaths in a week. I smelled sulfur. I'm going to investigate." I pulled my wallet out of my coat pocket and paid for my coffee. I got to my feet then met Atticus's eyes again. "The way a gargoyle should."

"It's crucial that you return with us. You need to be trained in your abilities and meet the other males at the very least," Atticus said, his voice strained.

"I'm not going with you," I said politely. "As for my abilities? I'm trained." I pulled on my jacket. "It was nice meeting you." I turned and left the cafe.

∼

Zahur

I WATCHED as the female walked away before turning to Atticus. He was rubbing his eyes with one hand, his mouth a tight line. I bit back a smile. It wasn't often the strongest gargoyle in existence was reprimanded by someone not even half his age. It was rarer still for Atticus not to fire back. I looked back at the door she left through. When I had come in Atticus seemed oddly relaxed yet tense at the same time. Interesting.

The waiter brought my coffee. I added sugar as Atticus sat quietly, his unfocused eyes on the window. Atticus sighed deeply and picked up his tea.

"Tell me about the Necromancer," he ordered. I finished my sip before answering.

"She's seventeen," I admitted. His gaze snapped to me, his eyes sharp. "I found her while she was trying to reach her Center. Before that, I had a word with her True Self." Atticus's face was blank as a board.

"Is she up to the task?" he asked directly.

"Without a doubt," I answered. "It won't be an easy road for her. But she... has an interesting future ahead of her." Atticus looked at his tea, his gaze unfocused.

"Why did she need to meet with her True Self?" he asked. Damn. I'd hoped he'd missed that one.

"She unmade a soul and it affected her," I admitted. Those golden eyes flashed at me. "It was trying to kill her, Atticus. What else could she have done?" I went back to my coffee. The girl did nothing but use the knowledge she had at the time to survive. We sat in silence as I finished my coffee quickly then looked back to him. "Now, how did you piss off our latest female?" Atticus gave me that blank face of his.

"She didn't react the way I expected," he admitted in a controlled voice. "The other females we've found were happy to give up fighting to go home."

"Who is she?" I asked. Atticus took a drink of his tea.

"Her name is Evelyn. She was raised out among humans it seems," he said. "Her parents are dead. One of us needs to follow her." I nodded.

"I don't think it should be you," I told him. "You seem to make her angry." Not to mention that I wanted to see if I could get more information out of her. I got to my feet and dropped a five on the table before heading out to the street.

Atticus

As soon as Zahur was out the door I took a deep breath. It was her. I looked at my tea and tried to think. A part of me was still reeling. The other was trying not to smile. For the first time in centuries, there was a reason to hope. My mind ran over our conversation. I closed my eyes and cursed. 'What kind of music do you enjoy?' Really, Atticus? What is wrong with you? You are almost five hundred years old. Normally, seducing females was easy; it came naturally. But with her? I sighed and looked out the window. Talking to her, all my experience disappeared in a puff of smoke. My entire life had just changed, and for once, it was for the better.

Wanting to smile, I pulled my phone out of my suit jacket pocket. I hit the name I was looking for and waited.

"Yes," the male's voice demanded.

"I've found her," I stated. And she was more than I ever expected.

Cyrus sighed. "Good. Bring her home tonight."

"She doesn't want to leave. There's what looks like a demon kill in the city; she intends to investigate," I explained, trying not to bristle at the order.

"I don't care what you have to do. Get her back here," Cyrus growled. He might not care, but I did. I wasn't about to drag her back to the community if she didn't want to go.

"She's also my Match." My body grew tense as the silence stretched.

"Listen to me, Atticus." Cyrus's tone was hard. "You are in a dangerous situation. Keep her at arm's length, otherwise you risk losing your self-control. Do you understand?"

The world stopped. No. I wouldn't ... not with her. This was my only chance. I swallowed hard. "I'm not my parents," I told him.

"But you are of your parents' bloodlines," he reminded me. "Remember what happened to them?"

"Yes," I answered. I'd never forget it. Cyrus made sure of it. Everything in me was screaming that he was wrong. That I could handle it. But if I was mistaken, she'd be the one to pay the price. He was right. I couldn't have her. I closed my eyes as every hope I ever had flickered out. What did I expect? Something good in my life? That was for other gargoyles, not me.

"You can't be with her and keep control," Cyrus lectured. "Do you understand?"

"Yes, sir."

Evelyn

As I DROVE out of the garage in my '68 Shelby Mustang my skin crawled. I knew that feeling. I was being followed, again. I checked my mirrors but found no car sticking close. Then I adjusted my sidemirror to look up. About eight hundred feet above someone was flying, though I couldn't see their wings. Odd. I drove to the parking lot behind the hospital and parked. I was getting out as I watched a dark figure drop to the ground, landing out of sight. I leaned against the car, crossed my arms over my stomach and waited.

Zahur stepped out into the light, pulling on his shirt.

"You're not very good at tailing someone," I pointed out.

"My specialty isn't flying," he bit out.

I raised an eyebrow. "Then what is?"

Zahur started to button his white linen shirt. While he got dressed I couldn't help but take a peek. Broad muscled shoulders, tapered waist, narrow hips, big arms and ripped beyond belief. I waited as he finished buttoning his shirt over all that bronze skin. Those silver eyes met mine. With Atticus gone my body had finally calmed down. What was it about that male? I eyed Zahur. And why didn't Zahur affect me that way? Did we have to touch for it to really affect me? I wish I knew.

"I mainly work in the Ether, the plane between this world and the others," Zahur announced as he tucked his hand into the pocket of his jeans and pulled out his cellphone, "so I don't get a lot of flight time." He texted while I stepped away from my car and headed for the back door of the hospital. He followed.

"Why are you following me?" I asked as I reached the door and pulled out my wallet.

"One of us needs to stay with you until we head back home," he grumbled, putting his phone back. I turned and gave him another smile, hoping he'd warm up.

"I'm one hundred and eighty-six years old," I informed him. "I can take care of myself." Zahur eyed me.

"Most gargoyles die before they reach two hundred simply because they are cocky," he informed me. My smile disappeared. "Besides, it's protocol for all females now." I didn't know what to say to that. It wasn't that I didn't want Zahur around. Having another gargoyle around was a nice change, even if he was crabby. It was just... odd.

"It's not my protocol," I pointed out as I found the card I was looking for.

"Technically, it is," he said. I shook my head as I ran the card through the slider. The light turned green, I opened the door and walked in. He followed. I flashed him a grin over my shoulder.

"I grew up with humans, remember?" I reminded him.

"How is it that you grew up away from our home?" he asked as he walked beside me down the hall. I thought about how to answer.

"My parents left your people behind and Mom had me

after," I summed up as we entered the stairwell. I headed for the basement.

"Must have been lonely, not getting to play with other kids," he offered. I smiled.

"I played with other kids, they were just human." I opened a door and left the stairwell.

"Really?" he asked, intrigued. "What happened when you flashed fang or your wings?" Voices echoed down the hall. I grabbed his arm and managed to pull him into the closet and close the door before the two police officers came around the corner.

"Huh," I muttered. I eyed him, surprised I didn't have the same reaction to Zahur as I did to Atticus.

"Why are we in the closet?" he asked dryly.

"The police and I don't have the best working relationship," I said quietly as I listened at the door.

"That explains the dash." He joined me at the door. "Now what was with that look?"

"Nothing," I said absently. "I just expected the same reaction I got with Atticus." He straightened. The police were gone. I stepped out of the closet and started down the bare hallway. Zahur followed.

"What reaction was that?" he asked quietly as we turned another corner.

"Oh, nothing, just a ... jolt," I hedged.

"Have you ever heard of the term The Matching?" Zahur asked casually.

I shook my head as we kept going down the hall. "No, I don't think I have. Why?"

"No reason," he muttered. "Since I *am* in charge of your safety, would you mind telling me where we're going?"

"The morgue," I explained with a sweet smile. "I need to get a look at the other victims."

2

EVELYN

The morgue reeked. With my heightened senses I smelled everything: decomposing bodies, antibacterial soap, the chemicals the janitor used tonight. And it always gave me a headache. It was my lucky night though as Brian, my favorite orderly, was working tonight. I opened the door to the morgue and stuck my head in. There was only Brian at one of the tall tables with a black body bag on it. Since it was clear of police, I walked in.

"Hi, Brian," I greeted cheerfully. He jumped, then chuckled. Brian was your average guy: dark brown hair, nice puppy dog eyes in an oval face. His addiction to video games in his off hours hadn't helped his physique any. At twenty-three he was already sporting a small beer belly.

"You scared the hell out of me, Evie," he told me, shaking his head. "Can't you make some noise?" His gaze went over my shoulder to Zahur.

"Sorry, I had to duck into a closet to avoid the police. I was worried there were still some in here," I admitted as I moved to stand across from him at the table. "I need to examine a few strange deaths."

Brian's gaze hadn't left Zahur. "Who's that?"

"Don't worry. That's Zahur," I stated. "He's like me."

"Evelyn-"

"Another P.I.?" Brian played dumb as he turned back to me. "I've never known you to work with a partner." I shrugged.

"Well, he is rather handsome company. What girl could say no to that?" I offered, smiling. Brian looked at Zahur and gave him the once-over.

"Not me, honey," he admitted. I smiled at the dumbfounded look on Zahur's face. Poor guy. I turned back to Brian.

"I need to look at the murder victim from tonight, near West Madison Street, and the other two that are similar," I announced. Brian's smile faded.

"The one from tonight hasn't been through forensics," he said. I pulled gloves out of the box on the wall.

"I'll be careful," I assured him. "You know me - paranoid."

He sighed. "I'll get the other two out." Brian walked off.

Before I did anything else I pulled a hair tie out of my pocket and put my long hair into a tight bun on top of my head. The last thing I needed was one of my hairs to get picked up in a murder investigation. That'd just bring up all kinds of trouble. After my hair was secured, I pulled on my gloves. Zahur moved to the head of the table.

"What exactly are we doing here?" he asked. I reached out and began unzipping the body bag.

"We are looking at the bodies of the victims to figure out what kind of demon did this. We're also getting solid evidence for Atticus," I explained as I finished unzipping the bag. I looked at him and pointed. "Please, don't touch anything." I went back to the head of the table and began to open the bag. Brian joined us just in time to help me lift the flap of the bag carefully.

The body was that of a young woman; she couldn't have been older than nineteen. I sighed as Brian went to get the paperwork. I looked at the body of the victim. Her chest was a mass of red meat and white bone. I brought the light over the table down further so I could see into the chest cavity. Some of the tissue was burned black, the rest was normal.

"Her name was-"

"Brian," I warned absently. "My face is practically in the chest cavity. It would be a bad time to give it a name." The ribs were broken and hinged, some of them twice, facing two different directions. I angled the light again to get a better look at her organs. Her heart was missing, all that was left were three thick scorched lines in the surrounding tissue and organs. I blinked. Three? My stomach dropped as I stood up. Three, not five.

That wasn't good. I walked around to the next table where Brian had brought out another victim. Another girl around the same age. I adjusted the light and looked into the pulverized remains of her chest cavity. Same as the first. Troubled, I straightened.

"Three, not five," I mumbled as I walked around the table to the next body. Another young girl. The same destroyed chest cavity, the same missing heart. Three more burns against the surrounding tissue.

"Dang it," I bit out as I took off my gloves and threw them away. I turned to Brian. "I need copies of their files, please." Brian simply nodded and walked out the door. I gestured to the newest victim. "Can you take a look and tell me what you see?" I asked him. He gave me a patient look.

"There are other ways to determine if it's a demon kill," he lectured me. I gave him a patient smile.

"We already know it's a demon kill, we're looking for what kind," I reminded him. "Now, look at the wound, please." He adjusted the light and looked closely into the remains of the chest cavity. When he stood up his face was dark.

"Three scorch marks," he said. I nodded. He went on to examine each body. When he was done, he cursed in another language. It sounded old, ancient even. He turned back to me. "They all have it, which means-"

"It wasn't done by a possessed human," I finished for him. "A full demon got through the barriers."

His gaze ran over me with approval. "It would seem so." He looked back at the bodies, his face drawn. I moved back to the freshest body and pushed up the sleeves of my shirt and coat. I took several deep breaths and reached out to touch her forehead. A dark hand stopped me. I looked up, surprised.

"What are you doing?" he bit out, his eyes hard.

"Looking at her last memories," I answered. Wasn't it obvious? Zahur looked at me, his face furious.

"Do you understand how dangerous that is?" he asked as he straightened to his full height. "They can suck you in and kill you too."

"If you make a mistake, yes, it's dangerous," I explained as I met his eyes. "I don't make mistakes." He stepped between me and the gurney.

"No," he stated, an accent starting to come through. "It is too dangerous. Especially for..."

"For?" I asked.

He clenched his jaw. "For a female. Right now, there are only a few of you left." I blinked in surprise. "I know if you do this, you could find out exactly what killed these women. But I still can't let you."

"You just met me, Zahur," I reminded him. "You don't really know me or my abilities."

"I'm aware of that," he whispered. "My job is to keep you safe. Letting you do this wouldn't be keeping you safe." The look in his eyes was serious. He wasn't going to let me do this. I pulled my hand from his.

"Alright," I said, my voice resigned. "I won't look at her memories. Let's just get the files and go." When he looked at me relief filled his eyes, it almost made me feel guilty. He moved away from the gurney towards the door to the coroner's office. When he was far enough away, I turned and put my hand on the dead girl's forehead.

"No!"

I dove my mind into what was left of hers. It was dark, her mind was decomposing, the memory banks dying out. It was like spelunking with a candle, and it took time. I dove deeper until I found the last flicker. I cupped my mental hands around the spark and breathed into it, giving it the energy it needed to come back to life. When it was large and glowing in my hands I threw it above me.

I was on the sidewalk, coming home from a party. Drunk and weaving, I decided to take the shortcut through the alley. It was dark, but I could see because of lights from the buildings. It wasn't so bad. I wiped the tears from my face. The picture of Brent in bed with my best friend Stacy filled my mind again. How could she do that to me? My heart ached as I weaved through the alley. A loose brick dropped from one of the buildings and smashed onto the concrete. I jumped, my pulse raced. I walked faster. We'd been friends since we were four, how could she do that to me? There was a sound. A scrape of something on stone. I went still, fear crawling through me. A warm breeze ran over the back of my neck. I froze. Then turned slowly. It was huge; long-limbed with black eyes. I jerked. It was hard to breathe. I looked down and couldn't understand what I was seeing. Its forearm was against my chest as if... Agony tore through me as the monster started digging around. It jerked its arm out of my chest. Time to go!

I jerked myself out of her mind and back to mine. I fell backward. Warm arms caught me against a hard body. I shook as I tried to stand, only my legs weren't having it. Someone was saying something in an old language as they picked me up and carried me away from the table. It came back to me. Oh yeah - the morgue, Zahur. He was so not going to be happy with me. He set me down in Brian's desk chair. His hands went to my face; I opened my eyes. He knelt on the floor, his eyes angry.

"I'm alright. Just give me a minute," I told him wearily. "It's not every day you feel your heart ripped out." His hands dropped from my face to the chair's armrests.

"What were you thinking?" he growled. He waited until I was ready. It didn't take long.

"It's a Hunger demon," I announced. "This one obviously likes hearts."

He closed his eyes, sighed, then he looked at me again. "Why did you risk it?" he asked, his voice firm. His question bothered me.

"Because what matters is finding what killed those girls and dealing with it," I reminded him. "That's our job. Our purpose." I ran my eyes over his face before meeting his again. "Or have other gargoyles forgotten that?" Brian came through the door before he could answer. I didn't look away from his gaze until Brian held the files between us. I took them and gave Brian a smile. "Thank you, Brian." Zahur got to his feet and stepped away.

"No problem," Brian said as I got to my feet. I headed for the door, Zahur not far behind.

We were halfway out of the hospital before he broke the silence. "I agree with you." I was so surprised I stopped in the middle of the empty hallway. I simply looked up at the male who was almost a foot taller than me. "I want to find the Hunger demon that did this and do my job," he stated as he met my gaze. "But we can't disobey an order from the Elder Council. There are rules we have to follow, procedure, red tape-"

"Those are rules *you* have to follow," I reminded him. "I don't know the Elder Council and they don't know me." I started walking for the exit again. He sighed.

"You make a fair point," he said. "Are you really a Private Investigator?"

"Yes and no," I explained. "I got the license so I have a cover for being here and poking around."

He eyed me. "By the way, where did you get that card that let you into the hospital?"

"I borrowed it," I hedged.

"You stole it."

"I did not." I waited a beat. "Brian did." He chuckled. I smirked.

"Brian stole it?" he asked as we turned into another hallway.

"Not really. He gets one every few months, gives it to me and then goes to the office and says he lost his." I shrugged.

He was quiet as we stepped outside. My smile dimmed. Atticus was leaning against a Mercedes with his arms crossed over his chest. Why did he have to be so good looking? I took a deep calming breath as I strode towards him. He straightened. Why did he look so much taller now? He was only a half a foot taller than me. How did I not notice that before? Why was I noticing it now? When I was close enough, I handed the files to him. He took them reluctantly.

"It's a Hunger demon and I'd say it's just getting warmed up," I said. "Do you still think there isn't any evidence?" Atticus adjusted the files before he examined them. It didn't take long before he looked at me again.

"No, you were right. There's a demon in the city," he admitted, his voice colder than before. He turned to Zahur. "We're going to need a base of operations."

"Do we have property left in the city?" Zahur asked.

Atticus shook his head. "No, we sold everything when we pulled out."

"If you're going to investigate this, then you and your team can stay at my place until you can find your own," I volunteered before I realized what I was doing.

"Thank you, we appreciate it," Atticus accepted before I could take it back. Dang it. I gave them my address as I took a key off my chain and handed it to Zahur.

"Where are you going?" Zahur asked as I walked to my car.

I opened my driver door. "I'm going to spread the word, let the other species know what's going on." And I really needed some space from Atticus. My body was practically humming. "I'll meet you at my apartment."

STILL SEEING the memories from the dead girl, I drove over to my favorite bar, The Bloody Moon. It was actually a were-wolf bar, but my best friend owned it and had my back whenever I was in need of a night out. I parked my car across the street from the bar and headed in.

The bar was in the basement of what had, at some point, been a bank. Astrid kept the safe for a cool off room when one of her pack members got a little rowdy. As I walked up to the door I passed werewolves who were three feet taller than me, but they mostly ignored me. A couple of the nicer ones recognized me and said hi. I said hi back before opening the door. Inside it was a different story; grumbling ran through the crowd as I moved through it. I ignored the werewolves. No one sane would lay a finger on me here. First, I've already proven that I could more than hold my own. Second, I gave them a heads-up whenever something nasty was in town. Third, Astrid would ban them from the bar. And wolves loved their beer. I made my way to the bar and snagged a stool. Astrid was down at the other end of the bar. I let out a loud whistle.

"Hey, sexy momma, can't I get a little love?" I called down the bar. Astrid turned and flipped me off. I smiled. Astrid was a beautiful werewolf. Crazy, but in a good way. In our world you'd have to be crazy to be friends with a gargoyle. Astrid finished with her customer and made her way down to me. Her skin-tight jeans showed off her long legs, and her blood red tank top accented the red streaks in her blonde hair. She stopped to fill a glass on her way over.

"Hey, hot stuff," Astrid greeted me as she handed over the frosty glass. Her eyes ran over me. "You look as pale as a blood-sucker. What's going on?"

"Did you hear about the two dead girls in the last week?" My voice sounded tired even to me. She nodded. "It's now three. I just went through the latest victim's death memory." Astrid's eyes grew wide as I took a deep drink.

"Ouch," she said before reaching under the counter and putting a tumbler in front of me. Astrid grabbed the best bottle of whiskey in the bar and poured me a double. "On the house, baby." I took it gratefully. The liquid burned my throat, but I welcomed it. It was a good distraction from the images running through my head.

"How bad was it?" Astrid asked. I set the glass down.

"Ever wonder what it feels like to get your heart ripped out of your chest? Literally?" I asked dryly. "Because I don't need to wonder anymore."

Astrid responded by pouring me another double. I drank it down. "Did you figure out what it was?" I nodded before I met her hazel eyes.

"It's a Hunger demon in full form." I didn't bother to whisper. They were werewolves, they'd hear me anyway. The males next to me were suddenly interested. "His victim profile is female, around nineteen years old. He finds them alone and takes the heart." I looked to my right to Edgar. The large man had triplet daughters who were around eighteen. "Keep your girls at home after dark," I warned him.

The big burly werewolf nodded to me before putting his beer down and heading out. His girls were probably out tonight. Several other customers made a beeline for the door. When the rush was over the bar was half empty.

I looked up at Astrid. "Sorry."

She shook her head. "Are you kidding? If they didn't go on their own I would have closed down the bar." I took another drink of my beer.

"There's also a squad of gargoyles in town," I told her quietly. Astrid's jaw dropped.

"Bloody moon, did you get to talk to them?" she asked, excited. Astrid knew that I hadn't met another gargoyle except my parents. I nodded.

"It didn't go the way I thought it would," I admitted.

Astrid lost her smile. "What's going on, sexy?" I looked around the bar at all the ears listening. I pulled out my cell and texted Astrid.

Evelyn: Don't tell anyone but our species is dying out. They came to investigate, but once they met me the mission changed, to take me with them.

Astrid cursed at her phone. She typed away, hitting the screen harder than she needed to.

Astrid: And just leave a fully formed Hunger demon here to feed? Seriously?

Evelyn: Right? Anyway, I convinced them to stay and investigate the demon.

Astrid's laugh had me looking up from my phone.

"Where are they staying?" she asked with a smirk.

I cringed. "I kind of volunteered my place."

Astrid gaped at me. "Seriously?"

"I don't know what happened. They were talking and all of a sudden the words came out," I admitted. She slammed her fist on the bar in a fit of laughter. I shrugged. "I'm blaming Atticus."

She was wiping the tears from her eyes as she asked, "Who's he?"

"Their squad leader. There's something different about him," I admitted.

"What?" She smiled.

"I don't know, we shook hands and I... was affected," I hedged, my face warming.

"We have something like that. It tells us who our Mate is," Astrid said, her eyes bright with mischief. "Let me guess, you got all hot and bothered?"

"Hot and bothered is an understatement," I muttered before taking a drink. Astrid smiled. I giggled.

"Did your mom ever talk about how she married your dad?" she asked before taking a drink of her beer.

"Nothing out of the ordinary," I summed up. There was more but that's not what she was asking about.

"I wonder if your species has something like we do for finding our Mates." She smiled. "Oh, this should be fun to watch. It's been a while for you."

"Astrid," I chided. She just winked at me. My face grew warm. "He's rather arrogant."

"I think you can handle him." Astrid smirked. "Go have some fun."

I smiled and took another drink. I had just set down the glass when a big body moved to the side Edgar had vacated. I looked up. It was Chad Harrison. Werewolf and jerk extraordinaire. The guy hated me and the feeling was mutual.

"Chad, to what do I owe the honor?" I asked dryly. The werewolf was tall and burly. His face had a large brow and jaw.

"What are you doing here, gargoyle? Shouldn't you be off sitting on a church somewhere?" Chad asked. I almost choked on my beer. That was actually funny. My species could hibernate for centuries, and since we turned to stone when we did, we used churches as a way to hide in plain sight. At least, that's what Dad had told me.

"That was a good one, Chad," I admitted. "Shouldn't you be chasing your own tail somewhere? Licking yourself?" Astrid started laughing as did a few others. Chad's jaw clenched. I'd gotten to him.

"You shouldn't be here," he growled. I was suddenly surrounded. I kept my eyes on Chad.

"This is my bar and I say who is welcome and who isn't," Astrid growled.

"It's a pack bar, and she's not pack," someone growled from behind me. Great. I tucked my phone into my pocket and stood up. Three of Chad's lackeys surrounded me.

"Do we really want to do this, boys?" I asked in a patronizing voice. In response the one behind me grabbed my shoulder. I instantly raised my foot and slammed it into Chad's gut, knocking him away. Astrid jumped over the bar. The hand on me disappeared. I turned to the last one. He swung, I tasted blood. Adrenaline burned through me. I turned back to him. He swung again. I blocked and sent my right hook to his cheek then landed an uppercut to his side, hearing the satisfying sound of ribs breaking. The force of my hit caused him to double over; I took the opening he left and broke his nose on my knee. He groaned as he crumpled to the ground. A hand dug into my hair and yanked me back.

"Hair pulling? Really?" I growled before I drove an elbow into his gut. His breath whooshed out of him as I turned and clocked him. Chad's nose burst as he went into the bar. Another tried to grab me from behind. I flipped him over my shoulder to the floor, then kicked him in the face. I turned around; the bar had broken into an all-out brawl. I spotted Astrid and started to stride in. A hand grabbed me and spun me into a tall, hard body. Heart slamming, I looked up into a pair of turquoise eyes. He was striking, there was no other way to describe him. Wide cheekbones, a strong jaw. Wild, thick, dark blonde hair that was down to his shoulders. And he was a gargoyle. Those eyes were sharp as they ran over my face.

"Stay safe and out of the fight, lass. Let us handle it," he told me, his Scottish accent thick. Adrenaline burned through my veins.

"I don't sit on the sidelines," I growled. He smirked.

"You've already gotten hit, any more and it'll be my hide," he stated before letting me go. I went to move around him. He blocked me. "Falk," he barked. Another gargoyle moved out of the shadows of the bar. His wavy, brown hair was wild and jaw length. He was a foot taller than me with broad shoulders, a lean build and dark eyes that stayed on me. It was, however, the thick band of scar tissue that ran the width of his throat that caught my eye. He planted himself in front of me as the other gargoyle turned and waded into the fight. I went to walk around him. He blocked me. I tried again, he stopped me again. I growled in frustration. He really wasn't going to let me back in the fight.

It wasn't long before the fight was over and the blonde and Astrid were throwing the unconscious werewolves into the back room.

The blonde male was huge, two feet taller than me I'd guess. His black shirt showed me broad shoulders and a barrel chest. His black leather pants showed off his thick legs. When he finished throwing the unconscious wolves around as if they weighed nothing he strode over to me.

"Ranulf and Falk, I presume?" I asked tiredly.

"Aye, I'm Ranulf." The big guy smiled at me. Falk just nodded.

"Are you following me?" I asked.

Ranulf chuckled. "Now, what kind of guards would we be if we didn't?" he asked, his accent thick. I sighed then walked over to Astrid.

"I'm sorry, hon-"

"Don't even worry about it, those assholes had been riding the line for days now," Astrid said. She tilted her chin at the males waiting near the door. "Those them?"

"A pair of guards apparently."

"The tall one's sexy as hell," Astrid said, smiling. I glanced back. Not my type really, but perfect for Astrid.

"I think I need to go and deal with this guard issue," I said as I paid for my beer.

Astrid smirked. "Good luck."

I shot her a playful look before I headed towards the door.

When we were out in the snow I kept walking towards my car. "How did you find me?" I asked as I buttoned up my jacket.

"We were already on the roof of the hospital when you took off," Ranulf explained. "Didn't take much to follow." I unlocked my door.

"Well, I'm going home," I announced.

"We'll see you there," Ranulf said before backing away a couple steps.

"Not if I get there first." And lock Ranulf's butt outside for sidelining me like that. This time Falk turned and eyed me.

"You're on," Falk said, his voice gravelly and hoarse. I couldn't tell if it was damaged or if he just didn't use it much. He wanted to race? This should be fun. I got in my car and peeled out of my spot.

Heart pounding, I sped through town, dodging traffic, slipping through spaces barely big enough for me. But I made it to my apartment in record time, only to find Falk leaning against the wall next to the door of my apartment building. Impressed, I pulled into the parking garage across the street. I made sure to lock the door before walking back.

"How did you do that?" I asked as I crossed the street. Falk shrugged.

"I'm fast," he said in that coarse voice.

"You need to teach me how you got that fast." I stopped at the door to the building as he eyed me.

"Do you ever fly?" he asked, his voice getting quieter as it got rougher.

"Not as often as I'd like," I admitted as I pulled out my keys. His gaze ran over me before meeting my eyes again.

"Still faster than Ranulf," he pointed out, his voice now barely above a whisper. Ranulf dropped to the sidewalk behind me. His wings were brown and his feathers were large but I didn't have a chance to get a really good look before they were again in his skin in a wings tattoo down his back. When he stood I noticed that scars covered the sculpted muscles of his barrel chest and abdomen. I wonder what caused them.

"She didn't have to avoid the high rises, I did," Ranulf pointed out before he pulled his shirt out of his belt loop and pulled it on.

"Excuses, excuses," I taunted. He shot me a look that made me smile. I turned, opened the door with the key fob and headed upstairs to my apartment. "I take it you guys are staying with me too?"

"Aye, lass."

I was still smiling as I reached the third floor. My apartment door was unlocked and open. Recognizing the voices coming from inside, I stepped through the door and began to take my jacket off. Atticus and Zahur were talking in the living room area. My apartment wasn't that large. The ivory walls glowed with light from the sconces around the room. The galley kitchen area with a breakfast bar was to the left of the small foyer. The brown leather couch was across the room, facing the television over my fireplace and the floor to ceiling bookcases that flanked it. Matching leather armchairs were to the right and left of the couch. The door to my bedroom was across the apartment. With the mahogany coffee table and end tables the whole effect was homey. Atticus glanced at me as I hung up my jacket on a hook.

"You know, you guys can close the door," I stated dryly.

Zahur looked my way then did a double take as the others stepped around me.

"Are you alright?" Zahur asked, his eyes narrowing on my jaw.

I shrugged as I dropped my keys into the bowl I kept on the table near the door. "Bar fight." I walked into the apartment but didn't make it far. Zahur met me and lifted my chin. I awkwardly pulled his hand away. "I'm fine, it's only bruises. Just let me go get cleaned up," I assured him.

"Aye, she handled the werewolves rather well," Ranulf told them. Zahur and Atticus's gaze shot to Ranulf.

"Werewolves?" Atticus asked. He turned to me. "You were attacked by werewolves?"

"No, it was a bar fight in a werewolf bar," I corrected.

Atticus shared a look with the others. "We'll handle it tonight."

"What is there to handle?" I asked. "They were drunk, and they're already being punished by being banned from the bar. And you know how wolves like their beer," I said with a smile. I headed toward the bathroom to the left of my bedroom door. "I'll be out in a sec." I closed the door behind me and started the water in the faucet. I looked in the mirror. It wasn't bad, a split lip with a bruised jaw and cheekbone. I've had worse.

Atticus

SOMEONE HAD HIT HER! I reined in my temper as I turned back to the others.

"You let her go into a werewolf bar?" I asked in a deadly calm voice.

Ranulf sighed. "*Let* really isn't the word for it, boss. She was already inside before we got there." Falk shot him a look. "Fine, before *I* got there."

I turned to Falk. "Why did you allow her to go in?" Falk's posture grew tense as he pulled out his phone. My phone vibrated.

Falk: Several wolves said hi to her outside. It seemed like nothing new. I saw no safety issue.

Falk must have used what was left of his voice to talk to Evelyn. I couldn't blame him, she was ... I shoved that thought away.

"And the bar fight?" Zahur asked.

"She held her own until we got inside. And she would have been fine even if we didn't interfere," Ranulf explained.

"You don't know that," I pointed out. "From now on, she doesn't go anywhere without an escort. Understood?"

Everyone said yes. I didn't care if she liked it or not. She couldn't go walking around unguarded.

The bathroom door opened. Evelyn came out, the blood gone from the corner of her lips.

Her eyes ran over the squad. "Is anyone hungry? Thirsty?" she asked, nervously pushing up the sleeves of her blue V-neck. Everyone said no. The room was tense as she moved between all of us to the sofa.

The right side of her face was starting to bruise a little. A wolf must have gotten a shot in before Ranulf and Falk could interfere. The injuries on her face made me struggle for control. Damn it, Atticus, lock it down. Cyrus's voice rang through my mind. I planted my feet in front of the fireplace. I wasn't going to her, I wasn't going to be The Matching's bitch.

Ranulf headed to the kitchen while everyone settled on the sofa and chairs.

"Are you dizzy? Any nausea?" Zahur asked.

"I'm okay," she insisted to Zahur. Ranulf dropped to the sofa on the other side of her, then handed her the ice pack. She smiled as she took it.

"Is it starting to show?" she asked dryly.

"Aye," Ranulf said as he rested his arm along the back of the couch behind her. I fought back the impulse to knock it off the couch. Rein it in Atticus!

"Thanks." She held the pack to her face.

"We've got a Hunger demon in the city with three kills," I announced. My gaze went to Evelyn. "I want one of us with you at all times, as a precaution." Her shoulders grew tense as she let out a calming breath.

"I don't think that's necessary," she said.

I ignored her. It was the only safe thing to do. "We'll be using Evelyn's apartment as our base of operations."

"Until you find your own place," she added quickly.

"So, we're staying?" Ranulf asked. My eyes ran over Evelyn. Her presence here concerned me.

"Since Evelyn is refusing to leave, we have to stay and protect her," I explained. "Which gives us the chance to stay in the city and take care of the Hunger demon."

"Is the Council going to go along with that?" Zahur asked from his end of the couch.

"They understand that a female not raised in our culture will need to take time to trust us," I hedged before looking at all of them.

"You didn't mention the Hunger demon, did you?" she asked with a mischievous grin.

I ignored her and continued. "In the morning, we'll go to the local Templars and see what they know."

"The Templars? Who are they?" Evelyn asked. Everyone looked at her in surprise.

I was the first to recover. "The Templars have been the eyes of our species since their inception in 1278. Their purpose was to help us control all supernatural races." I turned to Zahur. "Zahur, find where it came through the barrier and seal it."

"I will." Zahur's voice was hard. Evelyn frowned then looked back to me.

"And how is he going to do that?" she asked.

Zahur explained "Remember, I work in the Ether between dimensions. With the Veil shut-"

"Wait, what's the Veil?" she asked instantly. Stunned, I ran my eyes over her. This was basic education for any gargoyle. What had her parents taught her?

"It's the, well, portal, for lack of a better word. It's where the dead cross over into the next world," Ranulf explained. "And someone has closed it off. Which means-"

"The dead can't cross," she finished for him. He nodded. She was quick.

"Right. With it closed, the energy level in this world is building and causing cracks to form in the barriers between Earth, Heaven and Hell," I explained, trying to be patient. "And these cracks are the perfect opportunity for demons and angels to cross into this world."

"My skills keep me in the Ether as a guard," Zahur added. She looked up at him.

"You stop them," she said. He nodded.

"It hasn't left me a lot of time in this world. I'm rarely here anymore." Zahur told her dryly.

"I get why no demons, but why keep angels out?" she asked. There was silence as I exchanged looks with Falk. I had to know.

"Evelyn," I got her attention. "What exactly did your parents teach you?" She sat a little straighter.

"My education was focused in a different area," she hedged.

"And what area was that?" I asked politely. She looked up at me, her eyes shadowed.

"How to stay alive," she said quietly. She looked at each of us. "I'm not going to be much good for this meeting, so I'll just go get ready for bed." She got up before I could say a word. "The couch is a pullout and there are sheets, blankets and pillows in the linen closet to the left of the bathroom," she offered before walking into the bathroom.

Everyone was silent until we heard the shower turn on. Then we all cursed.

"She doesn't even have the basic education," Falk snapped in his gravelly voice, furious.

"But she has training in her abilities." Zahur offered. "She jumped into that girl's last memory like a pro."

"Aye, and she handled herself in the bar," Ranulf added. "There's training there too." I shook my head. This didn't make sense.

"She knows what we were created for. Even reminded me that our job was to protect humans," Zahur told us.

"All advanced education but no basic," I muttered. I rubbed my eyes with one hand. It made no sense. "We'll definitely need to keep a guard on her."

Zahur eyed me. "Anything you want to tell us, Atticus?"

Ranulf raised an eyebrow. My face was hard as I met Zahur's eyes. "I don't know what you mean."

Zahur smirked. "Anything about a certain female who's in the shower?"

"What are you going on about?" Ranulf asked, looking from Zahur to my hard face.

"How do you know?" I growled. How did he figure it out?

"Observation," Zahur said. "She doesn't know." My shoulders relaxed.

"What the devil are you two talking about?" Ranulf snapped.

"Nothing," I said coldly. This was none of their business and it had even less to do with their jobs.

Zahur smirked. "She's his Match."

Ranulf's jaw dropped. "No ... no, not that little spitfire." He looked back to meet my hard gaze. His eyes grew wide, then he started laughing.

"And she doesn't know?" Ranulf asked, still laughing.

"I asked if she knew the term The Matching," Zahur explained. "She said she didn't."

"And she won't," I announced. Everyone went still.

"You're not going to tell her?" Ranulf asked incredulously.

"This is just going to get in the way," I told him. Ranulf looked at me as if I had lost my mind.

"Aye, a female who could become your Mate after centuries of being alone," Ranulf said sarcastically. "What a pain in the arse." My gaze snapped to his.

"That's not what I said," I pointed out calmly.

"You're going to have to take her out on a date," Zahur stated.

"Dates? Like the fruit?" Ranulf asked. Falk let out a laugh that sounded more like a cough. Ranulf grabbed the small pillow behind his back and threw it at him. Falk caught it as his shoulders were shaking, telling me he was still laughing.

"You're over thirteen hundred years old," Zahur said, his voice exasperated. "Tell me you've actually taken a female out on a date."

"If it's not the fruit, then what the hell is a date?" Ranulf growled. Everyone but me bit back a smile. My mind was on the sound of the shower. How long did we have before she got out and could hear us again?

My phone vibrated. I pulled it out and checked it.

Falk: It's when you take a female out, to a meal, a movie, and you get to know her. It's how modern couples get to know each other.

Why did he send this to *me*? I read out loud what Falk sent.

"Oh," Ranulf grumbled as I looked up at them. "Scots don't date. We're rather upfront about it all."

"It's not your problem," Zahur reminded Ranulf. Ranulf chuckled.

"Falk and I will take the first watch," I announced. "Get some sleep."

I stepped away from the fireplace to a window and looked out while they started making room to open the sofa bed. I watched the traffic on the street.

My mind was busy running through ways to keep her from finding out about The Matching and Mates. The others would keep their mouths shut, but Zahur ... that male liked to meddle.

The shower shut off. Standing this close to her bedroom wall I had no choice but to listen to her get ready for bed. She hummed softly as she moved around her bedroom. It was a nice soft sound. I pulled back from that thought.

As time passed, she moved around in bed enough that I wondered if she was ever going to go to sleep. When her breathing finally became deep and even I let out a deep breath.

As the night went on I thought about those shadows in her eyes, and wondered what put them there.

3

DECEMBER 16

I woke up to sunlight shining on my face. I rolled over and stretched. There were already noises on the other side of my door. The males must be awake. I stared up at my ceiling and thought about them. Or, about one of them in particular. I rubbed my eyes and tried to understand what it was about him that kept getting my attention He'd been on my mind since I went into the bathroom. Then to bed. And while in bed. It had taken a while to fall asleep, but exhaustion had finally won out. Well. Lying in bed all day wasn't going to get me any answers. I got up and went to get dressed.

A while later I came out of my bedroom in dark jeans, a white long-sleeved scoop neck shirt, and dark tan knee-high boots. My hair was back in a pony tail down my back.

Atticus was washing a dish in the sink. He was in another suit, a severe black one, with a white button-down shirt and no tie. His white hair was styled the same as yesterday. Again, he was perfect. Not a wrinkle or hair out of place. How did he manage that?

"Morning," I greeted him as I pulled out my kettle.

Atticus moved around to sit on a stool at the breakfast bar while I filled the kettle with water.

"Morning," he said gruffly. Was he having a bad morning?

I set the kettle on the stove and turned the burner on high. I pulled out my good tea bags. By the time I dished up my plate with eggs and toast the kettle was whistling. I set my plate down and picked up the kettle.

"Where is everyone?" I asked as I poured boiling water into my mug.

"They are running a sweep at the moment," Atticus said absently. I picked up my plate, silverware and tea before I moved around the counter to sit on the stool next to him.

"Why so early?" I asked before taking a bite.

He took a deep breath. "We run a morning sweep to find any demons taking cover from the dawn."

"Good idea," I said as I continued eating. They weren't going to find anything. I had my own people out doing patrols. Well, not exactly *people.*

I could feel his eyes on me as I took out my teabag, then added milk and sugar to my tea. His silence was unnerving. "How'd you sleep last night? I know a sofa bed isn't the most comfortable place to sleep," I said as I tried to make conversation.

"We managed." He picked up his coffee and took a drink.

"Alright." I gave up, he was just going to be grouchy this morning.

"We've already managed to rent the apartment across the hall," he announced. "So, you will have your privacy. But there will still be one of us in here at night to guard you."

I ignored the guard part, I didn't want to argue about it

right now. "And you won't be sleeping on a couch," I reminded him. He nodded cautiously.

"That is also a benefit," he admitted quietly. I went back to eating my breakfast and drinking my tea. When I was finished he broke the silence.

"Evelyn, the team has a meeting with the Templars in thirty minutes," he said carefully. "Would you like to join us?"

I thought about who could take an emergency shift at the store. "If I can get someone to cover the store that soon." I pulled out my cell phone.

"What store?" he demanded.

"The one downstairs in the building, to the west."

"The bookstore? You work there?" he asked, surprised.

"No, I own it." I looked down my phone and called Rina.

"Hey Evie." Rina's voice was sleepy.

"Hi, I need an emergency cover." I didn't bother beating around the bush.

"Another shift? Hell yeah," she said cheerfully.

"You're a life saver. Mr. Gallagher should be coming in to pick up Ulysses by James Joyce. It's the 1935 Limited Editions Club signed by Matisse. It's sealed in the sold safe. If he wants to examine it-"

"Make him wear the gloves," Rina finished for me.

"Yes, and the price is set. No negotiation. If he tries, call me," I reminded her.

"I got it boss."

"Thanks hon, bye." I hung up the phone then turned to Atticus. "Thank goodness for great employees." He was watching me. "What?"

He narrowed his eyes on me. "I thought the big book-stores would have put all the smaller ones out of business by now. You must have loyal customers."

I smiled. "I sell antique books, first editions. I even broker deals between customers all over the world occasionally." He ran an assessing gaze over me. "And yes, I do have loyal customers."

"Hmm." He turned his attention back to his coffee. "You know, if you came back with us you would have unlimited resources for books."

I smiled, hesitating. "That sounds nice," I hedged. "But, I'm still not leaving with the demon on the loose."

He nodded once. "That's understandable."

I got up and took my dishes to the sink. When I turned around he was on his feet.

"We need to go," he announced before turning and heading for the door.

As I followed, Atticus picked up my gray wool pea coat and held it out for me to put on. I smiled to myself as I let him help me with my coat.

"Thank you," I said quietly. Atticus didn't have a jacket, just like the others last night. I turned around and asked. "Why don't you or the others wear jackets?"

His gaze snapped to mine. "Because we can regulate our body temperature at will," he said matter-of-factly. His eyes narrowed on me. "Did your parents not teach you that?"

I finished closing my jacket. "Yes, but coats help you blend in," I pointed out. "Anyone not wearing a coat in winter is going to garner some attention."

His face was thoughtful he held the door open for me. I stepped into the hallway and waited for him to close the door. I followed him downstairs and outside. He had managed to find parking on the street last night, which seemed like magic to me. I climbed into the sleek Mercedes. It smelled new; I was betting it was a rental. Atticus slid in on the other side and started the car.

"How old were you when your parents died?" he asked. I looked at him in surprise.

"Seventeen," I answered. "I still miss them sometimes." The car grew silent.

When the car was warmed up, he pulled out into traffic. "'Death is not the greatest loss in life. The greatest loss is what dies inside us while we live,'" he muttered under his breath so softly I barely caught it.

"Norman Cousins. Interesting choice," I said, looking out the window. "I would have gone with Longfellow. 'There is no grief like the grief that does not speak.'" I turned back to find his eyes running over me, surprise lighting them.

He turned back to the road. "'Loss is nothing else but change, and change is Nature's delight.'"

"Really? You're going with Marcus Aurelius?" I asked, surprised.

"I started on the subject of loss," he pointed out.

I huffed. "And I countered with grief. Your turn to pick a new topic."

"There are rules to this conversation?" he asked, his brow drawn down.

"It's a game some of the book collectors play," I explained as I looked back out the window. "I call it Quote Wars. A new topic must be picked after each quote, but it has to also apply to the quote before. So, a quote about death brings a quote about loss and so on and so forth."

"Where would you have gone after loss? You'd go right back to grief," he pointed out.

I smiled to myself. "I would have gone with healing. Hippocrates. 'Healing is a matter of time, but it is sometimes also a matter of opportunity.'"

"I see," he said quietly.

The rest of the drive over to Saint Patrick's Catholic

Church was quiet. I climbed out and followed him up the steps to the large stone church. The others were at the doors waiting.

When they saw me, Zahur was surprised, Ranulf smirked and Falk frowned. I guess not everyone wanted me here.

When we reached them, Atticus cleared his throat. "Everyone, as usual, let me do the talking inside. These Templars haven't heard from a gargoyle in fifty years, according to our records," he announced.

"They might not believe us," Zahur pointed out.

'Then we'll just flash some fang, a little wing," I offered dryly. "They'll believe it in no time." Ranulf laughed, Zahur eyed me. Falk chuckled. Atticus just shot me an icy look.

"Don't even think about it," he said in his cold voice. Wow, did he think I'd really do that?

"I will handle this. Is that understood?" Atticus was silent until I nodded. Atticus opened the door and gestured for us to enter the church. Slightly insulted, I followed Ranulf into the church hoping this wouldn't take too long.

THREE HOURS later

WE WERE STILL at the dang church. We weren't trying to convince them that we were gargoyles anymore. That only took two hours. The last hour we'd spent being brought up to speed on what the Templars had taken on since our species had cut off contact. It was pretty much exclusively dealing with demon possession. And the Templars were furious.

I sighed deeply and looked at the Templar who was talking. He must be a Templar because he sure wasn't a priest. His black military cargo pants and t-shirt hugged a muscular body. But it was the bronze and black Latin scrolled along his body that caught my eye. It ran from below his ears, down both sides of his neck and into his shirt. It reappeared on the outside of his arms to run to his wrists. I bet it was like that down the outside of his entire body. I wanted to examine those tattoos more closely but restrained myself. There were several Templars here, all in the same black, all with the same tattoos. There were even some women in the group.

I wanted to talk to them, see what they knew about what was going on around the city. But Mr. Lead Templar, whose name was Travis, was on a tirade, asking why they should help us after we deserted them. Atticus handled it like he seemed to handle everything. With cool, calm politeness. I, on the other hand, was getting impatient. It was already past noon and we still had a Hunger demon on the loose. I wanted to hunt it down before nightfall. And I wasn't the only one. Ranulf was looking up at the ceiling of the rectory, clenching his jaw. Falk kept shifting from foot to foot. And Zahur was trying not to fall asleep. Travis started his speech again and I lost my patience.

"Oh, will you stop your whining already?" I snapped. The room fell silent as all eyes went to me. "So you had to deal with the human possessions, I'm sorry. But I've been here for forty-five years taking care of your bigger issues." One of the priests in the corner grinned. "So, unless any of you Templars are over fifty, stop complaining. You've had the light end of the workload while I dealt with the rest of it." Travis went to open his mouth.

"No, Travis, she's right," the priest from the corner announced. He stepped forward and took the chair behind the desk carefully. His hair was silver and his eyes a sparkling blue. He carried the tattoos as well. He looked at me. "We struggled for five years before the demon population suddenly dropped and the other species stopped warring with each other. It took us three more years to understand it was you. You didn't try to contact us, but you managed to bring peace among the supernatural species of the city."

"I wasn't raised with my kind," I explained. "I didn't even know about Templars until last night."

He nodded. "That makes sense. We didn't know what you were; you were helping, so we left you be." He smiled. "And you were a gargoyle the whole time." The priest looked to Atticus. "Talk about irony." I grinned. The priest continued talking to Atticus. "I'm Father Xavier. Whatever you need, the Templars will answer." Travis muttered a curse behind the priest but everyone ignored him.

"Here's the current situation. Someone has shut the Veil." Atticus announced. "Which means-" I tuned Atticus out as I got up and started pacing. I needed to stretch my legs. I paced from Ranulf on one side of the room to Falk on the other. Ranulf would smirk at me or wink before I turned. Falk ignored me completely. My mind was running through ideas on how to catch this demon before anyone else got killed.

I was on my thirty-third lap when I sighed. I knew exactly what I had to do. I'd need some back up. I eyed Ranulf. He looked about ready to explode. I caught his eye then tilted my head out toward the chapel. He raised an eyebrow. I headed to the door, muttered something about a restroom and slipped out into the chapel. Ranulf wasn't far behind. I waited until we were in the middle of the chapel before saying anything.

"I'm ready to go demon hunting. How about you?" I asked cheerfully. He chuckled deep in his chest.

"And here I thought you'd snuck me out for a chance to hit a pub," he said with a grin.

I laughed and shook my head. "Sorry, Ranulf. Maybe later." He shrugged.

"Demon hunting? Always, lass. But we need Atticus on board," he advised. I sighed.

"He's in a meeting that doesn't seem to be ending and we only have until nightfall before it kills again," I reminded him as I started to back up. "I'm leaving, so if you want to take down a demon, this is your last chance," I offered before turning around and heading out of the church. I was almost to the curb when the church doors opened.

"You're not going alone, lass," Ranulf called. I turned, smiled and waited until he caught up. "Where's your weapon stash?" he asked.

"Back home," I told him. He grinned as I waved down a cab. I gave the driver the address of my apartment.

When we arrived we didn't go to my apartment. Instead we walked across the street to the parking garage where my car was parked. My '68 Shelby Mustang was a beauty, black and chrome with a perfect body. And a spacious trunk loaded with weapons. I opened the trunk to show Ranulf. He whistled appreciatively.

"Lass, I think I'm in love," he said quietly.

"I'm not selling the car," I told him dryly. He chuckled then looked from the broadaxe to me.

"Are ye sure? I can make an excellent offer," he tried again. I shut the trunk and moved to the driver side.

"Not even for the lost libraries of Alexandria."

4

The drive to the latest crime scene was more comfortable than I thought it would be. We talked about demons and methods of killing them. Basic hunting strategies. It was nice to be able to talk to another gargoyle about it. Then we talked about hitting a pub tonight to celebrate the demon kill. It sounded like fun to me.

I drove into the alley and shut off the car. We both got out and went to the trunk. I took off my wool coat and put it away. I slipped my leather harness on, then pulled on my old trench coat that I kept in the trunk specifically to hide weapons in public. I slid my short sword into the sheath down my back. I put on my belt with a couple smaller blades and throwing knives that had been dipped in holy water. I even put salt into the pockets of my coat and jeans. Ranulf gave me a look.

"Ever throw dirt in your enemy's eyes?" I asked. "This is a more painful version for demons." He raised an eyebrow.

"I've haven't used those tactics before," he admitted. I chuckled.

"You're two feet taller than me and outweigh me by at least a hundred pounds. You've never had to," I pointed out.

"Good point, lass." He smiled as we headed towards the alley.

It wasn't hard to find where the girl died; the red stained cement was a big clue. I knelt down on the cement, pulled out a small knife and scraped up some of the dried blood. Disgusting, I know, but I needed it for tracking. I made a small ball of flame in my left hand and held the dried blood in my right. When I was focused on my objective I added the flecks of blood to the flame. The yellow flame turned red. I held it in both hands and brought it in close.

I gave it direction quietly. "A life was taken. Justice I seek. Track the one who did the deed. Let only gargoyle eyes see." I dropped the flame onto the blood-stained cement. The flame spread over the rest of the blood before shooting down the alley and turning left. I got to my feet and stepped out of the flames.

"Impressive, lass," Ranulf said. "It's not often I don't hear magic in Latin."

"It's not really magic. It's energy manipulation." I grinned. "And I've never had to use Latin." We started walking down the alley, following the line of red flame. Ranulf stayed by my side.

"Truly?" he asked, impressed. I shook my head.

"My mom insisted on me learning it along with spell work. But I always found it faster to just tell the energy exactly what I wanted." I shrugged. "It used to drive her bonkers." He chuckled as we came to a stop. The trail went up to the roof of the building before us. I sighed and headed for the rusted fire escape.

"What are ye doing, lass?" Ranulf asked. I turned back to him.

"I'm climbing the fire escape," I pointed out. Ranulf smirked then crooked his finger at me. Suspicious, I went to him. He turned me around and pointed to the roof ledge.

"I can get you up there on my back," he stated. I looked up at him over my shoulder.

"You can do that?" I asked, surprised. He nodded. "Wow, females got ripped off in the strength department." He chuckled.

"But ye females have us beat in powers," he reminded me, smiling. Yeah, he was right. The split was about even.

"Alright, so how are you going to get me up there?" I asked. He moved around to squat in front of me.

"Hop on."

I chuckled then wrapped my arms around his neck and leaned on him.

"Okay, hold on," he warned before he stood up.

I clung on, even wrapping my knees around his waist. His hands adjusted my position until he was comfortable. "God, you're short. Ready?"

"I'm 5'7', you're just a giant. And yes. Just don't smash me into the wall, please," I said. He chuckled. His body bunched under me, then he exploded in a move of raw power. I clung to him as we flew through the air. He landed on the roof with no problem.

"Okay, that was fun," I admitted. He chuckled as he bent down so I could slide down off his back. I turned to see the flame trail crossed several roofs.

We picked up our pace the rest of the way, we were burning daylight and I really didn't want to fight a demon at night. The buggers were stronger and harder to see. An hour later we finally found where it went to ground. The flame line ran down a large storm drain on a deserted street. I went to the nearest manhole cover and pulled out the small crowbar I kept on my hunting belt for such occasions.

"Let me do that, lass," Ranulf said. I handed him the bar without complaint. "Since we're going in to battle here," he said as he removed the manhole cover, "can ye tell me what your powers are?"

"I've been clearing out demons for over one hundred and fifty years. Alone," I told him as he put the cover down. "What does that tell you?"

He went still, then looked up at me. "Alone?" he asked, surprised. I nodded.

"Yes."

A grin made its way across his face. "That tells me you're a bad ass female that can more than hold her own." My face warmed.

"Come on, let's take care of this before the others catch up," I suggested before looking down and dropping into the manhole. I landed in a crouch and moved so Ranulf could follow. He grunted as he landed, then straightened to his full height. I pulled my short sword from my back sheath and followed the flame line. Our night vision made it easy to find the way.

We walked in silence for a while. We were in a long tunnel when the scrape of flesh against cement caught my ear. I went still and listened carefully. There it was again, and coming towards us. Ranulf put his battleaxe back across his back and took out two smaller, double-sided hand axes.

"Ghouls," I stated. He nodded. Ghouls were what happened to humans if a fully formed demon fed them their blood. They turned into rotting, mindless zombies that followed orders. We moved forward, my pulse picking up. We stepped into a four-way junction. "This is a good spot."

"For?" he asked in a whisper. I turned to him.

"Drawing them out," I explained. "My usual method is to draw out most of the ghouls before I get to the demon. The demon's usually on its own by then. It splits up the fight." His gaze ran over me.

"Alright," he said. "Let's play this your way." I eyed him mischievously before gesturing to the tunnels on the right and in front of us.

"I'll take these two," I said. I raised an eyebrow at him. "Want me to barrier off one of them for you?" A bloodthirsty grin crossed his face.

"No lass, I think I can manage," he countered. I smirked before I turned to my tunnels and let out a shrill whistle.

"Ghoulies, ghoulies, ghoulies!" I shouted. "Fresh meat!"

"Oh, that was subtle," he observed. I shrugged.

"Subtle doesn't get their attention," I pointed out as white, deformed bodies started to shamble towards us. I hit a lever on my short sword which split it into two blades.

"If ye get into trouble-"

"Call," I finished for him. "We want as many in the tunnels as possible," I explained, watching the ghouls pick up speed. "So, make noise."

"Ye sure you can handle two tunnels?" he asked. "I can take another."

I chuckled. "Oh, believe me, I can deal with two little tunnels full of ghouls."

That was all the banter we had time for. The ghouls were on us. Ghouls were incredibly strong but stupid. You were fine if you could keep them from getting their hands on you. The first to reach me didn't last long. I sliced through one arm and took its head. The next took a boot to the face and lost a leg, then a blade through the skull. I pulled the blade and swung at another coming at me from the left. Ranulf's grunts and cursing told me he was fine. I kept my movements fluid and fast. Then something flashed out of the corner of my eye. I didn't think, just threw the short sword in my hand at the ghoul going for Ranulf's back.

He turned in time to watch it go down with my blade in its eye. His gaze moved to me. "Down!" I dropped to my knee instantly. His axe decapitated the ghoul that had snuck up on me. I moved forward, grabbing my short sword on my way, to take his tunnels while he moved to take mine. I checked the numbers.

"Is that side full?" I shouted before I severed another head.

"Aye!"

"Good!" I dropped a blade, gathered energy to me and gave it shape in my left hand. "Get down!" We both dropped to a knee as I threw the ball of light into the air. The energy took form and conjured blades of white light raced down each tunnel, decapitating every ghoul in their path. Once the last body dropped I got to my feet and looked him over. He had patches of black ghoul blood here and there.

"That's a neat trick, lass," he told me, his eyes sparkling. I winked at him.

"You haven't seen anything yet," I countered. He grinned at me before cleaning the blood off his axes. I cleaned off my short swords and started making our way down the corpse-laden tunnel where the flame trail led.

We walked for what had to be several blocks under-ground before I smelled it. Sulfur. Ranulf smelled it at the same time I did as we reached a corner. I started to build a ball of light in my hands. He saw it and grinned. Demons hated light and I was about to use this to drive one crazy.

"It's a Hunger demon, so we'll have to slit the throat," Ranulf said quietly.

"If you can distract him, I'll sneak in for the kill," I whispered. He nodded. It was a good strategy, I was smaller and easier to forget with a big gargoyle like Ranulf trying to kill you. I slipped my head around the corner. There it was, sleeping. Its body was solid black. Tendon and bone, long limbs, and sharp claws on his feet and hands that made its reach even worse. I turned back to Ranulf, worried he wouldn't be able to stay out of reach. He saw it.

"I'll be fine, lass. This will be easy," he whispered. I nodded that I heard him. I had to take him at his word.

I met his eyes, he nodded that he was ready.

I turned and threw the ball of light up to the ceiling, making it as bright as noon in the desert. The demon screeched as Ranulf charged out to catch its attention with his battleaxe drawn.

"Hey demon!" Ranulf bellowed, both his top and bottom sets of fangs showing in his mouth. He made a few striking moves against the demon, getting him to turn his back to me.

"Your heart is mine, gargoyle," the Hunger demon hissed.

"Only if ye can get to it!" Ranulf shouted back. I moved out from the tunnel into the room. The demon made a lunge for Ranulf. He dove to the side, dodging its claws by inches, then rolled to his feet and made his own strike. My heart started slamming against my ribs as the demon moved to follow him.

I moved out of the shadows and leaped to its back. I dug my talons into his flesh as I slid on its oily skin before I drove my blade into the side of its neck. It cried out in pain, twisting its body to the side, just like I wanted it to. I jumped, keeping my grip on the blade, gravity working with my body weight to drag the blade through the meat of its throat. It suddenly twisted. I hit the ground on my side under it.

Demon blood poured over my shoulder and down my arm, burning like acid. I cried out as the demon dropped over me, dead. The blood ate through my jacket, shirt and skin as I reached for my holy water. It wasn't there! The demon's body was thrown from me. Ranulf was there instantly, his arm around my back, lifting me until I rested against his chest.

"Demon blood," I bit out as I watched the muscle of my shoulder start to dissolve. My shoulder was on fire and it was spreading. Ranulf pulled out a large flask and poured it over my shoulder. It was like pouring water on a smoldering log. Smoke rose, and the wound hissed as he poured the holy water over the blood. When it was finally over, I fell limp against him.

"Don't ye carry holy water, lass?" he snapped. I wiped the tears from my face before I looked up at him.

"I left it in the car," I admitted. He was the first to start laughing, I wasn't far behind.

We were still laughing when Falk strode into the chamber, his face hard, his eyes dark. When he saw me covered in blood, both ghoul and my own, his face became deadly. Probably not good.

"Looks like we've been caught," Ranulf observed.

"Oops," I quipped. We both started laughing again. Falk's face was murderous as he reached down, grabbed my good arm and yanked me to my feet.

"Hey! Careful of her arm!" Ranulf snapped. Falk just started pulling me out of the room, his fingers digging into my arm.

"Falk, you're hurting me," I hissed, one second away from blasting him off my arm. Falk gentled his grip but didn't let go. I didn't try to fight him; the guy was furious right now. Ranulf followed close behind as I was marched back to the manhole we'd used. Falk gestured for me to follow.

I sighed and started to climb the ladder. When I was almost out Falk reached down and offered a hand to help me out of the hole. When I got to my feet I spotted the others. Atticus was standing with his arms crossed over his chest, his face cold as a glacier. Zahur came to me and started looking over my shoulder.

"Demon blood?" Zahur asked quietly.

"Yes, it was my own dumb fault," I admitted. Zahur took my good arm and brought me over to the side of the Mercedes. He pulled out a first aid kit and began pouring holy water over it. It hurt a great deal.

"What the hell were you thinking?" Atticus demanded, his voice low and icy. I looked up. Only Atticus was glaring at Ranulf. "Going after a fully formed demon on your own? Are you trying to kill yourself?" Atticus's eyes glowed as he walked to stand across from Ranulf, his posture rigid. "It's not bad enough that you risked your life, you had to risk hers too? What kind of male does that?" That made me angry.

"It wasn't his idea," I announced. Atticus turned those piercing eyes on me. "I was going after the demon myself; Ranulf figured I shouldn't go alone."

"Lass, let it be," Ranulf told me softly. I shot him a look. His eyes were calm and accepting as they met mine. What did he want, me to stay quiet while Atticus went after him over something that wasn't even his plan?

"This wasn't your idea, it was mine," I reminded him. "Why should you be the only one getting in trouble for it?" I turned to Atticus, who had closed his eyes and was taking deep breaths. "The Hunger demon is dead and we're not.

That's all that should matter." Atticus turned his back on me, his shoulders still rigid.

"Zahur, take her home and patch her up," Atticus ordered, his voice cold. Zahur touched my arm and started to steer me into the Mercedes.

"Evelyn, if you leave the keys, I'll bring your car home," Ranulf offered. I dug into my pocket and tossed him the keys. I gave him a small, apologetic smile before sliding into the car. Zahur took the driver's seat and drove away.

～

Atticus

SHE WAS GONE. She was hurt and heading home. My blood boiled as I began to pace. No one moved as I ran a hand down my face. They went after a fully formed demon, with only two of them! Were they insane?

That moment I realized she was gone was burned into my mind.

I was discussing what aid the Templars could offer when I realized I hadn't heard Evelyn's footsteps for some time. I turned and my chest seized. She was gone. Just... gone!

My hands began shaking when I told Zahur to take her home. He didn't argue; he knew me. He got her out of the line of fire.

Ranulf stepped forward and put his hand on my shoulder. "Breathe, Atticus. She was pretty bad ass in there."

I smacked his arm of my shoulder. "She was injured!"

"She's a gargoyle; she's going to get hurt. It's part of the job," Ranulf reminded me. A job she shouldn't have.

"Over my dead body," I growled low. When I got back to

that apartment I was going to make it clear to her. No more fighting demons.

Ranulf smirked. "Good luck with that, boss." Falk snorted in agreement.

"Get your asses down there and clean up that mess," I snarled. I needed them gone so I could calm down. Both of them disappeared down the manhole.

I leaned on the hood of the car and took deep breaths. She was alive. She was being taken care of. It's fine.

It wasn't fine. Feeling *this* over her... that wasn't fine. I didn't need this shit in my life! The way her eyes sparkled as she quoted Hippocrates... I'd never met anyone who could keep up with me until her. And it had to be my Match! I growled as I started pacing again. Feeling was off my menu. It was what kept me calm, and she was fucking with it! I took several deeper breaths, trying to dislodge the vise in my chest. She was fucking fine! Why was I still shaking like this? The ridiculous Matching! Control, Atticus, you need to find your control. I closed my eyes and focused. Control, control, control. My phone rang.

I pulled it out of my pocket and cursed. It was Cyrus.

"Yes?" I answered.

"Did you kill the demon yet?" Cyrus demanded.

"Yes. She was injured, demon blood," I bit out.

"Why was she there?" he growled.

"She didn't give us much choice," I stated. "Zahur is taking her back to her place."

"Keep her off the front line," Cyrus ordered.

"I will," I growled.

"And keep your distance," he reminded me. "I can already hear the emotion in your voice."

I closed my eyes and forced myself to speak normally. "Yes, sir."

Evelyn

WE STOPPED across the hall so Zahur could get the large med kit, which ended up being a large duffle bag. I was quiet until we walked into my apartment.

"This is unbelievable," I grumbled. It was freaking ridiculous.

"What?" Zahur asked.

"I was the one who decided to go demon hunting, Ranulf backed me up, the demon's dead and now Atticus is angry with him?" I shook my head. "I don't understand. The demon's dead. Be happy."

"But Ranulf needed to clear it with Atticus before breaking off like that," he explained. "Especially if you are involved."

"Atticus was in that meeting that took, what? Until sunset to get out of," I pointed out. "Just standing around was useless." I pulled off my ruined coat and harness. My white shirt was destroyed. Zahur eyed my shoulder again.

"Let's go to your bathroom, I want a better look at that," Zahur said. Still steaming, I headed into my bathroom. "You're going to need to get that fabric off of you."

I grabbed a clean towel from the built-in cupboard.

"I don't understand, what is Atticus's problem?" I asked. "Could you turn around, please?"

He did immediately.

Still muttering about Atticus, I pulled off my now destroyed shirt. Even my bra strap had been destroyed. They both took a flight straight to the garbage bin.

"Ranulf has a history of going off on his own," he explained as he set down the first aid kit on the counter. I kept my back to Zahur and wrapped a towel around my chest. "Okay, I'm covered."

"Counter. Now," he ordered. I hopped up on the counter under the lights.

"You were saying before?" I asked. He began to really look at the wound on my shoulder. The demon's blood had covered my shoulder from front to back and ran down my arm. The skin was gone, the muscle beneath was red, pitted and overall, rather disgusting to look at.

"It wasn't really about Ranulf. It was about you," Zahur said absently as he began rinsing my shoulder with cold water. It felt amazing.

"What?"

"That's why Atticus was so angry." He pulled out a jar of green goop from the kit and opened it. "What do you know about how our females pick a husband?" He added some herbs from a small bag with a label to the mix of green and stirred it.

Stunned by the change in topic, I answered. "Um, you meet, you fall in love, then you get married," I said as if it were obvious. His eyes ran over my face before going back to the jar in his hands.

"That's how humans do it. Not gargoyles." His voice changed, it became clinical. "We have something different. It's called The Matching." He stopped stirring the goo in the jar to meet my gaze. "A female meets a male, they touch, usually shaking hands. Then a surge of hormones is felt by both of them." My pulse picked up as he continued. "That's called The Matching. It tells you who your Mate is and starts a process."

"Mate?" I asked quietly, my handshake with Atticus running through my mind.

"The human term is husband, or wife," he explained.

"Our species is different than most. We usually only get one Mate in our long lifetime. And Atticus is yours."

My heart lodged in my throat and my nerves jumped. "Wait. So, Atticus is the destined love of my life?" I asked, hoping he'd say no.

"It doesn't work that way," he began. "Our species numbers have always been on the low side. The Matching tells us who we can have children with. It does make you more sensitive to each other, more aware. But that's it. The rest is up to the both of you." He began stirring the goo again. "They do almost always form a deep emotional connection."

"Wait," I said, stunned. "So, we live for hundreds, if not thousands, of years and we only get one Match? One person we can have children with?"

He nodded. "It is rare, but occasionally a female will have two. But in our history, I know of only two females who have had that occur and it was when she met both close to each other."

I sat there trying to absorb what he was telling me. "Atticus doesn't-"

"Care for you?" he snapped. His eyes narrowed on me. "How would you know?" I closed my mouth. He continued. "You don't know what it means for a gargoyle to find their Match." His gaze was shadowed as he continued. "You're his hope, Evelyn. Even if he doesn't know it yet."

"Pardon?" I asked, because I couldn't have heard him correctly. Me? Atticus's hope? I started to shake my head. His fingers on my chin stopped me.

"Our people live in a world of war for centuries," he explained calmly as his fingers dropped from my chin. "It goes on and on. Our duty never ends, and as centuries go by we watch our friends die, they turn into people we don't recognize anymore, caring for others becomes too much of a risk. We become alone in a dark world." His eyes were shadowed when they met mine. "Then a gargoyle meets their Match and everything changes. We feel emotions we haven't felt in centuries simply because our Match is with us. Because for once in our lives we have a chance to not be alone anymore. A chance to have a family, happiness. A chance at a life full of more than battle and death." He went back to stirring the goo in the jar. "That's why Atticus was so furious with Ranulf tonight. Because Ranulf knows what you mean to Atticus, and he still didn't tell us you were going after the Hunger demon." He looked back down at my shoulder and started applying the green goo to the wound.

Guilt hit me hard. If what he was saying were true, and he had no reason to lie to me, Atticus cared about me, more than I ever thought he could in two days. But... "He doesn't seem to even like me," I pointed out.

He sighed. "Atticus is young. He hasn't quite dealt with some of his own issues yet. Nor has he spent a thousand years alone, which is normally when we meet our Mate," he explained. "And Atticus is stubborn. With him, you'll have to watch his actions, they'll show more about him than what he says."

The goo cooled and soothed the damaged tissue better than anything I could imagine. It let me start thinking again.

"Why didn't he tell me?" I asked quietly, when he finished bandaging my shoulder.

He washed his hands and began cleaning up the med kit. "You should ask him when he gets back. He's going to want to talk to you about running off."

A thought occurred to me as he zipped up the large kit. "Do Matches always get together?"

He paused, then met my eyes. "No. Sometimes personalities clash and they decide not to complete the binding."

"What happens to them? Do they get Matched again?" I asked.

"If they live long enough, maybe. So far in our history it hasn't happened," he answered quietly. He picked up the kit and headed out of the bathroom. "I'll be in the living room if you need me." He closed the door behind him.

In a daze, I went into my bedroom and changed out of my blood-spattered jeans and into a pair of black leggings and a burgundy sweater. When I was dressed I sat on my bed, Zahur's words running through my head. Why didn't Atticus tell me himself? He was my Match. Was I going to marry him? How was I even going to bring up the subject? Why didn't Mum ever mention it? Frustrated, I laid down and snuggled with my pillow as it sank in what Atticus being my Match meant to my life. If I was ever going to have a family, it would be with Atticus. I took a deep breath and wished I could speak to my mum.

∾

Atticus

I STRODE into Evelyn's apartment. Only Zahur was in the living room, reorganizing the med kit. Her bedroom door was closed.

"She's in her room," Zahur announced, putting away the contents of the large first aid kit.

I walked further into the apartment. "Her shoulder?"

"Fine. Probably won't even scar," he stated as he straightened and slung the bag over his shoulder. He started for the door. When he reached me he stopped, his entire body rigid. "I told her."

My head snapped around and I growled, "Why?"

His jaw clenched and unclenched. "Because you need her." He left it at that as he strode out the door. The apartment was silent.

He told her. I bit back a curse. If he had just kept his mouth shut I could have taken her back home and left it at that. But now... now she's going to want to try and make it work. I ran my hand over my face. And I had to keep her from trying. Shit.

I went to her door and knocked. "Evelyn?"

"Come in," she called.

I opened the door as she sat up on her bed, tucking a stray curl behind her ear. It was such a feminine gesture that it caught my attention. Changed the way I was thinking. I looked around her room to give myself a moment to recover. Her walls were a light lilac color. Her dresser was on the other side of the room, old white wood with chips here and there. It matched her nightstands and headboard. A closet was on one side of another door across from her bed. I turned back to her. She was sitting up against a mound of pillows in different colors; pink, purple, white. The quilt under her was a pale green. Her burgundy sweater was too big for her, sliding down her bandaged shoulder. Finally, I looked at her again. She wrapped her arms around her knees.

"Have a seat." She gestured to her bed. I unbuttoned my suit jacket and sat near the end of the bed, a safe distance from her.

"Are you alright?" I asked, trying for neutral when I felt anything but. The urge to touch her, examine every inch of her so I would know that she wasn't injured was nearly over-whelming.

She sighed. "Yeah, I just miss my mom. I could use her advice right now."

"About?"

"You," she said quietly before meeting my eyes. "Zahur told me about The Matching, and what Mates are. Why didn't you tell me?"

"Because you didn't need to know," I replied, keeping my voice empty.

Her eyebrows went up. "I didn't need to know?" she asked, her voice dry. "I meet the one person I can have a family with, and you don't think I need to know?"

"I didn't believe it was dire information with a demon on the loose. I was going to tell you when we headed home," I lied. I needed her off this topic.

"And if I didn't go with you?" she asked, her voice sharp.

"Then that would have been your choice," I hedged.

"You would have left me in the dark?" she demanded, her voice rising.

"You wouldn't have known-"

"Do you think that matters?" she shot back. She shook her head, her cognac eyes glowing. "It was obvious to you that I had no idea what was going on, and you decided not to tell me even though it would affect the rest of my life. You don't get to make that decision for me."

"The Matching is nothing more than nature making you vulnerable to a stranger and making you feel things you don't want to. And it doesn't matter. Right now, what matters is what happened this afternoon," I stated. "You and Ranulf went after the demon alone and you got hurt because of that choice."

"I got hurt because it jerked in a different direction before it died," she countered.

"You both could have been killed. It was reckless and impulsive," I told her.

"You were stuck in that meeting that didn't seem like it would end before sundown." She took a deep breath before continuing. "I didn't want to have to look into another chest cavity because of it. I needed to do something proactive."

The shadows in her eyes bothered me. Her eyes should never be shadowed. Damn it, I needed to stop thinking like that. "Evelyn, if I'm in a meeting and you want to tell me something, all you have to do is touch my shoulder to let me know you need to speak to me," I explained, my voice hard. "But going off like that, disappearing, is unacceptable. Do you understand?"

Her eyes flashed at me as she continued to meet my gaze. "I understand I scared you. But I'm not a child to have to ask permission to do something, nor do I need you making decisions for me."

There it was, the ammunition I needed. I looked away from her to the lamp on the nightstand. "Don't act like a child and I won't treat you like one," I said, my voice as cold as I could make it. My gut knotted, hating what I was doing, but it was necessary.

"Yes, I agree that I won't disappear like that again," she said carefully, drawing my gaze back to her. Her cheeks were pink, her eyes hurt. "Next time, I'll just leave a note on my way out the door." She shifted to the other side of the bed.

"That is not what I meant," I said, almost growling, my temper waking up.

"It's what you asked for," she said calmly as she pulled on her boots. "Not to disappear. And I've agreed." She got to her feet and moved around the bed. "I'm going to head down to the Chinese restaurant on the corner. I'll bring back dinner for everyone." She opened the door and walked out into her apartment.

I rose to my feet and went to the doorway. "You're not going alone."

"Watch me," she called over her shoulder as she grabbed her coat then walked out the door, slamming it behind her.

Growling, I was across the room and in the hall in seconds. I slammed open the door to our apartment. The others looked up. "She's on her way to the Chinese restaurant on the corner," I growled. "One of you go with her."

The others shared a look.

"Now," I ordered.

"Atticus, she might just need a few minutes to herself," Zahur offered. "She hasn't exactly been alone since last night."

I didn't care. At least that's what I told myself. The other part of me was shouting to go after her and apologize. I ignored it. "Falk, if she's not back in ten, go get her. Drag her back if you have to."

I turned from them and headed down the hall to my bedroom. I made a point to close the door behind me carefully.

I sat on my bed and fought back the rage that flowed through me. I hated having to do that, call her a child when she was anything but. But it was what was best. She just kept getting under my skin. Pain registered. I looked down. My talons had slipped out and dug into my thighs. I cursed, then went about changing.

5

I was waiting in a booth at the Chinese restaurant, my mind running in circles, when my cell rang. Glancing down I saw Astrid's name.

"Hey," I said.

"Hey hottie, what's going on?" Astrid asked. I sighed as I ran over what just happened again. Where to begin?

"Well, we got the Hunger demon, so you can spread the word on that," I said. Astrid promptly announced it to the bar. There were cheers. I was almost smiling when Astrid came back.

"How'd it go with the guys?" Astrid asked.

"Remember when you said your species has something to find your Mate?"

"Yeah?" I could hear the smile in her voice.

"Well, we do too. And guess who it is," I said.

"The arrogant one?"

"Yes. The arrogant one, who wasn't even going to tell me I was his Mate," I announced.

"What?" she asked, her voice stunned.

I explained how Atticus had kept it from me and how he

would have left without telling me. That it was Zahur who told me. When I was done, I was tired.

"Oh, that is fucked up," she stated, stunned.

"Yes, I believe it is too." I took a deep, slow breath then I admitted what I was thinking. "I don't think he likes me."

"Well, do you like him?" she asked pointedly. I thought about it.

"I don't know him well enough to say one way or another," I admitted. "I'm angry with him, but I don't know him."

"Well, if I was in your shoes, I'd try and see if we could make it work," she said quietly.

"Really?" I asked, surprised. I expected her to say 'tell him to go to hell.' That was her usual go-to.

"Yeah, you only get one Mate in a lifetime sweetie, do you really want to give up on him so fast?" she asked gently. I sighed. She had a point. But....

"He said I was acting childish," I stated.

"Impulsive, I'll give you," Astrid said. "But childish? I think you both have that award."

"What?" Was she serious? *I* was being childish?

"You left the apartment alone just to prove a point," she reminded me.

"Yeah, but it was a point that needed to be made," I countered.

"I agree completely." She paused. "But what was him not wanting you to leave alone really about?"

I sighed as I thought about it. Dang it. "It was about my safety," I grumbled.

"Yep," she said. "He's worried about you getting hurt."

"I've done just fine for-"

"He doesn't know that," she reminded me. "He doesn't know what you are capable of, so he wants to protect you.

Cut him a little slack on that until he sees you in action. Then you can get pissed at him."

I hated it when Astrid was right. I hated it even more when she had to lay it out like that to get me to think.

"I'll give it a try," I said.

"Good. Now, how's that tall hottie from the bar?" she asked.

I rolled my eyes. "You mean Ranulf?"

"Ranulf? Hot name," she said, her smile in her voice.

I rolled my eyes. "I'll see if I can bring him by the bar to meet you before they leave."

"You're the best!" The background noise on Astrid's end rose. "Shit, gotta go sweetie, talk to you later!" Astrid hung up before I could say goodbye.

My skin crawled. Someone was watching me. I lifted my eyes from the table. A man was sitting in the second booth down from mine, facing me. His golden blonde hair was stylishly cut. His face was strikingly handsome. He looked up in time to catch me eyeing him. His dark blue eyes sparkled. I gave him an awkward smile before going back to my phone. Something about him put me on edge, worse than anything I'd ever felt. I went through my contacts to look busy. Apparently the males had gotten ahold of my phone and put their numbers in it.

"Waiting for food?" a rich voice asked. I looked up. It was blonde man.

"Yes, I'm just waiting on a big order," I offered politely. His head tilted to the side, his gaze ran over me.

"A big order for a small woman like you?" he asked with a grin. It sent shivers down my spine, and not in a good way. What was it about him?

"I have family in town," I hedged. "What about you?" He sighed.

"I just moved here," he said. "My family's back home. So, order for one."

"They deliver if you order over fifteen dollars worth. You'd have lunch for a few days," I offered. He smiled an amazing smile that made my stomach knot. I didn't know what it was. He was handsome, polite, he was the usual kind of man I went for, when I dated humans at least. Why was he giving me the creeps? Was this because of the Matching? Did it make other males less attractive? Was that why friendly, idle chit-chat was bothering me? Because it was another male?

"That's a good idea," he said. I looked back down at my phone and found Atticus. They really put everyone in here. Maybe I was just in a cruddy mood?

"Texting a boyfriend?" blonde guy asked. I looked up and eyed him. He was still striking, and had an amazing smile. But ... nothing. I felt nothing.

"No, I'm just not used to talking to people I don't know," I said. He chuckled. I kept eye contact until he finished laughing. Was I going to be this way the rest of my life? Only reacting to Atticus?

"You could ask questions back," he offered, still smiling. I smiled politely at him.

"Why would I ask you questions?" I asked.

"Because we're both stuck here waiting for food. Small talk never killed anyone," he replied. I gave him a small tense smile. He hadn't done anything creepy, he was just being polite. This had to be all me.

"I'm not very good at small talk," I told him. My number was called out. I got to my feet. "Have a good night," I said before I went to the counter for the large order. Two stacked boxes worth. I picked them up and was out the door before the blonde guy could say another word.

It was snowing outside again. I headed back down the block towards my apartment. How did I feel about only being attracted to Atticus? He was handsome, no doubt about it. The first time we spoke he was warm and nice. Now? He barely looked at me in my room. I was still struggling with it when a big figure in black came towards me. I recognized Falk's gait and met him on the sidewalk. He took both boxes without saying a word.

"Thanks," I said before we started walking back towards the apartments. He said nothing. I eyed him out of the corner of my eye. A foot taller than me, he was trim, but muscled. The guy never really spoke. I eyed the thick scar tissue across his throat. It looked like someone had almost taken his head off. Maybe his vocal cords were damaged? His face was usually unreadable. I peeked up at him again. His thick eyebrows were low on his brow, and his lips were in a tight line.

He truly didn't seem to like me. He stopped walking to look down at me. Busted. He raised an eyebrow, asking me without words.

"I'm just trying to figure out if you can stand me," I admitted. "Your face is usually blank or frowning at me and I can't tell." His brow drew down.

"You're not bad," he said in a rough voice. I gave him a small smile as we started walking again. I didn't know what to say to him.

"So," I began awkwardly. "What do you do for fun?"

"Carpentry. I like working with my hands," he said, his voice getting rougher.

"You do?"

"Takes my mind off things," he said, his voice getting quieter. Was it the scar tissue? It must be.

We were almost to the apartment when Falk's arm shot

out. I jumped as his hand rested on my stomach just above my belly button. I looked up to him with a raised eyebrow. His obsidian eyes met mine.

"Ice," he said, his voice hoarse and barely audible. It took me a heartbeat to realize what he was saying. Looking down, I found my part of the sidewalk was iced over.

"Oh," I said absently. Falk gestured for me to go ahead of him. I slipped by him. When we were past the ice I tried to understand what had just happened. Falk had been worried about me slipping on the ice? I hadn't expected that from the quiet male.

When we reached the building, I held open the door so he could go first. We headed upstairs and into the males' apartment.

The building owner had converted what had once been a loft into a four-bedroom, two bath apartment, which he rented out at an atrocious rate. The apartment was set up like mine only with much more room. Surprisingly, the apartment had furniture. Two large leather couches and a leather arm chair in the living room, a coffee table, lamps, heck they even had a huge TV on the wall that was showing a rugby game. It was noisy as the guys argued over the plays.

"Hey!" I shouted over the TV. They all turned. "Food." Atticus turned the TV down to a reasonable volume as everyone came to the kitchen. I got out of the way of the others. "How is it you have furniture already? And cable?" I asked them.

"Bribery," Zahur answered. I rolled my eyes. Ranulf got my attention, then tilted his head towards the door. I smiled. The pub. I had almost forgotten about it.

Zahur and Atticus were talking about a play when Ranulf and I slipped out the door and hurried downstairs.

I was trying and failing to hold back my laughter as we

stepped out into the snow. Ranulf chuckled as he took my arm and hurried me down the street. We were a block away before we slowed down.

"So, how long until we're missed?" I asked, smiling.

Ranulf looked back over his shoulder before answering. "About five minutes. They'll figure it out though."

He turned us around the corner.

"Well, I have to leave a note so...." I pulled out my phone and texted Atticus that I had left. And wasn't alone. This was going to push his buttons. I showed Ranulf and he let out a belly-deep laugh as he read it over.

"What's the plan?" I asked, smiling.

He smirked down at me. "Ever had real Scottish food?"

TWO HOURS later

WE WERE SITTING in the back corner of the best Scottish pub in the city. I was full and laughing when Ranulf signaled our waitress for another round of scotch. He continued his story.

"So, there was my baby brother, Hamish, in the court-yard of the farm," he said, "naked as the day he was born. His Match, Alia, was dressing as fast as she could in the barn. And my father was questioning Hamish to within an inch of his life."

"What did he say?" I asked. Ranulf chuckled.

"That training naked with a practice blade was a new training method he heard about," he said. We both chuckled. "My mother was listening to this, sighed, then headed straight for the barn."

"Hamish must have stunk as a liar," I said before taking my last sip of scotch. He shook his head, his eyes shining.

"No, our mother was just that smart," he admitted. I grinned at him.

"So, what did you do? You helped him out, right?" I asked, the curiosity almost killing me.

He nodded, his eyes on the table, his cheeks turning pinker. "Aye, I did," he groaned. "I dropped my kilt, pulled off my tunic, grabbed our practice blades and walked out into the courtyard bellowing at Hamish for being late for training." I was howling with laughter, the image he painted was just.... By the time I had control of myself, our drinks had arrived. Ranulf took a deep drink as his face turned crimson.

"D-d-did your mother figure it out?" I asked as I was trying to get my breath back.

"I think she knew that day. Hamish and Alia were Mated not three days later," he told me. He was smiling when I finally got my breath back.

"Oh, that was good one," I said as I wiped tears from my eyes.

"Your turn, lass," he said as he smirked down at me.

I finished taking a drink. "My turn?"

"Aye, what's one of your crazy stories." His gaze ran over my face before meeting mine again. "You have to have some."

I sighed. "Most of mine include hunting demons and killing rogue vamps or shapeshifters," I admitted, feeling completely relaxed and at ease for the first time in weeks. "I didn't have any brothers or sisters to go on crazy adventures with."

"Oh, don't try to play innocent with me," he chided. "Come on."

I grumbled, but gave in. "You know that whole Jersey Devil myth that started in the early nineteen hundreds?" I asked, biting back my smile as I turned my tumbler on the table.

His grin grew bigger. "Aye."

I raised my hand. We burst out laughing. I dropped my hand.

"That was you? How'd ye manage that?" he asked, still smiling.

"I was really bored," I admitted emphatically. "And I wanted to have some fun. I didn't think the myth would keep going like it has though."

"That can't be the only one," he prompted, grinning down at me. I leaned back in the booth and looked up at the ceiling.

"I might have a few more," I admitted. I looked up at him, my head still on the back of the booth. "My mom would have killed me. My parents never really got my sense of humor."

"It's a good sense of humor," he assured me.

I smiled. "Atticus doesn't seem to get it."

He chuckled, lifting his head to look around the pub. "Atticus is under five hundred years old. He is still working on his own issues. Not to mention the stick up his arse."

I grinned before taking another drink.

"So, how'd you like Scottish food?" he asked with a grin.

"It's not exactly my first time eating haggis, or scotch eggs," I admitted.

"Really?" He signaled to the waitress for another round.

"We might as well have her bring the bottle," I pointed out.

He chuckled. "You can hold your drink, lass. I thought you'd be passed out by now."

I scoffed. "I may not be Scottish, but I did spend some time in Scotland."

His eyes lit up. "When?"

I looked up at the ceiling as I thought about it. "Around, 1870. It was about thirty years after my parents died. I worked in a pub for a bit." I turned back to him. "All you Scots love to drink, and buy drinks for pretty English girls just to see them drunk."

His brows went up. "You're English." He eyed me. "I never would have guessed. Where were you born?"

"London," I said. "1823."

"Have you been back?" he asked gently.

I took a long, deep drink. "No, I haven't." The waitress came with our tumblers. I took another drink. I needed to change the subject. "This is my limit though. Any more and you'll be carrying me home."

"I'll make sure you get home," he promised.

I eyed him playfully. "Are you going to hold my hair back if I'm sick?"

He grinned. "Lass, I'll even carry your purse if you need me to."

"I don't carry a purse," I pointed out.

"Why is that?" he asked.

I rested my elbow on the table and propped my chin in my palm. "I kept losing them," I admitted without embarrassment. We both chuckled. I took a sip of mine before continuing. "All I really need is my phone and my wallet anyway."

"And weapons," he reminded me before taking a drink.

I nodded. "That's what the car is for. It's harder to lose a car." He let out another deep belly laugh. I was smiling until he took a drink from his glass.

His turquoise eyes were shiny from the scotch, he might not have been wasted, but he was buzzed.

"You're fun, Ranulf," I stated.

"I try." He smiled. His phone rang and he reached into his pocket, then answered. "Yeah?" I took a big drink out of my glass. "We'll head back now," he growled. He hung up, cursing as he put his phone away. "We're being ordered back."

I peeked up at him and met his gaze. "I say we finish these drinks, then we leave."

He grinned down at me. "And walk slowly back. It'll irritate the hell out of him."

I lifted my glass and tapped his. "Sounds good to me." We finished our drinks.

He slid out of the booth, then moved so I could climb out. The room spun.

"Whoa, okay, more drunk than I thought," I admitted, clinging to the booth.

He lifted my chin so he could see my face. "Are you good to walk to the door while I pay the check?" I thought it over as I eyed the distance. I could probably manage it.

"Yes, I will meet you outside," I said as I looked up at him "The fresh air will help."

He nodded. "I'll only be a few minutes." He waited until I started walking before he went to the bar. I made my way through the crowded room rather well, considering I was a step away from slurring. I managed to get to the door without running into anyone in the crowd, which I thought was quite a feat. I pulled on my jacket and slipped outside. Snow was still falling, it was pretty. I moved out of the doorway and sat on the bench just outside the door. It was a beautiful night. The snow fell softly, and for once the city was quiet. I thought about Atticus and wondered again why he didn't tell me. I took a breath and let it out slowly. The pub door opened and Ranulf stepped out, his gaze instantly finding me.

"Ready?" he asked. I nodded before we started down the street.

We walked in comfortable silence for a couple minutes, my fuzzy mind running over the stories he'd told me. Most of his stories had been about his family. Out of his seven brothers only two were still alive. His one sister had died in childbirth centuries ago. Apparently, female gargoyles had a lot of difficulties during pregnancy. He had enough battle stories that I began to understand him over dinner. He'd joined squad after squad and watched as the others found their Mates and left, while he stayed behind and did his duty, often alone. For 1336 years. He deserved his own happiness. Most of his stories had been about his family. Did he want one? I was curious.

"You want a big family," I said softly as we walked, "don't you?"

"Aye, but it's not likely to happen. Not enough females to go around," he replied.

"And you haven't met your Match," I pointed out.

He looked down at me and smiled. "So, he finally told you about that?"

"Yes, if by *he* you mean Zahur," I said pointedly. Ranulf sighed.

"Atticus... don't take it to heart. He's the prickly sort," he suggested.

"Atticus is a prick. Got it," I repeated, fighting back a giggle.

He chuckled as we turned the corner.

"You aren't what I expected," I admitted.

"What did ye expect?"

I smiled. "Someone much crazier."

He grinned. "Aye, I am that too."

I smiled to myself. I was walking down the street with a

friend who was a gargoyle. It felt good. No, it was amazing. I wasn't alone anymore. In fact, for the first time in years I was far from it.

~

Ranulf

THE SNOW WAS FALLING FASTER, by morning there would be another three inches on the ground at least. The snow reminded me that it wasn't long until Yule.

"Christmas is only a few days away," I said as I looked down at her. Her shoulders instantly tensed, her gaze on to the sidewalk. I watched her carefully as her smile disappeared. Her apartment had been bare. No decorations, not even a tree. "You don't celebrate Christmas, do you?" I asked, already guessing the answer. She shrugged her shoulders, her eyes on the sidewalk.

"I don't really have anyone to celebrate it with," she said, her voice small.

"Well, lass, ye have a Match and three others here to celebrate with you this year," I pointed out. Screw being subtle. "Evie?" She looked up and met my eyes. "I'm trying to find out if I need to get ye a gift." She smiled sweetly, though her face grew a little paler at the word gift.

"No, please, don't get me a gift," she said adamantly. "I don't celebrate Christmas and I don't do gifts." Her refusal of Christmas bothered me. Yule had always been a special holiday for our family. Even now my brothers, Angus and Fergus, and I got together every year unless some duty kept us from meeting. It was the only time we ever saw each other. Why wouldn't she like Yule? "Besides," her voice pulled me out of my head, "I think you'll be gone before Christmas anyway."

I looked down at her. Her face was somber as we turned the corner. "What do you mean?" I asked.

She gave me a small, sad smile. "Atticus wasn't going to tell me if I didn't go back with everyone. He was just going to leave me in the dark. So, I think you'll be leaving soon."

Anger burned in my gut, I wanted to hit him. "That son of a-" I shook my head. "I don't get it. If I found my Match I'd be busting my arse to make sure she was happy. I'd be shouting from the roof that I'd found her. You wouldn't be able to drag me away from her."

She chuckled.

"He's being a moron," I grumbled. I held up my phone. "I expected him to be calling every ten minutes. But no, he texted twice to check on you."

She raised an eyebrow. "Is that why we went to a pub? To worry Atticus?"

"That and because I needed to get away from him," I admitted. Otherwise I was going to hit him. Atticus had always been cold, but he had been worse since meeting Evelyn.

"That reminds me," she said, "Astrid wanted me to say hi for her."

Huh? "Who's Astrid?" I asked. I was buzzed but I wasn't drunk. I would remember if I had met an Astrid.

"Oh, just the blonde werewolf you fought beside at the bar," she said casually. My heart slammed in my chest. That blonde. God. Legs for days, and talk about curves! Damn! She had been beautiful.

"Oh, her," I muttered, trying to get the image of her punching another werewolf out of my head.

She started laughing. I ignored it until she weaved into me. I caught her before she could lose her footing.

"I shouldn't have had that last one," she said, her voice starting to slur.

I wrapped an arm around her waist to steady her. The steps to her building were just ahead.

"Shite," I grumbled. "I'm sorry, lass, I thought you might have a higher tolerance. You had scotch at your place."

She leaned into me, her balance off. "I do," she admitted. "That last one just hit me."

I cursed as I kept her on her feet. "Come on, lass, I'll get you inside."

"And if I'm sick, you have to hold my hair." She looked up at me playfully. "You promised."

"Aye, I promised," I assured her. "Now, let me get you inside." She looked at the stairs and glared.

"Oh. Stairs, my nemesis, we meet again," she said dramatically. I chuckled as I helped her walk up the snow-covered steps. She pulled her keys out and opened the door. She held on tight to my arm as we walked in.

"That last one really is hitting you," I observed as I closed the door behind us.

"Yes, I am sloshed," she said with a smirk.

"Are you feeling sick?" I asked, worried. She shook her head.

"No. Just dizzy," she said.

I set her against the wall then crouched in front of her. "Hop on, lass. It'll be faster." She laughed as she climbed on my back. She rested her chin on my shoulder next to my ear. My hands went to her thighs before I stood and started up the stairs.

"Oh, this is much better. The stairs hate me when I drink," she giggled.

I chuckled. "Don't worry, lass. We're almost there." She wrapped her arms around my shoulders to rest her hands on my chest. Poor thing was going to be hung over in the morning.

When we reached the door, I opened it and carried her in. Atticus looked up from his laptop in the living room.

"What did you do to her?" Atticus growled. He got up from the couch and stalked towards us.

"I'm just drunk," she explained, her voice matter of fact. "And when I'm drunk, stairs hate me." I set her down to stand on her own. She moved towards the sofa. I helped keep her straight until she was leaning against the back of the couch.

"You got her drunk?" Atticus snapped as I stepped back from her.

"I got myself drunk," she countered before turning to me. I kept watch on her out of the corner of my eye as Atticus glared at me. "Can you get me to my room, please?" I chuckled.

"Oh no, you're not my Match. I only promised to get ye home," I said, putting my hands up in surrender. I met Atticus's furious gaze. "This is your Match, you take care of her." I walked backwards out the door. The look on Atticus's face was murderous before I shut the door, laughing.

～

Atticus

I GROWLED AS RANULF LEFT. That asshole! Get her drunk then leave her here for me to deal with. She giggled behind her hand. I turned to her only for her to stop trying to hide it. She started laughing.

"Your face is priceless," she managed between giggles. I sighed. She really was drunk. Shit. She held up her hand and got herself under control. "Don't worry, I can get myself to bed," she slurred, an English accent suddenly evident. She started moving toward her room, using the sofa to help her along.

I sighed then moved to help her, reaching her just as she let go of the sofa. She didn't stumble but she wasn't stable. Not wanting to take a chance of her falling, I scooped her up off her feet and held her against my chest.

"Whoa," she said. Her hands went to my shoulders. "A little warning would be nice." I bit back the urge to lecture her on getting drunk. She probably wouldn't remember this in the morning anyway.

When we reached her room and I set her on her feet, she immediately went to the bed and laid down.

"Thank you, Atticus," she mumbled.

"Not yet, Evelyn," I told her. I took her arms and pulled her into a sitting position. She grumbled. I held her face until she opened those beautiful eyes and looked at me. "You need to drink some water."

"A cuppa and biscuits sounds better," she countered, a London accent slipping out. I bit back a smile at the sound.

"You won't be awake that long," I reminded her.

She pointed vaguely to the bathroom door. "I keep a glass in there."

When I was sure she wasn't going to lay down, I went into the bathroom. I found the glass by the sink. As I filled it she moved around in her bedroom, humming. At least she wasn't going to sleep. I looked at the small womanly things here and there on the counter. A lovely, blue-tinted glass container for cotton balls with a silver lid, a matching one for make-up brushes. Even her soap dispenser matched. It all had a certain feminine feel. Smiling to myself, I shut off the tap and walked back into the bedroom. She was leaning against her carved headboard with her arms around her drawn up knees, her cheek resting against them. Her shoes and leggings had disappeared, but her sweater was still in place. I tried not to notice how soft her skin looked.

I sat next to her and handed her the water. "Drink this and you can go to sleep."

Her eyes ran over my face. "You're taking care of me," she said softly, that accent sending chills over my body. "Why? You weren't even going to tell me."

Guilt ate at me. "And that would have been a mistake," I admitted quietly. Leaving her without telling her what had happened would have been cruel. I am many things, but cruel has never been one of them. Over the last couple hours I had come to a decision. I might not be able to be her Mate, but that didn't mean I couldn't make sure she was alright. If I kept my distance, she'd be safe.

She smiled then leaned forward and kissed me sweetly. My cock grew heavy from that one sweet, chaste kiss.

When she pulled back she had a soft smile on her lips. "Thank you."

"Drink," I reminded her gruffly, my heart racing in my chest. My body burned. Why the hell did she do that? Fucking Ranulf! He had to get her drunk. She quickly drank the water then handed me the glass. I set it on the night stand. "Now you can go to sleep."

She nodded, she was half asleep already. I stood and slid the blankets out from under her. She laid down and was almost out before I even covered her with her blankets. She snagged the blankets, snuggled down and curled up. Unable to stop myself, I brushed her hair from her face. She smiled softly. I clenched my fist.

I had to leave. I needed time away from her. I shut off her light before closing the door and heading out of her apartment. I took several minutes out in the hall to give my body time to calm down. By then, I was tempted to kill Ranulf.

In the living room of our apartment, Zahur, Falk and Ranulf were talking. They turned to me when I shut the door behind me.

"You got her drunk," I growled.

Ranulf rolled his eyes. "She's a grown female, she can handle herself."

"You're not watching her tonight," I stated. "Zahur, go over and take guard duty."

Zahur chuckled. "Guard another male's Match? At night? No, thank you." He shook his head. "If you want her protected, especially at night, you do it."

"Zahur," I warned.

Zahur shook his head. "I'm not stupid enough to do that. There are higher and older rules than you and your orders, Atticus."

I cursed and turned to Falk. He held his hands up and shook his head.

"Fine," I growled before turning around and walking out into the hall. I stepped into my room to get some pajamas for tonight. I was going to have to wear a shirt. I cursed the others as I stopped and took several deep breaths. Control, control, keep control.

When I was calmer I walked over to her apartment and grabbed a pillow from the linen closet. Not bothering to pull out the sofa bed, I set down my night clothes then took off my jacket and sat down. Looking down at the floor, my mind went back to that kiss.

Why the hell did she have to do that? And why the hell did she have to taste like fresh berries in the summer?

6

DECEMBER 17

I was in the middle of a delicious dream involving a naked male when my phone rang. I jerked myself up and grabbed the phone out of reflex. I was barely awake when I answered.

"Yeah, I'm here. I think," I half slurred into the phone.

"Evie, you need to get your ass down here." Brian's voice was panicked. That woke me up instantly.

"What's going on?"

"I've got a vamp body here that's been torn to pieces," he said quietly. "It looks like a werewolf kill." Damn it! I jumped out of bed and headed for my bedroom door.

"Has anyone else seen it?" I asked as I moved into the living room. Atticus looked up from his book and spotted me, his eyes growing wide.

"Yeah, his 'next of kin' who happened to be a vampire," Brian told me.

"I'll be there in five!" I hung up the phone, grabbed my keys and headed for the door. Atticus grabbed my arm. His touch brought me to a stop, my heart slowed as calm slid through me. What the ...?

"What's wrong?" he demanded.

"There's a vamp body in the morgue that looks like a werewolf kill, and the vamps already know about it," I told him quickly. "So, I have to go down there and figure out if it really is before the two groups go to war." Atticus was only quiet for half a beat.

"Alright, but you need to put on pants first," he pointed out. I blinked and looked down. I was in a pair of purple hipster panties and my sweater from last night.

"Damn it," I growled as I ran for my room. I quickly pulled on jeans and stuffed my feet into sneakers. I didn't bother with the bra and ran back into the apartment. The others were standing in the hall now, Atticus explaining what was going on. I grabbed my wool jacket, ran between them and headed down the stairs while I searched my contacts. There were curses behind me as they followed. I put my phone to my ear as I slammed my shoulder into the door. I searched the empty street and found Atticus's car.

"Someone get me to the morgue," I ordered. Everyone got moving.

"I expected to hear from you, Evelyn," Craig, Lemora's personal assistant, was practically joyful.

"Put her on, Craig!" I snapped as I climbed in the back with Zahur and Falk. Atticus took the driver's seat as Ranulf took the front.

"I'm sorry to say she's a little busy at the moment," Craig said his voice sickeningly sweet. Atticus cursed, reached back and put my seatbelt on me before he gunned it down the street.

"I know, that's what we need to talk about," I pointed out calmly. Atticus took a corner too fast, throwing me into Zahur. "I know about the dead vamp, I'm heading to the morgue now."

"Oh, don't worry about that," Craig preened. "We've already investigated. It was a wolf kill, we're just preparing an appropriate response." That's it.

"Put. Her. On," I growled into the phone, "or I'll rip your guts out and use them as decorations for my Christmas tree. All thirty feet of them." The car went silent. So was Craig. He knew I wasn't messing around. I wasn't known in this city for making empty threats.

"I'll transfer you to her immediately," Craig said in his professional tone.

"Thank you," I replied in the same manner. It wasn't long before there was a voice in my ear.

"Ms. De Haven." The vampire Queen of Chicago's voice rolled through my ear like fog.

"Ms. Lemora, I'm aware of the situation that has occurred," I said in a polite, professional voice. "I'm on my way now to investigate the incident."

"We've already investigated, dear. It's a wolf kill," she said in a cool voice with a slight southern accent. The accent was fake; the vamp was from France.

"We have an agreement, Lemora," I reminded her, my voice firm. "Any altercation between species in the area and you go through me first. Control your people until I figure out what happened." There was a long silence.

"Alright," Lemora sighed. "Investigate, but I want news before dawn and proof by dusk."

"You'll hear from me before sunrise," I said before I hung up.

Atticus pulled into the parking lot at the hospital. Falk was the first to get out of the car. I went to follow only to be brought up short by the seatbelt. What the ...? Oh, yeah. I unbuckled myself and slid out of the car. Not wanting to waste time, I jogged to the back door of the hospital and swiped my card. The light turned green, I tore open the door and hurried down the hall. The guys had no problem keeping up with me.

I shoved the doors to the morgue open and strode in. Brian was already at a gurney, waiting. His eyes grew wide as we strode in.

"Stop me if you've heard this one: five gargoyles walk into a morgue," Brian teased. I rolled my eyes as I went to the bloody sheet covering the body.

"You know about us?" Atticus asked calmly.

"Relax, Atticus, he has the Sight," I told him absently as I took the file Brian handed me. "It's why I got him a job in the morgue." I looked through the file quickly. Multiple lacerations to the stomach, chest and throat, right arm torn from the socket, left leg amputated. The list of injuries went on and on.

"Any organs removed?" I asked as I shut the file.

"We haven't gotten that far, he was decapitated," Brian answered. I looked down at the sheet. There seemed to be a head there.

"His head wasn't taken?" I asked.

"Nope, it wasn't too far from the body either," Brian informed me. I looked at the guys.

"Okay, gentlemen, things are about to get ghastly," I announced as I pulled my hair up into a bun. "If you have a queasy stomach, please leave now." I reached for a pair of gloves and pulled them on before looking up. No one had budged. "Okay, don't say I didn't warn you." I reached for the sheet and pulled it down off the body. Or what was left of it. There was so much damage that it was hard to tell what was what or where it belonged. In short, it looked like a were-wolf kill. I pulled the light down, took a deep breath and let it out. Then I slipped my hand into what was left of the

stomach cavity. This vamp wasn't a small man. The weight
had to have been put on after he was converted. I eyed that
belly, wondering how much blood it took to get yourself a
big belly like that. I had a feeling I didn't want to know. My
hand moved through a plump fat layer. Then I got stuck.
Oh, disgusting.

"Brian?" It was all I had to say. Brian was on the other
side of the gurney with gloves already on. He reached in and
separated the tissue so I could feel around the cavity. Blood
coated up to my elbow, my stomach rolled. My fingers found
every organ still there. I pulled my hand out. "All the organs
are still there," I said absently.

"Which means?" Ranulf asked.

"It wasn't a werewolf. They like taking parts of their kills,
even if they won't eat them," I muttered as I moved to the
head on the gurney. A smell hit me. I took another deep
breath. Sulfur and smoke filled my lungs. I followed the
smell to the victim's hair. It was stronger there. "Brian, I
need a lock of his hair in a bag." I straightened and took off
my gloves while he did that. "His hair smells like sulfur, so it
might be a demon kill." Brian cut off a large chunk of hair
and put it into a plastic bag, then sealed it. "But to be sure
...." I put my hand on the dead vampire's forehead.

"Don't," Atticus warned. I dove into the victim's mind
and looked for that last memory. It wasn't as dark as usual;
some memory banks were still glowing. After such a long
life, it took longer for those memories to die. I focused on
the one at the far end of the area. It was already a big ball,
still full of energy and glowing. It only took a touch and I
was standing on the snowy sidewalk.

I was enjoying the walk, Lemora was cracking down on
us about feeding on humans. 'Use the clinics.' God, her voice
was annoying. Blood from a bag wasn't the same as blood

from the vein and it never would be. I turned the corner then I felt it. Rage pouring over me. It's those wolves and that gargoyle who are to blame. My hands shook as I strode down the alley. If they weren't here, we'd be free to do what we want. I needed to do something about it. Tonight. I smiled, my fangs slipping out. We'll kill the gargoyle tonight, and tomorrow the wolves. A hand caught my shoulder and spun me around. I gaped up at the creature that towered over me. Its black skin was smoldering. It had a muscular build and horns scrolling back from its bald scalp. Its black eyes were empty as it tore my arm off. I screamed. Time to go!

I pulled back into my own mind. I fell back into a hard body, arms holding me up. Shouting echoed through the room.

"I'm fine," I gasped. The room fell silent as I tried to get my bearings. The scent of parchment filled my nose. I opened my eyes and looked up to find Atticus holding me against his chest. The warmth that filled me wasn't overpowering, it was soothing, comforting. It was just what I needed right now.

"What did you see?" he demanded. Well, it *was* comforting. I sighed, pulled away from him and headed for the sink.

"It's another fully formed demon," I announced as I scrubbed my arm and hands until they were pink. "This one is a Deava."

Zahur cursed.

"What kind?" Ranulf asked.

"They start wars, create trouble where there wasn't any," Zahur answered for me. I dried my hands with a paper towel as I turned back to them.

"Why do we have another fully formed demon after just killing the last one?" I asked them.

"That's a very good question," Atticus said. I threw the paper towel away.

"We'll figure it out. But right now, I have to convince the big bad vamp of Chicago not to go to war," I announced. Brian held up the plastic bag. "Thanks for the heads up, Brian. Can you have that couriered over to Lemora's?"

"Your wish is my command," he said sarcastically. I shot him a look before I headed out the door with the guys following. I pulled out my phone and called Lemora back. This time Craig put me through immediately. I focused on my call while we moved through the hospital.

"It's a demon. A Deava." I didn't bother with the niceties.

"Proof?" Lemora asked.

"I checked out his death memory, and a hair sample that smells like sulfur and smoke is being brought to you today," I countered as we walked outside to the parking lot.

"Alright," she said. "I'll tell my people to stand down."

"Have a nice day, Lemora."

"You as well, enjoy the hunt." Lemora hung up as we reached the car. I put my phone away.

"We need to hurry."

"Sunrise is in twenty minutes," Ranulf pointed out. "It'll go into hiding."

"Yeah, but what if it chooses somewhere that's populated?" I countered.

Ranulf's brows went up. "Good point."

"Let's go back to the apartments," Atticus bit out. "I have some questions for you." His face was blank as a wall as he climbed into the car. The others exchanged looks before getting in. Wondering what had Atticus so grumpy, I got in too.

The car ride was full of tense silence all the way back to our apartments. He pulled into a spot in front of the building door. I got out and headed up, not bothering to wait for any of them.

The others caught up quickly as I walked into my apartment. I started for my bedroom door when the front door closed.

"Evelyn," Atticus called, his voice cold. I turned back to find all of them in my apartment. Zahur was sitting on a stool at the breakfast counter, Ranulf was leaning against the back of the couch, Falk was still next to the door. All of them were somber and watching Atticus.

"What are you doing? Go gear up," I reminded them. We had a demon to catch and I wanted to get it soon.

"Why are you mediating between vampires and were-wolves?" Atticus asked in a deadly, calm voice. Wasn't it obvious?

"Because that's what they agreed to when I got them to stop fighting forty-five years ago," I explained. "Each side agreed to stop fighting, take their side of town and any problems come to me."

Atticus ran his hand down his face, his shoulders tense. "You made deals with these species?" Zahur shifted on the stool, his feet moving to the floor.

"I guess you could call them that, we call them Treaties," I explained, not understanding why Atticus was clenching and unclenching his fists.

"We don't do that," he declared, his voice icy.

"You don't make deals?" I didn't understand.

Atticus strode towards me then stopped four feet away. "We police these creatures, keep them in line," Atticus growled. His piercing eyes met mine. "We don't make friends with them, we don't talk to them on the phone. We hunt them down when they break our laws, that's it."

"Why did you make these Treaties?" Zahur asked. I

turned to him. His eyes weren't judging, just curious. It was a nice change from Atticus's blank face. I opened my mouth to explain but Atticus talked right over me. My own temper started heating up.

"It doesn't matter why, it's against the laws set by the Elder Council," Atticus declared. I shut my mouth and looked at him. His face was hard, his eyes cold.

"First, I was never taught those laws," I explained, trying to stay calm. "Second, the Treaties I've made work."

Atticus cursed. "You only think they work because the vampires and wolves want you to think it. They are probably still out there killing and you have no idea because they are hiding the bodies or converting."

"I'm not an idiot, Atticus," I bit out as I tried to explain how it worked. "They can't convert without my consent."

Atticus grew still. "Have you ever given it?" Tension filled the room.

I knew he wasn't going to like my answer. "Once."

His furious gaze met mine. "Do you know what would happen to you if the Elder Council ever found out?"

"They aren't here," I snapped. "They pulled out of this city before I even got here. They left chaos. I fixed it. Who cares what this Elder Council thinks? I don't know them and they don't know me."

"You've given permission for conversion. There is no reason good enough to sink to that level," he growled as he came closer. His golden eyes were full of disgust as he answered. "It's against a millennium of tradition that has kept the world from disaster." He shook his head, his disappointment clear. My stomach knotted at the sight.

"You're done," he announced. "You are clearly not capable of understanding the repercussions of the decisions you've made here. You obviously don't understand what you're doing." That hit me hard in the chest, as if a blade had been driven deep. My lungs grew tight as I fought to hide the hurt. Damn. This Matching stuff was starting to irritate the heck out of me. His eyes met mine again. "You'll have a guard from now on, at all times, no question about it. Any decisions that need to be made, I will make," he declared. My heart sank. Did ... did he not even respect me as a person? I looked away from him to the window above the sink as I fought back tears. The sun was rising. I needed to get to work, but first I had to get control of myself.

"Atticus, it's a dangerous situation, yes. Though..." Zahur started.

"You can't just ..." Ranulf trailed off to silence.

When my emotions were under control I met Atticus's eyes.

"Good luck with that," I said, my voice tired. If he thought he could just take over in Chicago, if he thought that little of me .... I pushed it away as I headed for my bedroom.

"We aren't done, Evelyn," Atticus growled.

"I didn't think we were," I called over my shoulder as I started to close the door. "I'm just changing." I shut the door. The males started arguing in the living room.

I took a shaky breath as I sat on the bed, braced my elbows on my knees and buried my face in my hands. My throat was tight as I swallowed hard. The way he looked at me. I took a deep breath. It wasn't as if I had much choice. Yes, I can be too trusting but I wasn't foolish. I knew every species in the city, I knew their weaknesses and strengths. Dropping my hands, I lifted my head. Zahur said to pay attention to his actions not his words. He was making that rather difficult.

Dawn began to lighten my room. I needed to get to work.

I went to my closet and pulled on my usual demon hunting gear. My worn, scorched, black leather pants, y-back black tank top and my hardened, black-leather, armored vest. The leather fit me like a glove, with extra armor over my heart. Lots of demons liked to go for the heart. I fastened the silver buckles at my side and pulled on my black leather, knee-high boots. The voices in the living room were getting louder while I put on the same belt from the trunk of my car. I pulled on my shoulder harness, thankful only my emergency harness had been destroyed. I tied it tight. This one was thicker and more comfortable to be honest.

I went to my closet and pulled out my jacket, more black armored leather. I slipped it on and buttoned the three buttons below my chest. The coat was fitted through my arms and torso, then flared down to my knees. It hid my weapons from view and covered my body when I wasn't using magic. I slid my second short sword into the sheath at the back of my neck.

The males weren't even trying to be quiet now. Ranulf's voice was clear through the shouting. I ignored them as I pulled a dented, round, metal flask of holy water out of the chest at the bottom of the closet. I slipped my phone into the breast pocket of my jacket. I pulled my hair out of the bun and quickly made a tight braid that reached the middle of my back.

When I was done I moved to the door and listened. The others were arguing with Atticus, Ranulf cursing the most. Falk, of course, said nothing.

I couldn't take these guys on a Deava hunt. It'd have them tearing each other apart, not to mention the damage I could do to Atticus right now.

I went to my nightstand and grabbed my spare keys for the Mustang, then walked softly to my large window, opened it and slipped out onto the fire escape. I closed the window and moved quickly down the metalwork, my mind already going over what I would need to do to kill the Deava.

IT WASN'T LONG until I was at the murder scene. Another alley. With all the dead bodies found in alleys you'd think people would steer clear, but no. They kept taking that shortcut at night. It wasn't hard to find the blood spatter. I knelt down and used a blade to scrape up some blood. I created a ball of fire in my left hand and dropped the scrapings into the flame. The flame turned red. I dropped it on to the blood-stained cement. Flames spread over the splatter then shot down the alleyway and towards the street. Great, we are going where the people are. I started walking. My mind wandered back to Atticus, the way he had looked at me. I knew it was the whole Matching thing, but it hurt. And I didn't like that it hurt. He didn't even give me a chance to explain. It was just, 'You're breaking the laws, you're doing it wrong.'

I sighed as I followed the flame down another alley. Never mind that I've done just fine over the past hundred years. No, I had to be wrong.

The flames moved further into the warehouse district. Super. I kept walking. Did the male even like me? As a person? I thought about it. No, I didn't think he did. I sighed and kept going. Did I even like him? I liked the Atticus I first met, the one that was in the car yesterday morning. The one who could challenge me with quotes. The one that took care of me last night. Where had that Atticus gone?

The flame led straight to a large warehouse at the end of

the long block. My phone rang. I pulled it out. It said Zahur. They must have finally noticed I was gone.

"Hello?"

"Where are you?" Zahur asked, his voice strained.

"Oh, just hunting down a demon," I said matter-of-factly. "You know, my job."

"This isn't a good idea, Evelyn," he advised.

"No, it's a great idea," I said cheerfully. "A Deava feeds off creating trouble between people. Taking a group into that would be incredibly stupid. It'd have us killing each other in no time. This is a one gargoyle hunt and you know it." He was quiet as he thought about it.

"That doesn't mean it has to be you," he countered.

"I know, but I have some anger I need to work out. This is just good timing," I offered. I wasn't lying, I was rather angry at Atticus.

"Atticus is furious," he said quietly. Surprise, surprise. Atticus is angry with me.

"I don't care if he is," I told him honestly. "He can't barge into my life, try to take over and bark orders." I reached the rusted warehouse door. "Look, I appreciate the concern but I've found its hidey-hole and need to go."

"Don't do something suicidal because you're angry at Atticus," he cautioned. I smiled to myself.

"Zahur, you guys don't really know me, but I don't do suicide. I need to go." I hung up the phone, frustrated. I tucked my cell back into my pocket then took off my jacket. I carried it with me to the door. I rolled my neck until it popped then charged my powers. The markings in my skin, which were usually invisible, glowed bright blue. Long lines down my arms and across my chest lit up. It only ever happened when I used a lot of energy, and I had a sneaking suspicion that I was going to need it today. My body practically thrummed with energy as I walked into the warehouse.

It was the office, and it was a mess. The stench of copper filled my nose as I let the door close behind me. Desks were overturned, papers were scattered over the blood-soaked floor. Three bodies littered the floor of the office, one with a letter opener sticking out of her neck. One had a tie wrapped around her throat, her lips blue. It looked like she'd been strangled. Another was further along the floor with his head caved in, brain matter and bone exposed to the air, a bloody stapler on the floor beside him. Damn it. Were there more people in the warehouse? I walked over the bloody floor and opened the door to the main warehouse. Large crates blocked my view of the main floor. I moved behind them until I came out into the center. A body was draped over the railing of the catwalk, several others had been ripped open. But I only had eyes for the large demon waiting for me in the center of the warehouse.

He looked like your stereotypical monster, hunched over with its claws digging grooves into the cement floor. Its obsidian skin was on fire, flames rising and flickering in the dim light. Its red eyes were watching me out of its sharp, almost wolfish, face. Its black tongue licked its lips, or what there was of them.

"Come to play, little gargoyle?" it asked, its voice dark and deep. I dropped my jacket and walked out from between the crates.

"How could I ignore such an invitation?" I asked politely. It circled left, I went right. "You could have had a feast. The city could be ripping itself apart by now. Yet you stuck to one vampire. Why?" I asked. The demon scoffed.

"My reasons are my own," it growled deeply. It was a

growl meant to run down your spine and make your skin crawl. To me, it was just irritating.

"A Deava like you? How long have you been stuck in Hell? You must be starving. Or did you just come for the scenery? Why limit yourself?" I asked.

"Orders are orders." It eyed me. "Now, let me see what your insides look like." I formed a ball of lightning in my palms, the lines on my skin glowed brighter in the dim light of the warehouse. My mouth burned as both sets of fangs slipped out.

I gave him a bloodthirsty smile. "Let's."

Heart racing, my grip was tight on the wheel as I drove through a deserted alley and followed the flame line into the warehouse district. She'd gone hunting alone! I was going to kill her the second I saw her! If she was alive. My chest grew tight at the thought of her dead. Fucking Matching!

I didn't even know what the hell happened in her apartment. I just remember thinking about what would happen to her if the Elder Council ever found out about her allowing conversion. Execution. There was no other option. And I lost it. I fucking lost it. The next thing I knew the others were arguing with me and Zahur was checking on her. She was gone. I waited only long enough for Zahur's call then I was out the door and in my car faster than the others could keep up. They were back there, somewhere behind me in the SUV.

Fear ate at my gut as I pressed down on the accelerator. I needed her to listen, to follow the rules. Otherwise, I wasn't going to be able to get a handle on this.

It didn't help that I didn't know what her abilities were.

She always sounded confident, but was that arrogance or experience? Something told me I was about to find out.

I sped through the warehouse district. There! At the end of the lane the trail stopped. The flame flickered out. My heart dropped. Either the demon was dead or she was. I sped up. Terror clawed at me, making me shake.

It was only a minute before I screeched to a stop in front of the warehouse. Then I was out and running through the door. An office; she wasn't there. Panic took over as I kept running further into the warehouse. I came out from between the large crates and slowed.

The demon was across the main warehouse, dead, but that didn't matter. She was on her knees, out of breath. She looked up and met my eyes. Those beautiful eyes. I didn't think. I started striding towards her.

"What the fuck do you think you're doing?" I shouted. "You could have been killed!" I dropped to my knees in front of her, grabbed her chin and immediately began examining her. Her face was fine. A burn on one arm, legs fine. Blood, there was blood on her throat but it wasn't flowing.

"My job!" she shot back. "I'm fine." She tried to pry my hand off her chin. Her eyes met mine, fire burning in them. More than half crazy, my mouth crushed hers. Cherry blossoms filled my senses, I didn't wait for an invitation. I dove in and took her mouth, claiming her roughly, leaving nothing to doubt. She was mine. My Match. My Mate. My female. She met me stroke for stroke as heat burned through me.

Before I could lose myself completely, I grabbed her arms hard and pulled away. Those wild cognac eyes met mine. "Never again," I growled before pulling her back against me. My mouth took hers again. Her body pressed against me, her curves fitting perfectly. She was heaven. Her taste seared into my memory.

Tires screeching outside brought my control back. Barely. I pulled back, got to my feet and dragged her to hers. Emotions rioted through me as I marched her back outside with my hand locked around her arm.

I ripped the door open. Sunlight blinded me only for a second. The others started getting out of the black SUV. I all but dragged her out of the warehouse and to my car. I stood her beside it and met her eyes. "Stay. Here," I bit out before letting go. "Zahur, take care of her neck." I turned back to the warehouse, grabbing Ranulf's battleaxe out of his hands on my way. Control, control, control. I kept hold of my fury until I was standing over the demon. Then I let it loose. I swung and swung, dismembering the demon, then chopping it into smaller pieces. Those three bloody claw marks on her obliterating my control.

~

Evelyn

WHAT THE HECK JUST HAPPENED? Atticus strode back into the warehouse without another word. He kissed me .... He yelled at me, then kissed me again. My body was still throbbing from those kisses. And he walked off like nothing happened? What?

Zahur stopped in front of me and put the small med kit on the hood. "Any other injuries?"

"I'm fine, just scratches," I said, confused by Atticus. He tilted my head to the side and wiped the blood away. Zahur's touch cooled my body off faster than ice water.

"Scratches my ass, those are claw marks," Zahur countered as he pulled out antiseptic wipes.

"You alright, lass?" Ranulf asked, his voice warm. He moved to lean against the car beside me.

"Yeah, just a little mad he got through my shield," I admitted, angry at myself. "I mean, the claws I get, but he got through my shield with fire. That's irritating as heck."

Ranulf chuckled as Falk leaned against the SUV, waiting.

"Hold still, this will sting," Zahur warned. He held my face in one hand and cleaned my neck with the other.

"So, what happened in there?" Ranulf asked. I sighed.

"Well, it looks like when it went to hide from dawn, there were a few workers inside," I began. I looked up to meet his eyes. "They're dead."

"Killed each other, eh?" Ranulf asked.

"Yeah," I said, "Before the fight I asked the demon why it stuck to one vampire and not the city. It had an interesting answer." Zahur finished cleaning my neck and gave me his attention. "He said 'orders are orders.'"

Zahur blinked then put the trash back in the kit. "You think it was summoned?"

"Possibly." I shrugged. "But that's all I got before he got uppity and I had to put him down." Ranulf chuckled, Zahur raised an eyebrow.

I stayed put as Zahur looked over the burn on my shoulder. It was red and about as big as a softball. It had just been a graze. He cleaned it then put aloe on it anyway.

When he was done I glanced at the door to the warehouse. What was he doing? There was nothing left but burning the body and it shouldn't take this long.

"Evie, why don't you take the SUV and head back to your place," Zahur suggested.

I pulled my eyes from the door. "Sure, I need pick up my car, then change and open the shop."

"Falk, would you go with her?" Zahur asked. Falk nodded, pushed away from the car and went to the passenger side. I opened my door and looked back at the warehouse, wondering if Atticus was alright. Remembering his kiss, my body warmed.

"Evie." Zahur got my attention. "He's fine." I doubted it, but I didn't argue because I needed to get some distance between myself and Atticus. I nodded, then slid into the car.

IT WASN'T LONG until I was in my room changing. Wanting to feel better, I took a shower before pulling on a pair of black slacks, a white button up and a long, dark-green cardigan. I undid my braid and left my hair down, strands curling softly around me. I didn't look amazing, but heck, I didn't look bad. I was comfy and going to work. It's what I needed right now. I slipped my feet into black ballet flats and left my room.

Falk was quiet as I picked up my keys off the counter and headed for the door. He followed like a large shadow.

We went downstairs and outside. I quickly found my key and unlocked the outside gate. Falk lifted the gate, and put it away without me having to ask.

"Thank you," I muttered before unlocking the front door. I hurried inside and turned off the alarm. Falk closed the door as I started turning on lights.

I loved my store. The counter, shelves and staircase were all of the same rich, dark mahogany that darkened with age. On the left wall were shelves bulging with books to the ceiling, stairs to the second floor and the balcony. Rows and rows of books were upstairs, and the walls covered by them downstairs. I smiled and took a deep breath. The smell of old books calmed me like nothing I've found in my life.

I flipped the open sign around and headed to the back where my small office was. I turned on the electric kettle needing to make tea, and sat down. I used my office phone to check my messages and put it on speaker. Three were requests for rare books, two of which I already had. A request to find a buyer for three volumes of Don Quixote here in the States. It was my usual morning. Until the eighth message.

"Ms. De Haven, this is Mr. Gumner, the new owner of the building your bookstore currently resides in." I rolled my eyes. I had been dodging this creep for weeks. "I would like to meet with you regarding your late rent for the last three months. Please call me back at 555-2424. Thank you."

I growled at the phone and shut off the speaker. I knew exactly what Gumner wanted, he had jacked up the rent on my shop to kick me out so he could do whatever he wanted with the space. I hadn't been able to make the rent for the last three months. My plan of avoiding him had been working so far. But it looked like my time was running out. Crap.

I turned on the computer in my office and checked my schedule. Two deliveries from that estate sale a month ago. The man had been a world renowned collector and his catalogue of books had been amazing. I closed my eyes and sighed. I had put a lot of money on the line for those books, and now I had to find buyers. If I wanted to stay in business, that is.

The kettle whistled. I got up and went to it. "Falk, would you like some tea?"

Boots moved over the worn wood as he came to the office.

"Please," he said. I set about making tea.

"So, what would you be doing now if Zahur didn't order you to watch me?" I asked, looking for a way to break the silence.

"Investigating," he said, his voice hoarse.

"Sorry I'm keeping you from it," I said.

"I don't mind," he said, his rough voice quiet. I looked over my shoulder to him. He was leaning against the doorjamb. Okay... I finished making his tea then passed him his mug before making mine. When I was done I moved to step through the doorway. "Excuse me." I slipped by him and moved behind the counter, then took a sip of my tea. Ooh. Goodness. Coffee was wonderful, but it really took a good cup of tea to start my day. I set my mug down as I started up the front counter computer.

"Who's Gumner?" he asked, his voice only rough this time.

I focused on opening the safe behind the counter. "He's the new owner of the building." I opened the safe and checked to see if I had room for the rarer books. I didn't. I sighed.

"And you're avoiding him?" His voice was moving.

"He raised the rent on the store space, so I'm probably going to be forced to move out. But now I'm three months behind and he's adding fees and I-I need to pay it off in full for even the possibility of staying," I explained as I carefully pulled out several of the less rare books. "I really don't want to lose this space, I've been here forty years. So I need to sell quickly, which means less money for each book-" I turned, and all but ran into him. He took the books from my arms carefully, then set them down on the counter.

"What can I do to help?" he asked, his voice growing gravelly again. The backdoor buzzer rang through the shop.

I sighed. "You can help me get these crates in and the books inventoried."

He nodded.

"Thank you," I said gratefully before heading to the back of the shop. Falk was one step behind.

It wasn't long before the crates were in the back of the store. Falk didn't even bother with the dolly. He just picked one up and took it inside. The delivery guys were stunned when he came back and did it again. I just thanked them before they left. Since I didn't have a store room, Falk had left the crates in the back of the store near my office.

I pulled out a crowbar and started opening one of the large crates. Once it was opened, I carefully took out the padding. There they were. My last hope for the store. I pulled them out carefully, one by one. Excellent bindings, gilding, they were in beautiful shape. I started thinking about the fastest way to sell, or the most profitable. Weighing my options. I took a stack of books to the counter and began adding them to the inventory and my online catalogue. When I was done with that stack I looked up to find the counter covered. Falk had been busy.

"Falk?" I called. I didn't get an answer but my phone vibrated. I checked it.

Falk: Yeah?

I blinked at the screen. He was barely over fifteen feet from me, and he texted?

"Um, thank you for bringing the books up," I said uncertainly. My phone vibrated again.

Falk: You're welcome.

I tucked my phone away and went back to adding books. But it kept bothering me. He texted me instead of saying anything. It had to be the scar tissue on his throat. How did he manage without being able to speak? I walked out from behind the counter and its stack of books. Falk was still unloading the crates as I walked up to him.

"Falk, does it hurt to talk?" I asked carefully. He turned, his dark eyes finding me as he nodded. "So, if I started asking you questions, then I'd just be annoying you?" He frowned, pulled out his phone and typed. My phone vibrated.

Falk: No, it's just frustrating that I can't answer. And I hate typing. Big fingers, small buttons.

I smiled at that. His lips twitched as he looked at the shelves. Was that an almost smile? It was. Wow. Falk could smile. He looked back down at his phone and typed. My phone vibrated.

Falk: Ask anything you like.

I smiled as he leaned against the crate. He must have known Atticus for years, so the urge to ask about him was almost overwhelming. As I tried to come up with a question a thought occurred to me. I could do something to help communicate with Falk.

"Falk," I said quietly. He met my eyes. "There is something I can do to make it so you can communicate easier. But it could feel ... invasive." His brow drew down before he began typing.

Falk: What can you do? And what do you mean by invasive?

I licked my lips before answering. "I could heal some of your internal scar tissue."

He raised an eyebrow then began texting.

Falk: The healers at home said there is nothing that can be done.

"They aren't me." I hated to say it, but I was good. Darn good. I could use telepathy, but that was much more intimate than I wanted to get with Falk. He started texting.

Falk: Can you explain more?

I smiled and looked up at him. "I can heal a wound in minutes. With scar tissue it's more difficult and takes longer, but I can make it easier. And soothe your throat."

He thought about it for several heartbeats before sighing and texting me.

Falk: I'll try anything once.

I tucked my phone into my pocket and stepped closer. "Okay, I'm going to touch your throat and see what I am working with."

He raised an eyebrow.

"I use energy to see what is going on in your body, like a sonogram does with sound," I explained. He nodded.

I rested my hands awkwardly on both sides of his throat. I closed my eyes and focused.

I poured energy through my hands and into his throat. The tissue soaked up the energy like dye and showed me what was there. He had suffered one deep slash across his larynx, cutting the vocal cords. As I looked at the damage I was amazed that he survived. A healer had to have been nearby when it happened, otherwise he'd be dead.

I opened my mental barriers a little and reached out with a thought.

"You have a lot of scar tissue on your cords. It's limiting their movement," I sent to him. *"I'm going to try and smooth some of it out. It might feel warm."*

He swallowed hard but didn't say anything or take my hands from his throat, so I assumed that was permission. I channeled more energy through my hands and into his throat. Like a river over rock, I gently poured energy over the scar tissue. The irritation I could soothe any time he needed, but this I needed to wear down over time so I didn't do more damage. I watched his cords carefully, I lost track of time.

When the increase in blood flow started working for his vocal cords I stopped. I closed my barriers, opened my eyes and braced myself for a moment against the crate. "Give it a shot. Tell me how it feels."

He swallowed hard. "I'm not really one for small talk." His voice was slightly rough. "It's easier to talk."

I smiled. "Good. Over time I might be able to get it so you can talk all the time, but until then I can soothe the irritation any time you need." His obsidian eyes met mine.

"Thank you," he said. "You don't know what-"

"Yeah, I do," I said. "It would be a nightmare not to be able to say my piece." I looked around at the store. "Let's get back to work."

Atticus

IT WAS three o'clock and I was standing across the street from the bookstore. Falk had called asking someone to bring lunch for him and Evelyn. Falk had called.

Apparently, Evelyn had training in healing as well as fighting, and tracking... and telepathy. It left me wondering what other abilities she had. My mind flashed to the warehouse. Stop it, Atticus.

I stood across the street holding two boxes from the deli a few blocks away, watching her through the store window as she worked on the computer at the counter. She occasionally said something to Falk, but otherwise she worked quietly.

I didn't want to go in there. Yeah, Falk was hungry, but

he could order his own damn lunch. But when Falk said Evelyn forgot to even take a lunch break, I had no choice. I needed to make sure she was taken care of. I fought myself for over an hour before I gave in and went to the damn deli. Now I was stalling before going into the store. I had kissed her. What the fuck had I been thinking?

That was the problem, I hadn't been thinking. Seeing her on the floor of that warehouse hit some switch inside me. One I didn't even know I had.

When my anger finally cooled, there wasn't much left of the demon. Decimated flesh had been scattered over the warehouse floor, the blood everywhere. Clean up after that was simple.

She tucked a flyaway hair behind her ear absently. Her fingers moved down and ran over the claw marks on her throat. Even from here I could tell when her eyes unfocused. Was she thinking about the near miss? Or me kissing her? Her face softened a little as she stared at the screen. Shit, it wasn't the demon. What did I start back there in the warehouse? She blinked several times, dropped her hand to the keyboard and went back to work. Which is exactly what I was going to do.

Our investigation after this morning had found nothing. It looked like the Hunger demon had simply found a crack in the barrier to slip through. And the Deava? Nothing. We searched the buildings around the kill site and didn't find a hint of a summoning circle. The demon had just been messing with Evelyn. It must have come through the same crack as the Hunger demon. And Zahur was on it.

Which meant we had no reason to stay here. We could leave tonight. Except... she wasn't going to want to leave. But I had to bring her back. And Zahur was right. I couldn't force her to leave, no matter what Cyrus said. It wasn't in me. That look of hurt in her eyes this morning had been enough to show me that.

I cursed as I realized the truth. We were going to have to stay until we could convince her to leave with us. And I was going to have to stay on that damn pullout until we did.

Ranulf spotted me as he came down the street. I crossed the street and met him outside the apartments.

I handed him the boxes. "Take these in to the bookstore. I'm not their damn caterer."

Ranulf took them with a smirk. "No problem, I wanted to see what they were up to anyway." I went to the doorway to the apartments and left him on the sidewalk. I needed to stay away from that female as much as possible. Maybe I could convince her to come home with us tonight?

~

Evelyn

FALK and I spoke on and off for hours. I returned my calls for books and made arrangements for the buyers to come in. I even made an appointment with Mr. Gumner for tomorrow afternoon.

By the end of the day I was frustrated. I had lined up three books sales, which would give me a total of twenty-two thousand dollars. But I had spent eighteen thousand on those books. Yeah, four grand was great, but not with a debt of six digits. I could have made better deals if I had the time.

"Evie? What's wrong?"

I looked up to find Falk in the doorway. "Nothing, I'm just tired," I lied. He raised an eyebrow.

I sighed. "I'm worrying." There was only one way I could see to get out of this debt with enough to start over again. I was hoping I was wrong. I got to my feet and started shutting everything down for the night. I made sure to grab the file I put together before locking up. Falk pulled down the gate and locked it for me. When we reached the landing my front door was slightly open. I was getting so used to everyone being in my apartment it didn't even surprise me. When I stepped inside I hesitated in the doorway. Atticus was examining the books in the bookcases, alone. Wondering where the others were, I took off my cardigan and left it on the breakfast bar as I went to fill the kettle with water. Falk, however, stopped in the doorway when he saw Atticus. His eyes met mine before he stepped out into the hall and closed the door behind him, leaving me alone with Atticus. Silence filled the apartment as I set up my mug for tea. I hesitated then sighed.

"Would you like some tea?" I asked, not turning around.

"Yes, please," he said. I pulled out another mug as footsteps came closer. Taking a deep breath, I turned around. He was at the breakfast counter sitting on a stool, his eyes unfocused as he looked out the window over the sink. I had set out sugar and milk on the counter by the time he said something.

"Evelyn, there are a few things I'd like to discuss with you," he said. I took a breath and let it out. Our kiss from this morning. We *should* probably talk about it.

"Alright." I started playing with my locket.

"We've spent the day investigating how the demons came through. Zahur has found the large crack in the barrier that they utilized," Atticus announced. I was stunned for a few heartbeats. That's what he wanted to talk about? Not me hunting alone, not kissing me, but demons? I let out a breath.

"That's good news," I said, my voice uncertain. The

kettle whistled. I went back to the stove and filled the mugs, brought both to the breakfast bar then set his in front of him.

"It is. And since this seems to have been a rare double incident," Atticus took a breath. "It's time to head back."

My eyes jumped to meet his. "You're leaving?" I asked carefully.

"There is no reason for us to stay except for you," he explained. "We all have responsibilities back home and I can't keep the others away from theirs because of you."

He was right. I looked down at my tea, my throat tightening. "That wouldn't be fair," I agreed.

"Evelyn, you have a place with us in our community," he said carefully. I looked up from my tea to meet those golden eyes. "Come with us. You can have a home there. Friends. We might even be able to find out if you have distant relatives."

What he was describing sounded wonderful, but there were things he didn't know. "I have obligations here."

He looked out the window, his jaw clenching and unclenching again. "What obligations?"

"The city will fall apart if I'm not here," I explained. "Those Treaties are with me, not with the other species. If I left, a war between the vamps and wolves could start. The city could turn into a war zone."

"You have a responsibility to your species," he reminded me. "If you go, depending on your bloodline... you might find that you have more than one Match."

His words hit me like a blade to the heart. He must really not want me. Then why did he kiss me? His concern, the kiss ... was it all just the Matching? I swallowed hard before I met his eyes. "No, thank you. One is more than enough." I needed to get away from him. I picked up my file and headed for the door.

"Evelyn," he tried again.

"I have some business to take care of with Astrid. Have a safe trip home," I told him before I closed the door behind me and started down the stairs.

Atticus

THE DOOR SHUT QUIETLY, leaving the apartment in silence. I closed my eyes and sighed. Nice job, Atticus. Why don't you slaughter her cat while you're at it? Probably because she didn't have one. I hurt her again, only this time I don't know how. I ran over our conversation again, then cursed.

I tried every argument I could think of. Except the Matching. There was no way to use that without lying about what was going to happen. That would just hurt her even more and I couldn't do that. I was already taking away any chance she would get to have children, that didn't mean I had to add to it. But I was getting desperate.

Whenever she was around my emotions were every-where. They were sharp, painful and overwhelming. And as I had learned this morning, just being in the same room tested my control. Every time those eyes met mine she made me feel ... everything. And I didn't want to feel. It was dangerous. Cyrus made it clear. Keep emotion out of your life and you'll stay in control. You won't become a monster like the rest of your family. Cherry blossoms filled my lungs. I opened my eyes and found her sweater. Sighing, I picked it up and headed for her bedroom.

I opened her small closet and began putting her sweater

on a hanger as I thought about her. She was beautiful. Completely different than I'd ever imagined my Match would be. I expected a female who would be happy with being mine, who would do as I asked without question and let me keep her at arm's length. Instead, I got a female who was stubborn, argued with me and was ... different. Who tasted like my favorite summer berries. I hung up her sweater and closed the small closet.

I went back into the kitchen, poured out the mugs and started running the water in the sink. I kept pushing her away like Cyrus told me to. But the longer I was around her, the more my control slipped. My lungs became tight. I washed the few dishes with shaking hands. I despised myself for it. I kept hurting her on purpose to push her away and it was probably working. I should be glad, not hurting this way. I put the mugs in the drainer and shut off the water, then leaned my hands on the counter and looked down at the floor.

Instead, I'm fighting the urge to go after her and make sure she's safe. Only her staying away from me would make it stop. But I didn't want her gone. I cursed at the thought. I had to stay the course. I had to keep her away and get her to go back. It was safer for everyone. I just needed to get her back home, where things made sense.

I turned and looked around her apartment. How the hell was I going to sleep on her couch and keep my distance? I cursed myself. I shouldn't have kissed her. I shouldn't stay here at night. But the idea of her being alone in this apartment at night haunted me. I found myself going over her books more often than I'd like to admit. It was an impressive collection. I know I should stay out of her apartment when she wasn't home. It's just ... I sighed. This was the closest I would ever come to being with her. And I didn't know how I felt about that. I cursed.

I straightened and headed out of her place, berating myself the whole way back to our apartment. The others were in the living room watching TV. They turned to me when I came in.

"Someone tail Evelyn to Astrid's and make sure there aren't any more bar fights," I ordered. The others shared a look before answering.

"It looks like we aren't leaving," Ranulf said under his breath. Falk smirked.

"I'm not feeling up to it," Zahur announced. "My arthritis is acting up. You know how us old males are."

I shot him a look. Gargoyles didn't get arthritis. Before I could call him on it, Ranulf spoke up.

"I've gotta wash my hair, boss," Ranulf said, getting to his feet and heading into the kitchen. "These luscious locks don't take care of themselves you know."

I wanted to kill him.

"Can't, think I'm getting the flu," Falk rasped. I was going to kill all of them.

"Knock it off," I snapped. "One of you get out there." I started heading for my room, fuming.

"Sorry, we're all busy. Why don't you watch your Match?" Zahur asked.

I stopped walking. Fucking Zahur. The meddling ass. I turned back to the room to yell at them.

Zahur checked the time on his phone. "She should be getting close to the bar, it's not too far away."

Fuck! They weren't going to do it. "I'm reporting your asses," I growled on my way to the door.

They started laughing before I even slammed the door behind me.

8

My throat was tight as I drove over to Astrid's bar. It was almost empty, her regulars wouldn't be here for a few more hours. She was behind the bar when I walked in.

"Hey," I said as I reached the bar.

Astrid's smile faded as she saw my face. "What's wrong?"

"I need your advice," I admitted.

She dropped the towel on the bar and headed back to her office without a word. I followed. The space was cluttered. I had no idea how she could find anything in here, but if I asked her for something she would know exactly where it was. She leaned on her desk. I took the chair across from her.

"What's going on?" she asked, worried. I handed her the file I brought with me.

"I'm going to lose the store." I finally admitted it out loud. My eyes burned as I continued. "It's not detrimental, I already do a large portion of my business online-"

"Why do you think you're going to lose the store?" she asked, opening the file.

"Remember how Mr. Gumner passed away?"

"Yeah. He was a sweet old bag," she said absently as she scanned my finances and inventory.

"Well, his son isn't. He tripled the rent and I'm three months behind," I admitted.

"How much?" she asked, still looking over the papers.

"One hundred and eighty thousand."

Astrid's head shot up, her face horrified. "What? For three months' rent? That's fucking ridiculous."

"Sadly, it's a prime commercial spot. Lots of foot traffic." I shrugged. "I can only see one way out of this, and I'm hoping you'll see another way."

She eyed me suspiciously before she went back to the folder. She found it a minute later. "Evie, this list includes your private collection."

I looked down at my lap and started cleaning my nails. "Yes, it does. I could get more for them if I had the time, but he wants to meet this week and I can't dodge him again."

"How long do you think you have before he evicts you?" she asked seriously.

"Maybe two weeks," I said. "And if I pay it off, I'll still have nothing to start up again."

"What about your apartment? You could sell," she offered.

I looked up and shook my head. "Not in time, and not without a huge loss and no way to get another place."

"You could stay with me," she reminded me.

I gave her a smile. "I can't, you know that. Your pack would get on your back for it."

"Fuck my pack, you're my best friend." She snapped the folder shut. "If you do what you're thinking, you'll have nothing to start over with. You won't have inventory."

I nodded.

"Fuck, Evelyn." Her face was pained. "What about a loan? Pay it all off at once. Just to give you the time you need to get a good price for the books."

"I tried last month," I admitted. "No bank will touch me with my limited credit score."

"You still dealing with that shit?" she asked.

"They think I'm a twenty-two-year-old who inherited her mother's business," I reminded her.

"Fuck." She got up and went to her filing cabinet. She pulled out a bottle of scotch and two tumblers. She poured me a drink and handed it to me. I smiled my thanks before taking a sip. "Hell, maybe you can fake your own death again," Astrid offered, sitting on the desk and taking a drink.

I raised my eyebrows at her. "Take the books and run?"

She nodded with that mischievous smile on her face. "Yeah, you can empty the store then 'have an accident' and start over in another part of town."

I smiled. "You know that won't work. I don't have an identity set up and I can't get one that fast."

"I can hope," she grumbled before taking another sip. "I say clear out of the store and make payments to the fucker."

"I'll try when I see him. But if he doesn't agree ...." I met her eyes.

She gave me a sad half grin. "You'll have to sell everything." I took a big drink. "Or fake your death and move across the world," she added dryly. I stared into my drink.

"Well, I can't go anywhere," I said, a knot forming in my throat. Even if I wanted to. I started turning the glass in my hands.

"What else brought you over?" Astrid asked insightfully. She knew me too well.

I lifted my head. "Atticus." I swallowed hard. "We kissed this morning."

"Oh my God!" Astrid giggled. "How was it?"

"Mind blowing," I admitted. If the others hadn't shown up I might have had him right there on the warehouse floor. Then he ...

Her smile faded. "Okay, I'm all happy here. What's with the gloom?"

"He tried to get me to leave with them tonight." I turned the tumbler in my hand. "He pointed out all the benefits of going. Even said I might have another Match if I go back."

"He said what?" she spat out. "What did he say exactly?"

I repeated Atticus verbatim.

She clenched her teeth. "Oh, that shit better not come near me or I'll rip his balls off." My heart was beginning to lighten. She wasn't done. "He's trying to pressure you to leave."

"I know, and I'm not going." I met her furious gaze. "That doesn't mean they won't leave tonight."

Her face softened. "Oh honey." She was off the desk and hugging me by the time the first tear ran down my cheek. I held tight to her, my throat one large lump, my heart aching. "I know you feel alone, but you're not." She pulled back and wiped my face.

"It's stupid, I know. I just met them but ...." I took a deep breath.

"But they are your own kind," Astrid finished for me. "Believe me, I get it." She pulled back, reached for the tissues on her desk and handed them to me. "It's the only reason I stayed with the pack after David and I imploded." David had been her long-time boyfriend; they were going to get married, only three days before the wedding David met his Mate. Things were tense in the pack after that.

"I can't go, and they can't stay." I shrugged and cleaned

up my face. "It was nice to at least get to know a couple of them."

"Even that tall blonde is leaving?" Astrid asked with a grin. I shot her a look. She smiled mischievously. "What? That male is tasty looking." I chuckled at the wistful look on her face.

She grew serious. "Do you think they'll be there when you go home?"

I shrugged. "No clue. But if they aren't I can give you Ranulf's number." I chuckled as her face lit up in glee.

She sat back on the desk and held up her glass. "To one hell of a bookstore." I tapped my glass to hers before drinking down the rest of my scotch. It was official. If I couldn't get Gumner to take payments, I would have to sell. Everything.

I CLIMBED the stairs of the apartment building, my mind on the store. I had just stepped onto my floor as Atticus stepped off the stairs to the roof. His eyes ran over me before meeting mine.

"Did you get your business done?" he asked stiffly as he buttoned his suit jacket. I eyed him, then the stairs to the roof.

"I thought you were leaving," I said as I went to my door. It was locked. I pulled my keys out of my pocket and focused on unlocking it. "Did you follow me?" I asked, not quite believing it. He said he was leaving .... I focused on unlocking my door.

"You're supposed to have one of us with you," he reminded me.

"I haven't really had someone with me most of the time," I pointed out as I walked into my apartment.

"Believe me, I'm aware," he growled. Biting back a grin, I moved into the kitchen and turned on the burner under the kettle. I went to grab my mug, only to find it in the dish drainer. Did he ... did he wash the mugs? I picked up the one I used. He did. Not knowing how I felt about it, I set it on the counter.

"Would you like some tea?" I asked over my shoulder.

"Yes, please," he said, his voice polite. I pulled the other mug out of the drainer.

When I turned around I paused. Atticus's elbow was on the counter, his eyes were closed as he rubbed his temples. He seemed tired. I crossed my arms over my stomach. "Do you have a headache?"

He sighed. "Yes." He dropped his arm to the counter.

I hesitated only a moment. "Would you like me to fix it or an aspirin?"

His eyes met mine. "You can fix it?"

I nodded.

His eyes ran over my face before he nodded. "I'd appreciate it if you could fix it."

I gave him a small smile as I stepped closer to the counter. "Lean forward so I can reach you, please." He rested his elbows on the table and leaned closer. Parchment filled my lungs, I swallowed hard before reaching over the counter. Carefully, I rested my fingers on his temple. I closed my eyes and poured energy into his body, soaking into his nerves and veins. It took a few heartbeats but I found the problem. I cracked my barrier a little.

"Knots in your neck are restricting blood flow. Give me a second," I sent, then closed my barriers quickly so I wouldn't go too far into his mind. I focused the energy over those knots, heating the muscles until they loosened and let go. Once the blood was flowing again I pulled my mind back

and opened my eyes. Gold eyes met mine. I dropped my fingers from his temple as the kettle started whistling. Ignoring the way he was looking at me, I turned and made tea.

"So, you can heal," he stated.

I turned and set his mug in front of him. "Yes."

"You're very good. Did your mother teach you that?" he asked.

I focused on dunking the teabag. "The control, yes. The rest I had to figure out since she didn't have the ability."

There was a long silence. "That's rather incredible."

I glanced up at him wondering if he was being sarcastic. He seemed sincere.

"Thank you." My tea was ready. I added sugar, milk and stirred it.

"It's rare to find someone who is that precise while healing," he said. "If you came with us, you'd probably end up teaching healing."

I sighed. "That's not exactly what I like to do." I took a sip of tea and looked at him. "What do you do back when you aren't out in the world?"

He added sugar to his tea then stirred it. "I'm the Historian for the Council."

I raised an eyebrow. "Really?"

He nodded. "I handle the historical library, artifacts, documents." He paused for a few heartbeats. "You would be an amazing asset to us."

I sighed and met his eyes. "Atticus, I'm not leaving with you. I can't."

"What is so important that you stay?" he demanded, clearly frustrated.

"Why is it so important that I go?" I countered. "Why is it

so urgent that I go with you?" Silence stretched as he didn't answer.

"You're my Match," he stated. "Your safety is my responsibility."

It felt like a hit to the heart. "Responsibility, right ...," I muttered looking down at my tea. "Well, I release you from that responsibility."

"It doesn't work that way," he said, his voice tired. I lifted my head to meet his gaze.

"If you don't want to be here, then I don't want you here," I told him. "I deserve someone who is going love me for me. And I'm never going to settle for less than that. So, if that's not you ... then leave." My chest ached. I picked up my tea and took it into my bedroom. I sat on the side of my bed and took a deep breath. Why was that so hard to say? I already knew the answer. They'd be gone by morning. And life would go back to normal. My eyes burned. Why did it hurt so much?

9

DECEMBER 18

I was hurrying down the house stairs, I couldn't wait long enough to change out of my dressing gown and into a proper dress and stockings. Dad said there would be a special present under the tree this year. I was hoping it was the dress we saw in a shop window a fortnight ago.

"Mum? Dad?" I called, smiling as I reached the landing. No answer. I hurried to the closed parlour doors and pulled them open-

I jerked awake, gasping, sweat running down my body as I looked around my bedroom. The sound of traffic outside reminded me of the year. I wiped my sweat soaked hair off my face as I tried to get my breathing under control. Christmas was getting close. The nightmares would continue to get worse as it got closer. I pushed them to the back of my mind as I climbed out of bed.

I did my normal routine and got dressed. Blue jeans and a purple oversized sweater that liked to slide down my shoulder, boots and my hair up in a messy bun. Then I headed into the living room and froze. Atticus was still here, at my bookcases, browsing my collection. It took me several heartbeats to process. What did this mean? Why was he still here? Did this mean he cared? Or was he just being stubborn?

Not knowing what to say, I left him alone as I went to the kitchen and began cooking breakfast. I pulled out my large skillet and put it on the burner. When I looked in my fridge I smiled; there was a large slab of bacon that hadn't been there before. Falk. It had to be. He had said he loved bacon yesterday. Shaking my head, I pulled it out and turned on the oven. I was setting the bacon out onto a cookie sheet when Atticus turned around and watched me.

I ignored him as I finished then put the remaining bacon back in the fridge. I didn't want to fight and I sure didn't want to be hurt this morning. I turned back and took a deep breath. Atticus was putting the bacon in the oven and setting the timer. Surprised, I didn't know what to say, so I stayed quiet and texted the others that breakfast would be ready soon. It didn't occur to me that they might not be here until after I pulled out the eggs and a large mixing bowl. Deciding not to ask, I set them on the breakfast bar on the kitchen side then began cracking eggs and leaving the shells in the carton. He pulled down a loaf of bread and began making toast. I finished cracking eggs and began whipping them.

"Have you ever added milk? I've found it makes them smoother," he offered quietly with his back to me.

"I normally do. I ran out," I replied just as quietly. He went back to making toast. When the eggs were ready and the pan was hot enough, I poured the eggs into the pan.

"Do you like cooking?" he asked. Since I was at the stove and he was at the toaster we were almost standing next to each other.

"Yes, actually." He said nothing. He probably expected

his Match to be a gourmet chef. Well, I'm not a chef, but I'm not horrible. He's probably disappointed in me again. My stomach knotted at the thought. I stayed quiet as I kept cooking. I didn't want to fight this morning.

~

Atticus

STANDING next to Evelyn while making breakfast was ... nice. We weren't yelling at each other. We weren't arguing. We were just making breakfast. I decided to keep quiet since whenever we spoke lately we fought. I just wanted a few minutes where we didn't fight. I might not be taking the position of Mate, but I wanted just a few minutes of quiet with her to last the rest of my life. Please. I stepped around her and started the coffee pot. I made a large one, assuming the others would be up soon. I walked back around her, her cherry blossom scent filling my lungs and making me want to touch her. I focused on making toast.

"Would you like some coffee?" I asked. She looked up at me with those cognac eyes, surprised. Those eyes did something to me every time.

"Um, yes please," she murmured before going back to the eggs. I pulled out a couple mugs then poured coffee. I added the cream and sugar to hers before stirring it and handing it to her. She took it and went still. She was staring at her mug.

"Is something wrong?" I asked carefully. She blinked then looked up at me, her face confused.

"You remembered how I like my coffee," she said, stunned. I went back to pouring my own.

"I have an excellent memory," I hedged as I put the

carafe back. She didn't need to know I took note of every-thing she liked or didn't like. When I turned back she was looking down at the eggs, her lips pressed together.

"Of course you do," she said, her voice barely a whisper. It was another minute before I realized I had pushed her away again. I leaned against the breakfast bar and reminded myself it was for the best. Though, the more time I spent with her, the more I questioned if Cyrus was right. Was this the right thing for her?

The timer went off for the bacon. She picked up a pot holder, opened the oven and pulled out the baking sheet. As she straightened she made a pained noise and set the pan down. She pulled her hand off the pan, hissing. I was there before she finished hissing. I took her hand and immedi-ately pulled her to the sink. I started the water, stuck her hand under it and held it there. I didn't realize what I had done until she let out a long breath.

"Bacon grease?" I asked, suddenly tense. Her skin was soft under my fingertips.

"Yeah, when I pulled out the pan it came over the edge," she said quietly. Her gaze was like a touch on my skin. I kept my face blank. "Why did you react that way?" she asked quietly. Surprised by the question I looked down and met her eyes. "Why would you care if I got hurt? You don't even like me," she asked, her face puzzled.

"I dislike seeing females in pain," I admitted before I could think about it. I turned back to examining the burn on her hand. The red was fading from her skin.

I realized what I was doing. I let go of her, turned away, grabbed my coffee and moved to the other side of the break-fast counter, feeling her eyes on me the whole time. I ignored it. She shut off the water then took the eggs off the burner. She pulled out paper towels and a large platter. She had just begun to put the bacon on the paper towels to drain the fat when the apartment door opened. Ranulf strode in. He stepped up behind Evelyn and looked down over her head.

"Bacon?" Ranulf asked.

She shook her head. "No, it's cows tongue." She elbowed his stomach and he chuckled as he moved to the coffee maker. Jealousy ate at me. The fact they spoke so easily was irritating.

Evelyn kept putting bacon on paper towels. The front door opened again. Falk walked in wearing his usual all black. His eyes went to Evelyn and stayed there, or more accurately, on her hands. He strode over and leaned against the counter with his back to me. She looked up to meet his eyes.

"Morning," she said. "I found bacon in my fridge. Was that you?" Falk nodded. Her eyes narrowed on him. She wiped off her hands on a towel before reaching up and wrapping her hands around Falk's throat. Her markings glowed in her skin as she closed her eyes and pulled energy to her. It was only a couple minutes before she opened her eyes and smiled. Falk patted her arm. I resisted the urge to knock his hand off her.

"Thank you," Falk said in his rough voice.

The corner of her lips twitched as she looked back down at the bacon pan and went back to setting the bacon to drain. "No problem. We'll do a real session later today."

Ranulf moved away from the coffee maker and came around the breakfast bar to take the stool beside me.

"So, how was crashing on the couch?" Ranulf asked. I ignored him and watched Falk get his coffee. He hadn't asked her to help with his throat. She did have telepathy; did she talk with Falk that way?

"Fine," I finally answered when Falk finished pouring his coffee. The door opened again.

"I hear there is breakfast?" Zahur asked as he zombie walked into the apartment, wearing only a pair of sweats and a white undershirt. She nodded.

"And coffee, all ready to go," she announced.

"Oh, you're a goddess," Zahur muttered as he went to the coffee maker and pulled down a mug.

"I won't debate that," she said with a small grin. The others chuckled. She covered the last layer of bacon with a paper towel. "Okay, dish up, the bacon is still draining."

The kitchen became chaotic as everyone dished up and ate breakfast. Zahur eventually woke up and joined the conversation Ranulf and Evelyn were having. Occasionally Falk would jump in with something to say. How did they talk so easily with her? The question bothered me all through breakfast.

After breakfast everyone helped with the cleanup and thanked her for cooking.

She shrugged. "No problem, but one of you are taking a turn tomorrow."

"Aye, I'll take care of it," Ranulf volunteered. Zahur caught her eye and shook his head. She smiled, her eyes lit with laughter. I couldn't sit and watch this anymore.

"It's time for a sweep," I announced. The room grew silent as all eyes moved to me. "Load up." The others pushed away from the counters or stood straight. Both Ranulf and Falk looked at her with concern before they went to load up. It bothered me. She was my Match, not theirs.

Then it was just the two of us in the apartment again. "Would you like to join us for the sweep?" I asked carefully. She eyed me.

"Um, thank you, but I have to work," she said in a neutral voice. I bit back my disappointment. She really had no interest in becoming part of the team.

"At the bookstore?" I asked calmly. Her eyes sparked.

"Yes," she said, her voice still neutral. Her eyes were sad before she turned and filled her coffee mug again. What was that?

"Evelyn, I think your work at the bookstore is distracting you from your duty," I informed her. As she put the carafe back, her sweater slipped down, showing the skin of her shoulder and the crest of a wing marking. She turned back to me with a strained smile.

"I have to work, Atticus," she began, her voice tired. "It pays for my apartment, food. You know, living expenses." I reminded myself to be patient.

"Gargoyles have unlimited access to funds," I explained. "All we have to do is bring you home and have you register. Then you can come back and you'll be able afford anything." She was stirring the cream and sugar in her coffee, her mouth a tight line.

"I'm not sure that's a good idea," she said softly. She looked up and met my gaze. It still impressed me that she could; most turned away from my eyes. "And I like working, I like making my own way."

"There's no reason you have to stay." I tried again to get her to understand. Her eyes narrowed on me.

"You and the other gargoyles have pulled back," she stated, her voice firm. "You left the humans to the predators of this world. You abandoned them. I'd say that's a good enough reason to stay." She pressed her lips together and looked away from me.

"It wasn't an easy decision for the Council," I replied, my own temper rising.

"How would you know?" she asked directly. "Were you in the room when they made the decision?"

"Yes, my position as Historian comes with a seat on the Elder Council," I announced. She eyed me and sighed.

"That explains a lot," she said to herself. She tucked a loose hair behind her ear and shook her head. "I don't know what you want from me, Atticus."

"I would like you to go on this sweep with us," I told her. "I want you to start learning how we do things. Become part of our team."

"Why? So, I might go back with you?" she asked, her eyes flashing. That had been the idea.

"We're doing the sweep," I told her, my voice cold. "Are you coming or not?" She rolled her eyes and shook her head.

"Hate to break it to you, but this sweep is a waste of time," she announced with a small smile. "It's covered already."

I bit back a curse. I know for a fact she never left the apartment since going to her room last night. The door opened, Ranulf leaned in.

"We're ready to head out," Ranulf announced. I turned away from her and headed for the door. When I reached it her voice made me pause.

"Please, don't kill anyone or anything without calling me first. There are things you don't know about this city. There's a balance. Please, don't mess with it," she warned. I bit back my reply and walked out the door, fuming.

TWO HOURS later

.   .   .

I took a deep breath and let it out slowly. During the sweep we had found traces of a nest of Red Caps in the Orange subway line. A nest of goblins directly under Evelyn's nose. It worried me that the nest was within fifteen city blocks of her apartment. I didn't care if it was a hundred, I wanted them out of the city. As far from her as possible. It was the entire point of the sweep. Clear out as many pests and risks as possible before we were called back. Cyrus won't keep us out in the field for long. I only had a couple weeks at most to convince her and it didn't look like she was going to leave with us. Cyrus was going to be furious, but I refused to put her in chains and drag her back.

She was right, she deserved someone who would love her for who she was. All I could do now was clear out as many dangers as possible and ask her to call if she ever needed help. It ate at me that this was the most I could do.

As the others arrived my anger with the situation hadn't diminished. She wanted me to call before I did my job. I shook my head, that wasn't going to happen. There wasn't time, not if we were going to clear the city as fast as possible.

"Let's talk strategy," I began. "Ranulf and I up front as usual. Falk, I want you above us. And Zahur-"

"It wouldn't hurt to have some magical back up on this one," Ranulf suggested.

"She wasn't interested," I announced. "Besides, she's not really trained."

Ranulf scoffed. "I've seen her in action, she's trained."

"She wasn't interested, and we need to move fast to get the city cleared," I told them coldly. They all shared looks.

"Why?" Falk asked, his voice rough.

"Yeah, you're being more of an ass than usual," Ranulf added.

"Instead of talking strategy, we're talking about her," I snapped.

"He's right," Zahur agreed.

I took a deep breath and let it out slowly. "We still need to get her back home as soon as possible. If she won't go-"

"She might be compatible with even more males, have any of you thought of that?" Zahur asked the group. "You might want to keep her away until you're Mated."

"Why would I do that?" I asked pointedly.

Zahur's eyes narrowed at me. "What are you doing, Atticus?"

"We have a nest of Red Caps to take out," I reminded them. "We need to clear the city. Now let's get to work."

~

Evelyn

I WAS HAVING a pretty off day. First the argument with Atticus, and then I remembered my appointment with Gumner was today. So when Zahur strode through the door with some green blood on his shirt sleeve, dread filled me.

He eyed me, his face growing concerned. "What's wrong?"

"What happened?" I asked immediately.

"There was a nest of Red Caps in a subway line." He said, his eyes running over the almost half empty shelves and the stack of shipping boxes waiting to go out. My stomach dropped.

"Which line?" I asked carefully.

"Orange," Zahur answered. I closed my eyes and counted to ten.

I dropped the book in my hand and headed for the door.

When I opened it, I turned to him. "Come on." I barely kept myself from snapping. Zahur came through the door. I locked the shop, then brought down the gate and locked it. I was headed up the stairs in a few heartbeats. Noise came from the guys' apartment, jeering and cheerful. It hit my temper hard. I opened the door and strode in. Ranulf and Falk were on the couches cleaning their weapons. Atticus was at his desk typing away on his laptop when he turned and met my gaze. "I told you to call me before you killed anyone or anything," I reminded him.

"You had a nest of Red Caps in your city," he said. "We took care of them." My veins boiled with fury.

"You have no fucking idea what you've done," I said, my voice cold. The others stopped cleaning their weapons. Yeah, I cursed. I turned on my heel and walked out of their apartment and into mine. I went to my room to get a weapon. I was packing light today.

I pulled out my harness and slipped it on, then took out my short sword from the chest in the bottom of the closet.

"We got them all, lass, you don't need to arm up," Ranulf assured me as he came to the door. I just shook my head. I was too angry to talk yet. I pulled on my long, fitted leather coat to hide my weapons then strode out of my bedroom. Everyone was in my apartment now.

"You didn't take out a nest," I told them, my voice hard. "You took out an outpost." I crossed my arms over my chest as my heart slammed. Ranulf moved away from my bedroom door and joined the others near the couches. "You see, I've had a deal with the Red Caps for the last forty-two years. They could stay as long as they followed certain rules and kept the subways clean of rats." I met Atticus's eyes. "I told you I had a balance here and to call me before you killed anyone or anything. What happened?"

Atticus's face was hard as he answered. "We're clearing out the city of pests. We don't make deals with these creatures."

I scoffed. "You've had back up your entire life," I reminded him. "Out here I'm alone. I've had to do things differently. The Red Caps were part of that." My gaze ran over his blank face. "You just screwed me over in ways you can't even imagine."

"Tell us about this deal you had with the Red Caps." Zahur's face was worried.

"They could stay and colonize without fear of me as long as they followed my rules," I told him before looking back to meet Atticus's eyes. "And now, thanks to you, I have to go renegotiate with their King." I looked at each of them. "And you're all coming with me." I headed for the door. When I didn't hear footsteps following I turned back. They were still in the living room area. "Get your butts in the car," I snapped. "You get to see the outcome of your actions."

"We're not going to feel bad for taking out some Red Caps," Atticus said. I met his gaze.

"I know. Bring the big med kit."

I WAS silent the entire drive to the nearest Red Line station. We took Atticus's Mercedes, I had insisted. This whole thing was his fault, so he could deal with the mess afterwards. I had the guys park at the mouth of a 'sealed off' section of track that led underground. I got out and took a deep breath to find my calm again.

Negotiating with Novak was never fun. It didn't take long, but what the Red Caps valued was vastly different than money or luxuries. I turned to the guys.

"Zahur, are you the squad's medic?" I demanded.

"I am," Zahur said. I nodded.

"You're coming with me. Bring the kit," I announced. Zahur went to pull it out of the trunk. I looked to the others. "The rest of you? If you can follow my instructions and keep your mouth shut, then you come too."

"Are you planning to tend the wounded?" Atticus asked dryly. I shot him a look.

"I doubt you left any," I countered darkly. Ranulf sighed and joined Falk and Zahur.

"I can't not go in with ye, lass," Ranulf announced emphatically as he stepped forward.

"Just ... don't say or do anything, no matter what." I looked at the three of them. "You don't know their culture, and you don't know the rules. Staying quiet will keep you safe." They nodded. I didn't expect Atticus to come, that's fine. He'll still see the aftermath. I turned and headed to the metal door. Opening it, I walked into the dark with the others a step behind.

The Red Cap lair was a fifteen-minute walk through the tunnels. I used those fifteen minutes to educate the others.

"The deal I made with the Red Caps was simple: War only with themselves, no kills outside their species, keep the subways free of rats, report any demon or strange activity immediately and act as back-up if I need it, which they don't mind. They actually fight over who gets to back me up. It's become an honor. Since they work better as a nest when they have purpose, they do my sweeps and report anything they find." I stepped over the third rail and walked down the center of the abandoned line. "For that, they get to stay, nest and in general live their lives without fear of me hunting them down."

"What do they eat, lass?" Ranulf asked directly. "Because I doubt rats be keeping 'em fed."

"You're right, they don't," I admitted. "Which is why I arranged for a butcher on the north end to bring in meat twice a week." I looked over my shoulder. "The Red Caps even pay for it themselves." I turned back around and kept talking. "But now that blood has been spilled, I have to renegotiate with Novak." We were almost there. "And Red Caps don't value the usual things." The gate was up ahead. It was a patchwork of welded metal that made up a wall and gate. "Here's the hard and fast rules. Don't speak to anyone, only to me. Don't touch anything and don't stare. Don't accept food or drink and if I bow, you bow. You stand up if addressed," I whispered quickly. "This is a negotiation. Do not interfere, no matter what you hear. Got it?"

"Yeah," Zahur said.

Falk nodded.

"I got it, lass," Ranulf added. When we reached the gate, I knocked. I took a deep breath and let it out. I needed to be calm. The gate was opened by one of my favorite Red Caps, he was the only one I knew of with a sense of humor. Helix was a good 6ft 5 and over 260 pounds of muscle encased in black jeans and a black tank undershirt. A red cap's skin was usually brown and as thick as a rhino's. It looked about as good too. Some even had plates of armor sewn into their flesh. Helix's red cap was shaped like a ski cap, only it came down to his jaw and had cut outs for his pointed ears. It was still sticky from his last kill. Helix's four yellow eyes ran over my company before resting on me.

"It's good you came, little one. Novak is furious," Helix warned in his deep, growly voice.

"Hey Helix, I figured he'd be angry. That's why we came," I admitted. He smiled down at me with his razor-sharp teeth. I smiled back before hugging him. Helix was careful not to hurt me as he squeezed me back. Even though

I could slaughter his kind, Helix was always worried about hurting me. It was sweet.

"I missed ya, big guy," I told him as I pulled back. "When are you coming by for a movie night?"

"When are you going to serve good food?" he countered, gesturing for the others to come in.

"I'm sorry mister food snob, I don't have the budget for Kobe beef tartare," I said dryly. Helix chuckled as he closed the gates behind the others.

"Well, after today, it won't be for a while," he said, becoming serious. His eyes ran over the guys.

"These are the ones who killed my people?" he asked.

"All but one," I admitted. The guys' faces were blank, but their posture told me they were expecting trouble. Helix nodded.

"It's good that you came," Helix told them. "It will help Evelyn show her sincerity. And it takes a strong warrior to admit they fucked up."

I looked to the guys and explained. "That you showed up will prove you are honorable. It'll help my negotiations and give you standing. Without standing in the Red Cap's world, you're just meat."

"And you don't want to go through what Evelyn did to get that standing," Helix offered. I rolled my eyes as Helix began to open the inner gates.

"It wasn't that bad," I grumbled.

"You almost bled to death and had to turn to stone until you healed," he reminded me.

"I did not," I denied dramatically. "I simply decided to hibernate when I was fed up with Red Cap rituals." Helix laughed at my lie.

Helix led us through the nest, which was really more of a city. The Red Line nest was their main home, their presence in the other lines was simply to keep the vermin down and keep an eye out for demons. Their city was surprisingly beautiful. The streets were clean, and the buildings had a style all their own. Red Caps liked curved edges for some reason, and it was reflected in their architecture. What had once been pieced-together housing had become stone and plaster. What had once been a dark section of tunnels and unused infrastructure was now a bright home for a hidden species. I eyed the stained-glass window-front of a shop as we walked into the village.

"Remind me to ask Undy to price what it would cost him to create a stained-glass window for my apartment," I said absently.

"How close are you to these Red Caps, lass?" Ranulf asked quietly.

"Well, Helix here is one of my favorite people in the world," I admitted. He stopped asking questions.

As we got closer to the town square more Red Caps became aware that we were here. Glares and whispers filled the streets as everyone hurried to the town center to get a good seat for the show. Bloodshed for the Red Caps was their favorite entertainment. Especially when other species were involved. My stomach was knotting as we got deeper into town. I took deep breaths and let them out slowly. I had no choice. I had to do this thanks to Atticus, the arrogant ass. My anger came back. It helped me calm down. Helix stopped before we would step out into the square. He knew me well enough to know I was going to need a minute. Every Red Cap was already there, the stone amphitheater packed. I took several deep breaths and let them out slowly. Helix's hand came down on my shoulder and he squeezed gently, watching the amphitheater as Red Caps found a place to sit.

"You know what he's going to want," Helix reminded me. Yeah, I knew.

"He's not getting that," I assured him.

Helix smirked down at me. "Don't let Novak get under your skin."

I nodded. It would be a cold day in hell before I let Novak win. Helix dropped his arm before turning to the guys.

"If you want to help her, say nothing to anyone but her. And keep your weapons sheathed," he warned them. All their faces were hard.

"How many did you kill at the outpost?" I asked them.

"Twenty-seven," Zahur answered. My breath came out in a huff. Great.

"Let's get this over with," I growled. Helix nodded before leading us into the sand arena that was the town center.

King Novak was already on the low dais. Novak was an odd Red Cap. He was only six foot three, short for his species, but his armored body and incredible strength won him his crown centuries ago. It was hard to kill something when you couldn't get past their armored skin to their flesh. Add his four, fully-functioning arms and you couldn't even get close enough to try.

Novak's three eyes were on me the second I emerged from between the buildings. He began to pace along the dais, his arms crossed over his naked chest. His long legs were encased in skin-tight leather and boots.

"Warrior Evelyn, of the Gargoyles. And the slayers of Outpost Lochlin," Helix announced. Though he stayed at the edge of the sand, I led the others into the small arena. When we reached the right spot, eight feet from the dais, I went to one knee and bowed my head. From the sound in the sand, the others followed suit.

"King Novak, I've come to rectify the grave error that was made this morning," I announced, projecting my voice. Novak stepped off the dais and strode towards me.

"Get up Evelyn and explain yourself," he growled in an extremely deep, harsh voice. I got up instantly, so that by the time he reached me I was on my feet.

Oddly, Novak would be a good looking human if it wasn't for the three eyes and razor sharp teeth. He had a strong jaw and chiseled features. Even his pointed ears looked good on him. I looked up into two of his three eyes and explained the situation.

"A squad of gargoyles have come into the city. I warned their leader that we had a balance going and to contact me before they took any actions. He chose to ignore that," I began. "They had no knowledge of our Treaty. I've come to make amends for their actions." Novak's gaze ran over me, a cunning light sparkled in his eyes. His gaze went to the guys behind me, still kneeling.

"Are these them?" he demanded.

"All but one," I replied.

His eyes came back to me. "They came willingly?"

"Yes, once I explained the situation, these three wished to make it right," I said calmly. Novak's massive shoulders relaxed a degree. He looked down at them.

"Get up," he snapped.

"Novak," I growled. His gaze snapped to me. "They are my people, and if you speak to them that way again I'll rip out your throat." The corner of his lips twitched. Red Caps loved females that held their own. Especially, when they held authority.

"Please rise," he said in a calm voice. Falk, Zahur, and Ranulf got to their feet. His eyes stayed on me as he added. "I want their heads." He turned to walk toward the dais.

"No," I stated in a hard voice. Novak turned back.

"They are responsible for countless deaths," he began.

"Twenty-seven is hardly countless," I countered before he got rolling. "I'm here to make amends, not to give you my people." Novak strolled towards me, he only stopped when he was close enough that I had to strain my neck to keep eye contact with him.

"You're not really a queen, but you could be," he whispered to me. My stomach rolled. There was shifting behind me. I shot Ranulf a hard look. He settled back down, his eyes burning. He really hadn't liked Novak's offer. The Red Cap King had been trying to get into my pants for years. I was used to Novak's proposals. Now they just made me feel sick.

"You know the answer to that, Novak," I reminded him quietly. It wouldn't be smart to deny him loud enough for the others to hear. I'd like to not have to fight my way out of here.

"You know what we value, Evelyn," Novak reminded me.

I kept eye contact. "I haven't forgotten."

"One night," he offered. "You, in my bed, and I'll make sure all is forgiven." This time there was no shifting behind me. It was actually a very sweet offer, by Red Cap standards.

"That's an extremely generous offer. But you know my answer," I stated. His eyes narrowed on my face.

"Are you sure about that?" he asked. "Twenty-seven deaths. That's a lot more than what you went through for your standing."

"I'm aware," I said calmly. He cracked a grin that I hated.

"I could deny that choice," he threatened. I smirked at him.

"I'd challenge you, Novak," I reminded him. A challenge must be answered, and even though he was bigger than me, he knew I'd win. He cursed as he looked away from me only to turn back. "Wouldn't one night be easier to give up than what you'd have to go through for twenty-seven deaths?" he offered. "It'd certainly be more enjoyable."

It was flattering the way he kept going after me, but it wasn't happening. "No," I stated simply. He sighed.

"Fine," he bit out. "A wing."

"Novak," I chided playfully, "you know your own laws. These circumstances don't qualify for crippling."

He growled. "The hip."

"Too high for regeneration," I told him. "How about two or three inches below?"

"Both?" he asked. When I hesitated he added, "Twenty-seven families."

I sighed, he was right. "Agreed."

"Done," he agreed, then turned around and bellowed, "Bring the long table!"

My stomach lurched as I turned to the others and began unbuttoning my jacket.

"Evie, what's going on?" Zahur asked as I began pulling my jacket off and handing it to Ranulf.

"I'm really glad the three of you came," I admitted as I took off my boots and socks.

"Why?" Zahur asked suspiciously.

"Because you'll be able to carry me out of here," I said absently as my hands went to take off my harness and sword.

"Why are we going to have to carry ye, lass?" Ranulf demanded. I handed him my harness.

I looked up at him and told him. "Because I won't have my legs."

10

"What?" Ranulf demanded.

"I won't have my legs," I repeated. I explained more fully to them as I took off my jeans. "Red Caps value one thing above all else: Flesh." I folded my pants and put them on the pile in Ranulf's hands. Now I was standing around in black, hip hugging panties and my purple oversized sweater. "Sex or meat. And I'm not giving him the first. So, meat it is."

"Why you? You didn't do anything!" Ranulf snapped. I met his eyes.

"Because the deal was with me," I told him. "And because Atticus didn't check with me like he should have, I have very limited options right now."

"What are the other options?" Zahur asked.

Getting irritated I listed them off on my fingers. "Marry Novak, sex with Novak, sex with one male from each of the families of the twenty-seven Red Caps killed. Or, I chop my legs off, the twenty-seven families eat them and I regenerate in the next twenty-four hours." They were speechless. "*This is the consequence of Atticus not making a simple freaking* phone call," I snapped, becoming furious again. Two Red Caps brought the long, wooden table made specifically to take lower limbs. I took a deep breath as adrenaline flowed through me. "Zahur, by any chance do you have any major pain killers in that bag?" Novak took the huge ceremonial battleaxe and began sharpening it. I appreciated it. The sharper the blade, the faster the cut, and I had to do this twice. Oh God.

"Is there any way to get you out of this? Can one of us take your place?" Ranulf asked. I met his eyes.

"No, it's me or nothing," I told him. He clenched his jaw, closed his eyes and took deep breaths.

Zahur pulled out a vial of liquid and a syringe.

"Gargoyle strength morphine." Zahur began drawing up a dose. I wrung my fingers as I watched them wipe down the long table.

"Have it ready for right after they take my legs, please," I told him.

He looked at me like I was insane.

"I can't have drugs in my system when this happens. It's a Red Cap rule" I explained.

"Screw this, let's just leave," Ranulf stated. I shot him a look.

"We can't, it'd make the Treaty void," I explained. "Their numbers are one hundred and eighty-two; do you want to take that on yourself?"

"One hundred and eighty-four," Helix corrected as he joined our group. "Mytara had her twins two days ago."

"Oh."

Helix looked at the table as he held out a pen to me. I took it, then began to mark where the cut line should be on both of my legs. When I was done, Novak was disinfecting the blade with alcohol. I really appreciated that. I didn't need a huge infection knocking me on my butt right now. I handed the pen back to Helix, then looked at the others. Each of them looked furious. Well, they could join the club.

"I need someone to hold me down," I admitted. Zahur and Ranulf cursed and shook their heads.

Falk just stepped forward. When I turned back around everything was set up. Novak looked to me.

"Ready, Evelyn?" Novak called. I nodded and started walking over with Helix and Falk at my side. Zahur and Ranulf brought up the rear.

"Thank you for holding me down. I hate asking, but I know me," I told Falk, my fingers playing with my locket.

"I wish I could take your place," Falk said, his voice rough.

"I know." My body was shaking when we reached the table. This was so going to hurt.

Novak met my eyes. "I imagine Helix is your chosen?"

"Yep, the guy's fast with a blade," I joked. Novak handed the axe to Helix. I let out another breath and laid down on the birch-wood table. "Just got a freaking pedicure too," I grumbled as I placed my arms over my head. Falk's hands went to my wrists and pinned them to the wood.

I took big deep breaths as Helix made sure to iodine my legs around the pen marks. I met Falk's eyes. His hands moved from my wrists to my hands. He still kept me pinned, but it was more comforting for me. I gave him a small, grateful smile.

"I'm going to do this fast, little one," Helix told me. I nodded.

"Don't stop for screaming," I reminded Helix. Hands went to my ankles. I recognized Novak's grip. I actually didn't mind. "Thanks, Novak. I didn't think of that."

"You'd make a formidable queen," Novak replied quietly.

"Eh, too stubborn," I reminded him. Novak chuckled. I looked at Helix. "Do it."

~

Ranulf

I CURSED AGAIN and again as Falk and I carried Evie between us. This was a fucking nightmare. She just had her legs chopped off. When the axe fell, I had to turn away. Her scream as the axe fell again would haunt my dreams for years. Zahur had been quick with the drugs and the tourniquets, but she was still losing blood.

"I'm killing Atticus the minute I see him," I growled as we turned another corner, picking up the pace.

"After we take care of her," Zahur snapped. Falk and I gripped Evie between us, pale and unmoving. She was still conscious somehow, and panting through the pain. This was entirely too close to losing my little sister, Meryl, who had died in childbirth. It didn't help that Evie's breathing was short and shallow just as Meryl's had been. Only now I was carrying Evelyn.

"One more turn and then the door," Helix assured us.

"Thanks for helping us get her out of here," Zahur said, as we all but ran down the tunnel.

"Of course," Helix said. "Her recovery will be much easier this time with you males around."

"This time?" I growled. Helix nodded as we turned another corner.

"To earn her standing the first time, Novak took her arm," Helix explained. The door was in sight. He opened it for us. "Take care of her, and if your leader does something like this again, I'll be taking his body pieces instead of hers." Zahur and I agreed instantly as we carried her through the door into the sunlight.

❧

Atticus

WHAT THE HELL was taking so long? I shifted against the car. The things that could have gone wrong kept running through my mind. I should have gone with them. Why didn't I go with her? I'd know what was happening right now.

She didn't understand what I was trying to do. When we get back to her apartment I'll sit her down and explain what happened. And how gargoyles usually run things. Would she even listen?

How could she make deals with the creatures we were supposed to be keeping in line? I didn't understand it. But if it worked for her, if it kept her safe here when I was gone ... I'd take it.

The door to the tunnels opened. About damn time. I straightened as Falk and Ranulf hurried out carrying ... Evelyn. It took me a moment to process what I was seeing. Evelyn's legs were gone, only bloody stumps remained. I moved towards them.

"Open the doors!" Zahur shouted as they ran towards me. "We need to get her back to the apartment now!" I turned around and opened every door to the car. Falk and Ranulf slid into the back seat with a bleeding, pale Evelyn. Zahur climbed in and straddled the console so he could work on Evelyn.

"Drive!" Zahur shouted. That snapped me out of my shock. I started the car and gunned it.

"What the hell happened?" I demanded.

"SHUT UP!" All three of them yelled at me. Stunned, I focused on driving. My Match was in the back seat, without her legs. I pushed down on the accelerator. Evelyn gasped.

"Dose her again," Falk growled. Zahur cursed as he worked to draw up another dose.

"She's streaking!" Ranulf shouted. I cursed. Streaking meant that her veins were starting to turn to stone. There was so much damage that her body was shutting down, trying to save itself.

"I'm on it," Zahur assured him. I weaved through traffic and blew through stop lights without a thought. She whimpered as they tightened the tourniquets. My chest tightened at the sound.

"Sorry, lass, but we have to stop the bleeding before you turn to stone," Ranulf explained.

"I know," she bit out.

A beat later Zahur sighed. "Thank God, she's unconscious."

"Now, what the hell happened?" I growled as I took a corner too fast and almost went into the other lane.

"You fucking happened!" Ranulf snapped. I glanced back at him before looking back at the road. He was serious.

"What are you talking about?" I demanded.

Zahur was bandaging what was left of her legs as he answered. "Remember that deal she had with the Red Caps? Since you didn't call and talk to her before ordering us to go in and take out that outpost, she had to make amends for their dead."

"And guess what the Red Caps value?" Ranulf growled.

"She had to give up flesh because of you," Zahur told me. "And since there are twenty-seven dead at the outpost she had to give up enough flesh to satisfy those twenty-seven families. Guess what they're munching on right now." My stomach churned. What the hell? I screeched the car to a stop in front of the building. Everyone worked together to get her out of the car and into her bedroom in the apartment. Ranulf sat on the dresser, Falk leaned against the wall next to the door and I stood at the end of the bed with my arms crossed over my chest.

We watched and waited while Zahur worked on her. When he had her stable and comfortable Zahur sat down on the side of the bed and sighed.

"She should be out for a bit," Zahur announced. "I can keep her sedated if she wants while her legs regenerate. But I want to ask her first. We need towels or more sheets if we aren't going to destroy her bed."

"I'll buy her a new one. Now, someone, explain to me again how this happened." I ordered. Ranulf was pale. Falk was somber as Zahur explained, in detail, everything. By the end of it I was swallowing back bile.

"So, if you had just listened to her and called before we went into that outpost, she'd still have her legs," Ranulf summed up for me.

I shook my head. It shouldn't be this way. "I just wanted to clear the city. We were going to leave when Cyrus ordered us back. I just wanted ...," I said absently as I looked at her. Her skin was deathly pale, I could barely see her chest moving.

"Then maybe you should have been listening when she spoke," Ranulf reminded me.

"She went down there knowing exactly what was going to happen," Zahur announced. I ran my hand down my face.

I ... I just couldn't. I walked out of her bedroom, then out of her apartment.

I hurried up the stairs and out onto the roof.

The fresh air helped, but it wasn't a minute before I was sick over the side of the building. When I thought I was done, the image of Evelyn in that bed hit me and I was sick again. When I finally stopped, my pulse was loud in my ears.

I sat on the waist high ledge and tried to think. Why hadn't I listened? Why didn't I just fucking listen? I closed my eyes and hung my head as my chest threatened to explode. I took deep breaths as what I did sank in.

I was the reason she had to sacrifice her legs. It was all my fault. It was nothing more than not listening. Because we were going to leave. Because I wanted her safe. Pure fucking stupidity. I cost her both her legs. Guilt tore through me, ripping me to pieces. I deserved it. She asked me to call, and I ... my eyes burned as I opened them. My talons were digging into my thighs. The pain didn't even register. Why didn't she tell me? I cursed myself as it hit me. She tried to tell me. I obviously wasn't listening or even willing to listen. How could I do that to her? To my Match, my Mate? Emotions tore through me, eating me alive, breaking through every barrier I had ever created.

Desperate, I picked up my phone and called Cyrus.

"Yes?"

"She lost her legs," I told him, my voice dead. "She had some deal with the Red Caps and I fucked it up. She lost her legs because of me."

"Well, that's what she gets for being stupid enough to even think of making deals with the Red Caps," Cyrus growled. Anger surged through me.

"She isn't stupid. She's resourceful and clever," I growled

low. "She's managed to keep every species in this city in line. Something we've never managed."

"Is that emotion I hear Atticus?" he demanded.

"Yes," I snarled. I couldn't stop it. It was storming through me and I was lost in it without a compass.

"Get control of yourself, you little wanker," Cyrus ordered. "Use those exercises I taught you. Put away the emotion. The last thing you need is to feel emotion for this stupid female. You owe this female nothing." I couldn't believe what I was hearing. It was nothing he hadn't said before, but now ... it was like I was hearing it for the first time. And I realized the complete bullshit he was spouting. Furious, I hung up and barely resisted throwing my phone into the alley below. The weight in my chest grew heavier as fear took hold. One emotion moved to another and another, tearing through me, leaving chaos in the storm's wake. What was right? What was true?

A hand came down on my shoulder. "Breathe Atticus, slow deep breaths." Zahur's voice was soothing. I did as he said. It helped. I could breathe but my chest still burned. He sat down beside me on the ledge. "I thought you would be having a problem, your Match is injured and you had a hand in it."

"I don't understand," I said, my voice thick.

"Well, the contract-"

"Not that," I snapped, turning to him. His dark eyes ran over me, assessing. "She brings up everything I've buried. I can't stop it. Can't bury it again. She just ... leaves me in chaos, with no idea where to go."

Zahur raised an eyebrow. "Is *she* hurting you that way? Or are you?" I didn't understand.

"What?" I bit out.

His face was understanding. "I've known you since you

were adopted into the community, Atticus." Zahur turned to look out over the rooftops. "I've watched as Cyrus taught you to bury every emotion, every feeling. Over and over. I saw it. And I've stood by, mostly because it seemed to work for you." He turned back to me. "But now it's all coming back, isn't it? Every emotion eating you alive?"

I closed my eyes and nodded.

"That's not her. That's everything you've chosen to ignore. Chosen not to feel," he explained.

"Cyrus said-"

"Fuck what Cyrus says," he snapped. I turned to meet his angry gaze. "Cyrus's own Match didn't want him. That male is a robot. You aren't." Was he telling the truth? Did Cyrus's own Match refuse him? Reeling, I turned back to look down at the alley.

"I don't know what's right anymore," I admitted, still fighting to find an anchor to grab onto in the storm.

"Ignore Cyrus's lessons and feel," Zahur instructed. "What do you want?"

"Her," I admitted, my voice barely there.

"Atticus, you know I was Mated." Zahur sighed. "I only had her for a year before I lost her. That female...." He swallowed hard. "I would trade every day of my life since to have one more hour with her."

"But what's best for her? Since we all know it's not me," I pointed out.

"How do you think she should be treated by her Mate?" Zahur asked.

"Like she's precious," I answered instantly, without thinking. "She should be appreciated for being who she is."

Zahur gave me a half grin. "Then why aren't you doing that?"

I swallowed hard as his question hit like a kick to the gut.

Why wasn't I? I looked down in the alley. Cyrus's lessons aside ... she was my Match. And I was treating her like .... bile rose in my throat.

Zahur sighed. "Your Match, your Mate, is downstairs, drugged, injured and hurting," he pointed out logically. "What do you want to do?"

My mind racing, I muttered, "I should make a report-"

"Atticus," he snapped. I turned and met his demanding gaze. "What do you *want* to do?"

"Be there. Take care of her. Make sure she's not in pain," I admitted.

"Start there," he advised before turning and stepping back onto the roof. "I need to check on her. She should be waking up in a couple minutes." Before Zahur left me on the roof he handed me a small container of mints.

With the storm tearing through me, only one thing was clear: her I wanted to be with her. The pain in my chest eased, I took deeper breaths. She probably wouldn't take me now, but she deserved better. And from now on, that's what she was going to get.

I popped a couple of mints into my mouth, got off the ledge and crossed the roof. I was down the stairs and in her apartment in a minute. When I walked into her room the others were still there. Someone had gotten towels to place under her. Zahur was checking the veins along her legs for streaking as I took off my suit jacket.

"How is she?" I asked, setting my jacket on the dresser beside Ranulf.

"She agreed to sedation," Zahur announced. Some tension inside me eased. At least she wouldn't be awake through the pain of regeneration. My eyes ran over her. Her breathing was shallow and short, her face strained even while drugged. Was the dose not high enough? Was she still in pain?

"Zahur, look at her face. Check the dose," I ordered.

Zahur turned on the bed and took her hand. "Evie, squeeze my hand if you can hear me." I watched, my pulse in my ears as there was no response, just the flicker of her eyes moving under her eyelids. She wasn't responding to Zahur.

I moved to the side of her bed and put my hand on his shoulder. "Move."

Zahur didn't argue as he got up and I took his place. I picked up her hand and rubbed my thumb over her knuckles. "Evelyn, answer me. Squeeze my hand if you can hear me." My voice wasn't soft or gentle. It was demanding and rough. Her fingers gently squeezed mine. Shit. "Evelyn, if you're still in pain, squeeze my fingers again." Her fingers squeezed mine weakly. "She's hurting."

Zahur moved to the dresser and went through his medical bag. "Some sedation will practically paralyze you instead of putting you out. With us, it's a different drug for everyone."

He drew up a new dose and injected her with it. I watched her face, worried it wouldn't work. When her face finally relaxed, I sighed in relief. She wasn't hurting anymore. I stayed where I was and kept her hand in mine.

"Everyone else out," Zahur ordered, "she needs to rest."

"Sorry excuse for a Match," Ranulf muttered as he got off the dresser and walked to the door. I didn't argue, he was right. Falk said nothing as he followed him out the door.

Zahur drew up several more syringes, capped them and set them out on her dresser. "She'll wake up in a couple hours. Give her one shot. It'll knock her back out."

I nodded, though my gaze was on her chest, watching the rise and fall with every breath.

"Call if she gets a fever or she starts streaking," Zahur told me. I nodded again. "She's going to be okay." He left and the room fell into deep silence.

I traced her fingers gently, not wanting to disturb her.

During the long hours of the day I memorized her face, her eyelashes, her lips, even her nose and ears. She was stunning. Kind, funny, sweet ... and much more than I ever deserved.

Cyrus called my phone three times in the following hours. Each time I let it go to voicemail. I needed to think, not listen to his bullshit. And that's what I did.

During that time, I thought about everything Cyrus had ever taught me, what I could remember of my parents. They were loving, and respectful to each other. I remember Mom arguing with Pa, but there was never shouting. It was always a calm discussion. I wanted that with Evelyn. I blinked as I realized it. I'd made a decision. I'd do whatever it took to be the Mate Evelyn deserved. Fuck Cyrus.

Around three o'clock sweat began to roll down her skin, she whimpered in her sleep. I called Zahur. He came in and checked her out. She had developed a fever due to the regeneration. Zahur pulled out several bags of herbs and a jar of his general salve. He began grinding a mixture of herbs together. When he was done he handed me the jar.

"Rub that into her skin; forehead, neck, and inside of her forearms. It'll take a little while to kick in so she's going to burn for a bit. It's normal."

"I still don't like it," I told him as I started to gently rub the salve on to the skin of her forearm. Zahur pulled his stethoscope out of his bag and moved around the bed to listen to her heart. I focused on getting her to cool off.

Zahur took off his stethoscope and straightened. "Her heart is doing great."

I moved to her neck. "Good."

Zahur left. I continued to rub the salve into her skin whenever she started sweating again.

It was getting dark when Falk came in with a container of Chinese takeout. He said nothing as he handed it to me.

"Thanks," I said, leaving it to sit in my lap. He smacked my shoulder. When I turned back to him he pointed at the container in my lap. "Fine, I'll eat." I let go of her hand and started eating.

When I was almost done, she whimpered. I instantly handed him the container and checked the time. It was time for another shot. I grabbed a sedation syringe and was cleaning her arm with an alcohol swab when she opened her eyes.

"Atticus?" she whispered. Her glazed eyes found mine. "I … don't feel … well …." She closed her eyes, as if that was all the energy she had.

"I know," I said gently as I used the needle on her arm. "I'm fixing it, luv." My accent slipped through. Her lips twitched at the corners before she was still again. I tossed the syringe in the trash and started cooling her off with the salve again. The heat coming from her regenerating legs was intense. I applied the ointment to her thighs above the cut line. She sighed in her sleep. I made a point to keep covering her legs as well.

Evelyn

THE PAIN WAS GNAWING, burning bone deep. I shifted on the

bed. A cool hand touched my face. I opened my eyes. Atticus? His face was worried ... it must be bad if he was worried .... The sharp jab of a needle barely registered with the amount of pain I swam in.

"Eve," he said softly. "I just gave you another dose. It'll take effect any minute." I nodded. That cool hand worked something cooling into my forehead. It felt so good.

"I'm sorry I didn't listen to you," he said quietly.

I turned my head and met his eyes as the pain started to ease. "Why do you hate me so much?" I asked, my voice cracking.

His face grew pained. "I don't hate you. Far from it," he whispered. That cool hand held my cheek, it felt so good. It settled something inside me. I snuggled into it as everything disappeared.

11

DECEMBER 11

I woke up slowly. My body didn't want to move, I didn't even want to wake up. But once I started waking up there was no going back. I reached down and scratched my leg.

My legs! I opened my eyes then lifted my foot to examine my leg. It looked good; no scarring, no hideous deformities. Just a normal leg. I wiggled my unpolished toes to make sure they worked. They did.

"Checking to make sure all your toes are there?" Zahur asked quietly. I smiled as I brought my leg back down. He got off the dresser.

"Maybe," I said innocently. He chuckled. I looked up at him, not bothering to move. "Thank you for taking care of me." His amber eyes were warm as he smiled.

"I didn't," he said. Huh?

"Then who...?"

"Atticus took care of you," he said. "He wouldn't leave your side until your legs finished regenerating."

I rubbed my eyes with one hand. "Why ... why would he do that? He hates me."

Zahur smirked. "It is what Mates do," he explained as he moved around to my side of the bed. "And it wasn't hate I saw yesterday." Before I could ask about that he took my hands and pulled. Suddenly I was sitting on the side of the bed. His eyes ran over my face. "How are you feeling?"

"Tired. Sore and a little groggy, like I got my legs chopped off," I muttered, deciding to put that new information away for now.

"Good, but I still want a look at your legs to make sure the nerves regenerated correctly," he told me. I raised an eyebrow.

"That sounds like doctor speak," I pointed out. He smiled.

"Probably, because I am a doctor," he admitted.

"Really?"

"Yes," he assured me. "I graduated in nineteen twenty-five, nineteen fifty, nineteen seventy-six— "

"Alright, alright, you're a doctor. An old one at that," I teased.

"Says the female who is almost two hundred years old," he chuckled. I looked up at him.

"Says the two-thousand-year-old male," I countered. He grinned down at me.

"Respect your elders, child," he told me as he knelt in front of me. Both his hands took my right foot off the floor.

"Can you wiggle your toes for me?" he asked in a professional voice. I wiggled my toes for him.

"Good." He put that foot down and lifted the other. "Again?" I wiggled those toes. "Good, any pain?"

"Nope," I answered. His eyes met mine.

"I want to check the nerves in your legs," he said. I nodded. His examination was made up of tapping on my legs and asking if I could feel it. By the time he was done I was feeling the need for a shower.

"Everything looks to be in good working order. You're cleared to go back to your normal routine," he said. "And I have some business in the Ether to take care of." He got up and headed for the door. He paused and turned back to me. "Don't let Atticus scare you off. He needs you more than he knows." Before I could reply he left my bedroom, closing the door softly behind him.

Feeling disgusting, I went into my bathroom and took a shower. I was rinsing the shampoo out of my hair when Zahur's words ran through my mind. Atticus had taken care of me. There was no reason for Zahur to lie to me, so he must have. I didn't know what to think of that. Atticus had stayed after I told him to go, what did that mean? Did he want to try? Or was it just the Matching forcing him to stay? I didn't want to ask. Maybe I really didn't want to know. And what was that about Atticus needing me? I wasn't going to find answers hiding in here. I quickly finished my shower.

I pulled on a pair of jeans and a teal long-sleeve shirt. I blow dried my hair, left it down and headed out my bedroom door. Atticus was in the living room. He was looking at the books in my bookcase again. He was his ever-pristine self in a gray suit and a white dress shirt. His hair was perfect, as usual. Was Zahur wrong? He seemed perfectly fine. Not knowing what to think, I headed into the kitchen.

I went to the full coffee maker and poured a cup of coffee. I was stirring the cream and sugar when he spoke.

"Evelyn, can we speak?" he asked, his voice polite. I turned back to him. There were bags under his eyes, and his mouth was a tight line. Maybe yesterday had hit a nerve?

"Yes, we should probably talk," I admitted. I moved into

the living room area and sat on the couch. Atticus hesitated only a moment before he walked around the coffee table and sat on it in front of me. The silence grew longer as I sipped my coffee, waiting for him to start. I finally looked up at him. He opened his mouth to say something, then closed it again with a grimace. I waited. After several more attempts to speak, he growled in frustration before he met my gaze.

"The things I say never quite come out correctly with you," he said, his voice quiet. "I'd like you to enter my mind, so that this time I can show you." I blinked at him in shock. He wanted to give me access to his mind? To everything he was? I couldn't believe it.

"Do you understand what that means, Atticus?" I asked gently. "Are you prepared for what I might see?" His eyes were piercing as he held my gaze.

"You won't look without permission, that much I do know about you," he said. I weighed the pros and cons. On one hand, I might get a better understanding of Atticus. On the other, I might learn that he hates me. But all my debating melted away when he spoke again. "Please?"

"Alright." I set my mug on the floor, then scooted forward a bit more until I was close enough that my arm wouldn't hurt while touching his face. My knees ended up between his thighs. I met his gaze again and reached up. He wrapped his big hand around my wrist and brought my palm to his face.

I closed my eyes and focused. I slipped into his mind gently, like slipping into a lake.

I was standing in a room, a giant room, with blank white walls and fluorescent lights above. Everywhere I looked there were filing cabinets. Some were open, the contents spilling out, some were closed. Papers and files were stacked high on top of some of them. The floor was littered with papers. It was a mess.

"You've worked with a telepath before," I said, not knowing where he was. There was a creak behind me. I turned. Atticus was getting out of an old wooden desk chair. His inner mental projection was shocking. His hair was disheveled. His face had at least a two-day growth of stubble. His grey slacks were wrinkled, his shirt sleeves rolled up to his elbows, showing the tattoos that ran down both arms to his wrists. He leaned against the old wooden roll top desk and ran his hand through his hair.

"Yes, once. She taught me how to make it easier to communicate with a telepath if I ever needed to," he admitted. I was still stunned by the way he looked. His gold eyes wandered around the room. I walked over to stand in front of him. "This is my mind since I met you. Everything was fine, orderly, I had control. Everything had a place and a purpose. Then you came and everything is ...." He turned his head to meet my eyes with his. He was lost behind those eyes. "I'm sorry I didn't listen to you yesterday," he said softly. "I'm sorry about all my criticism. I'm sorry about the way I've been with you since we met." His eyes dropped to my legs. "Is there any lasting damage?"

"No damage," I assured him. "I'm just sore."

He looked away to the room of files again. "I thought keeping you away would help me keep control. Keep my emotions under control. But it hasn't. It's just made it worse." My heart ached. In here, I could feel the strain he'd put himself under.

"There's control, Atticus, and then there is too much control," I said softly. "You can't control every emotion. You can control how you react to it, but-"

"You don't understand, I have to have that control," he said softly.

"You can't control whether or not you have an emotion or a feeling. If you're stabbed with a blade, it's going to hurt. There's nothing you can do about that, it's a fact. All you can do is deal with it," I told him. His shoulders sagged a little as he exhaled.

"Why not?" His voice was barely a whisper. I moved closer, reached up and cupped his neck.

"Because you have a heart, Atty," I whispered back.

"But I have to have that control, otherwise ... my family ...." He stopped and swallowed hard. "I'm the most powerful male of our species."

"Could you end the world?" I asked. He blinked at me. His eyes clearing.

"No."

"Then why not let yourself feel?" I said softly. His hands moved to my waist as he pulled me closer, until I had to tilt my head back to see his face.

His eyes were on me but not really seeing me. "I grew up being taught that emotions were dangerous. That I had to control them or I'd hurt anyone I cared about."

"You were actually told this?" I asked, incredulous. Who would tell a child that?

He nodded. "Often, and if I forgot the lesson ... there were repercussions."

"What kind of repercussions?" I asked, not sure I wanted to know. I moved my hands to his chest.

He looked over my head, his lips tight. "Once, when I was eleven, I found a rabbit. It was young, hurt. I took it home, kept it secret and took it to a healer. They fixed its leg." His eyes met mine, pain filled them. "That's when I got caught." My heart dropped. "The man who adopted me wanted me to kill it. And because I refused, he killed it, cooked it, and then forced me to eat it with him for supper."

Horror tore through me. "Oh my God." Atticus clenched and unclenched his jaw as he took deep breaths.

"He taught me that caring for the animal was wrong, that being upset that he killed it was weakness, that being forced to eat it was good for me." He met my eyes. "He taught me everything I felt was wrong and that I shouldn't feel anything."

"That's cruel, Atty," I said gently, my fingers reaching up to stroke his jaw. "Emotions are normal. They make life worth living. Otherwise it's just-"

"Dull, and never ending," he finished for me. "The only emotion I've felt for so long was anger. It was the only emotion I could hide." He met my eyes. "Then I followed you into an alley, shook your hand"—his hand cupped my jaw, his thumb caressing my cheekbone— "and everything I've buried came back. Now I have no idea how to deal with it."

"Atty...." I didn't know what to say. In here, I could feel the stress and pressure he felt himself under. The confusion, the war inside him. In here, I could see him. The one who recited quotes in the car. The Atticus who kissed me in the warehouse, the one I first met in the alley.

"I'm sorry. For everything." He swallowed hard. "Am I too late, Eve? Have I fucked up too much for you to even consider...?"

"Atticus, you hurt me a lot," I admitted, looking at his chest. "I didn't want to be hurt by the things you said, but I was. In here, I can feel what you've been dealing with. It doesn't make it okay, but I do understand." I toyed with my locket before looking up and meeting his eyes. "So, no. It's not too late."

I was crushed against him, his arms around me, his nose buried in my hair. I smiled, wiggled my arms free and hugged him back. He let out a deep breath that made his body shudder.

"Just be honest with me, okay? If you're having trouble, tell me," I said quietly.

"I'll try," he whispered into my hair. He held me for another few heartbeats. "Alright," he said, letting me go. He was all business Atticus again. "We should get back. We have things to do." I stepped back, gave him a smile and slipped out of his mind.

I was sitting on the couch again. Atticus was still across from me, perfect as usual. Only now I saw it for what it really was. Control, too much control. Before I could move my hand away from his cheek, he turned and kissed my palm gently. My heart skipped a beat at the brush of his lips.

Atticus didn't say anything as I scooted back onto the couch. He got to his feet and buttoned his suit jacket.

"Let's get going, we have an appointment," he announced. I looked up at him and wondered where the real Atticus was.

"What appointment?" I asked. He looked down at me, his face blank.

"According to Falk, I owe you a pedicure."

I smiled. He was going to get me a pedicure? That was ... sweet. I got to my feet and met his eyes. "I would love one, but I have to go open the store. Give me a few days and I can take some time off."

His eyes became hard, his shoulders rigid. He was pulling back already.

"Honestly, I want to go. The shop is just slammed," I told him quickly. His eyes searched mine.

"A few days it is," he agreed, his eyes warming. An

awkward silence filled the living room. Not knowing what to say I played with my locket as the silence stretched. He began to say something then stopped himself. I started to ask what his plans were for the rest of the day, then stopped. I was just in his mind, it was intimate and personal. And now I had no clue what to say to him. The silence stretched.

He cleared his throat. "Um, what time do you have to open the shop?"

The shop! "Around five minutes ago." I admitted. "I'll-I'll see you later." I turned and all but fled out the door.

I went downstairs and unlocked the store. Before I even turned on the computers, I went into my office and sat down in my chair. I took a deep breath and let it out slowly. What just happened? Atticus wanted to try. I could barely believe it. I thought he didn't even like me. Then again, there were the little things he did. He helped me with my coat, walked between me and the street, he even buckled my seatbelt before driving to the morgue. But when he spoke ... Zahur had been right.

It took some time, and a cup of tea, to clear my head and focus. Out in the store there were still boxes from yesterday that needed to be picked up. I had just turned on the computers when the store phone rang. I answered.

"De Haven Books, how can I help you?"

"Ms. De Haven, this is Mr. Gumner," an irritated voice announced. I sighed.

"Mr. Gumner, I am so sorry I missed our appointment yesterday. A friend ended up in the hospital and I'm her emergency contact," I said.

"Sure," he said. I rolled my eyes.

"She's going to be alright, by the way." I barely controlled my voice. "Tomorrow, however, I will be in the store all day if you'd like to come by."

"I already have appointments tomorrow. I'll be there the twenty-first. Make sure you are," he snapped before hanging up the phone. I resisted the urge to throw the hand set. I sat behind the counter and looked at my emptying shelves, a knot of dread filling my stomach. I looked at the list I had printed from the website. I had to ship out half my books today. At least it wasn't my private collection, yet. I got to work.

THE BELL over the door chimed. Corrina Soryn strode in, muttering under her breath. The twenty-two year old Romani was a pretty woman. Her long, warm, dark hair was pulled back off her face. Her olive skin was flawless, her square face was stunning. A thin silver nose ring glinted in the store light. Her leather jacket covered a deep green shirt that matched her eyes. Her dark blue skinny jeans were distressed and hugging a body with curves every woman would want. Rina had offers for modeling contracts, but she continually refused so she could go to college to study computer science. She turned and frowned at me as she took off her gray scarf.

"What happened?" I asked. I knew that look on her face.

She began to take off her coat. "My roommate has the loudest brain on the planet," she announced angrily.

"Couldn't sleep?" I guessed

"No," she snapped as she came around the counter and hung her stuff on the hooks there. "It wasn't bad enough hearing her when I'm studying. I have to listen to her come out to her parents in her dreams too." I bit back a smile. Rina was a human telepath and was still struggling with her control. I'd been teaching her for the last six months.

"Did you shield before you tried to sleep?" I asked.

She sighed. "Yes. I seem to be missing something." She leaned on the counter next to me as she eyed the books on the counter.

"We'll go over it again before you go home today," I reassured her.

She turned and met my gaze. "What is with the books?"

I looked around the store. "I have to close the store."

Her eyes grew wide, her mouth opened. "What... why?"

"Gumner," I said simply. She muttered something under her breath her mother would no doubt have scolded her for.

She sighed. "I'm sorry, Evie." She wrapped her arm around me and squeezed. "You can still work online."

I hesitated. "If I can pay off the debt to Gumner without selling my private collection? Yes."

She squeezed me again. "Have you started calling collectors?"

"Some, I'll be reaching out to a few others today," I admitted. "Losing the store is painful, Evie. But it's just a place. It isn't a person and it's not the end of the world. And it's not over yet," she said as she took her arm off me. "Come on, let's kick some butt so you'll still have a business."

I nodded. That was Rina. No tears, no pity. Just empathy and motivation. The woman was amazing. I took a deep breath and let it out. Then we got to work.

~

Atticus

I WALKED into the werewolf bar that Evelyn had gone to. According to Ranulf, Evelyn had a friend in the owner. Hoping to get information I stepped into the almost empty bar. A few of the regulars turned to eye me, including the tall blonde werewolf behind the counter. A friend of Evelyn's if Ranulf's information was correct.

She watched me with hazel eyes as I moved to the bar across from her.

"Pardon me, I'm looking for Astrid," I said politely. I needed a favor from the wolves and being rude wouldn't help.

She ran her eyes over me, her gaze assessing, before her eyes met mine. "That's me." She narrowed her eyes at me. "And you must be the asshole who was responsible for Evie getting her legs cut off." I grew still. She set down the glass she was cleaning.

"Unfortunately, you are not incorrect. I'm Atticus," I admitted. "News travels fast in this city."

"How is she?" she asked, bracing her hands on the table. "She didn't call me so I'm assuming your group took care of her."

"She's healed and is back at her store," I replied.

She shook her head. "Do you even give a shit about the pain you put her through? The damage you did?"

My temper surged, I held it back. This was Evelyn's best friend, she had the right to be angry. I looked her straight in the eye and told her the truth. "I regret it more than you can imagine."

Her eyes searched mine and seemed to find what she was looking for. "You care about her?"

"That's none of your business," I snapped without thinking.

She smirked. "That's a big yes." I reminded myself not to kill the wolf. She leaned on her hands. "Now, what do you want?"

"Information," I said simply. "Have any of your pack encountered a demon or anything odd over the last week?

Heard any rumors of summoning?"

She tilted her head to the side, her brow drawn. "You should go through Evelyn for this."

"Why is that?" I asked.

Her eyes narrowed at me. "Evelyn runs this city. She has Treaties with every major species here. If you, a gargoyle, want to ask me, a wolf, questions then you have to go through Evelyn; otherwise I don't have to answer shit."

Stunned, it took me a moment to reply, "I know about the Treaties but ... Evelyn runs the city?" I couldn't imagine it. How?

She smiled. "You really haven't taken the time to get to know her," she said, surprised.

"It's none of your business," I reminded her.

"Oh, it is if you hurt her. And I already know you have." She leaned forward. "I'll make you a deal. You answer one of my questions truthfully, and I'll answer one of yours."

I clenched my fists at my side. This was ridiculous, but it was the fastest way to get answers. "Alright."

She smiled. "I'll go first," she announced. "Do you care about her?"

"She's my Match," I hedged.

Her eyes narrowed at me. "Yes, or no."

I swallowed hard. "Yes." A smile spread across her face. "Now, have you or your pack seen anything strange?"

"No, nothing more than the usual. The city has been quiet except for those murders," she said. "My turn." She eyed me. "It's not a question, more like advice."

"Such as?" I asked. She smirked.

"Evie has enough trouble on her plate with her store at the moment. If you care about her, be supportive right now," she said cryptically.

I clenched my jaw as she picked up the towel and hung

it over her shoulder. "As to the rest of your questions, no. No one's heard any rumors about a summoning. But," she met my eyes, "you might want to talk to the witches and warlocks. They've pushed the limit of their Treaty more than a few times." She grabbed a napkin and pen, then wrote on it. "This is the only witch I know, she can get you in touch with the others." She slid the napkin across the bar. "That's everything I got."

I picked up the napkin, my mind back on Evelyn. "Thank you." I tucked it into my breast pocket. I stepped back and headed for the door.

"Evelyn usually works through lunch," Astrid announced, stopping me in my tracks. Falk had said the same. I turned back to her. "She loves the fish and chips from Sam's pub on Ninth. Best in town." Astrid turned her back on me and got back to work.

I left the bar and got into the Mercedes. Fish and chips ... she had said it wasn't too late. I decided to give the others the witch lead and try to have lunch with Evelyn without being an ass.

12

I was on the phone with James Demer in London. He wanted a specific book of mine but he was lowballing me. My fingers were getting sore from tapping on the desk.

"James, I know what this book is worth, so stop lowballing me," I snapped into the phone. I closed my eyes and licked my lips. Alienating one of the most successful collectors who would be interested in this particular book wouldn't be smart. "The price I'm asking for is half of what it's worth; you can turn around and double your investment."

"I know, Evelyn, but you seem to be in a bit of a bind," James said, gloating. James and I had been rivals since I bought this particular book out from under him. I propped my elbow on the desk and rested my forehead in my hand.

"So, you have to take advantage of it," I muttered.

"Of course, it's just business," he assured me, his voice cheerful. It wasn't just business, they were my books.

I sighed. "James, I'm not just going out of business." The silence on the line was thick. "I'm three months behind on the store rent, which is six digits at this point. I have to sell everything just to pay off the landlord. I might be walking away with nothing here. No books, no money. So, either you buy this book or I'll have sell it to some low life like Joe Burgess." Burgess was a creep; he was known to screw over anyone at any time. He bought low and sold high. And he didn't give a damn about the books.

He cleared his throat. "You're selling your *entire* private collection?" he asked, his voice polite.

"Over the next few months, yes." The bell over the door rang telling me someone was here. Rina had already taken off to her classes.

"I'll take that book. I'll buy it off the site immediately. And Evelyn, don't tell anyone else about your private collection for twenty-four hours, I'll see what kind of offer I can get together," he said.

"Thank you."

"I didn't say I'd buy, Evie," he warned. "I'm going to see what kind of offer I can come up with in that time."

"I know. But thank you anyway," I said, my voice tired.

"I'll let you know by three p.m. your time tomorrow," he said before hanging up. I hung up the phone and hid my face in my hands. I made the sale, and Demer might be able to buy the rest. *I* wouldn't have them, but my books could go to a good collector.

"Evelyn?"

Atticus's voice had me lifting my head. He was standing in the doorway, his brow furrowed. His eyes ran over me.

I plastered on a smile. "Hi, um, what are you doing here?"

He finished his assessment and met my eyes. "Are you alright?"

I took a breath and let it out. "Yeah, I'm fine. That was

just a particularly surly collector." His gaze didn't leave mine. "What are you doing here?"

He held up two styrofoam containers. "I thought we could have lunch. Falk mentioned that you usually work through it."

I caught a whiff of something delicious. "Do I smell chips?" I asked with a grin. My accent clear.

His eyes warmed. "From Sam's pub, I heard it was the best for fish and chips." He stepped into the small office. He picked up the only other chair in the office and set it beside my desk. He held a container out to me. I took it with a smile of thanks and sat down. Making sure to move my order list, I set it down on my desk.

He unbuttoned his suit jacket and sat down. "I like your office."

I smiled as I opened my container to find perfectly fried golden fish and chips. Oh, so tasty. "Thank you. I'm a little over organized when it comes to my business." I looked up and met his eyes. The corner of his lips lifted into a grin. It instantly lightened my mood. I opened my stash drawer.

"These are good chips," he said. "You know, the only thing missing is-"

"Malt vinegar?" I asked as I pulled it out of the drawer and showed him. He did smile this time.

"You are English. I had thought so," he said. I drizzled the vinegar over my food before passing the bottle to him.

"Yes, I'm English. I was born in London. You?" I asked, letting my accent out again. I popped a piece of fish into my mouth. Realizing we didn't have napkins I reached down into my stash drawer again and pulled a few out.

"I was born in Northern England, the Manchester area," he said, his northern accent slipping out. I smiled to myself.

I had always liked a northern accent on a man. I handed him some napkins. "Thank you."

"So, when did you first guess I was English?" I asked curious.

He grinned. "When I watched you make a proper cup of tea."

I chuckled. "Ah, that always gives me away. I can't not make tea properly, it's just not in me."

"You say that like it's a bad thing," he countered.

I shrugged. A couple heartbeats went by before I asked, "Atticus, tell me about yourself?"

His face was closed off as he wiped his mouth on his napkin. "What would you like to know?"

"Anything you're willing to share."

He took a deep breath before answering. "I come from a rather well-respected bloodline, I was an only child, my parents died when I was ten. Then I was adopted by-"

"I didn't mean cold hard facts, Atty." I grinned as his eyes narrowed at the nickname. "I meant, tell me about you. What's your favorite food? Color? What do you love to do?"

"That diminutive isn't going anywhere, is it?" he asked, slightly irritated.

I smirked. "Nope."

"I like books," he admitted quietly. "As the Council's Historian I spend a lot of time with books and preserving our records."

"That explains the parchment," I said to myself.

"Parchment?" he asked. I looked up to meet his gaze.

"You smell like parchment. I had wondered why," I admitted before going back to my meal. There was comfortable silence for a few minutes.

"What about you?" he asked. I lifted my head. "We never

got to finish talking about your family, or what you did after they passed."

"They were ... normal, I guess," I began, trying to remember. "They loved each other. They still acted like teenagers in love by the time I came along."

"When were you born?" he asked as he tore off a piece of fish.

"1823."

He grinned as he looked up from his food. "Perhaps I should have asked, when is your birthday?"

"Oh." My face warmed. "May twenty-eighth. When's yours?"

"April seventh," he said as he used his napkin.

I raised an eyebrow. "What year?"

His left eyebrow twitched. "1534."

"That's a lot of birthdays," I teased.

"You were telling me about your parents," he reminded me.

I bit back a smile. "They were great. Both were determined to prepare me in case something happened to them. So, a lot of studying and lessons." I looked down at my chips. "Turns out they were right."

"I'm sorry, Eve, I shouldn't have brought it up," he said quietly.

I looked at him. "It's alright." I leaned back in my chair and continued, "After that, I sold the house. I traveled here and there. Then I came to the States. Worked, killed demons, and anyone who broke the laws."

His eyes ran over me. "So, you just traveled?"

I nodded. "Scotland, Ireland, Siberia, even China and Japan. I just never stayed in one place for too long. A month at most."

"Until Chicago?" he asked, wiping his fingers his napkin.

"Until Chicago," I admitted. "I'd been collecting books for years, selling them as I traveled. Even working here and there." I met his eyes. "I got tired of never having a home. So, when I got here, I stayed."

His eyes were shadowed as he watched me. "You were alone the entire time, weren't you?"

I finished my bite before answering. "I met people here and there, but if you mean close friends? Then yes, I was alone." I shrugged as if it didn't matter as I went back to eating.

"Why Chicago?" he asked softly. How was I going to explain this?

"I got here and it... felt like home. It was the first place that made me want to stay," I tried to explain. I didn't know if he would understand, but it was the only answer I had.

"Which is why you didn't want to leave with us," he surmised.

"There are a few other reasons," I said quietly.

"Like Astrid," he offered. "She's the first friend you've had in over a century."

I resisted the urge to squirm under his gaze. "That's one of them."

The silence stretched as I went back to my lunch.

"Why have you forgiven me so easily?" Atticus asked. I grinned as I looked up from my meal. "I expected yelling, insults, recriminations. But you've just ... forgiven me." He looked baffled.

"What does the back seat of your car look like?" I asked, smiling now. He frowned.

"It's ruined. The blood stains were so extensive I had to buy the car from the rental agency just to avoid questions," he said.

I bit back a laugh. "That's why."

Understanding dawned in his eyes. "You've forgiven me because you've *already* gotten back at me." He picked up his napkin from his lap. "You knew what was going to happen and the mess it was going to make." I was struggling not to laugh now.

"Yes," I admitted. "That was my revenge."

"That was a rather brilliant way to get revenge," he admitted. I couldn't hold it; I started laughing and couldn't stop. He just grinned and shook his head.

We passed the rest of lunch in conversation, carefully learning about each other. I learned that after reaching adulthood he left the community for two hundred years, traveling with other gargoyles to other countries. The tattoos he wore in his mind had me wondering if he had them in real life. After he went back he spent the next three hundred years working in the gargoyle community. His love for books and history took him to the old historian who wanted to retire with his Mate. And when I handed him a mug of properly made tea he all but groaned at the taste. It made me smile. During that hour I got a peek at the real Atticus. He was ... nice, determined, and ... yeah, sexy as ever.

I told him about the places I lived before Chicago. Turns out we had been to the same villages in Asia, just centuries apart.

When we were done eating he took our containers to the trash. When he came back his serious face was on.

He sat back down and turned to me. "I learned today that you run the city."

I grew still, half expecting a lecture.

"Would you tell me how you've managed it?" he asked in a quiet voice. I took a drink of tea to hide my surprise.

"You know I have a Treaty with the Red Caps," I began.

"What you don't know is that I also have them with the witches, werewolves, vampires, other shapeshifters, and a few fey. Ninety-three species in all." His brow drew down but he didn't say a word, so I continued. "Every species is responsible for their own. And every species has to give up their law breakers to me. I make sure they are guilty, and sentence them."

"What sentences have you handed out?" he asked, his voice careful. He was actually listening while he rubbed the pad of his forefinger over the nail of his thumb.

"Death for the extreme violations, exile, some of the others I've given back to their leaders to punish as they deem fit. Those tend to be the worst punishments," I explained.

"How can you be sure that the leaders will hand them over?" he asked. I grinned.

"Because each Treaty I wrote out personally, and every Treaty except for the Red Caps', is magically binding. For the Red Caps, it's all about honor, so they stay true to their word."

He raised an eyebrow. "How does this magical binding work?"

"Most species have a connection to their Alphas, Masters, or leaders. I exploited that connection so that if one of their people break the Treaty, they'll know something is wrong," I explained.

"What happens if they still decide not to report it?" he asked.

I met his gaze and told him plainly, "The leaders will start to die. Slowly, and painfully."

His eyes filled with understanding. "That's why you trust them to hand over their own. Their own lives are at risk," I nodded. His gaze was assessing as it ran over me. "That is extremely resourceful."

"I've had to be." I hesitated only a moment before adding. "But it goes both ways."

"Both ways?" he asked, carefully setting his cup down on my desk.

"If I violate a Treaty, then I'll start to die the same way. Only a pardon from the leader of the offended party will stop the spell."

Silence fell between us. I played with my mug. I didn't know what else to say... His face was blank, his eyes were unfocused.

"You don't approve, or it's against some law, right?" I asked quietly.

His eyes focused as they met mine. "No, actually, I was just thinking how much I underestimated you. You're only a hundred and eighty-nine years old. And you've managed to not only control the city, but keep its humans safe. I've never heard or read of anyone your age doing what you've done here." His tone impressed. My face burned. I didn't know what to say.

But that didn't matter when his eyes met mine. "Evelyn, why are the bookshelves half empty?"

I pulled my eyes away from his and looked down, turning my mug in my hands. "Spring cleaning?" I offered, knowing that he would see through the lie.

A perfectly manicured hand covered mine, stopping the cup from turning. Warmth slid up my skin as anxiety slipped away. He took my hand off my cup and turned me in my chair. He knelt down to meet my eyes.

"Spring cleaning doesn't include shipping boxes," he said gently. His thumb ran over my knuckles.

I looked up and met his warm eyes. "I'm going out of business."

He frowned. "How's that possible? You're selling, and have a rather impressive collection."

"The original building owner died a few months ago and his son inherited the building. And as the lease allows, he's increased the rent to drive me out." I swallowed hard as his face softened. "I'm three months behind now and, in order to pay it off, I have to sell everything as soon as possible."

"Even your private collection?" he asked.

"Sooner or later, every single book."

"I can give you the money," he offered softly.

I instantly shook my head. "I don't want your money, Atty." He winced at the name. I explained. "I don't want to owe anyone anything. It's a thing with me." His hand squeezed mine. I continued, "I'm hoping I can convince him to take payments. Then I'll have more time to find buyers, and that means I can get a better price. If I manage to salvage my private collection through this then I can start over, selling online."

"Take the money, Evelyn," he tried again, his accent slipping through. "It means nothing to me and I have more than enough."

I shook my head again.

He sighed. "You're stubborn."

"Yes, I am," I admitted.

He smirked. "Well, so am I." He straightened to his feet and took off his jacket. "I assume you've got book orders?"

He tossed his jacket onto the empty chair. Stunned at his sudden disrobing it took me a second to answer. "Um, yeah, I, uh..." I turned in the chair and grabbed the list. When I turned back he was rolling up his sleeves, showing the tattoos woven over his muscular forearms that I had seen in his mind. Tattoos. On Atticus. Oh dear, that was ... Oh my. Not noticing my drooling, he took the list from me and scanned it.

"If you pack them and address them, I'll pull the books from the shelves," he suggested. I looked up at him in surprise. He was serious. He started to head out of the office. I barely caught up to him in time.

I grabbed his arm and pulled him to a stop. He turned and looked at me questioningly. I finally found my voice. "We just ate fish and chips, so let's go wash our hands before we touch the rare and antique books." He smirked and followed me to the bathroom. We had a lot of work to do.

IT TURNED out that Atticus and I worked well together in the bookstore. I was sealing another box when Atticus brought down another armful of books.

"That should be the last for today," I said, smiling at him. "Thank you for helping. I don't think I could have gotten through all this today."

"Being surrounded by books is something I'm used to," he admitted as he set the books on the counter. His eyes met mine. "You wouldn't have to if-"

"I'm not taking your money," I cut him off. He sighed but didn't ask again.

His phone rang while I was writing out the address label. Atticus was all business when he answered.

By the time he got off the phone he was frowning again. "There's some trouble at the head of the Witch's Council house."

I went still. "What?"

"Ranulf and Falk are there," he announced. My heart dropped, then I was moving around the counter. He didn't bother to grab his jacket before we strode out the door. I only stopped long enough to lock the door as he used the phone. "Zahur, get back to us now," he ordered, then we were getting in the car.

As Atticus drove I became worried. Ranulf and Falk were at Rowena's. My pulse raced.

"What are they doing there?" I asked sharply.

"They were questioning her," he countered, his voice hard.

"You don't meet a witch on her home turf. You meet them on neutral ground and in public!" I growled.

"Astrid said you had Treaties with everyone," he countered.

"I do!" I answered. "But if you meet them on their turf you have to go through ritual greetings and all sorts of loop-holes before you can even ask questions." I looked over at him. "Tell me you knew that?"

His jaw clenched and unclenched. "I didn't."

Oh no. At least the store was close to Rowena's. I tele-pathically reached for Falk. Since I was trying to heal him it should be easier to find him. Only I hit a wall. I knew the feel of that magic; it was Rowena's, and it was stopping me from reaching them.

"Drive faster," I growled. He pressed down on the accelerator.

"You think something has gone wrong?" Atticus asked.

"I can't find Falk, she's blocking me," I told him, "That could mean nothing, or it could mean something very bad." I wasn't seeing the car or the road. My eyes were closed and I was examining the barrier blocking me.

"So, you *have* made a telepathic link with Falk," he growled.

"No, since I've been working on his throat it's just easier

to track him." I focused; the wall looked like ice, thicker than a foot I'd imagine. It was a great barrier but I was better. I mentally knocked on it three times. A new voice rang through the car.

"Ah, Ms. De Haven. Why are you pounding on my barrier?" Rowena's voice crawled through the speakers of the car.

"You've blocked me off from my people, Rowena. Take the barrier down now," I said out loud.

She tsked me. "They came to my home, my rules."

"They have guest rights," I reminded her. "If you harm them, I'll tear you apart piece by piece."

"Oh, I wouldn't harm them." Her voice was sweet and cloying. "But the poor things seem to be hallucinating." If they were seeing things then she'd drugged them or she was throwing illusions.

"Guest. Rights," I reiterated.

"They haven't claimed them," she countered. We turned the bend. Rowena's mansion was up ahead, gates closed. I rolled down the window.

"Rowena. You know my rules" I growled again as I took off my seatbelt and shifted to lean out the window.

"What are you doing?" Atticus shouted.

"You have my people, and you haven't dropped the barrier. What happens now is on you," I declared as I pulled energy through my body and into my hand. "Don't stop, Atticus." We were speeding toward the gate. I focused and threw the energy blast at the iron gates. They smashed open, swinging wide on their hinges only to hit the stone of the fence. I slipped back inside as he drove the car around the curve of the gravel drive. He skidded to a stop, white gravel flying.

Rowena's home was enormous. It looked like it belonged in Europe, not the U.S. My gums burned as my fangs came out. My marks began to glow as I charged the rest of my powers, slowly burning through my shirt. Atticus met me on the steps up to the door. "Get them out. I'll deal with Rowena," I growled.

"It's one witch, I can handle one witch," he reminded me. I turned to him.

"We're on her turf," I stated. "I would bet my life that she has spells all over the place to make physical attack all but useless. I'll handle her. You get them out." I watched the struggle in his eyes before he nodded. We reached the doors. I didn't bother knocking. I blasted the doors off the hinges and they crashed to the stone floor of the large foyer.

Ranulf was to the left, staring off into space. Falk, to the right, was as still as a statue, his pain etched on his face. I reached for him and still felt that barrier. Two sweeping staircases led to a balcony where Rowena stood. She was a beautiful woman. A gorgeous oval face, cascading chestnut silk for hair. And russet eyes that were glowing. In contrast, the skin along her neck was already gray, the color spreading across half her face. The spell had begun some time ago. That didn't make sense .... Her lithe figure was in black slacks and a plum silk blouse.

I glanced back at Atticus giving him a knowing look. "Get them out of here." He gave a quick nod before moving around Falk. I turned, giving the witch my full attention.

"You drugged them. How?" I demanded. She grinned with glee.

"Oh, it wasn't hard. A large dose of spelled hallucinogen in their waters." She took a shaky, painful breath. "They were very trusting."

"Why?" I asked, my voice calm as I examined the gray veins crossing her face. Then I realized why. I threw a shield up blocking her from attacking Atticus or the others while he finished dragging Falk out the door.

She scoffed. "You know why, otherwise you wouldn't have sent them."

"You had something to do with the demons showing up," I stated.

"Maybe." She stated, her eyes burning. "It doesn't really matter; I finally get to do what I've wanted to do for months." She raised her hand as she said "Ignis." She threw a ball of flame towards me. The ball dissipated as soon as it hit my shield. Energy tingled over my skin as I threw a bolt of lightning; it hit the stone railing forcing her back from the balcony. The air was thick with the smell of a stormy summer night.

"Hurry up." I yelled at Atticus as I moved to the stairs, my eyes still on that balcony. Another ball of flame flew over the railing shaking my shield. I worked faster. Focusing on making the water molecules in the air heavier, and heavier. Rain began to pour from the ceiling. Rowena cursed and began throwing balls of ice. She couldn't keep this up much longer, not with the spell draining the life from her. The more magic she used, the closer to death she came. So, I stayed low as I moved up the stairs. When I reached the second story landing I peeked out. Rowena was leaning on the back of a couch, drenched and panting. Her face was beyond pale, black veins were starting to cross her skin. Her whole body shook as she fought to keep herself upright. I created lightning in my palm and pressed my hand into the water that covered the floor. She screamed as she jerked from the shock then dropped to the floor. I let the rain stop and allowed the lighting to fizzle out in my hand. I got to my feet and strode behind the couch, my face blank.

She was gasping, sweat rolling off her face, the blackness

of her fingertips now covered her hands. Her eyes grew wide as she lay there. I knelt in front of her. Taking her chin in my hand I examined her face. Her skin was completely gray now, black and gray veins marred her beautiful face. A large black patch was working its way down her throat.

"You had something to do with those deaths," I stated. "Did you summon these demons?"

She glared at me. "Grant me a pardon and I'll tell you." Her voice was dry and raspy.

"Tell me and I might consider," I lied. She was going to die for what she did to Ranulf and Falk. Not to mention the human victims.

"Pardon first," she gasped painfully.

I looked her in the eyes.

"No," I stated, my voice cold. "You hurt my people and you enjoyed it, you violated the Treaty. You do not get to walk away from that." Rowena cried out in pain as she fell to her side on the stone floor, clutching her chest.

"How ... long?"

I thought about it. "The less magical ability, the slower it works." I focused back on her. "So, for you? I'd say three more days, four at most." Rowena cried out as she lay flat on the floor, her body jerking as she fought for air.

I debated how wise it would be to enter the witch's mind. It would be easy, but as a witch, Rowena would have more tricks and traps up her sleeve than I had time to deal with. No, I couldn't get the answers from her.

I straightened to my feet and pulled out my cell phone. I called Rowena's second in command.

"Hello."

"Delia, this is Evelyn," I said quickly. "You should come to Rowena's house."

"Why? What's happened?" she asked, her voice hard.

"She violated the Treaty, you'll be the new Head in a few days," I informed her. "I thought you might like to round up some of the other witches so she doesn't die alone." There was silence for several heartbeats.

"I'll do that. Thank you."

"I need several questions answered now," I growled into the phone.

"Whatever you need," Delia offered, her voice professional.

"Are there any witches or warlocks besides Rowena who are strong enough to bring a demon, fully formed, through the barrier?" I ignored Rowena's crying as Delia thought about my question.

"Individually, no," Delia began, "but in a group, it's possible."

"Anyone new in town? Anyone Rowena has been seen working with?" I asked, looking out the large window across from the balcony.

"No, no one new. But ...," Delia hesitated.

"What?"

"Just rumors," she offered. "A few warlocks have gone missing. They could have gone on vacation or something, but it's the only thing out of our usual."

"Does Rowena work with them?" I asked as I ran my hand through my hair.

"Lately, yes," she answered.

"Could these warlocks and Rowena, together, pull something through?" I asked directly.

"I believe so," Delia answered. I cursed. Rowena started coughing.

"Send me their information, please." I made a point to keep my voice polite.

"I'll do that immediately." Delia hung up. I tucked my

phone back in my pocket and turned back to Rowena. A bit of blood was smeared on the corner of her mouth.

"That is the only mercy you will get from me," I told her. "The others are on their way. They'll do what they can to make you comfortable."

I turned to leave and paused. Atticus was leaning against the balcony railing, his gaze on Rowena's writhing form. I moved past him and began down the stairs. He followed.

"That was rather brutal," he observed.

"She broke the Treaty, she knew the repercussions." I hurried down the stairs. He followed silently behind me.

"I don't disagree," he said. Rowena let out a pained cry, stopping me at the bottom of the stairs.

My eyes went to the balcony. "Some days I feel like a monster." I barely breathed. I hated that spell, but I hadn't seen any alternative. I turned away and walked out the door to the car with Atticus.

ZAHUR MET us at their apartment. Atticus had Ranulf's arm over his shoulder and was leading him to his bedroom. Zahur took Falk from me. They moved through the door down the hall and on the left. Zahur let go of Falk. He dropped like a rock, half on and half off the bed.

I grabbed his legs and rolled him the rest of the way onto the bed then yanked off his boots. Zahur went to get his doctor bag, I stopped him.

"Just bring in a couple garbage bags, they're going to be sick." I warned. Zahur frowned then nodded and went to do as I asked.

I moved to sit on the side of the bed next to Falk. His face was still pulled in pain. I held his face in my hands and closed my eyes.

That barrier was gone. Rowena was too far away and too weak to hold it. Falk was in an old forest, and a woman was there; tall, blonde, and beautiful. She was yelling at Falk as he stood there, his head hung in shame.

"I shouldn't have been with you! You're not even human!" she shouted. Who the heck was she? It didn't really matter. I strode through the underbrush to his side.

"Falk," I called gently. He lifted his head to see me. Tears rolled down his ravaged face. The drugs were tearing him apart.

"You're not real," he murmured. I reached up, grabbed his chin and forced him to look at me.

"I'm the only real thing here, Falk," I whispered. He slowly reached up, his hand holding mine to him.

"Evie?" he asked softly, his voice shaking.

"It's me," I assured him. The woman kept screaming at him for wasting her life. He looked from me to her. "She's not real, you've been drugged," I explained. His eyes came back to mine. "Remember, you were at Rowena's house? You drank something?" He nodded slowly. His hands clung to my upper arms. "I'm going to force the drug out of you and you're going to be sick, so I want you to puke."

"You're really here," he said, as if to reassure himself.

"I'm really here." I pulled him closer until he leaned down, I cradled his face in my hands. I poured healing energy through my hands and into his body. With my eyes closed I followed it. Through his lungs, into his blood stream and to his brain. I spread the healing energy every-where I went as I pulled the drug from his system. When I was done, I pulled back.

Zahur was there with the bag when Falk rolled to his side and was sick. I ran my hand up and down his back trying to soothe him. When he was done, he couldn't even open his eyes as he relaxed into the bed. "Thank you, Evie," he rasped. I brushed the hair off his face and smiled down at him.

"No problem," I said. "Get some sleep." I covered him with his blankets and we left his room, closing the door behind us in time to spot Atticus leaving Ranulf's room. I passed him and slipped into Ranulf's room. Zahur a step behind me.

The big bear of a man was flat on his back, still in his boots and mumbling. I pulled his boots off then covered him in his blankets and sat next to him. Zahur silently took his spot near the side of the bed.

I held Ranulf's face and closed my eyes. I was in a room lit by candles. A woman was giving birth in the bed and it didn't look like it was going well. A younger Ranulf was kneeling beside her, holding her hand.

"The healer is on the way, hold on, please." Ranulf begged with tears in his eyes. The woman, who had the same blue eyes as Ranulf, turned to him. Her breathing was short and shallow.

"Save the baby..." She whispered before going limp in the bed.

"Meryl? Meryl!" Ranulf shouted as he tried to shake her awake.

"Am I dead?" Ranulf's voice came from behind me. I turned. He was standing in the corner, his painfilled eyes on the lifeless figure in the bed. "Is this hell?"

I went to him and stood between him and the bed. "No, you've been drugged." I explained. "Do you remember going to see Rowena? The Head of the Witches' Council?"

His eyes met mine as he nodded.

I reached up and held his face. "I'm going to get the drug out and you're going to be sick."

His hand wrapped around my wrists, his grip hard. "Get me out of here." He growled.

I nodded and focused. I did the same as I had with Falk, clearing the drug from his system. When I was done working, I pulled my mind back and got my hands out of the way.

Ranulf rolled to the side and threw up into the bag. I rubbed his shoulder as he heaved. When he was done he laid his head down on the pillow and sighed.

"Lass..." he mumbled. His hand shoved the covers aside so he could take mine.

"Rest," I said softly. Zahur left with the garbage bag.

"Thank you," he murmured before he sighed deeply and relaxed into the mattress. I held his hand until his grip eased enough that I knew he was asleep. I slipped out of his room quietly.

Zahur was in the living room, leaning against the wall. Atticus was pacing. I walked into the kitchen and started making coffee. It sounded good to me.

When I turned back, Atticus and Zahur were watching me with assessing eyes. It put me on edge. "What?" I asked from across the apartment.

"The spell you used for the Treaty," Atticus began, "I've never seen effects like it before."

I brushed the hair out of my face and just told them. "Because I created it." If it was possible, Atticus stood even straighter.

"What are your abilities?" he asked, his voice calm. I moved to stand behind the couch and met his eyes.

"Can you promise me that anything I tell you won't go past this room?" I asked directly.

"There are some things I have to report to the Council," Atticus reminded me.

I crossed my arms over my chest. "I know," I said. "That's

why I'm asking for your word." Tension filled the silence in the apartment as he contemplated my request.

"Why the secrecy, Evelyn?" he asked gently as he slowly walked around the couch to stand in front of me. "What are you trying to hide?"

I licked my lips before looking up into his soft, golden eyes. "Me."

13

E velyn's voice was sincere as she answered. I waited for her to elaborate, but she didn't. She truly meant her.

"Why are you hiding?" I asked gently. She pressed her lips together hard.

"I'll tell you if you both promise me that you'll tell no one," she said softly, making my pulse skip and blood flow to my groin. "Not even on your bloodlines. Just a promise to me." Shoulders relaxing, I took a deep breath. If I had to report what she told me, it wouldn't have any consequences with the Elder Council, just her ... shit.

Zahur nodded.

"Alright," I gave in. I had to know why she was hiding. "Now, what are your abilities?"

She swallowed hard before answering. "All of them." I stood there, stunned, for a full minute as her words sank in.

"All of them?" Zahur asked carefully.

"Yes." Her voice was quiet. "Air, fire, water, lightning, earth, telepathy, telekinesis, conjurations, spell weaving, and healing. I can manipulate energy, all kinds, any kind. Anything you can think of, I can do it."

"To what level?" I asked.

She kept eye contact with me as she answered. "Extremely high. Energy manipulation is like breathing to me. It's easy, it always has been." I was silent as I absorbed this information. Then confusion set in.

"Why would you keep that a secret?" I asked. "There is no reason to." The coffee finished dripping. She went to pick up the carafe. Zahur and I sat on the stools at the breakfast counter and watched her make coffee. When she put a mug in front of me she finally met my eyes again.

"A couple of reasons. First, what would your Elder Council do to a gargoyle with that kind of power, who they can't control?" she asked matter-of-factly.

I thought it over. If she didn't take orders, and she wouldn't if she didn't agree ... they would want her 'handled.' Which meant either dead or locked up.

"They'd either kill you or lock you away," Zahur stated.

"I see your point." I turned my mug in my hands on the counter. I watched her stir her coffee with a spoon. "And the second reason?"

"My parents were in hiding, from someone on the Council. A male named Cyrus," she began. My heart dropped. She continued. "Cyrus was a Match for Mom. She always said suitor though. She said he had a great bloodline, reputation, position. You name it, he had everything you'd think a female would want in a husband." She looked down at her coffee. "Except, my mom loved my dad. He didn't have the best bloodline, or any of the advantages that Cyrus did. But she picked him."

"Your mother was Tatiana Suvu?" Zahur asked. We both turned to him.

She nodded. "Yes."

"You know about this?" I asked, still reeling from Evelyn's story.

Zahur nodded as he met my gaze. "Yeah, it was a huge scandal about six hundred years ago." He looked to her. "Your mother was the last in the rarest, most powerful bloodline in gargoyle history." He turned back to me and gave me a meaningful look. "A match between Cyrus and the Suvu line would have brought two powerful bloodlines together. Instead, she picked the male she loved. Owyn Dalca."

My world was crashing down around me. That's why he sent me to bring her back. That's why he kept telling me to keep her at arm's length; he probably thought he'd be a Match for her as well. If he couldn't have the mother, he'd have the daughter. Murderous rage filled me, Zahur saw it in my eyes and nodded. He knew what I was thinking, he figured out why we were here. I was a fucking idiot.

"They were married, that's what she always called Mated I guess. It should have ended there, but it didn't," Evelyn continued, not noticing the tension between Zahur and I. "He had a higher position so he started to harass them and kept sending my father out on suicide missions."

I looked down at my coffee. My knuckles were white, I eased my grip on the mug.

"He kept surviving. After a close call my parents had finally had enough. They packed a couple satchels and left that night."

"All we ever knew was that they were gone one morning," Zahur said. "Then eventually, when our numbers dropped they were declared dead."

"They didn't die until I was seventeen," she said softly. Zahur reached out and took her hand.

"I'm sorry that they are gone. I knew Owyn." She met his eyes. "He was a good male, and utterly devoted to your mother."

He patted her hand before pulling away. "Thank you." Her voice was quiet, barely there. She cleared her throat, pulling me out of my own head. "So, that's what I haven't told you. I'm hiding from this male."

"Well, it's nice to know your real last name. Dalca. It's Romanian, isn't it?" Zahur made small talk, giving me the chance to get myself under control.

"Yes, it's old Romanian." She grinned as she took a sip of coffee.

Zahur looked at the clock on the wall. "So, what do you have planned for the rest of the afternoon?" He looked back down to her.

She checked the clock. "I need to get back to the store. Then tonight is girls' night. Astrid usually comes over." She met my eyes. "Would you mind not coming over until after she leaves?"

I thought about it. "You'll stay across the hall?"

"Yes," she said patiently.

"Then I'll give you your space," I agreed. I needed some time to think anyway. She smiled at me and it made my pulse jumped.

"Thank you," she said before she headed out the door.

We were silent for a full minute.

"You have to tell her," Zahur stated.

I scoffed at that. "We are just now talking, I don't think this will help."

"It doesn't matter," he stated. "She needs to know." He was right of course, I had to tell her. But... Shit. It was going to hurt. The way she'd look at me ...

"I'll tell her. Just... not now," I admitted quietly. Right

now, I wanted to explode, rip something apart and slam it into a wall. Well, more like someone.

"Then when? After she's your Mate? When she has no choice but to accept it?" he asked pointedly.

"If I tell her Cyrus adopted me, I'd have no chance anyway," I growled.

He raised a knowing eyebrow. "I think you'd have a better chance than you think, if you told her."

"Her mother is the one who refused Cyrus? You're positive?" I asked again, to be sure. He nodded. FUCK!

Zahur got up and headed for his room.

"You know what this means," I announced.

"We can't take her back," Zahur finished for me. I nodded. Fucking Cyrus! Furious, I threw my mug against the kitchen cabinets. It shattered, coffee splattered everywhere. It did nothing to cool my temper.

Evelyn

LATER THAT NIGHT...

I was just hanging up the phone when my door opened.

"Hey girl, I've got the booze, did you order the pizza?" Astrid announced as she strode into my apartment carrying a bottle of wine. Ranulf straightened, his eyes running over the tall, curvy blonde. Astrid's gaze found Ranulf. She smirked as her eyes ran over Ranulf, slowly. The silence was too sexually charged for me.

"Yeah, I just ordered the pizzas for everyone. Astrid, this is Ranulf, one of the gargoyles who came to town," I announced as I moved to the back of the couch and watched them continue to eye each other. Okay, this was taking too long. "Ranulf, it's girls' night," I reminded him.

He tore his eyes off Astrid to look at me. "I'm going, text us when the pizzas are here." He headed towards the door. Astrid watched him leave, turning to watch him go. She turned back biting her lower lip, her face pained.

"That male... I want to climb him like a tree," she stated emphatically. I chuckled as I picked up my 'girls' night' basket. It had everything we usually used. Mud masks, nail polish, all the other essentials. I moved to the living room and sat on the big sofa. I set the basket down and started pulling out polishes while Astrid went into the kitchen to grab wine glasses and a corkscrew.

She came back and sat next to me. "So, what's Ranulf's deal?"

I smiled as I found Astrid's usual red for her toes. "He's single. Thirteen hundred and some change old."

Astrid began to pour the wine. "That's old. Think his plumbing still works?"

I laughed as I handed her the nail polish and took the wine glass she handed me. "I imagine so." I turned to her, she had that light in her eye. "Astrid."

"What?" she asked innocently.

"We have a Mate thing, too," I reminded her.

She pulled off her boots and socks. "I'm not looking for forever here, Evie. Just a few great hot nights that leave me walking funny. I'm not the settling down type, you know that."

I rolled my eyes as I set my glass down and found my clear polish I liked to use. "Well, if you want to take a shot, go for it. They might be here a bit longer."

She stopped shaking the bottle and raised an eyebrow. "And why's that?"

My cheeks grew warm as I found my nail file. "I had lunch with Atticus today."

"And?" she asked with a grin.

"And ... it was nice," I admitted as I sat back on the couch and started filing my nails. "We talked. I got to know him. He got to know me."

"And?" she asked, grinning.

"I told him about the store," I admitted. Astrid's grin disappeared. "He offered to give me the money."

Her eye brows went up. "Really?"

I nodded as I started filing on my other hand. "Yeah, I turned him down."

"Of course you did," she grumbled.

"I don't want his money," I reminded her.

"Just him out of his pants," she countered. We both started laughing as my face burned.

"Atticus naked." I thought about it. Goosebumps ran over my skin. "That would be a sight." I tried to shake the image from my mind.

"You've only ever slept with humans, right?" She asked as she started painting her toenails.

My face warmed. "Yes."

"Wow." Astrid smiled mischievously, "You're in for quite a ride."

My face caught fire. "Astrid!"

She snickered. "I'm not kidding. At least with Atticus you won't have to worry about hurting him or STDs, right? Or is that just us?"

"No, we don't get diseases." I said absently, then quickly added "Besides, I didn't say I was going to sleep with him." I pointed out focusing on my own nails.

"But you want to." She teased.

I sighed and shot her a look. "You know what I want."

Astrid grinned. "Yeah, a guy who will love you for you."

"Can you blame me?" I asked.

"Not at all." Astrid began painting her toenails on her other foot. "I still don't know what you saw in that cop."

I shrugged as I started polishing my left hand. "Potential," I admitted. "I was lonely and as you would say, 'hard up.'"

Astrid winked. "I'll give you that." She finished her toes and put her feet on the floor carefully. "Now, tell me about Ranulf."

I laughed before I filled her in on what I knew. Nothing I told her eased her attraction to the gargoyle.

When the pizzas arrived, I answered the door only for Ranulf to open the door to the males' apartment. He took over and paid for the food, then, despite my protests, brought the pizzas into my apartment. The other males soon followed through the open door.

"So, what did we get?" Zahur asked as he joined us at the breakfast counter. I pulled the pizza for us and waited for the guys to leave. They all started to settle in, talking about a rugby game. My gaze met Atticus's. I mouthed 'please?'

His jaw clenched. "Grab the pizzas and take them over to our place. The ladies have plans," he announced. The males grumbled as they grabbed boxes and headed for the door.

"Thank you," I called quietly to Atticus before he left. He gave me a small bow from the neck before closing the door behind him.

Astrid started laughing. When we brought the pizza to the living room she was just getting herself under control. I opened the box and started eating while she got ahold of herself.

Finally, I'd had enough. "What is so funny?"

She stopped laughing. "That male is so hooked, it's funny to watch."

I finished chewing. "What are you talking about?"

She shook her head. "Nothing."

We turned on Magic Mike and went on with our usual girl night activities.

Halfway through the movie, Astrid's phone went off. She growled as she answered.

"Yeah?" Her head dropped back to the sofa. "It's not my job." She closed her eyes and gritted her teeth. "Fine." She hung up.

"David?" I asked gently.

"Yes, it was Alpha dick," she growled. "He wants me to put another female wolf in line because his fucking Mate is too weak to do it herself." She yanked on her boots.

"He still won't assign a new Alpha female?" I asked.

"No, because he wants his Mate to step up. Only she's not," she bit out. "She doesn't even have the guts to call and ask me for help herself."

"I'm sorry, Astrid," I said. "Is there any way you can refuse? Challenge her?"

She shook her head. "Some days I think it's time to look for a new pack." She turned to me. "You decide to leave, give me a chance to pack a bag."

I reached over and hugged her tight. "Of course. I need my Astrid." She squeezed me back before pulling away. She got up and headed out the door without another word. I sighed and turned off the television.

I got up and moved to my bookcase, looking for a book. *The Count of Monte Cristo*, I had started it earlier and since Astrid was gone, I figured I'd finish it. Finding it, I was just walking back to the couch when there was a knock on the door before it opened. Atticus came in wearing designer navy pajama bottoms and a long-sleeved white shirt that hugged the muscles of his chest.

"Ranulf told me Astrid left," he explained. He held up his book. "Do you mind if I read in here. The others are being extremely loud."

I smiled to myself. "Sure, I was about to start a night of reading myself." I curled up in the corner of the sofa as he sat at the other end. "What are you reading?"

"*The Iliad*," he replied, his nose already buried in the book. I smiled to myself. He really was a book geek. I went about reading my book.

The apartment was quiet except for the occasional shouts of joy from the apartment across the hall. It was soothing.

Eventually I got up to make tea, taking my book with me. I continued to read as I waited for the kettle. I was so engrossed that I set up two mugs for tea then waited, leaning against the counter. When the water boiled I poured it into the mugs and let it steep for a few minutes. I turned the page several times before I took out the teabags, then added milk and sugar to one. And only sugar to the other. My nose still in my book, I picked up both mugs in one hand and walked back to the living room. I stopped by Atticus and gave him the one with only sugar then moved back to my spot on the couch.

As the evening went on I ended up laying on my back on my part of the couch. Something touched my foot. Looking over my book, I watched Atticus as his hand absently massaged my left foot. My body warmed as I watched to see if he knew he had done it. When he stopped to turn a page, his hand went back to my foot, massaging again. It was sweet. I hid my smile behind my book as I started reading again.

When the lines began to blur I called it a night. I said goodnight to Atticus and went to bed, falling asleep quickly.

I was at the parlor door, I opened it to find it empty. Empty except for the gifts under the tree. And a note on the side table. I picked it up. "Darling, your Mother and I have taken ill. We're resting now. Please, open your presents- Dad." Strange, it didn't look like his handwriting. I turned toward the gifts, excited.

"Evelyn!" Atticus's voice tore me from that hell. I opened my eyes to Atticus's face, sweat rolling down my skin. Atticus was above me, his hands on my arms.

"I'm awake," I said in a trembling voice as tears rolled down my face. I closed my eyes as I tried to shove those memories back behind their door. I struggled. They kept coming back.

His hand cupped my face, his thumb running over my cheek bone. "You're still crying. What's wrong? Tell me." His voice was hard, with an edge of desperation. I shook my head, it was stupid. I always had these nightmares near Christmas.

"Bad memories," I told him.

He cursed. The bed shifted. His arms moved around me, pulling me on my side and against his chest. I buried my face against him and clung to his cotton shirt as I tried to stop crying. He held me close as his hand ran down my hair then down my back, over and over, his touch soothing. The scent of parchment filled my lungs, helping me calm down.

He held me until I stopped crying. When I calmed down he loosened his grip on me.

"What memories?" he asked quietly.

I shook my head. I just got them behind their door, I

wasn't about to open it up again. "It happens every winter. It's okay."

"You were crying in your sleep," he bit out. "That is not alright."

I sighed, then lifted my head to meet his eyes. They were concerned. He was worried. "I don't want to talk about it now."

Those golden eyes searched mine. "But you will?"

I nodded.

He pressed his lips together. "Alright." His arms moved out from around me, he shifted to sit at the side of the bed. I didn't want him to go.

"Atticus," I barely whispered before he got up. He half turned to look down at me. "Stay. Please?" I asked quietly.

He grew still, his eyes ran over my face, searching, before he nodded. I moved to give him room. He pulled the covers back and climbed in.

The bed shifted as he got comfortable. I rolled onto my back and tried to relax so I could fall asleep. I shifted a bit, trying to find a comfortable spot.

Once I did, I started to fall asleep, only to jerk awake before I could go. I didn't want another nightmare. I looked up at the ceiling, listening to Atticus's breathing, deep and even. Time moved along slowly, I started counting sheep. It didn't work. My body begged for sleep but my mind wasn't listening.

I was about to say enough and go read on the couch when the bed shifted. Suddenly I was face down in bed with Atticus's hand between my shoulder blades. I tried to move but that hand held me to the bed firmly. The fingertips of his other hand ran over my back.

"What are you doing?" I asked, on the verge of blasting him into the ceiling.

"Getting you to sleep," he stated. What? I was about to tell him to let me go when his hands moved and his fingers pressed into a spot on each side of my spine. My body tensed and relaxed at the same time as a wave eased up my back. It was both relaxing and a bit painful.

"Oh. Whoa," I breathed as I laid my head back down on the bed. He held pressure to those spots between my shoulder blades for several minutes. Then he moved his fingers down and pressed again. I groaned. I couldn't think at that point, all I could do was lay there as he moved down my spine, encouraging the muscles in my back to relax. Everything grew hazy as he moved his hands up to the back of my neck. His fingers pressed into a spot that had me closing my eyes. The last thing I remember was a blanket moving to cover my shoulders.

I woke up slowly, pressed against someone. Which was new... I rubbed my cheek against his soft fabric as I shifted my knee higher. As I floated there I realized I was snuggled up to his back, my arm around his waist, my knee bent and thrown over his hip. I took a deep breath and breathed in parchment. Huh. No .... that can't be right. No... I had to still be asleep.

As time went on, I became aware of a long-fingered hand holding mine against the middle of his chest, over his heart. I gave his fingers a squeeze. They squeezed back. He was awake.

"Comfy ..." I mumbled, wondering who I was next to. It felt like Atticus ... smelled like Atticus ...

"Do you usually take all the bed like this?" he muttered, still half asleep.

I rubbed my cheek against his skin. "Uh-huh. Sorry." I hugged him tight before slipping my hand from his and moving away from him to give him room. I rolled over to my back on my colder side of the bed. Was my heat turned on? I pulled my blankets up to my chin as I curled up on my other side. The bed moved. He shifted his body close to mine, his body heat warming me. I cuddled back into him until my body met his. His arm tentatively moved around my waist. He gently buried his face in my hair and took a deep breath. "It's alright," he whispered, his arm tightening on me a little before I fell back to sleep.

14

The sun on my face woke me up. I stretched as I rolled onto my back to find I was alone. Wait, that wasn't right. I rubbed my eyes and looked over at the other side of the bed. It was already made, perfectly. Still half asleep, it hit me.

Atticus. Atticus slept here last night. Then my memory came flooding back. My nightmare, him waking me up. Me asking him to stay. Then waking up wrapped around him. Him asking if I hogged the bed normally, even how hesitant and unsure he was wrapping his arm around my waist when I was cold. That was Atticus. I rubbed the morning gunk from my eyes as I absorbed that.

I asked him to stay last night. I looked at the closed door and wondered if he was going to mention it. Oh, I hoped not. I knew why I asked him to stay. My stupid nightmares. I took a deep breath and let it out slowly.

I hated Christmas. Grumbling about Santa and elves, I took a shower and went through my usual routine. I pulled on a pair of worn jeans, a gray scoop neck shirt and a navy cardigan. I pulled on my newish pair of brown leather ankle boots with just a bit of heel to them. I hadn't worn them yet and they did look good. I made sure to braid my hair and check my make up before leaving the bedroom.

When I came out everyone was already there. Zahur was at the stove making pancakes.

"Morning," I said as I moved to the coffee maker.

"Morning," everyone said at once. I smiled as I poured coffee. When I turned around Zahur handed me a plate of food and a fork.

"Thanks," I said, taking the plate. I went to the breakfast counter to stand at the end. Instead Atticus got up, giving his seat to me. "Oh, thank you."

"You're welcome," he said quietly as he headed for the sink.

I sat down and started eating.

"I want to go out and find these warlocks today," Atticus announced as he turned and leaned against the sink.

I lifted my head to meet his eyes. "Can we split up to get it done faster? I have a lot of orders at the store."

He nodded. "That sounds reasonable, and if they aren't at their homes it'll give us more time to find them." I looked down at my breakfast, suddenly not hungry.

"Sounds good to me, let's get started," Ranulf suggested.

Everyone got ready to leave, the males loaded up on weapons and I grabbed my coat.

I ended up with Ranulf at the third warlock's address. It was in the cruddy part of town. After I parked the Mustang I wondered if I'd come back to find it whole, gone or in pieces.

"Alright, lass. How do you want to play this?" Ranulf asked, making sure to stay with me as we crossed the street.

"I was thinking, 'Hi, I'm a gargoyle. What the heck have you been doing?'"

He chuckled as we reached the run-down building. "That'll work." He opened the door and let me walk in first. Immediately the smell of urine hit my nose.

"Oh, ew," I muttered. I plugged my nose as we moved further into the building. Trash was scattered here and there. Mindful of my shoes, I stepped over or around it. "Maybe I should have changed my shoes."

"You look like a librarian today," Ranulf pointed out as we started up the rickety staircase.

I looked over my shoulder at him and raised an eyebrow. "You have a thing for librarians, don't you?"

A grin spread across his face. "Nay, lass. I like the wild ones."

"Then you'll love Astrid," I teased as we reached the third floor. I checked the apartment number before heading down the dirty hall.

"The smell just gets worse," he muttered. I took a good whiff. The smell was rotten and thick on my tongue. I knew that smell. I turned and hurried down the hallway to apartment 311. The smell was thicker here. I tried the knob. Locked.

I stepped back. "Break the door, please."

"I smell it too," he muttered before taking his large booted foot and kicking the door clean off its hinges. The scent tripled. I held my hand over my mouth and nose. He cursed.

"Stay here." Ranulf stepped through the door.

"Not a chance." I carefully followed. He came up short, I almost bumped into him. I stepped out from behind him and bit back a curse.

Three bodies were lying on the floor of the mostly empty apartment. The south wall was covered in symbols I recognized. It was a spell to tear a hole through the barrier. The center of the circle was scorched, the wall-paper burnt away and the plaster beneath more than cracked.

"We'll call the others. Tell them we found all of them and the portal," I said absently as I examined the floor. White paint surrounded the three bodies, symbols and runes circled the warlocks in a protective circle, except ... I needed a closer look. I carefully stepped around the circle, trying not to step in the liquified remains.

Ranulf took my hand to help me keep my balance as he spoke on the phone with the others. I tiptoed around the circle, looking at the symbols. Ranulf came with me, helping me keep my balance. When I got to a cleaner patch of floor I bent down and took a closer look. No... Not believing what I was seeing I blinked hard, trying to clear my eyes. The image didn't change.

"I don't know these symbols," I said. "I mean, it's a protection circle, but against what, I don't know." I used Ranulf's hand to help me stand. I pulled out my cell and took pictures of the markings. Then I moved to the wall. The symbols for opening a tear were there, nothing was different on the wall. Ranulf hung up as I stepped back to his side.

"Atticus says to go open your store and see if you can figure out the symbols," Ranulf said as he put his phone away. "I need to stay until they get here."

"Okay, I'll head back"— I began to tiptoe again— "and get started on research."

Instead of helping me, Ranulf's hand turned me around. Then I was upside down, over his shoulder with his hand wrapped around the back of my knee.

"Come on, lass," he said cheerfully.

I laughed as he moved through the room. "Why?"

"You're moving too slow." When we were out the door he set me down. He straightened and turned to the doorway.

"Hold on," he said as he propped the door against the doorframe. "I'll walk you back to the car. I need some fresh air."

We headed back out of the building.

When we got outside I took a big breath of fresh air. Ranulf had me moving towards the car.

"It's not a good sign that you don't know those symbols, is it?" he asked as we crossed the road.

"No, it really isn't," I admitted. "My mom made darn sure I learned as much as I could every day."

"An overachiever?" he asked.

"If the subject was the difference between life and death, yes." I stepped up on the curb. "It wasn't just her though, I wanted to learn."

He walked me to the driver's door.

I opened the door then look up at him. "I'll see you later."

"Drive safe," he said. He stayed on the sidewalk until I started the car and drove off.

Atticus slipped into my mind. Not this morning's Atticus, but the male that slept beside me last night. Did I ever cross his mind? He seemed to be warming up to me. But this wasn't dating, it was ... like an arranged marriage. And I wasn't exactly the best judge of character.

It had just been a few years since my last relationship. And that had been a huge mistake.

Atticus, he was my Match. If I ever wanted to have children, it'd be with him. Did he even want kids? There was still so much about him that I didn't know, that he didn't know about me. We needed to start talking to each other; we couldn't just keep having small moments together.

As I pulled into the parking garage, I decided I would try to ask Atticus out on a date. I locked the door and hurried over to the store. Maybe I'll ask him over for dinner? The idea knotted my stomach. Would we be able to talk like we did yesterday? We were still being careful of how we spoke to each other. Would we ever be able to just talk without worrying about insulting each other?

I walked into the store with the phone ringing. I didn't bother to turn on the lights, I hurried to the counter and answered. "De Haven Books, how can I help you?" I asked, my voice hurried.

"Evelyn, it's me." James Demer's voice filled my ear. My heart jumped into my throat.

"Hi James, what's the news?" I asked, anxiously. There were a couple heartbeats of silence.

"I can't buy your entire collection, Evie," he said, his voice troubled. "I can maybe buy the best four you still have." My heart dropped. Damn.

"I'll take it," I said, my voice thick. "I'll send them to you today."

"I'm sorry, Evie." He really did sound sorry.

"Thanks." I hung up the phone. The shop was quiet, waiting to open. I took several deep breaths. Okay. I was going to have to convince Gumner to let me do a payment plan. Then I could save my private collection. It's okay, it will work out. I'll convince him.

I put away my anxiety and turned everything on for the day. I called UPS for a large pick up. They'd be here this afternoon. I looked at the orders on the site, then printed them out and got to work. I can do this. I can do this.

～

Atticus

THE MALL WAS loud and full of humans. I couldn't believe I was doing this. We had other things to do, more important things.

"I'm going to kill you," I growled at Ranulf.

He chuckled. "It's Christmas and you have a Match," he reminded me. "You have to get her a present."

I grumbled wordlessly as the others joined us. "And why do they have to?" I asked.

The others laughed and shook their heads.

"Because we like Evie," Zahur explained. "She's been a friend to us and friends give presents on holidays."

I wanted to punch him. I fought back the urge as I looked around the busy mall. I spotted Astrid coming down the escalator. "Did someone call her?"

"I did," Ranulf admitted with a smirk. "She's Evie's best friend. Astrid is willing to help us find things she'd like."

Books, she'd like books, you moron. But since I doubted there was an antique dealer in the mall... "Fine."

Astrid strode up to us, smiling. Mostly at Ranulf. "So, gifts for Evie," she announced. "I'm going to walk you through some stores and I'll point out things she'll love. Sound good?"

"Sounds good, lead the way Gift Goddess," Ranulf announced.

"Gift Goddess? I like it," she decided as she turned and led us further into the mall.

She took us into a kitchen supply store. "There are several stores she loves, so I'd suggest you buy from one store each."

"We only have an hour, then we have to get back to work. Everyone understand?" I asked.

The others murmured agreements as Astrid led us into a store. She began to show us the things Evelyn loved but would never buy for herself.

My phone vibrated. I pulled it out. It was a notice from Evelyn's bookstore website. I'd been outbid on several books.

Holding back a grin, I put in a new bid on a couple books, a few thousand over the last bid.

"What are you doing?" Zahur asked from behind me. The sneaky bastard.

I sighed. "Evelyn's business is going under." I shrugged. "I'm making some bids on a few books."

He scowled at me. "When did this happen?" He pulled out his own phone and found the site for the bookstore. "Shit. Her books are selling, though."

"It's a long story," I admitted as I watched Falk head to the counter with something. We followed. I was halfway to the counter when my phone vibrated again. I checked it. Someone had outbid me by several thousand dollars. I went to the site. I recognized that email: Zahur. I outbid him, again by several thousand dollars.

I reached the counter as they finished paying.

"Would you like this gift wrapped?" the woman asked.

"No," Astrid said instantly. "Do you have gift bags instead?"

"Of course," the woman said as she pulled out a gift bag.

Astrid turned to the rest of us. "Never give her a gift in wrapping paper. Especially not gold," she informed us. I was about to ask why when my phone vibrated again. I turned to see Zahur's satisfied expression. This meant war.

The hour went on like that. Going from store to store, Zahur and I outbidding each other. At least until the others found out. Then the bookstore site became a war zone.

I eventually slipped away to find my own gift for Evelyn. I was standing in a jewelry store looking at several lockets when Astrid found me.

"Thinking of a locket?" Astrid asked.

I took a calming breath and let it out slowly. "Yes." There, I had kept the annoyance out of my voice.

"I wouldn't do that," she said. "She already has one. It's a family heirloom, she wears it all the time."

I had noticed that small locket whenever she played with it. "Then perhaps a bracelet."

She leaned against the display and raised her eyebrow. "Have you decided to stay with her?"

My back stiffened at the question. I shot her an irritated look before moving on to the bracelet section.

She followed. "Come on, Atticus. Tell me. I'll even keep my mouth shut." She stepped in front of me, stopping me. "Are you going to stay and be her Mate?"

My heart slammed in my chest as the question lingered in my ears. I had already made this decision when I hung up on Cyrus, I'd just never voiced it out loud. I met her gaze. "Yes."

She smiled. "Her ring size is five," she said before stepping out of my way and leaving the store.

A ring? Astrid was mentally unstable. We were still trying to figure out how to talk to each other. I kept looking for something she might like. I found a nice pair of drop diamond earrings that would look beautiful on her. I was at the counter paying when a ring caught my eye. It was lovely, Victorian, a small ruby center stone with gold metalwork that surrounded two small diamonds. It was something Evelyn would no doubt love. What was I thinking? This wasn't the right time. I turned back to the cashier and paid. As the day went on, that ring stayed in the back of my mind.

~

Evelyn

IT WAS the end of the day when my cell phone rang. I finished the address on the label before answering.

"Yes?"

"Little one." Helix's voice surprised me. He only called when something was found on a patrol.

"What did you find?" I asked.

"We don't really know, but it's something you should see," he explained. "Meet us on the roof of 32458 Johnston Street and my scout will fill you in." I hung up the phone and tucked it into my pocket.

"Rina, can you close for me?" I called.

"Yeah, no problem," Rina answered from the office. I hurried around the counter, grabbed my jacket and headed out the door, straight to my apartment. Surprisingly, it was empty.

I changed into my hunting gear, only this time no coat. I also left the short swords behind and slid daggers into sheaths at my hips. I pulled my hair into a tight braid and headed up to the roof.

Thankful it was dark, I took a deep breath and pulled my wings out. They burst from my back in a shower of blood and sinew. My wings slipped through the slots in the back of my tank and armor. My wings were beautiful, at least to me. Raven black feathers from crest to tip. I pumped a few times to get my blood flowing.

I smiled, then ran across the roof and jumped. My wings flapped once, twice, and I climbed higher. I flew through the sky, the wind howling at me as I stayed out of human sight.

It only took ten minutes before I found the building. It

was at the back side of a dead-end alley. I dropped to a crouch on the edge of the roof. Movement to the right had me pulling a blade. A Red Cap raised his arms. One of Helix's scouts. I put the blade away along with my wings.

The Red Cap came forward to crouch next to me. He was a small thing, almost human sized. Only with spider legs. Perfect for running along roofs and staying hidden. His green eyes turned to me.

"Report," I whispered.

"I've watched this alley over the last three months," he said. He pointed at the manhole cover in the middle of the dead end. "A human comes out with meat and throws it down the manhole."

My temper sparked. "Why am I only hearing of this now?"

"It was cattle meat. Always," he explained. "Until a few weeks ago."

I watched the alley and took a deep breath. There was copper on the air, and the taste of something wet and moldy. "And?"

"I didn't say anything because I thought I might be wrong, but the meat changed," he whispered. "I thought at first chicken, or goat. Then I was assigned to another area for a couple weeks." I turned to him. His yellow eyes were on the manhole cover. "Now, the human brings out body parts. Human body parts. Every three nights."

I met his eyes. "This needed to be reported to me sooner."

He bowed his head in apology. "I apologize, Warrior Evelyn."

"Follow your instincts. You're a Red Cap; you know meat," I reminded him. He nodded. I turned back to the alley. "Go, I'll handle this."

"He won't come out until past ten," he warned. The Red Cap didn't wait, he took off into the shadows.

I stayed and sat on the ledge, my feet dangling over the alley. I threw an illusion over me that made me invisible to human eyes. And I waited.

It was around 9:00 p.m. when my phone vibrated. I checked it.

Atty: Where are you?

Oh no. I forgot to leave a note.

Evelyn: Got a call from the Red Caps, checking it out.

I sent him the address and tucked my phone back into my pocket.

It wasn't long before Atticus dropped beside me. I looked up and had to stop myself from gaping. His wings were scaled and leathery. There were no feathers to speak of. They were amazing. He pulled his wings into his back, sliding through the slots on his white button down.

"I have an illusion up, so you might want to get down," I told him. He sat beside me, his posture rigid.

"What the hell are you doing here?" he whispered harshly. I didn't bother explaining. I reached over, touched his hand, then cracked my barriers. I touched his mind gently and filled him in within seconds. He took a deep breath and let it out in a huff. I pulled my mind back and closed my barriers again.

"I forgot to leave a message," I admitted. "Sorry."

He sighed. "I know you can take care of yourself, but... a simple text to let me know..."

"Alright." I didn't argue. I was in the wrong. I forgot to tell him, it was that simple. Atticus shifted to sit on the ledge beside me, his thigh touched mine.

A streak of light caught my eye. I looked up in time to see the last of a shooting star. "It's a nice night out at least."

He looked up at the star filled sky. "It's a nice spot, not a lot of light pollution here."

I snorted. "This is the closest we've come to a traditional date."

"I brought you lunch," he said quietly.

I kicked my heel off the building as I looked down at the alley. "Was that a date?"

"It's the closest we've managed," he muttered, his voice strained. "Do you... do you want to go have actual dates?" My heart jumped into my throat. We were actually talking about us and what we were. I started fidgeting with my locket.

"I guess. I-I don't know how this is supposed to go with gargoyles," I admitted.

"We're screwed," he said dryly. I chuckled quietly. He grinned.

"I know with humans there are stages, but I don't think that will help," I said.

"We could always ask Zahur," he pointed out.

"Oh God, no." I denied that immediately. He chuckled.

"I feel the same way," he admitted. "What are these human stages?"

"Well, there's meeting, just getting to know each other on dates, then it's established you're in a relationship. Then from what I've seen... someone asks the other to marry them. Someone says yes, they become engaged and then married." I resisted the urge to squirm. Why was this so awkward to talk about?

"Well, I don't think the dating phase is quite accurate to our situation," he said softly.

"Neither is being engaged, but at the same time it is. Because we are Matched." I sighed. Why was this so hard?

"So... I guess we're at the established relationship

phase?" he asked, awkwardly. It was clear he'd rather be talking about anything else. And frankly, so would I.

"That sounds about right," I agreed. I wanted to end this conversation as fast as possible. Where was this human?

As if in answer to my question, a door to the alley opened up slowly. I automatically moved to a crouch. So did Atticus. It was a human man, around his thirties. His clothes were meticulous as he made sure the alley was empty. He went back through the door then came out carrying a large, wrapped bundle. A human shaped bundle.

"Atticus...."

"I see it," he whispered back.

We watched as he carried the bundle to the manhole. He dropped it to the cement carelessly. A pale leg fell out from the sheet it was wrapped in. Even from the roof I could spot the cuts and bruises on the skin. The human opened the manhole, cursing as he did.

"Stupid whore. Worthless, uncooperative, not right. Next time I'll get it right..." he muttered to himself. He dropped the cover to the ground. He lifted the sheet covered body and held it over the hole. "Dinner time," he called before dropping the woman's body into the manhole. A cry rang out, and it wasn't human. Then crunching reached my ears. My stomach churned as the feeding noises continued until he closed the manhole cover.

We watched in silence as the human walked back inside.

Then my temper burned. "What is down there?"

"Stay here," Atticus ordered. He dropped to the alleyway, silent as a shadow. I followed and landed beside him. He shot me a look, I shot him one back.

He sighed then moved to the cover and started pulling it off without even needing a crowbar. The stench was horrendous, rotting and foul. Before I could climb down he stopped me. He shook his head then began going down first. If he thought I was going to stay up here he was nuts. There was a splash. I began to climb down after him. His hands at my thighs stopped me from climbing down further.

"Don't. It's flooded down here," he warned. "I'll check it out. You go back up."

I turned on the ladder and looked down. The water was at his waist, it would be almost to my chest. Pieces of flesh and bone floated on the surface. Yeah. I wasn't going to argue.

"I'll go up top," I told him as I started climbing. He chuckled quietly.

"So, it only took waist-deep disgusting water for you not to argue?" he asked. I looked down at him.

"Waist high on you, but almost chest high on me. And females have a stronger sense of smell," I countered before climbing up the ladder, his laughter following me. I climbed out and stood at the manhole, waiting. As time went on I started pacing, my fingers playing with my locket.

What was taking so long? I hadn't heard him shout or anything.

It seemed like forever before Atticus's white hair appeared at the bottom of the ladder. He climbed, cursing under his breath. When he climbed out the stench of the sewer came with him. I fought the urge to pinch my nose closed as I threw a scent containment shield around him. Now no one could smell him, not even himself.

"What is it?" I asked.

"It's a trapped Qalupalik," he announced. "I broke the chains holding it to this part of the sewer. It'll head out soon."

I was stunned, Qalupalik usually only ate fish and loved large bodies of water. They were once thought to take children that came too close to the shore, but it was a myth told by mothers to their children. This made no sense. "How'd it get in the sewer?"

Atticus was looking at the door the human came out of with his jaw clenched. "I'd say the human lured it in and trapped it." He turned back to me. "He's been using it to clean up the bodies of the women he's killed." Anger burned in my heart.

I looked at the door. "Well, let's go pay him a visit," I said.

"Agreed," he growled

I headed for the door. I waved my hand; it unlocked and opened. Atticus slipped in before me, I rolled my eyes as I followed. I muffled our steps as we walked into the dingy back hall of a house. There were screams, but the low sound and pitch told me they weren't real. A movie? Atticus stopped in a doorway on the left. When I reached him I saw why.

A metal medical table sat in the middle of the kitchen instead of an island. It was covered in blood that dripped onto the floor. I stepped inside to get a better look at what we were dealing with. That's when I noticed the photos.

Pictures covered the top cabinets. Each and every photo was of a woman being tortured. Skinned, cut, burned. It didn't matter to this guy. I walked around that kitchen and wanted to get my hands on this bastard. Atticus went to the filthy instruments on the counter.

Finally, I had enough. I turned and strode toward the sound of the TV. I stepped into a dark family room doorway where the TV was the only light. It was enough light, however, to show me the human masturbating. The screaming on the TV grew worse. I looked. It was a video of the human raping a woman as she screamed in pain. Bile rose in my throat, my stomach lurched. I covered my mouth and turned away from the room. Atticus was there in a heartbeat. His hands on my shoulders, his eyes searching my face. The woman on the TV gave a horrible scream. I shuddered. Atticus looked over my shoulder. His eyes glowed, his face changed. The Atticus I knew was gone. This Atticus was pure rage. He stepped around me. Glass shattered and the screaming stopped.

"Who are-" The human's voice was cut off. I braced myself and turned back around. Atticus had the human's throat in his hand as he pinned him to the wall. The human had managed to get his pants up before Atticus had reached him.

"You sick motherfucker," Atticus bit out, his hand squeezing. The human's eyes bulged. "How many women have you tortured? How many did you kill?" he snarled. Atticus dropped him, he fell to the floor gasping. "A quick death isn't good enough for you." Atticus grabbed the human by the back of the neck and began to drag him into the kitchen. Atticus pinned the human's face against the cabinets, next to the pictures. "That's what you think women deserve? Huh? You disgusting fuck!" He shook him hard. "I know what you deserve," he growled. "Let's give it to you." He jerked the human away from the cabinets and out into the back hall. I followed, my skin crawling just being in the house.

Atticus dragged the human to the manhole and shoved the human's face inside. "Hey, want to finish this fucker off before you go?" he shouted into the sewer. I stepped beside him, hugging myself. Trying to get that image out of my head.

"No, please! I didn't do anything!" the human begged.

"I doubt those women thought so. I'll see you in hell," Atticus snarled before throwing the human into the manhole. The human screamed as Atticus stepped back. There was a loud crunch followed by more screaming. I covered my ears so I didn't hear anymore. Atticus covered the manhole again, cutting off the sound of crunching.

He turned back to me as I dropped my hands from my ears. His eyes were still raging as he came to me and pulled me into his arms. I buried my face into his shoulder and took deep breaths.

"I'm sorry," he whispered, his hand was in my hair holding me to him. I took a shaking breath. "You should never have seen that." His arms all but crushed me to him and I didn't care.

"I feel so disgusting just being in that house," I told him. He kissed my hair and held me tighter.

"Let's go home," he said gently. "You can take a shower." I nodded before pulling away. I looked at the house over my shoulder.

"I want to burn it to the ground," I admitted in a whisper.

He took my hand, bringing my attention back to him. "I'll call in a tip. The human police might be able to find out who those women were. Give their families closure."

I nodded.

The flight home was blurry. All I really remember was landing on the roof and the burn of tucking my wings back into my skin.

Atticus led me downstairs and opened the door to my apartment. "Eve, are you going to be alright to take a shower?"

I nodded. "I just... need to get the feel of that house off me." His hand ran up and down my back.

"Then go take your shower. I'll be over after I've taken

mine," he said. I nodded and headed in. He closed the door behind me.

I went into my bedroom and grabbed my usual sleeping clothes before going into the bathroom.

I took a shower with the water as hot as I could stand. I scrubbed and scrubbed until I finally felt clean again. I wished he had let me burn the place to the ground. Maybe after the police were done...

When I was finally feeling better I got out, dried off, then pulled on my lavender hipster panties and a gray cami. I opened my bathroom door and froze.

Atticus was in my bedroom. In my bed to be precise. He had his pillows behind him and was sitting up against my headboard reading, an old, leather-bound book in his hands. That wasn't what stopped me. What stopped me was the fact he was in nothing but a pair of navy, designer pajama bottoms that were riding low on his hips, the blankets down to his knees. His chest was muscled, but not overly so. His six pack was defined, his Adonis belt ... oh my. His body was ... whew. But it was his tattoos that drew my eyes. Two full, Asian-style sleeves ran up his shoulders and across most of his chest. One side was dark, stormy, with very little color as it rose up his arm and across his pec. The other ... the other arm was bright, vibrant, as it moved along his shoulder to cover his other pec. My fingers itched to trace the lines.

"So, we're doing this now?" I asked dryly, not knowing what else to say.

He lifted his eyes from the book. That gaze ran over my body just as thoroughly as I had ogled his. "Why not?"

Why not? The truth was, tonight I didn't want to sleep alone. Not after that house. I shrugged casually as I moved to my side of the bed. "It's too cold to sleep alone anyway," I reasoned as I climbed in the side furthest from the door and started fixing my pillows.

He smirked as he read his book. "You can control your body temperature."

I sighed wearily. "Don't poke holes in my story."

He chuckled as I laid down under the blankets. He set his book down and shut off his lamp.

The bed shifted as he laid down and got comfortable.

I closed my eyes and the image in that house came back. I took a shaky breath.

"Eve... come here," he called softly. I didn't hesitate. I turned into him, my body pressed against his side, my knee moving over his leg. His arms closed around me as I laid my head on his chest. Peace filled me as he kissed my forehead and held me tight. I relaxed completely and fell into a deep, dreamless sleep surrounded by the smell of parchment.

15

DECEMBER 21

I woke up slowly, the sun streaming through the window. I stretched as I rolled onto my back to find I was alone. I rubbed my eyes and looked over at the other side of the bed. It was already perfectly made, again. A leather-bound book on the nightstand caught my eye. I smiled to myself. Atticus must plan on sleeping in here again tonight. I wasn't really against the idea.

Last night ran through my head. After my shower I thought I would have been fine. But Atticus had known better. I played with my locket as I watched the sunlight cross the ceiling. He had put himself out there last night. He was there for me when I didn't even know I needed someone. That was rather... amazing.

I mentally shook myself and got out of bed. Knowing I was meeting Mr. Gumner at some point today, I dressed for it. I pulled on my dark-gray pencil skirt, a white-silk button-up blouse and a blush colored cardigan. I left my hair down and slipped on my black ballet flats. If I looked professional maybe Gumner would give me a chance. Even if I did miss our last appointment.

When I stepped out of my bedroom I wasn't surprised to find everyone there. Atticus's head rose, his eyes finding me from where he leaned against the counter next to the coffee pot. He was perfect again in another suit, not a hair out of place. I sent him a smile before moving towards the kitchen.

Ranulf and Zahur were on the stools at the breakfast counter talking about other leads they might try. Falk was leaning against the end of the breakfast counter, eating cereal and listening.

I went straight to the stove to start the kettle. Only it was already starting to whistle. I shut off the burner and peeked at Atticus. He was listening intently to the conversation. I went to grab a mug only to find two already out on the counter. Atticus was talking about meeting with some of the other species. I smiled to myself, poured the water into the mugs and went about making tea.

When I was done I handed his to him, he took it with a grin. "Thank you."

"Thank you for putting on the kettle," I countered.

He grinned at me. "It's Ranulf's turn to cook, so everyone is eating cereal."

I looked at him puzzled. "I don't have cereal, I haven't gone to the store this week."

Atticus was suddenly focused on drinking his tea. Suspicious, I walked around him and opened the fridge. It was stocked. Not just stocked. Packed with food. Laughter erupted behind me. I turned around to find everyone watching me.

"You guys didn't need to-"

"With how much we eat here?" Ranulf said. "It's long overdue." I shook my head and pulled down a bowl, then tried to find where they put the cereal. After I closed the fourth cabinet, Atticus reached up and plucked a box from the top of the cabinets.

"Seriously? How was I supposed to find that?" I asked as I took the box from him.

He bit back a grin. "Look up?" The others snickered.

I shot him a playful glare then set about eating my breakfast.

I was almost done when Zahur got my attention. "Evie, we'd like to talk to some of the other species in the city. Find out if they've seen any more odd demon events."

I nodded. "I can make you a list of addresses and give them a call to meet you on neutral territory. It's the safest bet if you don't know their customs."

Ranulf raised an eyebrow. "Aren't you coming with us?"

"No," I said carefully. "I have an appointment today that I can't miss."

Atticus met my eyes. His filled with understanding. "Alright, can you also make us a list of what not to do?"

"Sure. Can someone grab a notebook from my desk?" I asked. When I looked down at my breakfast my appetite was gone. Today was the day.

Zahur came back with a pen and notebook. I set my bowl aside and began writing out directions. As I did I explained what not to do with each species and why. By the time I had to open the store I was confident there wouldn't be any issues today.

My mind on the store, I put my bowl in the sink and began pulling on my jacket.

"I'll be back in a minute," Atticus announced, jarring me out of my head. He opened the door for me.

I stepped into the hall, we started down the stairs. "I thought you were going with them?"

"I am, I'm just walking you to work first." He held open

the outside door for me. I tried to hide my smile as I passed him then headed to my storefront. I unlocked the metal gate and Atticus raised it.

"Thank you," I said as I started unlocking the door.

"You're welcome." He began turning on lights as I turned off the alarm. When I turned back he was watching me closely.

"What?" I asked awkwardly.

"The landlord is coming today?" he asked, his eyes darkening.

I sighed as I pulled off my jacket and headed for my office. "Unfortunately." I draped my jacket over my chair and turned on my computer.

"I'm going to have the team scattered today so no one will be here to help," he said as he stood in the doorway.

"Don't worry, I can call in Rina if I need to," I said as I moved back around the desk to head into the store, only to come up short when Atticus didn't move. My pulse picked up as I met his eyes. "Atticus, I need to get to work."

His cheeks tinged a light pink. "Right..." He scratched his eyebrow and stepped back. "Um, yeah, and I need to go babysit. I'll see you later," he said awkwardly. He didn't look at me as he turned and walked out of the store.

I leaned against the doorjamb and groaned. I really needed him to kiss me again. But not now. Now, I needed to get orders shipped. I put Atticus out of my mind and got to work.

It wasn't until dusk that Mr. Gumner walked into the store. Rina couldn't come because she was stuck studying for a test tomorrow, so I was by myself when he walked in. I was bringing down a stack of books when I spotted him at the counter. Mr. Gumner Jr. was an annoyingly snobby man who didn't look much like his father. In his forties, his triangular face and pointy chin screamed his mother. He walked in wearing a navy wool suit with lines that told me it was expensive, probably Italian, and an elegant, long, black wool coat. His blonde hair was turning white at his temples and the permanent frown lines didn't help his looks.

I smiled. "Mr. Gumner, it's good to see you." He turned and watched me walk around the counter and add the stack to the 'to go' pile. When I turned to him he was eyeing the empty shelves and the stacks of packages waiting to be shipped. "I'm sorry for missing our last appointment. A friend of mine was in a car accident."

"It looks like business is good," he observed.

"In the book world, just because you're selling doesn't mean you're selling well," I said, with a polite smile. "Which I wanted to discuss with you."

He turned back to me and his deep blue eyes sent chills down my spine. Seriously, this guy was one monocle away from being a Bond villain. "You are three months late on the rent, there's not much to discuss about that."

"I agree, I'm already working on clearing out the space by the end of the month," I admitted politely.

"Good, then I won't have to serve you with an eviction notice," he said in a bored voice.

"No, you won't. What I would like to discuss is the payment for the last three months," I began.

"Ms. De Haven, a lady does not shirk her debts," he chided. "You will pay every cent of the total owed."

I straightened my shoulders and raised my chin. "I have every intention of paying every cent I owe you, sir," I said, politely. Pulling on all my etiquette lessons from my mother,

I continued. "However, I was hoping we could arrange a payment plan."

He raised an eyebrow. "A payment plan?"

"Yes, sir." I explained, "The issue with rare books is that if you want to sell a rare book quickly, you will get at most a quarter, or if you're very lucky, half of what it's worth since most collectors also sell for a profit."

"And?" he asked.

"If we can work out a payment plan that will give me more time, then I can get better prices for these books." He watched me with curiosity. "The price difference is so great that it would make up for any late fees I have already incurred, plus interest."

He looked around the store quickly then met my eyes. "No," he stated.

My heart dropped.

"You will pay the total of one hundred eighty-six thousand, eight hundred and ninety-three dollars and thirty-seven cents by the end of the month or you will incur more late fees. Do you understand?" he asked bluntly.

"Mr. Gumner. I'm saying I'm already vacating the shop, so you'll be able to rent it out. That with a payment plan, you will make a profit. Not just what I owe you but interest," I said carefully again, my stomach in knots, my hands shaking. He had to understand. I couldn't lose my books. "Doing this would save my mother's private collection. It's all I have left of her." A total lie, but I loved my books and I was starting to have trouble breathing.

He smirked, and it wasn't a pleasant one. "I understand perfectly. Quite frankly, I don't like you. I didn't even like your mother; she was abrasive." I bit my tongue at that. Abrasive my foot! You grabbed my butt and I smacked you for it. Of course, it happened twenty years ago and he didn't know that was me, he thought it was my 'mother.' But he was still talking. "I might have been willing to negotiate had you not already stood me up the other day. Now, vacate the premises by the end of the month. And make one payment. Is that clear?"

"Yes, sir," I said, stunned.

He smiled, satisfied. "Then good day." He turned and left the shop.

Thick silence fell. The world became slow. I looked at the mostly empty shelves, the books still there. The stairs to the second level. I loved every inch of this place. He had barely listened. I looked up at the second level. I needed to clear those books. I focused on walking around the counter and picking up several empty boxes, then walking up the beautiful, worn, dark wood stairs.

At the top I went to the first case. One by one I started taking books off the shelf, the pressure in my chest increasing with every book I added to the box. When the box was full I set it down. Then picked up another.

I failed. I was going to lose my collection. I was going to have to sell to that snake Burgess.

He had tossed a card with an offer for my private collection through the mail slot. It was pathetically low.

I lost... I put down the full box and picked up an empty one. Chest aching, I put the books into the box, my heart breaking a little more every time, until it finally sunk in. The tears fell faster. I held a book on the shelf for—I don't know how long—as I cried. My body shook from it, but I didn't make a sound. If I started, I'm sure I never would have stopped. I rested my forehead against a shelf on the bookcase and sobbed. I cried until it was hard to breathe, then when I could, I started again. I didn't know how to stop. Everything I had worked for over the last two hundred years... gone. I didn't even notice the bell over the door ring.

"Evelyn?" Atticus's voice caught my attention, barely. I took deep breaths, trying to ease the knot in my throat. A tread sounded on the staircase. A hand on my arm turned me. Atticus's face came into focus. "What's wrong? Are you hurt?" he demanded. Tears still falling I shook my head.

"He didn't agree," I barely said. "I have to sell it all." My chest was an aching void, a hole burned right through me.

His hands moved, one cupped my face, the other brushed my hair back behind my ear. "It's alright, luv," he said gently, his accent slipping in. "We'll make it right." His golden eyes were full of promise. A promise of what, I didn't know. "Just stop crying, take deep breaths for me." I did as he asked, but the tears kept falling. His face was pained at the sight of them. "Eve, please, stop crying." He stepped closer, his hands on my shoulders, his body pressing me back between the bookcase and him. Warmth moved over my body. My breath caught in my chest at the desperate look in his eyes.

"How?" I asked, my voice cracking. He leaned down and brushed his lips against mine. My heart skipped, the world stopped. Everything I am was focused on those lips. He gently kissed me, coaxing me. His hands moving down my arms, spreading heat. That... that felt good. That felt very good, my lips moved against his, my hands sliding up to his shoulders. He kissed me more confidently, moving his mouth a little deeper. His tongue traced the seam of my lips, asking. I opened them. He slipped in and took every thought away. My body burned as the kiss changed. My breasts grew heavy and aching. Hunger slipped in, need. I don't know if it was mine or his, but it took over and I was lost. His hands moved over me, my waist, my hips, my ribs.

One of those scorching hands finally cupped my breast over my blouse, his thumb stroking my nipple through my clothes. My pulse pounded in my ears as I gasped, as my body throbbed. His mouth moved down my neck making me cling to him. He groaned against my skin, sending hot shivers over my body. My heart raced as he kissed down my chest, his fingers unbuttoning my blouse until he could shove my bra out of the way. He left hot kisses that had me moving against him. His hot mouth took my breast, I cried out as flames licked my skin. I arched into him as my hands buried in his hair. My core throbbed with every heartbeat. Gasping, I tilted my head back. I wanted this... needed it. Please... His hand moved down the outside of my thigh, then under my skirt and up my inner thigh. I whimpered as he touched my soaked lace panties. His mouth came down on mine again, demanding everything. My toes curled.

His fingers slipped into my panties and stroked me. I whimpered against his mouth. Oh God! Lightning shot from between my legs to my breasts and over my skin. His other hand caressed my breast, his fingers massaging. His thumb found my clit and moved. I clung to his shoulders as my whole body shook. He slid a finger inside me, my body clenching around him. It had been so long... that one finger seemed enormous. My hips moved against his hand as I reached up and sank my fingers in his hair. He kissed me deeply, hungrily, as his hands made me burn. He added a second finger, and I had to cling to the bookcase so I wouldn't fall. His mouth moved to my earlobe.

"You're so beautiful, luv," he whispered, his accent thick. A wave of scorching heat rolled over me. I gasped, I was close. His fingers picked up the pace, finding every sensitive nerve I had and stroking it.

"Atty..." I cried out, my fingers clinging to the wood of

the shelf. "I'm... don't stop..." His mouth moved back to mine as his hand hit a new rhythm. Holy crap! I kept moving against him. The scent of parchment, his touch, his kiss, his body pressing me into the bookcase. It was all too much. Wave after wave of pleasure crashed over me. I cried out, my fingers digging into his shoulders as his mouth took every noise I made as I came so hard lights danced across my vision.

When it was over I was limp, Atticus and the bookcase the only reason I was still standing. He kissed me sweetly as he gently slid his fingers from me. I shuddered at the feeling. He set my skirt right then wrapped his arms around me and held me to him. I looked up into his eyes and found molten pools of gold. His hard body pressed against my stomach. Desire filled me. I didn't want to stop. I trailed my fingers down his chest. His breathing hitched as I reached his belt. He lowered his head and kissed me gently as I undid his belt. I leaned into him, my fingertips moving lower.

A bell rang. The world slammed back in sharp color. Oh my God. We're in the store. And we... Atticus... Oh dear. And he was going to leave. My heart ached.

"Hello! UPS!" someone shouted. I pulled away. Stunned at myself, I fixed my clothes, my face burning. I didn't look at Atticus as I stepped around him and headed downstairs to give instructions. What was I going to say to him?

Atticus

I WATCHED from the balcony as she moved around the store giving instructions. My cock finally stopped aching as time went on, though I still couldn't take my eyes off her. Her lips were slightly swollen, there was a pink tint to her cheeks as she signed paperwork.

I had come in determined to sit her down and tell her about Cyrus, but now... Finding her crying changed everything. I couldn't take that beautiful, tear-streaked face. It put my heart in a vise and squeezed hard. And now all I could think about was touching her again.

My cock grew hard, agreeing with the thought. I took deep breaths and tried to cool my blood down. Okay. Think about something else.

Cyrus. Cyrus had called almost every three hours since I hung up on him. He was starting to get suspicious. I had realized this morning that I needed to get off the grid before he figured out I wasn't coming back. I had already started using my personal accounts that he had no knowledge of. Everyone had turned off the GPS on their phones this morning, though they had wanted to know why. Luckily, Zahur made up a cover story. Ranulf was picking me up a pre-paid cell phone and as soon as that was in my hands I was going to pop the battery out of my old one. He was also picking me up a new laptop. I planned on creating several proxy servers tonight. I'd have to hook her computer up when she was asleep. I was almost off grid, at least in regards to Cyrus and his reach. And that was all I cared about.

The delivery men were almost done. I sighed and looked around the second floor. I picked up a half empty box and continued emptying the shelf Evelyn was working on when we... I quickly focused on loading the box with books.

When it was full I went back to the railing. The packages and delivery crew were gone. Evelyn was behind the counter packing more books into their boxes. I headed downstairs.

I set the box on the end of the counter and moved to stand across from her. She kept working. Dread filled me. Did... did I push her too far? Did she not want to...? I didn't know her history, I didn't know if she was a virgin or not. And I didn't care. I just didn't want to hurt her.

"Evelyn," I said quietly. I hated asking, but I needed to know. "Did I... did I go too far?"

Her head snapped up. "No," she said instantly. "It's just..." She looked around the store before meeting my eyes. "I'm at work and I'm a...." Her face turned scarlet, her voice strained. "I'm a keep-it-in-the-bedroom kind of woman."

I let out the breath I'd been holding. She wasn't mad or upset, she just liked privacy.

Before I could say anything, the door slammed open. Zahur strode in, cursing in Ancient Egyptian.

"What's happened?" I demanded.

Zahur came to the counter. "Any alcohol in here?"

Evelyn walked to her office and returned with a bottle of vodka and a tumbler. I raised an eyebrow at her.

"Hey, a girl could have bad days at work." She shot me a playful look. I bit back a smile as Zahur took them.

"We've got a big fucking problem," Zahur announced as he poured himself a drink. He quickly drank it down before turning to me. "I found where they are getting through, and it wasn't just a crack. There was a hole." I grew still, my shoulders tight. That's unprecedented. Cracks in the barriers we expected, but a hole? Zahur poured another drink.

"Were you able to shut it?" she asked as we watched him pound down another.

"Yeah, it's shut. A patch job, but it'll get stronger *if* we can keep them from coming through." Zahur ran his hand down his face. Evelyn started playing with her locket.

"The big question is, what came through?" I thought out loud. As if in answer, Evelyn's phone rang. She pulled it out and grumbled before answering.

"What's up, Brian?" she asked instantly. Her face grew pale.

"On my way." She hung up the phone and took a deep breath before looking at us. "Brian just came on shift, he's found something big. I need to get down there."

"Did you find those symbols?" I asked.

She shook her head. "I... didn't even get a chance to start."

Her eyes met mine. Should I go with her? I was about to when my phone rang. I pulled it out. It was Cyrus. It was time to handle this shit now.

"Zahur, stay with her," I ordered, my voice cold. I met his eyes. "I have some Council business that can't wait." Zahur nodded. He understood exactly what I was doing.

I turned back to her. Her eyes were shadowed as she eyed me. What? Where did those shadows come from?

"Let's get going, Evie." Zahur caught her attention.

"Thank you." She hurried out from behind the counter and out the door.

I answered the phone. "Cyrus."

"Where the hell have you been?" Cyrus snarled in my ear. "Report!"

My body shook with the rage burning in my gut. "Tatiana Suvu" Silence filled the line. "She was your Match, she refused you."

"You don't know what you're talking about." His voice grew deadly. "Whatever you think you've heard is hardly the truth."

"You sent me to bring back her daughter," I said, my own voice deepening. "You thought she'd be a Match for you."

"You've lost your mind," he countered. "I was simply worried about her daughter."

"Then why tell me to stay away from her?" I snapped. "Why did you tell me to keep her at a distance?"

"Because you, quite frankly, are dangerous and are going to kill everyone around you one day," he said, his voice matter of fact. "You are not fit to be her Mate."

I grunted. He was right about that. "No, I'm not. But for her, I'll try."

"That's not how it works!" he raged in my ear. "Bring her back now! That's an order."

I smiled. "Fuck you," I growled. "I'm going to spend the rest of my life keeping her out of your hands."

"Listen, you little prick-" I hung up on him. I didn't have a choice, I pulled the battery from my phone immediately. I stood in the silent store for several minutes breathing slowly, calming down. It was done. I was hers, if she'd have me.

I started shutting off lights and closing the store. Thankfully, she had told me where her extra key was hidden. I locked the door then pulled down the grate and locked that too. Oddly, I felt lighter than I had in years. It felt good.

Evelyn

WE WERE RUNNING through the hospital towards the morgue. Brian had sounded shaken on the phone. I'd never heard him shaken before.

By the time we reached the morgue doors my heart was pounding. I was pulled up short by the scene waiting for us. Every table had a black body bag. Every one. Shocked, I counted. Eight. Eight dead bodies since last night.

I finally noticed Brian at the farthest table. And he wasn't alone. Detective Matthew Green was with him. The human with a badge wasn't a stranger. I had known the tall, hot mess of a man for several years now. Even dated him for a few months. Matthew's black short hair was messy, his chiseled face was, as always, striking. When his brown eyes spotted me, he sighed heavily.

"Not another one of yours?" Matthew snapped. Zahur moved to stand slightly in front of me, as if to protect me from the detective. I rolled my eyes and stepped around him to stride down the room to Brian's side. Zahur stayed in step with me the whole way.

"Unfortunately, yes," I admitted. Matthew's suit was rumpled, there was even a mustard stain on his tie. The detective's eyes moved to Zahur, my large quiet shadow.

"Who's this?" Matthew asked, his eyes inspecting Zahur.

Before I could answer Zahur did for me. "Zahur, her fiancé's brother." I kept my surprise off my face as Matthew frowned at Zahur.

"Since when do you have a fiancé?" Matthew's eyes moved to me. I shrugged.

"You know me, I'm such a player that I could have several," I offered lightly. Both Brian and Matthew scoffed. I looked at the body bags. "What happened?"

"They were all found around three this morning. All within an eight-block radius," Matthew began. "It seems completely random at this point."

"All of them have different injuries, no murder was the same," Brian offered. I looked over the bags and sighed. This wasn't going to be fun.

"Have they been through forensics?" I asked, going to the wall and grabbing a pair of latex gloves.

"Yes," Matthew answered. "What are you doing?"

I pulled my hair up into a bun and pulled on the gloves. "I'm taking a look."

"Evie," Matthew warned. My eyes moved to his.

"You know this is one of my weird ones," I said calmly. "Take a walk, Green," Matthew strode towards me. Zahur moved faster than I could follow. He was suddenly between me and the detective. Matthew eyed Zahur. Zahur eyed him right back. "Hey!" I snapped, getting both of their attention. "Knock it off with the testosterone poisoning and play nice." Matthew backed up a few steps and Zahur relaxed as the distance between me and the human grew.

"You can't examine the bodies, Evie. We're not dating anymore, I'm not risking my ass for you," Matthew warned. I met his eyes.

"Do you want the killings to stop?" I asked pointedly. He frowned at me as he nodded. "Then let me work. Thirty minutes."

"Thirty minutes, and I want answers this time," Matthew growled before turning and walking out of the morgue. I turned to the body bag in front of me and started to open it.

"You dated that prick?" Zahur asked.

I sighed. "Unfortunately, yes. He's the reason I swore off humans. Now, let's get to work."

THE WORLD WAS TOO bright as I pulled out of the last victim's memory. Strong arms caught me, then lifted me off my feet. I was limp as Zahur moved with me in his arms, muttering in that ancient language. I needed to find out what it was. He set me down on a desk which forced me to open my eyes.

"Brian? Can you bring her some juice?" Zahur asked, without taking his eyes off me.

"Yeah, I'll be right back." Brian's voice came from somewhere behind Zahur. I blinked hard, trying to clear my vision before I looked around. We were in a dark office, the only light coming through the door behind Zahur. The victims' death memories ran through my head like a movie of agony. My chest ached, my throat felt like it had been torn out, not to mention all the other damage the bodies suffered. I felt like I was going to be sick.

"Talk to me, Evie," Zahur said, his voice gentle with concern.

"I think I need a drink," I admitted. "'Cause, damn." I closed my eyes again as images surged through my head. He backed up a step

"I wish you wouldn't do this," he said. "And I know Atticus is going to hate it."

"It's information we need," I reminded him as I sat up straight. I met his shadow filled eyes. "There are eight," I announced. "Eight fully formed demons that came through last night."

He cursed. "That explains the hole I found in the Ether," he bit out. I nodded.

"Someone is definitely pulling them through," I told him. "We have to find them."

"We will, but we need to talk to Atticus first," he assured me. I nodded. It wasn't long before Brian came in with a small bottle of orange juice. Zahur took it, opened it, then handed it to me with an order to drink. I didn't argue, I needed the sugar. I gulped down the juice as fast as I could. When I was done I felt better. I met his gaze.

"Eight, Zahur," I told him as I got off the desk and to my feet.

"I know," he assured me. "And we only have forty-two minutes till sunset." We started moving towards the morgue doors. There wasn't enough time...

. . .

EVERYONE WAS in my apartment and they were discussing our next move. With the warlocks dead, we had no leads about who had brought the eight demons through.

I was sitting in the corner of the sofa with my knees curled under me. Atticus had insisted on tucking one of the blankets from my linen closet around me. Ranulf had brought me a tumbler of scotch. Atticus constantly checked on me with his jaw clenched. Zahur had been right. He hadn't liked that I read that many memories in a row. Oops.

I was zoning in and out, and hurting when Atticus brought me a cup of tea. I set down the still full tumbler and took it gratefully as he went back to the conversation.

"You're saying that we shouldn't patrol?" Ranulf asked.

"That's right," Atticus said. Ranulf shook his head, growing agitated.

"That means more bodies in the morning," Zahur pointed out.

"There are eight fully formed demons out there. There are five of us," Atticus explained. He glanced at me then turned back to the others. "I don't like those odds if Evelyn is with us."

"And you know I'd go," I added before taking a sip of tea. They all turned to me with varying grins.

"I know," Atticus grumbled. "Which is why I'm suggesting no patrol for tonight."

Ranulf growled before walking into the living room area and sitting across from me on the coffee table which creaked under his weight. "Lass, I hate asking," he said, "but what kind of demons are we dealing with?"

I took another drink before answering. "A Fury, a Wrath demon, a Preta, a Wish demon, a Pride demon, a Succubus,

even a freaking Rakasha." I shook my head, stunned.
"They're all out there, right now."

"That was only seven," Atticus pointed out.

"The eighth," I took another sip. "That one, I didn't see him. But he told the victim its name." I looked at them. "Abaddon."

"Shit," Zahur said.

"Fuck me," Ranulf breathed. Falk was silent.

"The high-level demon of destruction?" Atticus asked carefully. No one had managed to kill a higher-level demon in all of history. The only way to deal with them was to send them back. And since they couldn't cross the boundary fully, they possessed a human.

I nodded. "That one... left a message," I said quietly. The tension in the room ramped up. Everyone walked into the living room.

"What was it?" Zahur asked.

"Come out, come out, wherever you are," I said, repeating the last thing the demon had said to the victim before punching through his chest.

"What is powerful enough to bring that many demons through the barrier at once?" Atticus asked absently, as if he was talking to himself.

"I could," I admitted, looking up at them.

"I think we can rule you out, lass," Ranulf said with a smirk. I gave him a grin back.

"What else do you think could do this?" Falk asked, his voice raspy. I sighed and thought about it.

"A very high-level demon," I offered, running through my memory. "Someone who doesn't need spells or too long to recharge. So, no humans."

"But this did start with a human summoning," Atticus pointed out. "So, let's figure out what they summoned."

"We need to figure out those symbols," I stated. "The protection circle failed, but that could have been because they summoned the wrong thing, or they just didn't have enough power to do the summoning and power the circle."

"Or they had the wrong symbols," Zahur offered. I nodded, looking down into my tea.

"The symbols will still get us into the ballpark of what came through, even if they were wrong," I explained, my voice tired. "I'll need my journals."

THREE HOURS later

I WAS STILL in my spot on the sofa. Everyone was spread around the living room with one of my journals. Ranulf had one of the armchairs, Zahur had the desk, while Atticus was on the other end of the sofa. Falk, the wonderful male that he was, was in the kitchen cooking dinner for everyone.

When I was young, my mother made a point to have me write every lesson down. Unfortunately, that meant lots of journals.

"Your mom took your education seriously," Ranulf announced. The others nodded.

I looked around the room. It was strange. I had gone from being alone most of the time to being surrounded by gargoyles who cared about me. I smiled to myself. I liked it. I liked having Atticus around like this, I even liked the others being around all the time.

I was still smiling when someone pounded on the door. Did Astrid lose her key again?

I got off the couch and went to answer. Matthew was

standing there in the same suit as earlier, only now he looked furious.

"What the hell, Evie?" he shouted. "I told you I needed answers and you just bailed!"

"You don't like the answers you get," I reminded him as I stood in the doorway.

"Are you going to let me in?" he snapped.

"No," I said as I stepped out into the hall and mostly closed the door for at least the illusion of privacy. They would be able to hear even if the door was closed.

"I need real answers, not some bullshit," he yelled.

"Stop yelling, Matt," I warned. If he went on much longer Atticus might decide to do something about it. Or one of the others.

"I'm gonna yell, Evie, because you need to talk to me," he snapped.

"I'll talk to you when you stop yelling," I countered calmly.

He took a deep breath and let it out slowly. "I need to know what you know about these deaths," he said calmly.

"I told you the truth once and you didn't like it. You said I was crazy, if I remember correctly," I reminded him.

"I want the killer, Evie," he repeated, stepping closer until I had to look up at him. He was frowning, his brow furrowed. He wasn't going to go away without something. I sighed.

"There are eight," I said. "Each victim was from a different killer."

He crossed his arms over his chest. "And how did you figure that out?"

"Different wounds, different cause of death and if you looked at the files, you'd know it's estimated that they all died within the same hour. The timing alone says multiple killers," I pointed out.

"Yeah, I saw all that," he said. "What did you see that I didn't?"

I met his eyes. "Absolutely nothing."

He cursed. "I knew you wouldn't tell me."

"Then what are you doing here? You already know you have eight killers, so go. Find them," I suggested dryly.

He didn't move. I waited as his eyes grew warm and curious.

"When did you get engaged?" He asked.

Oh, for crying out loud.

"How is that any of your business?" I asked, my voice tired. He reached out and grabbed my left hand. I could have dodged him, but I had always played the human with him.

"Let go," I demanded quietly.

He held up my hand. "No ring." He let me go. I clenched my jaw as he continued. "You're not the kind of woman who gets engaged without a ring."

I straightened my shoulders and lifted my chin. "You really don't know what kind of woman I am."

His eyes ran over my face. "I know you miss me," he said softly.

Oh, God.

"No, Matt. I really don't," I assured him. "I answered your questions-"

The door behind me opened. I looked over my shoulder to find Atticus stepping out of the doorway to stand close behind me. He didn't even spare Matthew a glance as he wrapped one arm around my waist, his hand resting on my hip. Then the other hand brought something around for me to see.

"Stop leaving this on the window sill over the sink or it's going to end up down the drain." His voice was warm as he lectured me. My heart stopped.

In his hand was a stunning ring. It was Victorian, the open gold filigree was delicately woven around the ruby and two small diamonds. "She's always taking it off when she washes her hands." Atticus's voice stopped me from going into shock. I held out my hand and he slipped the ring on my finger. It fit perfectly. How did he...? Not now. I can panic later.

"Sorry, I forgot," I muttered.

He kissed my hair. "It's alright, I'll just keep reminding you." He straightened to his full height. "And you are?"

Matt eyed him. "Detective Green. We were just discussing a case-"

"And she's told you everything she knows, correct?" he countered, his voice hard.

Matt straightened to his full height. "No, she hasn't."

Seeing my chance, I took it. "Actually, I have." I looked up at Matt. "So please leave."

"Evie-"

"My fiancée just asked you to leave." Atticus stepped around me to stand in front of me, and for once I was grateful. I didn't want to deal with Matt's ego today.

"Don't interfere in a police investigation." Matt's voice was furious.

"Investigation my ass," Atticus growled. I rested my hand on the middle of his back to calm him down. "She's answered your questions and now you're just harassing her. Get out of here before you leave the building bleeding."

Matt's eyes ran over both of us, accessing the situation as if he was at a crime scene. After several long heartbeats of silence, he turned then walked down the steps and out the door on the first floor.

Atticus's shoulders tensed as he turned around to face me. I gaped at him. He scratched his left eyebrow. "I know you probably wanted to handle him yourself-"

"I don't care about that," I told him, slightly in shock. I held my left hand up. "What is this?"

He looked away from me, his gaze darting around the hallway, clearly uncomfortable. "It's a ring."

"I-I-I grasped that," I assured him, still in a daze. "Wh-why do you have it?" He looked anywhere but at me, his cheeks pink. Was he going to propose? Was this....? My brain felt like it was going to explode. I... I couldn't even try to understand this right now. "You know what, don't answer that." His eyes shot to mine. "I... I can't even process this right now." I went to pull off the ring. His hand stopped me. I met his eyes.

"Keep it," he said, his voice had an edge I'd never heard before. I left the ring on as I looked up at him, confused.

"Let's... let's go back to work." I turned and walked back into the apartment, acutely aware of the ring on my hand.

I ROLLED over in bed again. I was exhausted but I still couldn't fall asleep. The demons worried me. How many more bodies would there be in the morning? The store weighed heavily on my mind. I didn't have long to get everything sold and out of the building. Then there was the new Treaty to make as soon as Rowena died. The witch probably couldn't hold out much longer. And then there was Atticus. I held up my hand and looked at the ring.

It was gorgeous. And perfect. I dropped my hand to my chest. But what did he mean by it?

By the time we had finished going through the journals everyone was exhausted. When I came to bed he was already asleep. I didn't mind, I didn't know what to say to him.

His deep, even breathing told me he was sleeping heavily. And I couldn't.

Giving up, I got up carefully. I didn't bother with slippers or a robe as I went into the living room. I went to my storage closet and pulled out a couple of boxes then walked to the bookcase. I sighed. It wasn't going to get any easier later.

I started putting the books into the box. The faster I went, the less time I had to think about it.

I was on my secondbox when the bedroom door opened. Atticus came into the living room in his navy pajama bottoms and nothing else. His eyes were confused as they swept over the boxes and books.

"What are you doing, Eve?" he asked.

"Um... I... I couldn't sleep," I muttered as I turned away, more for my own sanity than to stack books. "I figured I'd get started on taking the books down to the store."

He moved to stand in front of me. "Luv, when was the last time you checked your auctions?" His gentle voice had me looking up to meet warm eyes.

"I haven't really been looking, just printing out the orders," I admitted. I didn't want to know how little the books were going for. It was hard enough.

He picked my phone up off the coffee table and handed it to me. "Check."

Not understanding, I went to my website and logged in to check the sales sheet. I almost dropped my phone. "What...?" I ran through the lists of books that went out yesterday, and how much they went for. Tens of thousands over what they were worth. Every book on the site was sold, and the total was way over what I needed. "Who...?" I looked up and met his eyes. "You did this?"

He looked down at my phone. "It wasn't just me. The guys got in on it and it might have become a game."

I looked up at him, shocked. "I told you I didn't want your money."

His eyes flashed as they met mine. "You didn't want me to give you money. Those books are mine. They are going straight to my own collection."

I gaped up at him. "I... I don't understand you sometimes," I admitted. "The books... the ring..." I swallowed hard as he looked away at the word ring. "I don't know how to talk to you. Especially about us." My eyes burned.

He was looking over my shoulder at the bookcase as he answered. "You're not alone on that one." He let out a breath and met my gaze. "Right now, your private collection is safe. You can pay the landlord and not go out of business. He took my arm and brought me back to the bedroom. "That's enough for now, you need to get some sleep." He closed the door behind him.

I stepped further into my bedroom then turned around. "The ring." His shoulders grew rigid as he looked at it on my hand. My voice was quiet. "I need to know what it means."

He took a deep breath then met my eyes. "It means I'm staying." My heart pounded, the world faded as he continued. "I wasn't even going to give it to you until we figured this out. But what that dick said... I couldn't stop myself."

"What do you mean, you're staying?" I asked, telling myself not to hope. "Your whole life is back there."

He moved closer until I could feel the heat coming off his body, my senses full of parchment. His eyes stayed on mine. "My life is here," he whispered softly. His fingers held my chin, his thumb ran over my bottom lip. "I know I have more to learn about you, about how a relationship even works. And we have time to decide if we want to be Mated. But I want to find out." He swallowed hard as his eyes grew shadowed. "If you want me, that is."

My eyes burned as warmth poured through me. He was staying. That part of me that had been holding out broke right there. I went to my toes and kissed him deeply. His arms held me tightly against him as his mouth moved hungrily with mine. My body instantly caught fire, my core throbbing. Before I knew it, my arms were around his neck, my body melting against his. His tongue caressed my lower lip. I opened my lips and lost the ability to think. His hands moved down my hips to my legs. He lifted me and I wrapped my legs around his waist as his mouth drove me out of my mind. He lowered me to the bed beneath him, his weight going to his elbows, his hips forcing my thighs wider. His hard cock rubbed against me through our clothes. I gasped as my body clenched. His hot mouth trailed down my neck to my breast bone as I ran my hands over his back, needing to feel him. My skin was too tight, too sensitive. I needed him. He shifted his hands to my cami, pushing it up and pulling it off me. Cold air brushed over my breasts making my nipples ache, then his hard chest was against me, stoking the flames higher. His hands ran over me, his mouth taking my nipple, his tongue dancing along my skin. Lightning streaked from my breast to my core, I whimpered as the fire between my legs grew. I moved my hips against him and he groaned against my skin, making me shiver. He moved further down my body, his mouth and hands leaving fire in his wake. My body throbbed as he kissed low on my belly. His hands pulled my panties down my legs. He moved back, his hands running up my thighs. Unable to catch my breath, I looked down the line of my body. My fingers moved into his hair as he met my eyes a second before his mouth buried between my legs. I cried out and threw my head back as every nerve I had came alive. His tongue teased my clit, his lips taking it. His fingers found my core as he groaned against me, sending a bone deep shudder through me. He slipped a finger inside. Gasping, I started to tremble as my body coiled tighter. I cried out as he added another. So. Freaking. Good! It had been too damn long. His mouth worked as he stroked me, forcing me higher and higher. He shifted, then moved my knees to hang over his shoulders. His fingers thrust deeper.

"Atty...," I moaned as my hips moved against him. His tongue worked faster, with harder strokes that left me blind. He slid another finger inside me, stretching me. Flames streaked through my body, over my breasts and through my legs. "Oh, God... I'm...," I whimpered. It was too much but at the same time exactly what I craved. He picked up the pace, not letting me catch my breath. Wave after wave of pleasure poured over me. I cried out, my hands in his hair, holding his mouth to me as I came.

When it was over he kissed his way up my body. I convulsed as sparks shot through me with every touch.

He leaned back on his knees, his hands going to the strings on his bottoms. My body throbbed hard.

I sat up to help him undo the drawstring and shoved his pants down his hips. He was bare to me, his large dick was heavy with a pearl of liquid already on his tip. I reached out and stroked him. He growled and pulled my hand away. "If you keep doing that, we'll both be disappointed," he warned through heavy breathing. Oh, yes. Yes please.

His lips crushed mine. Hunger took over. I pulled him over me, his arms wrapped around me as his mouth devoured mine. His weight settled over me. His hand brushed my sweaty hair back from my face. He kissed me deeply as his hands moved over my body; my breast, hip, thigh, it didn't matter. As long as he kept touching me I burned.

He pressed himself against me, the heavy weight of his dick moving through my folds and over my clit making me whimper. I wrapped my legs around his waist, pressing harder against him. His hands slid up my arms to hold my hands above my head. His fingers tangled with mine. He pulled back to look in my eyes, his eyes asking.

"Yes," I breathed. His mouth took mine again as he shifted his hips then slid inside in one long stroke. Lightning streaked through every nerve I had. I cried out as he filled me, my body clamping down around him, my nails biting into his hands. He went still, lifted his head, his eyes stunned.

"Eve? Are you-"

"Not my first time," I gasped. His eyes closed as his forehead touched mine.

"Fuck, you're tight," he growled. I moaned as he settled his weight against me, pressing me into the bed. He took me at my word and moved. Flames licked my skin as he pulled almost all the way out of me. I cried out as he slid back inside, filling me slowly, driving me crazy. His mouth found mine again and he kissed me hard. He started making long, deep thrusts that had him stroking every already sensitive spot I possessed. My hips moved with his, my body tightening around him even more as he drove me higher.

He kissed me hard, hungrily. Wanting to touch him, I tugged my hands free as he shifted me a little. I wrapped my arms around him as he almost pulled out then thrust deeply again.

I cried out as he buried himself as deep inside me as he

could. He growled against my mouth before he lifted his head and met my eyes, then he pumped into me, harder, faster. The new angle helping me take all of him. Everything I was trembled as he pounded me into the bed. "Don't stop..." The noises I was making in the back of my throat were getting louder, I knew, but I didn't care. It didn't matter. All that mattered was his body in mine, his skin touching mine, his breath against my neck.

As long as he kept touching me, we were all that mattered. My body coiled tighter and tighter. Oh God... Flames burned every part of me. My body moved with his. He growled. I shattered into a million pieces. Ecstasy ripped through me, his body still moving. I cried out as I was torn apart by the waves of pleasure tearing through me.

His breathing turned ragged, desperate as he joined me. "Eve..." He gave a guttural groan, my name on his lips as his body became rigid against me. It was perfect.

We both laid there, trying to catch our breath. He stayed still inside me as aftershocks kept hitting me, making me shiver and shake. His forehead rested on mine as we tried to catch our breath. My legs dropped to the bed, my knees still bent and resting against his hips.

"Did I hurt you?" he asked, his accent thick as he lifted himself off me a little so he could meet my eyes. His shifting sent shivers through me.

Still flying and limp, I shook my head.

His hand cupped my face gently. "Answer me, luv."

I opened my eyes and looked up at him. His face was worried.

"I'm more than alright," I mumbled as I tried to get my mind working.

His thumb ran over my bottom lip, grabbing my attention. I kissed it, then opened my eyes to meet his. Keeping skin contact with me, he shifted, gently pulling himself from me. I caught my breath and shivered. Oh, God... even that was toe curling.

He hesitated to lay on me again. "Am I too heavy?"

I shook my head and ran my fingers over his face. "No, you're perfect."

He smiled down at me before kissing me softly. "You're lying."

I chuckled as he moved beside me, then off the bed to pull the blankets down and out from underneath me.

"You know, you're seriously killing my post orgasmic bliss here," I grumbled as he had me move up the bed.

"I'm just taking care of you," he said quietly.

He pulled the blankets over me, then disappeared into the bathroom. I took stock of how I felt. My body was sore; it had been a few years after all. So many muscles not used... My groin was a little sore from how rough we were, but I didn't mind. All in all, I was extremely good.

Atticus came back to my side of the bed with a warm wash cloth. He knelt down beside me, his hand moving under the blankets. I gasped as the wash cloth touched my still sensitive body, he leaned down and kissed me gently before cleaning the inside of my thighs. My face was burning when he pulled away, got to his feet then dropped the cloth in the hamper.

Atticus slid into bed, rolled on his side and pulled me into his arms. I happily shifted over to press myself against him, my head resting on his arm.

"Are you sure you're alright? I wasn't exactly gentle." He asked in a whisper.

"If it hurt, I would have said something," I told him.

His fingers ran up and down my spine as if he couldn't

stop touching me. His lips rested against my forehead. "Will you always tell me if I hurt you?" he whispered softly.

"Yes." I looked up at him. "Will you always listen?"

His eyes narrowed at me, his face changing. "Of course." His eyes ran over my face, his body tensing. "Did that prick not listen?"

I reached up and touched his lips. Most of the tension melted out of him. "He couldn't hurt me if he tried," I reminded him gently. The anger melted away. I had one question that I still needed answered.

"The ring?" I said softly. "It's not an engagement ring, right?"

He sighed deeply before meeting my eyes. "It is." My heart jumped into my throat. "But I hadn't planned on giving it to you so soon." I lifted my hand from his chest and began to take it off to give it back. "What are you doing?" His hand stopped me from taking off the ring.

I met his eyes again. "You weren't planning to ask. You should have it back. Then you can ask when you're ready to."

His hand didn't leave mine. There was a struggle behind his eyes. "Keep it on," he said gently. "See how it feels."

The air left my lungs. What? "As a gift? Or as...."

"No," his voice barely a whisper, "not as a gift." He kissed my forehead and pulled me close. "Now, get some sleep."

I laid in his arms as I tried to think, only his arms and body heat weren't going to let me. I fell into a deep sleep.

16

DECEMBER 22

I woke up curled against him. I wondered if last night was a dream until I realized I was naked under the blankets. I smiled to myself. That had most definitely been fun. I opened my eyes. He was on his back, my head on his shoulder, his arm holding me to him.

Seeing my chance, I took a closer look at his tattoos. They were beautiful. The lines flowed and the artwork was breathtaking. I traced my fingertip along one of the lines that ran along his pec. My body grew wet just from tracing his tattoo. Was that a Match thing or just an Atticus thing? Did it even matter at this point?

Wanting to explore, I ran my fingertip down his chest and over that mouthwatering six pack. I moved to his hip and the muscle line there.

"What are you doing, luv?" he asked, his voice sleepy, his eyes still closed. I smiled to myself.

"Playing," I said innocently as my fingertips brushed him. He gasped, then moaned as I touched him. He opened his eyes to look at me as I straddled his waist. His eyes flared with heat as his hands went to my hips.

"You want to play?" He smiled, his hand moving down my belly to the front of me. I grabbed his hand and pinned it to the mattress.

I shook my head, smiling. "Uh-uh." Heat flared in his eyes as I ran my hands down his chest. "You got to explore last night. It's my turn."

"God, you're beautiful," he whispered, as if it were fact. I focused on running my fingers over the muscles of his chest and stomach, enjoying the hard lines under soft skin I found. Then I moved back down his body, his legs parting so I could kneel between them as I ran my fingers over the muscles of his hips, his thighs, anywhere but where his body was standing at attention. He pulled the blankets to the side so he could watch me as I ran my fingertips over the inside crease between his thigh and groin. He groaned deeply. "You're killing me, Eve."

I smiled up at him. "And what were you doing to me last night?"

He smirked. "I sure as hell wasn't teasing you." My fingers ran gently over his balls. His head dropped back and he gave a deep groan as his muscles tensed. "Shit, Eve."

I smiled, "What were you saying?" My fingers very lightly ran over his shaft. His hips moved.

"Not a damn thing." He gasped as he watched me touch him. I wrapped my fingers around his thick shaft and moved slowly, my thumb rubbing the underside of his tip. His eyes closed as he gripped the sheets in his hands. I kept my hand moving slowly as I lowered myself. I blew over the large head. His eyes opened and shot to me. He watched as I licked a line from base to tip. He cursed, his eyes staying on mine. Then I slipped my mouth over him. His head fell back as his hips shifted. "Oh God... Evelyn..." I slid more of him into my mouth, surprising him. He cried out, his hands finding me.

One in my hair the other cupping my face gently as he watched me slide his cock out of my mouth then back down my throat. His body shook as his face changed. Wonder filled his eyes as I worked my mouth and tongue around him. His face flushed, his breathing grew heavy. His eyes turned to molten gold. My body throbbed hard from the look of promise on his face. Oh, I loved this, playing until I was ready to do as I wanted with him.

After a long slide back from my mouth, his hands stopped me. "Eve..." A note in his voice told me his control was shaky. I let go of him and slowly moved back up the bed to straddle him. His hands moved over my skin, my hips, thighs, then to my breasts where he stroked and massaged. I leaned down and kissed him desperately. My body on fire, I sat up. Causing that look on his face was enough foreplay for me. I rose on my knees, felt him, then rolled my hips until the head of his cock found my entrance. I lowered myself just a little. He gritted his teeth, his hands ran over my skin. Then I sank a little more onto him, his hard body sliding into me. I shuddered as he held my hips. My breathing grew heavy as I lifted myself then met his eyes. I sank fully onto him, his body filling me completely. I closed my eyes and moaned at the feeling of being completely full.

"Damn... Eve. You're killing me," he bit out between clenched teeth. His entire body was tense, his muscles bunching. I rested my hands on his chest, grinned, then moved slowly. He cursed again, his hands ran up my thighs as I rode him slowly. His hips began to meet me at the pace I set. The fire grew as I took him over and over. Heart slamming, I rotated my hips. He growled, his hands gripped my hips tightly, his finger biting deep.

My breathing grew heavy as heat rolled over me. Bracing my hands on his chest, I leaned forward, making his angle perfect for rubbing my clit against him. His hands ran up my sides to my breasts as I moved over him. His eyes stayed on mine as his hands moved over my body. I gasped as sparks shot from my breasts to between my legs where he was stretching me.

His eyes stayed with mine as the inferno built. I moved faster, his hips met my pace as his right hand moved to my hip, the other taking my breast, his thumb stroking the nipple. I moaned as I teetered on that edge.

The bedroom door opened. I instantly covered my breasts and dropped to his chest, hiding myself against him. Just as quickly Atticus covered me with the sheet.

"Whoa! Okay, you are in here." Ranulf announced, surprised.

"What the fuck are you doing?" Atticus shouted, wrapping his arms around me as I buried my burning face into the crook of his neck.

"I-"

Atticus grabbed his pillow and chucked it at him. "Get the fuck out!" The door shut quickly.

"Oh my God..." I said, my voice embarrassed. He held me close as he brushed my sweaty hair from my face.

"I'm sorry. I'm going to kill him later." he assured me before kissing my cheek. His hand ran down my spine then back again, comforting me as I tried to stop my face from burning. When I could, I rested my temple on his arm so I could look up at him. His face was soft, his eyes worried as he looked down at me. "Are you alright?"

"I'm embarrassed. And a bit mad," I admitted.

He frowned. "You're beautiful, you have nothing to be embarrassed about."

"I know I don't," I explained. "I've got a great body. But I choose who sees it and who I share it with. And Ranulf is definitely not on that list."

His face grew hard. "No, he's not." He grabbed the sheet and pulled it over me.

"I'll kill him now." He went to get up. I pulled him back to me because he didn't sound like he was joking.

"What are you going to do?" I asked. His face softened but his eyes were hard as his hand cupped my face.

"I'm going to beat the hell out of him," he stated. His fingers stroked my cheek. "No one else is allowed to see you naked."

I held his hand to my face as I thought about it. I was angry with Ranulf. Who didn't knock these days? "Just a little."

His lips twitched. "I'll beat him only a little." He hesitated before he leaned down and kissed me gently. I wrapped my arm around his neck and melted against him. His kiss grew softer, his lips taking more of mine. He pulled away reluctantly with a small grin. "Go get ready for the day, then come over to the other apartment for breakfast."

"Alright, I need a shower anyway. Someone got me all sweaty," I said innocently. He chuckled before he got out of bed. I watched that muscular butt bend over and pull on his pajama bottoms. He finished tying them, picked up a white shirt, then went to the door. He looked back, his eyes running over me, a small satisfied smile on his lips before he left the bedroom and closed the door behind him.

I laid back and grinned like an idiot. Last night had been.... wow. Amazing? World shaking? I couldn't even put a proper word to it. I had to get up. We had demons to kill, but at least this morning I got out of bed with a smile. A door slammed somewhere and I chuckled. Ranulf was in deep trouble.

∾

Atticus

As I closed Evelyn's bedroom door my smile dissolved. Ranulf. That stupid fucker had seen her, seen us. I took deep breaths as I pulled my shirt on, headed out of her apartment and walked into our apartment. Ranulf was pacing across the room. He turned when the door opened.

His eyes were wide. "I didn't see shit! I'm sorry-" Rage boiled through me as I slammed him against the wall, my hand on his throat cutting him off.

"You will forget what you saw," I snarled into his face. "You will never walk into that apartment or our bedroom again without knocking or I'll fucking tear you apart." My body shook with my rage. He violated her privacy, that would never happen again. "Do you understand?"

Ranulf nodded sincerely. Pulling back, I let him go. He gasped and stepped away from me. I stood still and it took several minutes of deep breathing before I calmed down enough to turn around. Zahur and Falk were in the kitchen leaning on the counters, watching me. I hadn't even seen them when I came in.

Zahur smiled. "Well, Atticus." He eyed me. "You've changed."

"Don't," I growled as I headed for my bedroom.

"Oh, come on Atticus, that female is good for you," Zahur lectured. I stopped walking. She was. She really was. It was time to tell them.

I turned to them. "Evelyn can't go back to the community," I announced. They grew quiet. "And I'm not returning either."

Ranulf and Falk's jaws dropped.

"What? Wait... you're messing with us, right?" Ranulf asked.

"No," I said. "After these demons are dealt with and we take care of whatever is bringing them through, you three are free to head home."

"Why can't she go back?" Ranulf asked.

I let out a breath then explained as I stepped up to the counter. "Cyrus." I met Falk then Ranulf's gaze. "We weren't sent to investigate demonic activity. Cyrus somehow figured out she was in the city and sent us to bring her in if he was right."

Ranulf eyed me. "What? Why?"

"Cyrus's Match was Tatiana Savu," Zahur announced, drawing Falk and Ranulf's attention. "She's one of only two females in our history to have two Matches. She saw Cyrus for what he was and picked the male she loved, Owyn Dalca."

Ranulf cursed. "I bet he didn't like that."

"No, he didn't. From what Evie has told us, he sent Owyn on suicide missions, harassed them, made life difficult for them. When they had enough they left," Zahur explained. "Evelyn is their daughter."

Falk didn't seem surprised but Ranulf cursed.

"So, he what? Thought he'd be a Match for Evie?" Ranulf snapped.

"That is my theory, which was substantiated by him when I told him I wasn't returning," I told them.

Zahur turned to me. "He said those words?"

"Enough to confirm my suspicions," I answered before turning to the others again. "So, when this demon situation is handled, you'll head home. By then I'll have Evelyn in another part of the city, in a more secure location and under a new name."

Falk snorted.

Ranulf shook his head.

Zahur sighed. "Do you really think that's going to happen?" What? Of course, it was.

"We're not going anywhere," Ranulf announced. "We're a team. More than that, we're family." He crossed his arms over his large chest. "We're staying."

I couldn't believe what I was hearing. It was idiocy.

"You have lives back there, families," I reminded them before turning to Falk and Ranulf. "If you stay, you will never find your Matches."

They absorbed that for several minutes.

Then Ranulf met my gaze. "If we don't stay, Cyrus could come for Evelyn and you," he countered. "You may be the strongest male in our species but even you can't take out several squads of gargoyles on your own."

"Cyrus wouldn't risk it," I told him. "He likes to keep things quiet."

"If he truly thinks she could be a Match for him, he'll send as many as he thinks he needs to," Zahur began as he met my eyes. "And they won't be males who care if they hurt her to get her to cooperate."

"We aren't going to abandon you or Evie," Ranulf repeated. Falk nodded in agreement. "We are staying here. Now go take a shower, you smell. I can't understand how your Match stands it."

Stunned by their decision, I walked into the bathroom and began to shower. What the hell were they thinking?

Evelyn

.   .   .

I TOOK deep breaths as I braced my hands on my knees. That Fury had been a particular pain in the butt. It had nested in the top floor of an office tower. Unfortunately, it had been the office of a popular defense lawyer with known mafia connections. The secretaries had escaped intact, the lawyer and paralegals—I looked at the bloody pieces around the office—not so much.

As I got my breath back, Ranulf got to his feet and glared at me. "You caught me on fire!" he bellowed.

"You got in my sight line," I pointed out. There were a few heartbeats before we both broke down and started laughing.

Ranulf patted his hair. "How's the hair? Any bald spots?"

I chuckled. "No, I just got your armor."

"Yeah, it'd be a pity if he lost his hair," Zahur taunted. Ranulf flipped him off.

I walked over to stand next to Atticus and Falk as they looked down at the dead Fury. The skeletal creature was curled up on its side, its wings disintegrated by the fire I threw at it. The only way to kill a Fury was to take its wings. This one had been fast and it had taken longer than it should have. It didn't help that I couldn't get a clear shot.

I looked up at Atticus. "I could just burn it to ash now."

Atticus nodded. They backed up as I gathered energy, my markings glowing blue. I sent a stream of fire over the body. The smell of burnt flesh filled the area. When the body had finally burned away, the floor below was deeply scorched.

"Just set fire to the office, it'll hide all the evidence," Atticus ordered.

"Alright. Back up to the stairwell," I warned. The males moved as I asked. I tossed fireballs here and there around the area as I went, hitting the copy room especially hard. By the time I reached the stairwell the office was turning into an inferno. Instead of running down the stairs, everyone pulled out their wings and jumped down the stair shaft. Flapping only occasionally to slow my descent, I hit the ground and pulled my wings back. Then we hit the fire alarm and were out of the building before anyone saw us. We strolled over to the SUV. I turned to them, clapped my hands together and smiled. "Next one?"

AFTER VISITING the Preta's crime scene, we followed the trail to a slaughterhouse. Fitting, since a Preta was a Hunger demon that could never be satisfied.

Before stepping more than a foot from the car, Atticus turned back to us. His eyes ran over me quickly before he said, "Evelyn, can you stay back with the car?"

I stopped walking and looked up at him. "The car?" I asked, hoping I heard wrong.

His eyes met mine. "Yes. If the Preta gets past us-"

"Atticus," my voice warned him. He sighed.

"Fine," he bit out before sending a look to the others and heading into the building.

The smell of blood and meat was thick in the air as we moved through the slaughterhouse. Cow carcasses were everywhere, the flesh gone from their bodies. We even walked past several human skeletons.

The sound of crunching bones echoed through the main floor. It was sickening. Ranulf spotted it first. He crouched down, we all followed.

"It's feeding off another cow," Ranulf said.

"Spread out and hit it from behind," Atticus said.

"I'll throw a barrier to keep it from running the other way," I offered.

Atticus met my eyes. "Otherwise, stay out of this one."

I narrowed my eyes at him. "Are you serious?"

"I agree," Zahur announced. "We need to focus, and you in the middle of the fighting distracts all of us."

"How am I doing that?" I demanded.

"Well, being set on fire distracted me," Ranulf countered.

I shot Ranulf a look. "Haven't you ever fought with females before? You need to keep clear of my line of fire."

He sighed. "Aye, but it's been years."

I scoffed. I couldn't believe this. "Is it really that bad?" I asked, trying to understand. I turned to Falk, hoping for a no.

"We're out of practice," Falk said quietly.

I eyed each of them. This wasn't the time or the place for this discussion.

I sighed. "Fine, I'll stay back."

Ranulf tilted his head to the side. "The noise stopped." Something dripped into the middle of the circle. We looked up. There, hanging upside down from the pipe, was the Preta; ancient, dry, cracked skin, its talons dripping with blood.

"Shit," Zahur snapped. Everyone dove out from under it as it dropped on top of us. A heavy weight hit me, fangs digging into my back before I blasted the damn thing off me. It screeched as it flew through the air and crashed into a large puddle of blood. Everyone moved—everyone but me. The venom of a Preta had paralytic properties. Not to mention that it hurt.

"Evelyn?" Atticus called.

"Bite..." I bit out.

I threw a barrier up around me in case the demon got close again. I closed my eyes and focused. I moved through my body much like I had with Ranulf and Falk. I manipulated my body, this time pushing the venom out through the wound. It streamed down my back as I focused. When it was gone I was ready to kill the demon. I opened my eyes and got to my feet. I followed the noises further into the building. I moved past a cow pen just in time to watch Atticus take its head. That wasn't good enough for me. When they backed up I torched the body. Everyone turned back to me.

"It made me angry," I admitted.

Atticus strode straight to me. "Zahur." He unbuttoned my jacket and pulled it off my shoulder. He was almost frantic to see the bite. I let him pull the jacket off. When his hands went to my buckles, I held his hand to stop him.

"I'll get it," I promised. Everyone else reached us.

"What happened?" Ranulf asked.

"I got bit," I grumbled as I started unbuckling my buckles. Curses went around them as Atticus pulled off my armor. When he peeled my shirt off my shoulder blade it hurt. I hissed then looked over my shoulder, trying to see the damage.

"Zahur, get the kit," Atticus ordered.

"It'd be more hygienic to take her to the kit," Zahur countered. "She's taken the venom out, all that's left is the bite. She'll be alright until we get to the car." I took my jacket from Atticus and started walking out of the slaughterhouse.

The males were quiet as they moved to walk around me like a guard. I sighed as we left the slaughterhouse and went to the car. I stripped off my harness and vest, stuffing them into the back of the car.

"Evie," Zahur called, the kit on the hood. I sighed and walked over. I faced the SUV as Zahur lifted my tank top to examine my back. I hissed as he pulled the cloth out of the wound. "Good job getting the venom out," Zahur said absently as he cleaned the venom from my back.

"Well, it was that or stay put," I pointed out. Zahur reached around me to grab the disinfectant and more gauze. I rested my arms on the hood.

"This is going to hurt," he warned. Zahur soaked the bite with disinfectant. It burned down to the bone. I grunted, closed my eyes and took deep breaths. I gritted my teeth as Zahur began to scrub the punctures.

"I'm sorry, I have to." Zahur's voice was hard.

"I know," I grunted. He stopped cleaning. I leaned against the car, breathing deeply to get my breath back. Zahur started to bandage my shoulder. "I-I can heal it now... just...in a second."

Zahur's hand touched the area between my shoulder and neck, his fingers on my collar bone. He wiped below the wound again. "Then do it, because you're still losing blood."

I nodded then closed my eyes. I focused on moving energy to the back of my shoulder. It took several minutes but I healed the wound completely.

Zahur wiped down my back and shoulder one more time. "That is handy."

I lifted my head from the hood. "Okay, come on, we have five more." I let my shirt drop and reached for my vest.

The guys shared a look before Atticus looked at me, his face hard. "Let's call it a day."

I raised an eyebrow. "Because I got hurt? There are five more demons out there."

"Not just because of that," Atticus countered. "You also have some other work to do, Falk as well. And Zahur has to hit the Ether."

"You want me out of the way," I surmised. Zahur started putting things away. Ranulf was looking anywhere but at me. Falk met my eyes, as did Atticus. I looked down at the ground, fighting back emotion.

"Fine, I'll head back and open the shop." I didn't know how I was feeling. Hurt, angry, sad it was all a jumble in my chest. "Take me back." I opened the door to the car and slid in.

"That went well," Ranulf said sarcastically.

"Not now," Atticus growled.

I ignored it. Everyone got in and we were on the road. I was quiet the whole way to the shop. When we got there, Zahur got out so I could exit the car. I didn't bother with my vest but I waited until Zahur got back in the car. I went to Ranulf's window and knocked on the glass. He rolled it down.

I met Atticus's eyes, my stomach knotting. "Just, don't go after the Rakasha or the Succubus without me. Please?"

Atticus let out a breath. "We won't go after them without you."

The knots in my stomach eased.

"Don't worry, lass," Ranulf smiled. "We'll go after the lower level ones."

Hating this, I stepped back. They drove off. I turned and opened the shop.

Inside I turned everything on and dropped my vest on the chair. I opened my stash drawer and fished out a big, comfy green cardigan. I pulled it on before I ran through the morning routine in the shop. I made a cup of tea and started going over the day's shipping list.

I was still in the middle of finding the books when my cell rang.

"Hello."

"Evelyn, it's Delia." The witch's voice was thick. "Rowena is gone."

"I'm sorry for your and the others' loss," I told her simply.

"She violated the treaty, she knew what she was doing," Delia said. "I'll be ready to sign a new Treaty tonight."

"I'll see you at the usual time."

"Bye."

I put the phone down and sighed. I needed to make a new Treaty. It took hours. I looked around the book store at all the orders to go out. I needed help.

I picked up the phone to call Rina, only for Rina walk right through the door, her face pale, her eyes wide.

"I jumped into someone's dreams last night," she announced.

I blinked. "That's nothing new, you've done it before."

She shot me a look as she dropped her book bag onto the counter. "Not the sex dream of the hottie down the hall."

I bit back my laugh. "Did you at least enjoy yourself."

Her face turned beet red. "That's not the point!"

I couldn't hold back my laughter.

She rested her elbows on the counter and hid her face in her hands. I leaned down to her level. "It's okay. It happens to every telepath at least once," I explained gently. She dropped her hands and met my eyes. "You didn't violate him. You never touched him."

"No, but it was *his* dream," she pointed out. "It's like..."

"Did he ever say no?"

She sighed. "No."

"Did you do it on purpose?" I asked.

"No," she snapped.

I smiled. "Then it's okay. It was an accident. As long as you don't jump into his dreams again, it'll be alright."

She sighed deeply and nodded, her face back to its usual color. "How do I stop myself from doing it again?"

"Shielding exercises before bed," I reminded her. "You haven't been doing them."

"I forgot," she admitted.

"Well, I'm glad you're here. I was about to call you," I said. "I need you to take over the store for the day. The Head of the Witches Council died today, I need to draw up a new Treaty by tonight. Save my butt?"

Rina smiled. "Of course, that's what I do."

I smiled as she came behind the counter while I gathered materials. It was going to be a long day.

17

It was more than two hours before I saw any of them again. Falk came into the store and he paused at the door. I got up and moved to the doorway of my office. Rina was typing away on her laptop with her earbuds in again, not even noticing that Falk had come in. Falk, however, was staring at her like he'd never seen a woman before. I grinned as Rina finally looked up from the computer and saw him. Her lips parted as her eyes ran over him before going back to meet his. She pulled out her earbuds.

"I-is Evelyn here?" Falk asked, his voice extremely hoarse.

"Um, yeah, she's in her office," Rina said, her face turning pink.

"Thank you," he croaked. He headed towards me, his shoulders tense. He had an odd look on his face as he met me at the door.

I reached up and held my hands to his throat. I poured energy through his throat, soothing the irritation. When I opened my eyes he grinned down at me.

"So, what have you guys been up to?" I asked, walking back into my office to sit down behind my cleared desk. The only thing on my desk was the long parchment that I was currently working on.

"Running errands, picking up groceries," he said, his voice only rough now.

"Fun," I said sarcastically.

"Not really." He leaned against the doorjamb and glanced over his shoulder at Rina who was also glancing over every once in a while, as if she couldn't help it. "Who's that?"

I smiled as I picked up the glass spelled pen I was using. "That's Rina. She's a human telepath who I'm teaching to control her abilities. She also works here while going to the university." I peeked up at him. He was trying not to be obvious about watching her out of the corner of his eye.

"What is she studying at the university?" he asked casually.

I smiled. "Computer sciences. She's planning on creating video games when she graduates." When he didn't say anything I added, "Would you like to meet her?"

His head snapped back around to me. "No, that's alright."

I smiled at the embarrassed look on his face. The bell to the store rang.

"Why not?" I asked.

"She's human. No real future there," he pointed out. I rolled my eyes as Atticus stepped to the doorway.

My eyes went straight to him and ran over him. No injuries. The tightness in my chest eased. "Hi," I greeted him. Falk turned in the doorway.

"Go help the others bring up our gear," Atticus ordered. Falk sighed then headed towards the door. Atticus stepped into my office and closed the door behind him. "What are you working on?"

I put the pen down carefully and closed the ink bottle as he came around the desk. "Rowena died today." I looked up at him. "I have to have the new Treaty ready by eight tonight."

"That soon?" he asked as he put a hand on the back of my chair and one on the desk. His eyes ran over the parchment.

I sighed. "Unfortunately, the witches usually have a funeral right away. The signing of the new Treaty is at the beginning of it."

"That's... interesting," he said.

"That's what I always thought," I admitted, looking back down at the Treaty. I was looking over the second parchment, my master copy, when hands spun me around in my chair. Surprised, I looked up at him. There was a light in his eyes I'd never seen before.

"How did hunting go?" I asked.

"We weren't hunting," he admitted, a small grin on his face.

"Then what were you doing?" I asked, suspicion filling my voice.

He grinned. "Come with me."

⁓

Ranulf

THIS WAS A BAD IDEA, bordering on horrible. Falk and Zahur

were in the middle of putting up a Christmas tree in Evelyn's apartment.

"Take it down," I tried again. The guys ignored me. "Guys, she doesn't celebrate Yule, and I don't think it's an accident."

"It's Christmas, Ranulf. It's time she got to celebrate it with others like her," Zahur countered. I ran over our drunk walk back to the apartment.

"I don't think that's why she doesn't celebrate," I told them.

"Sure it is," Falk countered in a rough voice. "Everyone hates Christmas when they have no one." I couldn't argue with that. But something told me this was a bad idea...

The apartment door opened. I sighed. It was too late. Evelyn walked in with a box in her hands, looking back at Atticus. When she turned the blood drained from her face. She dropped the box at her feet.

"Surprise!" Falk and Zahur cheered from behind me.

"Get rid of it," she said desperately.

"Come on," Zahur tried. "With us, Christmas will be fun."

"Then stick it in your own fucking apartment!" she shouted, her voice shaking, her eyes full of tears. She turned and strode out the door and up the stairs towards the roof. Everyone was silent.

"Take the tree down," Atticus ordered.

No one argued. Everyone worked together to take down the tree. Even Atticus took off his suit jacket to help get rid of it. What was it about Christmas for her?

Evelyn

I COULDN'T SEEM to stop crying. I wiped my face again and took deep breaths. It was ridiculous that a stupid tree could break me down like this. Over 150 years later and I still shook at the sight of a Christmas tree. Still broke into a sweat whenever I saw a wrapped present. I don't know how long I was sitting on the ledge of the roof when the access door opened. Atticus's scent reached me on the breeze. He stepped next to me, his hands resting on the brick.

"I'm sorry," he said quietly. "We thought you would like a real Christmas."

"It's not your fault." I looked out over the snow-covered roofs and still couldn't stop the tears from falling.

"Stop crying, luv," he said quietly as he stepped closer then leaned down to whisper in my ear. "You know what happens when you cry."

I chuckled as my face burned. It helped push back some of the memories.

"Why don't you like Christmas? Or gold wrapping paper?" he asked gently. I stared at a water tank on a far-off roof and began to talk.

"I was seventeen, we were in London. I went to bed on Christmas Eve and everything was fine. Mum was knitting, Dad was reading as usual." Tears fell faster. His hand took mine. It helped push the tears back even more. I continued. "The next morning I came downstairs early and went into the parlour. The presents were under the tree like they were every year, but my parents weren't there. They were usually up before me." I swallowed hard as my voice shook. "I found a note. It said they were both ill and to go ahead and open my presents." I took a shaky breath. "So, I gathered the gifts with my name on them." I hesitated. "All of them were wrapped in gold paper. I opened the wrapping, then lifted the lid." I took a breath and let it out. "It was my father's head." He grew still "I kept opening the boxes to see if my mother was there too. She was. A demon had cut them to pieces and wrapped them as a gift for me."

"I'm sorry, Eve. When you said you didn't celebrate Christmas I just thought it was because you were alone," he said, his voice filled with regret.

I pushed those memories back and wiped the last of my tears away before I looked up at him. "I should have explained."

"Is this what your nightmare was about?" he asked.

I looked back down at the alleyway. "It happens every year. I have more, and worse, nightmares as it gets closer to Christmas." He was quiet long enough that I sighed. "I'm sorry I yelled at you guys, I just..."

"There's nothing to be sorry for. This was our fault," Atticus told me.

"Not really, you didn't know," I reminded him. "You were trying to do something nice and I just couldn't handle the tree." I looked down at my hands. "I know I should deal with it. But I really don't know how." He carefully slipped his arm around my shoulders.

"What about a Charlie Brown tree?" he asked. I raised an eyebrow. "Do you believe you can handle one of those?"

"What's a Charlie Brown tree?" I asked.

He frowned down at me. "You are almost two hundred and you don't know what a Charlie Brown Christmas tree is?"

I shrugged. "I don't watch Christmas specials or even listen to Christmas music."

"It's a small tree, no more than two feet," he explained. "Do you think you can try that?"

I thought about it. He wanted to celebrate Christmas,

and I wanted to for him, but... I imagined a small tree and it didn't bother me. "I think so."

"Then we'll take the tree back and get a smaller one," he said. He hesitated. "You don't like gifts, do you?"

I closed my eyes and sighed. "You guys went shopping, didn't you?"

"Perhaps," he hedged.

"You guys shouldn't have, I-I can't go shopping right now," I admitted, my face growing warm.

"That's not why we did it," Atticus said quietly. "The tree is already gone. Come back inside."

I wiped my face and nodded. "I have to keep working on that Treaty."

He stepped back so I could get off the side of the building. His hand went to my lower back as we headed back inside. I still had a lot of work to do.

18

I finished putting on my lipstick then stepped back from the mirror. Natural, but effective. I smiled to myself. My hair was up in a chignon on the back of my neck, two smaller tendrils loose. My pearl earrings were classic, they'd go perfectly with the dress. I sighed and walked into my bedroom. I opened my closet and went still. Suits hung in my closet along with several pairs of men's dress shoes on the floor. I smiled to myself. It looked like Atticus had moved in. I went to my dresser and found his boxers and socks folded and tucked in with my panties and socks. I played with my locket as I tried to decide how I felt about this. He didn't ask me first... that bothered me. But otherwise... I didn't mind so much. Going back to my closet I pulled out my navy-blue lace cocktail dress. The neckline was modest, the hem below my knees. I loved the dress. I hated wearing it for this. It was a funeral but it seemed wrong to wear black considering I was the reason she was dead. Pushing the thought aside, I slipped the dress on and zipped it up. I slipped on my black heels, checked the mirror one more time, then opened my bedroom door. Everyone turned to me.

Atticus

APPARENTLY THE SIGNING of a Treaty between Evelyn and the Witches' Council was semi-formal. She had dropped that bomb on us an hour and a half before the event. Except for me and Ranulf, the rest of the team had to scramble to a department store and find what they needed. I wore a black on black suit without a tie. That was it. I wasn't wearing a damn tie. Hell, Ranulf was refusing to wear anything but his usual black leather pants and shirt. Falk had found dark gray slacks, a dark teal button down and a dark gray tie that matched his slacks. Zahur had khakis and a white dress shirt.

After our talk Evelyn had spent the rest of the afternoon weaving spells into the parchment of the Treaty. The parchment practically glowed by the time she was done with it. I checked my watch. We needed to get going and she was still getting dressed.

We were lounging around her apartment, either pacing like Ranulf or busying ourselves with a book like I was. What was taking so long?

Her bedroom door opened. I turned and all but dropped my jaw.

Evelyn was a vision. Her hair was up at the back of her neck. Small pearl earrings could be seen behind tendrils of soft hair. Her cognac eyes glowed somehow. And the navy-blue lace dress.... I had to take a breath and let it out slowly. It hugged her curves but left something to the imagination.

And I didn't need to imagine that body... Stop it, we're working tonight. I swallowed hard as she walked into the room. The dress flowed around her knees, showing off her legs. I took a deep breath and let it out slowly again. My Match really was too beautiful for words.

"Everyone ready?" she asked, looking around at each of us. She ran her eyes over me and smiled. My heart skipped a beat. "You guys all look great."

I got to my feet. "We're going to be late." Everyone moved toward the door.

Zahur stepped to her side. "What he meant was, you look beautiful."

I picked up her coat, cursing myself. I should have told her that. Her smile faded as she walked to the counter and picked up the Treaty. Her face was troubled as she rolled it into a tube. She came to the foyer. I helped her put her coat on as the others moved into the hall and down the stairs. I leaned down to whisper in her ear, "You do look beautiful." Her cheeks tinted pink.

"Thank you," she said softly. I rested my hand on her lower back as I walked her down the stairs and out to the car. I opened the front passenger door for her.

"Are you ready?" I asked gently.

She shook her head. "Not in the least."

Evelyn

THE FRONT DOORS had been repaired, the house was lit up like day. One witch was waiting in the foyer. Carlena was one of those women who looked better in black than most. Her black hair and green eyes were striking. Add in her pale skin and a face most models would go under the knife for and she was a vision.

I met Carlena before the stairs. "Carlena, you look stunning as always."

She bowed her head in thanks. "As do you, Evelyn." Her eyes ran over my dress then met mine again. "Never black. Why?"

Over the last twenty years, two Treaties had been signed with the witches. Carlena had been at both, though she didn't look it.

"It seems hypocritical when I'm the one who put her in her coffin," I admitted. She tilted her head to the side and eyed me.

"Do you regret not pardoning her?" she asked quietly.

"No," I stated simply. "She violated the Treaty and caused a death toll that is still climbing."

Her eyes ran over me again, her gaze appraising. She nodded before meeting my eyes again. "I would have done the same." She glanced toward the ballroom doors. "You won't find many who agree." She gave me a small smile. "Let's get this over with."

Carlena led the way. I followed, feeling the males spread protectively around me. Carlena opened the doors to the ballroom and stepped back.

The room was decorated in black and green. Death and rebirth. After the new Treaty was signed, the funeral would start. For them, I traditionally left as soon as possible. The ballroom was full of magic users, all dressed up. A center aisle was open allowing us to walk to the center of the room where Delia waited.

My stomach knotted as eyes ran over me. Whispers ran through the room. Several called me names. Most were murderer, but I pretended not to hear it.

Delia was in her thirties, but looked just out of her teens. She was a small, thin woman with white blonde hair. Her blue eyes were crystal clear. Her black gown left her arms bare. The round, white-marble topped table was in the center of the room, the ceremonial pen waiting.

"Ms. De Haven. Welcome to the Head House," Delia greeted formally.

"Ms. Delia, formerly Rowena's second in command," I answered as we reached the table. "Let me introduce you to my companions; Atticus, Ranulf, Falk and Zahur."

Delia looked at each of them. "It's surprising to meet you. Thank you for coming." She turned to me. "Shall we begin?"

My stomach rolled. I swallowed hard as I stepped forward and unrolled the long Treaty. Murmurs ran through the crowd. It was an impressive piece of work. When I finished rolling out the Treaty I straightened.

"The Treaty states as follows: Harm none, unless in the case of self-defense or in the defense of others," my voice rang out.

"We know the Treaty by heart, Ms. De Haven," Delia announced. I was grateful for it. Reading out the rules and laws was a long, arduous process. Delia slid the Treaty towards her.

She picked up the pen and signed. She turned it back to me. My heart heavy, I picked up the pen on this side then signed my name.

"It's done." As soon as the ink was dry, I rolled it up and tucked it under my arm.

Delia met my eyes. "Thank you, Ms. De Haven. Would you like to join us for Rowena's funeral?" Huffs and disgusted noises ran through the room. I ignored them again.

"Thank you, but I think it's best if we leave," I said.

Delia gave me an understanding smile. "I understand, have a nice evening."

I turned and walked down that aisle again. Mumbling ran through the room, more insults.

By the time we walked outside I felt beaten. "I need a drink."

I WAS deep in my mind as we walked into Astrid's bar. It was still too early for the usual crowd, which was fine. I just wanted a drink to drown out the voices calling me names and Astrid had the best. She spotted me, her smile disappearing. By the time I reached the bar she had a tumbler of vodka on the rocks for me.

"Thanks hon," I said before taking a sip.

"Rough?" she asked quietly.

"Nothing like being called a murderer over and over again to make you feel like a monster," I said quietly.

"You're not. She knew the laws and chose to violate them," Atticus reminded me as he stepped up to the bar.

I met his eyes. "It doesn't make it easier."

Ranulf came up to the bar. "So, Goddess, what kind of scotch do you have?"

Astrid smirked before pulling out the strongest bottle. "Lewis, I'll take care of Evie and her friends. You've got the rest."

Lewis nodded as he served a wolf a beer. Everyone ordered and sat down.

As the night moved on the more we drank, the more I forgot about Rowena. The guys made jokes, trying to cheer me up. Eventually it worked. As everyone drank, stories of past screw ups came out until it turned into a game of ratting out one of the others with a worse story about them. Oddly, no one told a story about Atticus.

"What about Evie?" Ranulf asked, his eyes glazed. "Come on, she has to have some embarrassing stories." The others joined in harassing Astrid.

My face was warm as I smiled and shook my head. Atticus's arm moved across the back of my chair. "Good luck," I told them. "I don't make mistakes."

"Not in a fight..." Astrid's smile grew bigger.

I shot her a look. "Don't you dare."

"If not in a fight, then when?" Zahur asked, his own face flushed.

Astrid met my eyes. I shook my head at her. "I know yours," I reminded her.

She smiled a big, drunk smile. "But I'm not embarrassed by mine. I call them lessons."

We both giggled as the guys chuckled. Atticus's fingertips trailed up the back of my neck making me catch my breath. The others didn't notice since Astrid was telling them a story about a night out at a bar years ago. I turned to look up at Atticus. Those golden, shining eyes met mine, he seemed relaxed.

I smiled, "Are you drunk?" My voice slurred a bit.

He grinned. "Perhaps." His eyes ran over my face.

"What are you thinking?" I asked in a whisper. He looked away to the others to see that they were all still talking.

He turned back to me. His eyes ran over my face before leaning in to whisper in my ear, "Have you thought about the ring?" His whisper ran over my skin. He pulled back to meet my eyes. Heat pooled between my legs.

"I'm... still considering it," I whispered back softly. His

eyes flared with heat. "We still have things to figure out." I didn't know if I was reminding him or myself.

"Still need to decide if we fit," he agreed softly, though the heat in his eyes grew. My pulse picked up.

His other hand took my chin, his thumb stroking my bottom lip. "What is a gargoyle wedding like anyway?" I asked, my curiosity taking over.

"I'm going to use the rest room," Zahur announced. Out of the corner of my eye I barely noticed Falk getting to his feet as well.

"Hey Goddess," Ranulf called, "do you have anything stronger than this?"

"Uh, yeah, at the bar," Astrid said awkwardly. They both left the table.

His hand left my face to take my left hand. He met my eyes again. "There's no ceremony, no public display. It's just the promises I make to you, and you to me." Heat rolled over my body at the molten look in his eyes.

He leaned closer, his lips brushing mine. I tried to think through the fuzziness in my mind.

"We...we still need time..." I reminded him. We still needed to talk about things; him moving in without asking, him pushing me out of the fighting. But all I could think about was my body throbbing with my pulse.

"You're right, and we're in no hurry," he admitted, pulling back a little so he could meet my eyes. "But right now, I need to get you alone." The hunger in his voice was too much. My body throbbed, my panties soaked.

"Then take me home."

Ranulf

I MET Astrid at the bar as the others became scarce. The heat Atticus and Evie were putting out was distracting enough. But when she asked about gargoyle weddings we all had to get out of there.

Astrid rested her elbows on the bar, leaning forward as she shamelessly watched the two at the table. "When did he ask her to marry him?" she asked.

"I don't think he did," I told her, holding back my laughter. I explained what happened with the cop and how Evie came back in with a ring on her finger. "I didn't hear him ask her."

"Are you fucking kidding me?" she snapped, turning my attention back to her. "Evie deserves a proper romantic proposal."

I smiled at her. "Agreed. Those two are still feeling each other out."

She eyed me then smiled. "You seem like an intelligent male; do you know how to treat a female right?" The heat in those electric hazel eyes had the blood flowing straight to my cock.

"In more ways than you can imagine," I assured her. She ran her eyes over me then stood up straight.

"I can imagine a lot of ways," she countered as she reached under the bar and grabbed a bottle of scotch. Movement out of the corner of my eye had me looking over my shoulder back to the table. Atticus had gotten to his feet, slightly unsteady. He helped Evie to hers. She leaned into him as they began to weave for the door. I shouldn't let them leave, they were probably going to fly, but with the way they were talking... I should probably go with them, talk to Atticus when she goes into her apartment.

"Here." Astrid's voice stole my attention from them. She held out a tumbler of scotch. I reached out and took it, my fingers brushing hers. Instantly my body was aching as heat washed over me. Electricity ran over my skin. I grunted as I met her eyes. The Matching...

~

Astrid

MY HEART SLAMMED as my body burned, my core throbbing. I met Ranulf's eyes, stunned. Mates. With a different species. I'd never heard of that happening in the history of werewolves. I needed to think... My body gave another hard throb. I couldn't think, not with my body begging to take his. I tilted my head for him to follow me and let go of the glass. I took controlled breaths as I moved through the bar to the office.

When we reached the office he closed the door. I turned and met those turquoise eyes. Gargoyle, werewolf, it didn't matter. Not right now. A wave of heat poured over me, taking my control with it. I grabbed his shirt and pulled his lips to mine. My whole body went up in flames. He dug one hand into my hair and held me still while he took control of the kiss. He dove into my mouth, plundering, taking what he wanted. His hard grip in my hair had my body soaking my panties. I moaned at the taste of him. My body trembled as wave after wave of heat ran through the center of me. He pushed me back against the desk, pressing his hard body against mine. The world dissolved. There was only Ranulf, his mouth, his touch, and the desire racing through me. I ran my hands over his chest. I couldn't take it anymore, I had to feel more of him. I yanked at his shirt, trying to pull it over his head. He growled against my mouth, making my hips shift against him. He pulled back and looked at me with fire burning in his eyes, his hands running over me as I pulled his shirt up. He took control again, pulling it off and dropping it before taking my mouth again. Gasping, I turned my face away. His hot mouth moved to my throat, his teeth grazing me. I ran my hands over the muscles of his shoulders, his arms. My breasts rubbed against the material of my shirt, the tight peaks ached for attention. His grip on my hair pulled me from the desk, turning me, pressing my ass against his hard body. He jerked my shirt down, his hand covering my breast and squeezing hard. I cried out as lightning shot through me.

"Oh God, yes." I moved my hips, stroking him through our clothes, my arms going behind me to weave around his neck. He growled against my throat again. As he pinched my nipple hard I threw my head back, crying out as my body throbbed. His hand moved down my body and up my skirt to find me. His hand covered my soaked thong. His lips moved to my ear.

"You like it rough," he whispered in a husky voice.

I nodded as much as his grip on my hair would allow. "Wolf thing..." I managed through my heavy breathing.

His fingers slipped into my panties. He groaned when he found me wet. I moaned as he stroked me.

"I'm going to bend you over this desk and fuck you till you scream," he growled in my ear. My body clenched, another shudder of desire tore through me.

"Please..."

He pulled his hand out of my panties and swept part of my desk clear. I was already bending over when his hand left my hair to press me to the wood top. His other hand pulled up my skirt, grabbed my thong and tore it off me. I whimpered in need as the inferno built inside me. The heater sent warm air over my exposed ass as the laces of his leather pants brushed me while he worked to free himself. I needed to see. I turned my head to see his dick but his hands were already at my hips, his head already pressing against me. He thrust into me in one hard stroke. I cried out as he filled me completely. Oh shit! He was perfect!

"You're so fucking wet, Astrid." He didn't wait for me to get used to him. He pulled out and started pounding me into the desk. Crying out, my body trembled as my hands scrambled over the desk for something to hold on to. He kept driving into me, hitting the end of me with every thrust. The sound of skin slapping skin filled my office as he continued to do exactly as he said he would. He grabbed my hair again and pulled me up until my hands braced on the desk. Sparks shot along my nerves, my body tightening around him. His teeth found my neck as his hand reached around my hip to the front of me. He stroked me. The firestorm grew hotter.

"Shit! Don't stop!" I cried out, not caring if I was loud. His teeth bit down hard. I screamed as my body exploded. My nails dug into the desk, my body milked his as he continued to pump into me. He thrust once, twice, then growled against my throat as he came deep inside me.

That's when it happened. Images flooded my mind. Memories. But they were his. Growing up in Scotland, his family, the ache of losing his brothers and sister. The jealousy that ate at him when he watched others with their Mates and families. The anger he felt when Atticus kept refusing Evie... I saw it all, felt it all. 1300 years of pain swamped me. I knew I wasn't alone, he was seeing my life too. It was the Mate Bond, it stripped you bare and showed your Mate the truth of you.

When the images stopped, he let my hair go. Gasping, my body limp, I laid down on the desk top as I slowly came back to earth. He slid out of me, making me groan deeply. He had felt so good. He leaned over the desk, his hand running up my spine.

Knowing I had to face him, I pushed myself up, fixed my shirt and turned to lean on the desk. He was there instantly, his hands going to my face, forcing me to meet his eyes.

His eyes were warm as they met mine. "Are you good?"

"Yeah," I said, my voice hesitant.

"What was that?" he asked quietly.

"The Mate Bond." I swallowed hard. "It shows your Mate exactly who you are. Your memories, emotions, mistakes. Everything."

His eyes narrowed at me. "Everything I saw... they were your memories?" I nodded. Now he would judge; every male I'd been with, every mistake I'd ever made. He knew it now, and he'd judge. I took a deep breath. If he couldn't handle it - it would hurt, but I'd be fine. I may never have children or meet anyone else who touched me the way he did, but I would be just fine.

His eyes ran over my face before meeting mine again. "You are amazing," he said, his voice in awe. My heart slammed in my chest as he pulled me into his arms and buried his face in my hair.

I let out the breath I had been holding as I clung to him, my eyes burning. "You're not so bad yourself." He let out his own breath, making me smile.

We were silent for several minutes, just holding each other. Then reality came crashing down. He was a gargoyle, I was a werewolf. Different species weren't supposed to be able to breed or bond with each other.

"How did this happen?" I asked no one in particular. He pulled back a little and brushed the hair from my face.

"I don't know," he admitted. "It shouldn't be able to."

"Our Mates, the bond is usually sealed after the first time they have sex," I admitted. I can see why now. Holy hell, I had been aching. "What about yours?"

He shook his head. "Ours requires vows said out loud." His eyes grew shadowed. "We have a bigger problem. If my Elder Council finds out, they'll probably kill us both." My heart ached.

"Same with our Alphas," I admitted. I met his eyes. "What are we going to do?"

His face was strained when he answered, "We're going to have to hide it."

19

DECEMBER 23

Atticus

Movement in bed woke me up. I buried my face into her hair to block the light. Wait, what? I opened my eyes and rolled onto my back to see the sun shining through the bedroom window. Evelyn started to wake up, rolling into me. Pressing her naked body against my skin. Hmm... oh, that's right... I wrapped my arm around her and used my left hand to take my phone off the nightstand. When I brought it back so I could see the time I went still. Not because of the time, but because of the new white vine marking that ran from my wrist and wrapped around my forearm then up my bicep. A single pink cherry blossom stood out on the vines and thorns wrapping over the black and gray tattoos that had already been there. Oh shit. We Mated last night. My chest grew tight as I scoured my memory for what happened. I remembered being drunk, coming back to her place, the feel of her. Sliding into her... then it was all a blur of sensation and then peace...

She stirred against me, moving to her back and rubbing

her eyes. "What's wrong?" she muttered. "You're tense." She opened her eyes and went still beside me. Oh fuck. "Atticus, what is on my arm?"

She didn't remember either... Shit, shit, shit! Vows were binding, and I had no memory of what I promised.

"Atticus!" she demanded, moving to sit up with her back against the headboard. I turned to find her holding the sheet to her body, her eyes wide.

"It's alright," I said calmly when I felt anything but. I reached over and took her left hand to examine it. Thin branches moved up the inside of her forearm. There on one of them sat a white ball of cotton. Cotton? I sighed. Yeah, that was me. I wasn't pretty or anything a female would want. I swallowed hard. What the fuck had I promised? My thumb ran over her markings gently, knowing that they wouldn't change.

"Atticus, what is this?" she asked again, her voice shaking.

I met her eyes and told her. "Sometime last night we promised something to each other and now we're... Mated."

Her face grew white, her mouth gaped. Her breathing became rough. "What?" she asked, panic filling her eyes. I wanted to join her but both of us couldn't lose it. I sat up next to her and wrapped my arm around her. I focused on calming her down. Perhaps it would help push back the tightness forming in my chest.

I brought my arm around to show her. Her marks on my skin were feminine, beautiful. Her fingers ran over the vines. "These marks are Mate marks. Vows and promises we make to each other get burned into our skin by magic. It also enforces those promises."

"I don't remember what I promised Atticus!" she said, her voice high. "We were so drunk it could have been about making you pancakes every morning!" She got out of bed, wrapped the sheet around her and searched the floor as if to find her clothes from last night.

"I vaguely remember tearing your dress," I admitted, scratching my eyebrow. She straightened and let out a breath. Then she started blinking fast, her hand covered her mouth as she took another shaky breath. My chest tightened even more. She didn't want me... I climbed out of bed on her side and wrapped her in my arms. She hid her face in my chest. "It's going to be alright." I whispered. "I know I'm not the male you deserve-"

She shook her head then lifted to meet my eyes. "Atty, we got married and I don't remember what I promised you. I don't remember getting married."

She was upset she didn't remember her promise? Relief filled me as it sank in. She wasn't upset she was Mated to *me*. Just that she didn't remember. The vise in my chest loosened.

"Well, it looks like we only promised one thing," I tried to reassure her. I had no idea how. "When we are ready to promise more we can... have a wedding? Humans do that, right?" She smiled through the tears threatening to fall.

"I don't want a wedding. I want to remember getting married," she explained.

"I... I can't give that to you. I don't remember either," I admitted. I looked at the bed. "I remember coming in here, tearing your dress, and...us." I met her eyes, my own panic threatening to rise. "And that's it."

Her eyes stopped watering, she took several deep breaths, then she gave me a small smile. "Well, it looks like you're stuck with me."

Relief filled me as I grinned down at her. "I don't mind." I pulled her close and kissed her forehead gently. My panic disappeared with that kiss. She rested her head on my chest and let me hold her. We were Mated. That was it. There was no divorce, there was no turning back. A part of me was thrilled that she was mine. Another... terrified of what she'd say when I told her about Cyrus. I kissed the top of her head. "Let's get dressed and get some coffee."

She nodded then pulled away. I dressed in my suit slacks and my usual white dress shirt. I was rolling up my sleeves while she pulled out her hunting gear.

By the time I was dressed, she had closed the bathroom door behind her. I opened the bedroom door and bit back a curse. Shit! Everyone was in the kitchen. Falk was at the fridge pulling eggs out. Coffee, I needed coffee. And tea, Eve liked tea in the morning. I closed the bedroom door behind me and went into the kitchen. I was filling the kettle at the sink when Falk stopped making breakfast. Out of the corner of my eye, I noticed him turning and signaling to the others. I mentally cursed him. I put the kettle on then started making a pot of coffee.

By the time I turned around Ranulf and Zahur were grinning like hyenas.

"So, Atticus," Zahur said, his eyes on my left arm. "Anything exciting happen last night?"

"Shut it, Zahur," I bit out through clenched teeth. Ranulf snorted and went back to texting on his phone.

"So, it only took getting her completely plastered to agree to be your Mate?" Ranulf asked, obviously distracted.

I had enough. "If any of you try to tease her this morning, I'll rip your wings off," I growled. Eyebrows went up around the kitchen. "She's already upset-"

"Why is she upset?" Zahur asked, frowning.

"Because neither one of us remembers what we promised," I bit out. Eyebrows went up again.

"Oh... yeah. That's kinda important boss," Ranulf said, cringing.

"No shit," I growled. "So back off the bullshit with her today."

Everyone nodded. The bathroom door opened. Evelyn came out with her hair in a braid over her shoulder and her face freshly washed. She looked up and hesitated.

"Look, it's the Mrs," Ranulf greeted cheerfully.

Fury boiled in my veins as her face turned red. She turned and walked back into our bedroom, closing the door behind her without a word.

I met Ranulf's eyes. "Run."

Ranulf didn't waste time, he took off out of the apartment. I let him run.

By the time the tea was ready she came back out of our room and moved into the kitchen. I handed her the mug.

"Thanks," she muttered.

"Are you alright?" I asked quietly.

She nodded. "It just kind of hit me when he said that."

"Don't mind Ranulf," Zahur told her. "He's currently running for his life from Atticus for that."

She looked up at me with an eyebrow raised. "Are you chasing him?"

"I just made him think I was," I admitted. She chuckled as she sat down.

Everyone made conversation as we ate. Zahur kept glancing at the markings on her arm. I made a note to talk to him later about it. Breakfast was almost over when I decided to call Ranulf back in to get ready for the hunt today. We had several demons to take out and my Match, no... my Mate was going with us. I was thankful for the agreement with the others to keep her out of the fighting as much as possible. My eyes ran over her as she sharpened a blade. This wasn't going to be easy.

Evelyn

ONE TRACKING SPELL and a lot of driving brought us to the Pride demon's day hide out. It wasn't a warehouse or a high-rise. This one was hiding out in a mansion in the poshest neighborhood in the city, which meant getting in might be a problem.

"We could just hop the fence," Ranulf suggested while we all stood on the corner of the block near the estate's back gate.

"In this neighborhood? The police would be called the second our feet left the ground," Atticus pointed out.

I gestured at the alleyway. "I could-"

"If Evelyn can hide us we could jump the fence or even fly over," Atticus said, talking right over me.

I tried again. "Or I could simply-"

"That's still risky, the demon could feel the energy being used," Zahur offered.

Giving up, I turned and walked down the alley toward the back gate of the property.

"Evelyn," Atticus called as he began to follow.

I ignored him. I reached the gate, opened my jacket and pulled out my tools.

"What are you doing, lass?" Ranulf asked, his smile in his voice.

"I'm getting us in without alerting the demon," I said patiently as I opened the combination lock box and looked at the wiring.

"You know how to do that?" Zahur asked.

"Yes. I was trying to tell you, but I kept getting talked over and ignored." I found the circuit I wanted. I slipped my tool in and bridged it with the power source. It shorted out the circuit board. There was a small click of the gate unlocking. I slipped my tools back into my jacket breast pocket and turned to the speechless males.

I met Atticus's eyes, then Zahur's. "Stop ignoring me when I have a suggestion. Otherwise, I'm just going to do what I was trying to suggest in the first place." I turned and headed through the gate. Ranulf and Falk both bit back chuckles as they followed.

The backyard was lush and large. It even had a long, modern in-ground fountain. We moved between the bushes and the fence toward the house. Atticus took the lead. I somehow ended up in back, again. Their concern was sweet, but on a hunt it was starting to irritate me.

In the tall brush halfway to the house Atticus stopped and crouched. He made hand gestures to the others. They moved off across the lawn and further down the side of the house. I assumed I was to stay with Atticus since he didn't give me instructions. He gestured for me to stay where I was. Was he seriously leaving me here? Outside?

"You want me to stay out here?" I whispered.

He moved closer, his lips going to my ear. "We need someone to keep an eye on our escape route. Keep it clear."

I pulled back and met his eyes. He was lying. It was a good idea, but still a lie. My temper sparked. I bit back my response because of where we were. "Fine."

The relief in his eyes was obvious. Of course, he didn't know about the argument we were going to have later. He squeezed my hand before he moved on to the back of the house.

I was mad and worried about him at the same time, it was an odd feeling.

I stayed in the brush and waited. And waited. I checked my phone. Ten minutes had gone by. Shouldn't they be done by now?

A small shuffle in the dirt to my right caught my ear. I went still. There it was again, this time from my left. I took a deep breath and got a lungful of rot. Ghouls.

I pulled my blade from my back and split it into two.

Ghouls rushed me through the brush. I took one head, spun, and took another from the ghoul behind me. Others came through the bushes. I needed more room.

I moved out of the bushes to the center of the lawn. The ghouls burst from the bush-line and charged me. It wasn't hard to take them down one by one as they reached me. I moved quickly and smoothly, taking heads or setting them on fire, whichever was needed. The ring of dead ghouls grew. At least they were coming after me and not after the others while they were busy with the demon. There was a loud crash from inside, multiple voices shouting. I focused on killing the supply of ghouls that never seemed to end. One tried to jump tackle me - he flew overhead and into the fountain. I threw a ball of ice. The fountain instantly froze trapping the ghoul where it stood, waist high in ice. I went back to dealing with the others. Finally having enough, I focused on blowing them apart before they could reach the ring around me. The explosions were silent but effective. Black blood and body parts flew around the yard.

When the last ghoul dropped I was breathing hard and surrounded by a ring of dead ghouls. A ring of black blood and limbs encircled that. I rested my hands on my knees as I got my breath back.

The back door of the house opened. The others strode

out smiling and laughing, no one looked injured. I straightened. Everyone turned to the yard and stopped dead in their tracks.

I began cleaning the blood off my short swords. "How was the demon?"

"Atticus almost killed Ranulf, but otherwise it was your typical demon fight," Zahur answered as he walked onto the black grass.

I nodded as I put my blade back together then slid it back into its sheath. "I think there is a large basement somewhere." I began to make my way out of the piles of dead ghouls. Atticus was there in an instant, his hand taking mine to help me keep my footing. When I stepped onto the black grass he didn't let go.

"Are you injured?" he asked, his voice hard.

"No, they were easy," I told him.

Ranulf pointed behind me. "Think ya missed one."

I turned and found the ghoul in the fountain. "Oh, whoops." I pulled energy, then threw a blast that blew the ghoul apart in a macabre firework display.

"Holy..." Zahur muttered. I ignored them as I set fire to the pile of bodies and the black grass. We were on our way out of the alley when smoke started pouring from the house.

I was quiet until we reached the SUV. I turned to Atticus and met his eyes.

"Do you still want me to stay outside?" I asked pointedly.

His eyes were hard as they met mine. "No. But stay in the back."

"Fine." I turned and got in the SUV. Everyone else piled in, we had more demons to hunt.

.   .   .

WE WERE at the crime scene of the Rakasha. Being canni-
bals that enjoyed blood more than flesh, it wasn't a pretty
sight. I did my usual tracking spell, only this time it didn't
work.

"Huh, that's new," I muttered as I squatted on the spot
and ran my hand over the area. The energy above the blood
was thicker. Only by a fraction, barely there, but enough. A
cloaking spell.

"What's wrong?" Atticus asked.

I closed my eyes and ran my fingers over the energy,
finding its shape. "This one has a cloaking spell. Interesting..." I focused on finding the energy connection, what was
fueling it. Certain magic needed to be performed and
powered only once. Cloaking spells were different. They
needed a constant stream of energy, and that energy was
usually from the one it was attached to unless someone else
wanted to power it. Since we were dealing with demons here,
I doubted one of them would be that accommodating. I
could blast the spell, overload it, or even cut it off from its
energy source, but then it'd know and could go on a killing
spree. I wanted this one to stay in hiding and away from
people. There. I found the energy line. I stood, focusing on it.

"We're going to have to feel this one out. This is going to
take some focus," I warned. "Please don't let me walk into
the street."

Atticus was beside me in a heartbeat, his hand taking
mine. I closed my eyes, concentrating on the energy line. I
started walking, following the line.

It took time, more time than I'd like. When I lost it we
had to turn back and find the trail again.

"This is taking forever," Ranulf grumbled.

"What? You have a hot date?" I bit out.

Ranulf was strangely quiet as we walked towards a school, an elementary school. Oh God. "Schools are out on vacation, right?"

"Tomorrow is Christmas Eve. Yeah, they're on vacation," Zahur answered. I let out a relieved breath. Then another thought hit me.

"What about the teachers?" I asked the group. They were quiet. That wasn't good. I moved faster, following the trail to the school steps. I sighed and looked to the others. Everyone's face was grim. I started up the steps first. The door was unlocked. Please let none of the children have come to play on the playground. The halls of the school were silent. The scent of blood hit my nose. Ranulf cursed.

I led them down the left hallway, past the office and classrooms. The spell led up upstairs.

"The third door on the right," I whispered. They all shared looks. Atticus made hand gestures.

"What the heck does that mean?" I asked, frustrated.

"He's just saying he'll take point and act as a distraction while everyone else surrounds it," Ranulf answered.

Atticus gestured to me and pushed his hand away from him twice. I understood that. Stay back. Yeah, yeah. That was already clear. I just nodded. Everyone pulled out weapons as we moved down the hallway.

When we reached the doorway I stayed in back as directed. Atticus moved through the door, quickly followed by the rest of us.

It was crouching on the head of a woman, its long nails cutting flesh and pulling it to its lips. Bodies were torn apart, pieces here and there. Blood soaked the floor so your feet squished when you took a step.

It turned to us, its long, sharp teeth bared in a gruesome

smile. "Gargoyles, so glad you could come. Your kind are tasty."

The guys moved in.

A pink sweater caught my eye. A little girl's body lay among the other body parts. Her face was towards me, her blue eyes frozen and unseeing. Fury built in my belly. I turned back to the fight just in time to watch it jump up to the corner of the ceiling, cackling. I snapped.

I raised my hand and reached out as if to grab him physically. I wrapped energy around its waist. I made the motion of slamming him to the floor. It was still cackling as it dove face first into the floor, splintering the wood around it. The guys turned to me as I walked up to the circle around it, my fury burning. I flipped my curled hand over. The Rakasha flipped then slammed down hard again.

It continued to cackle and squirm under my hold, at least until it saw me.

"It's you. He told us about you," it said in a hiss as it continued to squirm. "He's coming for you and you can't stop him," It sniggered, its hands gleefully clapping. Blood boiling, I closed my hand and turned it hard. Bones crunched as it screeched in pain. I met its yellow eyes.

"Who told you about me?" I demanded.

It cackled. "Abaddon..."

I debated going into a demon's mind to find the answer. Weighed the risks versus the reward. I sighed. Even I didn't like those odds.

"He'll make you his," the demon laughed. Before I had a chance to blow the thing apart Atticus's sword drove into its chest. The demon cried out in pain. My eyes snapped to Atticus, but this wasn't my Atticus. This gargoyle's eyes burned with fury. Zahur took my arm and moved me back as Atticus drove the blade into the demon's thigh. It screamed. Atticus continued driving his blade into the demon, keeping it alive as everyone else got out of the splash zone. He made the demon suffer, and the look in his eyes told me he felt no regret for it. And quite frankly, neither did I. Finally, when the demon was mostly meat and bone, he took the head, killing it.

Everyone was silent as Atticus cleaned his sword and put it back in its sheath. He lifted his head. His eyes were cold and hard when they met mine. It felt like a blow. He moved around the demon's remains.

"Burn it," he ordered coldly when he strode by, not even looking at me. I looked at the door he left through, stunned by the change.

I turned back and set fire to the demon's body before I followed the others out of the classroom and down the hall. Everyone was quiet as we walked down the halls.

"Where'd he go?" I asked.

"Probably bringing the car," Ranulf answered. "He's the fastest on foot."

When we walked outside Atticus was already back with the SUV running at the sidewalk. Everyone else climbed in back leaving me the front seat. I climbed in and closed the door. Atticus didn't look at me. His hands gripped the wheel tightly. I reached over to touch his shoulder but he shrugged me off as he pulled into traffic. The old Atticus was back, cold and silent. I didn't understand what happened. He tore apart a demon... why was he acting this way?

"Shit," Zahur snapped. Everyone but Atticus turned to him. "Something's wrong in the Ether."

Then he was just gone. Poof. Just not there anymore.

"Now we're one down," Ranulf muttered. Atticus said nothing as he moved through traffic.

I hadn't been paying attention to where we were going, not until we stopped in front of my store.

"What are we doing here? We have more demons out there," I asked from the passenger seat.

"We're one down," he said, his voice hard and cold.

"Seriously? We're calling it a day?" I couldn't believe this. When Atticus didn't answer, I'd had it. I wasn't going to put up with this again, he was my husband, damn it. I turned to the guys in the back. "Give us a minute?"

They both nodded and slipped out of the car. I waited until they moved away from the car.

"What's wrong, Atticus?" I asked directly.

"We have a job to do, and you have to work in the store," he said, his voice still cold as he kept his eyes ahead of us.

"Atticus," I snapped. "Look at me." His hands gripped the wheel tightly before he turned to me. Emotions fought in his eyes, they flashed cold, then hot, then cold again. "Tell me what is wrong." When he turned back to look out the windshield I pushed it. "Why are you acting this way?"

He was quiet so long I thought I might have to stay in the car all day, but he finally opened his mouth.

"I lost it in there," he said quietly, his voice strained. "When he said Abaddon was coming for you, I lost control." He clenched then unclenched his jaw.

"Atty, he threatened me. Of course you got angry," I told him gently.

"I lost control. I was furious and my anger just took over." His eyes went to the steering wheel as he shook his head. "He was right. I'm going to kill everyone I care about, just like the rest of my family."

I reached over and took his hand off the wheel to hold it in mine. "You didn't come near us, Atty." He lifted his head to look at our hands. I continued, "You didn't even cause arterial spray which, given the damage you did, is impressive and wasn't an accident."

He was quiet for several heartbeats before he asked, "I didn't?"

"No, you didn't," I told him gently. "Even when you 'lost control' you still made sure not to hurt your team."

His hand gripped mine tightly as he searched my eyes for something. If he found it or not I didn't know. He looked back out the windshield, his face still like stone. He pulled his hand from mine. I bit back the hurt from him pulling away.

"Atticus." He didn't look at me which lit my temper. "You aren't a monster that's going to hurt the people you care about." When he continued to say nothing, I snapped. "Are you listening to me?" he nodded.

"Do you believe me?" I demanded.

"I don't know," he said, his voice still cold.

"Atticus..." I tried again.

"You need to go to your shop. And we need to get going," he told me.

Still angry with him over his sudden change I grabbed my coat. "Just don't go after the Succubus without me. She'd eat you guys alive." Completely irritated with him I opened the door and climbed out, making sure to take my weapons with me. Falk and Ranulf were leaning against my store window. "Stay safe."

Falk reached out and squeezed my shoulder before heading to the car.

Ranulf smiled at me. "I know this is bullshit, lass. But he's my boss."

I nodded, letting him know I understood. He got into the car.

I watched them drive off. Then I smiled. For such

powerful gargoyles, not one of them noticed that the store was already open.

I shook my head as I stepped inside. Rina was behind the counter boxing up books.

"You are the best woman in the world, you know that?" I said as I came in.

"I know," she said with a smile as she taped a box shut. "It's not often you call in the morning begging me for help."

"And offering you triple your usual pay," I reminded her.

She chuckled. "I know." She eyed my gear. "Heading off to work your other job?"

"Yeah. Apparently I'm not allowed to play with the boys," I said dryly. She winked at me.

"So you're going to go out alone," she said in a knowing voice.

"Exactly." I pushed away from the counter. "I'll see you later." I headed out the door and across the street to the parking garage.

It wasn't long before I was at the Succubus crime scene in a cheap, flea-bag hotel. The poor man had probably thought it was his lucky night. I flicked my fingers to unlock the door, then pulled the yellow crime scene tape off the doorway. Making sure the hallway was empty, I moved inside. The hotel room was sparse, just a bed and dresser. You didn't need much else in this kind of hotel. I moved to the bed and waved my hand over it. A Succubus kill was bloodless, they simply drained the life out of you as you orgasmed, but they always left a trace of themselves behind. It was unavoidable.

My fingers found the small hint of energy. I smiled as I tuned into it and followed it.

It led me downtown, to one of the high-class hotels in the city. I garnered a few looks at my wardrobe but I kept walking through reception to the elevators. The trail left the elevator at the top floor. It wasn't long before I was at the door. I made sure the hallway was empty before knocking.

"Housekeeping," I said with a Russian accent.

The door opened. She was stunning. Thick black hair, big violet eyes and a body any man would drool over. I blasted her back into the room. I walked in and shut the door behind me. She got to her feet, smiling.

"It's been a long time since I've faced a gargoyle with that kind of power," she said, her voice was seductive but it simply slid over me without effect.

"Not gay, sweetie," I mocked.

Her eyes glowed bright. "This should be fun."

I STAYED where I was on the broken glass of the shattered coffee table, watching her body stop convulsing. I focused on breathing. That had hurt like hell. I groaned as I sat up. Wiping the blood from my face I flicked my fingers and her body went up like tinder. The hotel room was destroyed. Pieces of drywall fell from the ceiling, holes the size of people were through the walls. Almost the entire floor was destroyed. I needed to move before the humans called the cops.

As she finished burning I got to my feet and gasped. The stabbing pain in my side told me at least one rib was broken. Bruising was everywhere, but that I could live with. I sat on the torched bed and closed my eyes. The Succubus had gotten a lucky shot. I had just thrown her through the bathroom wall. Tile shattered as she hit and dropped. I was pulling more energy to throw a lightning bolt when the ceramic toilet came through the hole in the wall, slamming into my side. A toilet broke my ribs. I was never telling

Astrid about this. I poured energy through my body. Fixing my broken ribs, I whimpered as they sealed. I sat, trying to get my breath back, as I watched the body burn.

When her body was just a black mark on the carpet I got to my feet and made my way out of the hotel, trying not to stagger. Driving home had me breathing deeply from the pain. I needed to heal more of my bruises when I got home. Then hot chocolate and a soak in the tub.

After what felt like forever, I started climbing the stairs to my apartment.

Raised voices caught my ear. When I reached the landing, I found the males' apartment door open. Shouting was coming from inside so I walked in.

"Damn it. More gauze!" Atticus snapped.

"No, I need stitches." Zahur's voice was exhausted. My own pain forgotten, I hurried through the apartment and pushed a bedroom door the rest of the way open. Zahur was on his back in his bed, his shirt gone, his body slashed and bloody. His jeans were open so his hand could press against his lower abdomen. His other hand was holding just above it. Both were soaked in blood. Someone had tried to gut him. I stood there, stunned, as Zahur gave Atticus instructions on how to stitch him up. I had a better way.

I moved past the others and nudged Atticus out of my way. My hands covered Zahur's. I met his eyes. His sweating face was almost white from blood loss. "I've got you, old man." I closed my eyes and concentrated. My marks glowed as I pulled energy and moved it through my hands. "Move your hands," I muttered. When Zahur's hands lightened the pressure, I moved my hands under his. Round, slippery organs met my fingers. No one *tried* to gut him, they had succeeded. I concentrated on running that energy through his body, forcing tissue to knit and mend. Scars were inevitable with this kind of healing but at least he wouldn't be down long.

When his abdomen was sealed I concentrated on his bone marrow, forcing it to work faster to replace his blood loss. When his level was in the safe zone, I pulled back. I practically dropped to the floor. Hard arms caught me and turned me to sit on the bed.

"Just... one sec..." I gasped as I tried to get my bearings. Parchment filled my lungs as fingers lifted my chin.

"Where did you get these?" Atticus demanded.

I patted his hand before opening my eyes and meeting his. "Yell at me later. Let me finish fixing him up." I turned on the side of the bed to face Zahur. I wiped at the blood pooled over his stomach. Falk handed me a towel. I thanked him as I cleaned off Zahur's lower abdomen and stomach. A large ragged scar went from his pelvic bone up to his belly button, but the wound was closed and everything back where it needed to be. That's when I noticed he was practically hanging out of his pants.

Not even thinking about it, I covered him with a sheet before I moved up the bed to his side. His eyes were closed, his color better. Rapid healing of this amount usually required the body to rest. There were still deep cuts on his chest. I dug into the kit on the floor beside the bed and pulled out what I needed. I tore open the antiseptic wipes.

"So, what happened?" I asked them as I began to clean the cuts on his chest.

"There was a breach in the Ether," Ranulf answered. "That's all we got before he was giving instructions on how to fix him."

I finished cleaning the wounds on his chest. I reached out and touched a fingertip to the edge of the deepest cut. A bronze hand snatched mine, causing me to jump and my bruises to protest. Zahur's eyes met mine.

"Thanks." He swallowed hard before looking up at Atticus. "It's not a demon pulling them through. It's an angel." The room fell into stunned silence. But I didn't care; he was bleeding again.

I moved his hand from mine. "Let me finish the worst," I told him. Those chocolate eyes met mine with a small twist of his lips before he nodded. I put my finger on the worst cut again. "This might hurt." It was all the warning I gave. I focused the energy I had left and ran it over the cut. He grunted as I moved as fast as I could, sealing the gash. When I finished I was dizzy.

"I... I think that's all I've got left," I admitted.

"It's more than enough, Evie," he whispered, his eyes ran over my bruised face. "There are herbs in my bag that will help with your bruises."

I patted his shoulder absently. "Rest now," I told him. He nodded then promptly passed out. I reached for the bandages. A hand grabbed my wrist. I looked up to meet Atticus's worried eyes.

"Falk will bandage the rest of his wounds, we need to take care of you," he bit out. Oh, great, he was mad.

I didn't even argue. I just got to my feet and moved towards the door. Atticus was giving instructions as I stepped out into their living room. I didn't get far. I was leaning on the back of one of the sofas by the time he came out of Zahur's room. He took my arm and led me around the sofa. I sat down, careful of my bruises. He disappeared then came back with a smaller first aid kit. He lifted my chin with his fingers and assessed my bruises.

"Where else?" he demanded. I began to unbuckle my vest. His hands removed mine and did it for me. He pulled the vest off slowly. It helped not having all that pressure on my ribs. I shoved my tank strap down my arm. He examined my shoulder carefully.

"It's strained, it'll be fine tomorrow," I reassured him.

His piercing eyes met mine. "What else?" he growled.

"Ribs, back, legs. I'm just a bunch of bruises," I admitted. "They'll be gone in a few hours."

He took a deep breath; his hard eyes ran over me again before he got to his feet.

"Stay here," he ordered coldly. I carefully leaned back against the couch with no problem. I didn't know where he went, but it wasn't long before Ranulf was in front of me.

"What did you go after, lass?" he asked.

"Succubus," I admitted. "She was feisty."

He chuckled. "Is there anything you need?"

"A bath and a mug of hot chocolate," I said wistfully. He smiled as he examined my arms.

"Evelyn." Atticus was back, his voice hard. He took my hand and helped me to my feet.

Atticus ignored Ranulf as he led me into the bathroom. The room was hot, the mirror fogged over.

He closed the door behind us. I leaned against the counter simply because it hurt to stand straight.

"You're taking a bath. I've already put the herbs in the water," he announced as he came over, knelt down and began untying my boots. I was trying to figure out a way to ask him to leave when he got to his feet and started pulling the rest of my clothes off me.

"Atticus, I can get it myself," I told him.

"I've seen you naked, Evelyn," he reminded me, his voice cold as his hands went to my pants.

That's it. My hands stopped his again. He met my eyes. "You are not my Atticus," I told him. He looked at me confused. "When my Atticus comes back, the one who can actually talk to me without the room dropping fifty degrees, then you can see me naked. Until then, out!" His eyes flashed as his hands dropped from my clothes. Then he was slamming the door behind him. I sighed, not knowing if I had just pushed him away more or not. I stripped down, grunting and groaning as I pulled off my leather armor.

When I was finally naked I pulled back the frosted curtain and slowly slipped into the water in the deep tub. I hissed as the herbs stung my bruises and cuts. But when I was finally up to my neck the stinging eased. I let out a deep breath and laid my head back.

Not ten minutes later someone knocked on the door.

"I'm in the tub. If you need to use the lavatory go use my apartment," I called with my eyes still closed. The door opened. I quickly sat up and covered myself. "I'm in here!"

"I'm aware," Atticus announced dryly. "The curtain isn't transparent, you still have the privacy you wanted." I looked and realized he was right. I relaxed again.

"An odd kind of privacy," I pointed out. His footsteps moved across the tile. He moved the curtain a little to place a mug of hot chocolate on the edge of the tub then let it drop back. Surprised, it took me a few heartbeats to say anything.

"Thank you." I picked up the mug and took a sip. It was sweet, rich and chocolatey. Everything I was looking for.

"We need to talk," he said, his voice neutral.

I took a big drink. "Alright."

"You went after the Succubus on your own," he said carefully.

I looked up at the ceiling and sighed. "Yes."

"Why?" he asked, his voice strained. He was clearly trying not to yell.

I took another sip. "All of you are so worried about taking me out hunting that most of you don't seem to remember that I've been doing this for years," I said quietly, trying to be honest with him. "I've taken out Rakashas before on my own, and just about every type of demon you can name, yet you keep pushing me out of the fight like I'm a twelve-year-old." I swallowed hard. "It bothers me, frustrates me and yes, one of the reasons I went out on my own today was because I was tired of being told to stay back."

There were several heartbeats of silence.

"Then why did you come home bruised head to toe?" he asked.

I took another sip. "Because when you get two powerful energy users in a one-on-one fight we kind of... null each other out sometimes. There's no point in trying to be clever, at least not with some demons. It becomes more about how many walls and floors you can slam the other one through."

"How many walls and floors did you go through?" he asked quietly.

"I would prefer not to comment," I said dryly.

He chuckled. I smiled to myself. It was a good laugh. I pulled the curtain back enough so I could see him. He was leaning against the wall at the other end of the shower, his arms crossed over his chest with his gaze on the tiled floor. His suit jacket was gone but his sleeves were rolled back showing his tattoos again.

"I know we've been forcing you back out of the fighting," he said softly. "But it has nothing to do with your abilities, Evelyn. None of us have gotten used to you fighting with us, and during a fight your safety is the sole thing on my mind." He looked up and met my eyes. "We know you are more than capable of holding your own. This is my weakness, not yours."

I closed my eyes and prayed for patience. When I opened them, he was still waiting. "So, all of you had a meeting to discuss this and came to this conclusion? That I shouldn't hunt with you."

"Yes. Ranulf didn't like it, but eventually he agreed as well," he said.

I sighed as I met his gaze. "Atticus. Don't you think I should have been there for that meeting?" He blinked. "My Mate and teammates got together and decided what I would be doing without me even being there."

His gaze was on the floor again, his brow furrowed. There were several minutes of silence before he nodded. "I see your point." He lifted his head and met my eyes. "I didn't believe you would be open to the idea."

"Whether you believed that or not, I should have been there," I explained calmly. "To listen to what everyone thought, to say how I felt about it." I looked up at the ceiling again. "I'm a reasonable person, Atticus. If I had been at that meeting, I would have listened and understood everyone's reasoning."

"Would you have agreed?" he asked quietly.

I met his shadowed eyes again. "Yes. I would also have asked that you let me take care of the Succubus, considering none of you could."

He huffed. "So, we would have been on the same page."

"Looks like it," I said before taking another drink. A couple minutes of silence went by.

"You said I wasn't 'your Atticus.' What did you mean?" he asked carefully.

I sighed deeply, my head falling back against the tub. "You keep changing," I began. "You're warm, then you're cold. And I can't take it." My throat tightened. "Ever since the Rakasha you've been cold. You wouldn't look at me in the car, you would barely talk to me." I swirled the water with a fingertip. "You pushed me out. And when I tried to get you to talk, you might as well have given me frostbite." I laid my head back as my throat tightened. "I can't deal with that, Atticus. And I don't want to."

"That had nothing to do with you," he assured me.

I sighed and stayed calm. "Whether it did or not isn't the point." I looked up at the ceiling again, trying to make him understand. "You slammed the door on me, Atticus. I was trying to help and you shut me out. And it hurts when you do that." I put my mug on the bathroom floor.

"How?" his voice was quiet.

I looked down at the water as my eyes burned. "It makes me feel like you don't want me." My voice was barely a whisper in the room. "That you don't even like me."

The silence was thick in the bathroom. Would he ever say anything? I was about to give up and get out when he finally spoke up.

"I'm sorry, Eve. I didn't mean to make you feel that way," he said, his eyes meeting mine. "I didn't mean to shut you out, it's just... what I've always done. I truly didn't mean to hurt you. I never would, not again, not on purpose."

"Atticus, we need to not be afraid to talk to each other," I said. I shifted, pressing the front of my body against the side of the tub, putting my arms on the side and rested my chin on them. He met my eyes. "I promise to talk to you about what's on my mind or what I'm feeling and to listen with an open heart and open mind to what is on yours."

"And if I upset you?" he asked.

"If you upset me, then I'll walk away and calm down. Then I'll come back to you when I can have a calm discussion on the topic. But don't shut me out."

His eyes were warm as he walked across the room and

knelt next to the tub. His fingers held my jaw, his thumb running over my cheek. "I promise the same. And to always include you in our team discussions, especially anything regarding you or our lives." He took a deep breath. "And I promise not to shut you out ever again."

I smiled up at him. "Deal."

He grinned down at me before lowering his head. His lips brushed mine softly, my body relaxed in the water. When he lifted his head he looked... oddly settled. Calm.

My left forearm began to burn. I hissed as I shifted in the water so I could look at it. He grunted as he raised his arm. I watched as a few more balls of raw, fluffy cotton appeared on the branches. I looked over to find several more cherry blossoms were now along his vines.

"*How did I sleep through that the first time?*" he wondered.

"I don't know, you'd think that would have woken us up," I said as I looked back up at him.

He frowned in confusion. "What did you say?"

"You wondered how you slept through the burning the first time," I told him, not understanding. His eyes grew wide.

"*Evelyn, can you hear me?*" he asked, though his lips didn't move.

"Yes, I can," I said, sitting up in the tub. I closed my eyes and felt around inside my mind. There! A fresh link had formed. I opened my eyes and met his. "It's a telepathic link."

"What? How..." He closed his eyes. "Our promises."

"What was the exact wording?" I asked carefully.

"To listen with an open heart and open mind," he repeated.

"Oh my God." I dropped my face into my hands. "It created the link."

"Seriously?" he growled *"Are we ever going to get a vow right?"* he sent.

I groaned and dropped my hands. "I'm sorry, I didn't even think about the wording of what I was promising."

He reached out and held my bruised face gently in his hand. "Neither did I." He gave me a small smile. "We'll manage. But right now we have work to do. I brought some of your clothes, they're on the counter." He tucked a stray hair behind my ear, making my body warm. "When you're done with your bath, come out and we'll have a meeting about this angel that's summoning everything."

"I doubt Zahur will be awake," I pointed out.

"I'll fill him in tomorrow morning," he assured me.

I nodded. He leaned over me and kissed me gently. When he was done he got to his feet and headed for the door. *"Brilliant idea Atticus, kiss her when she's naked and then head out to the others when you're hard as a rock."*

I giggled. He stopped, then turned around and looked at me.

"You're the one who came into the bathroom while I was in the tub," I pointed out.

"This link is going to have a learning curve, isn't it?" he asked woefully.

"And probably a steep one at that," I admitted. He cursed mentally. I raised an eyebrow.

He cursed out loud before he left the bathroom, closing the door behind him.

I laid back in the water, smiling as I ran over our conversation again in my head. We promised to talk to each other and be open minded. Maybe I should have added calmly? I instantly dismissed the idea. When I lost my temper I truly lost it. A lot like my Mate. I looked down at my arm. We were married. I ran my fingers over the thin brown branches. The white cotton balls were spaced along them. I didn't know what to think about my Mate mark.

I soaked a little longer before pulling the plug and climbing out. I dried myself with a towel and looked at my body in the mirror. All of my bruises were darker, but they weren't hurting so much anymore.

I looked at the clothes he brought me and smiled. I pulled on the pale pink, hip hugger panties and a white cami. The light blue jeans were comfy, as was the oversized lavender sweater. I pulled my hair back into a bun before bending to pick up my clothes. I made it halfway down before gasping as pain shot through me.

By the time I reached my armor the door opened and Atticus was walking towards me. He snatched up my clothes from the floor, then took my arm and helped me back to my feet.

"Next time, call," he chided.

"Well, I thought I could get it," I muttered as we left the bathroom.

"This link might come in handy," he sent. *"I can keep a better eye on you."*

"Oh, great." Even my thought was dry.

He bit back a laugh as he tossed my armor into a bedroom I hadn't been in yet. I was too tired to ask.

We joined Ranulf and Falk in the living room.

I sat in the middle of the sofa next to Ranulf. Falk took my other side.

Atticus stood across the coffee table with his arms crossed over his chest. "Alright, we have an angel in the city summoning demons," he stated. *"And he's after my wife."* The anger coming from him was making my shoulders tight. I tried to block him and it helped, but it was more of a sheer curtain over a window rather than a wall.

"That's not something I thought I'd ever hear," Ranulf muttered, bringing my attention back to the conversation.

"At least that explains why we couldn't figure out those symbols," I offered, rubbing the bridge of my nose. "My mom and I never went over angels."

"That does explain why there was every kind of symbol for every kind of demon known. Not to mention all the information on almost every species we know of," Atticus said.

"I'm sorry, can you explain this to me," I asked them. "Why are angels bad?"

Ranulf's arm laid across the back of the couch. "It's not that they're bad, lass. It's that they are psychopaths." I raised an eyebrow at that.

"We don't know if they are still working for God or not, but they've become twisted," Atticus explained. "They have determined that humanity is worthless and should be eradicated. They are worse than demons at this point."

"Demons do like hiding and staying on earth," I shifted, trying to get comfortable. But between my bruises and Atticus's anger, it wasn't happening.

"Well, angels don't," Ranulf countered. "They only show up to destroy and kill."

"I'm amazed that it's managed to stay hidden this long," Atticus stated. "They are usually all for exposing themselves to the world while trying to set it ablaze."

"That is weird," Ranulf said. "This one's staying hidden while using demons to do the destroying."

"Clever," Atticus muttered before looking to me. "With an angel in the city... Evelyn, I would feel much better if you had someone with you at all times."

I sighed. "I can handle-"

"Lass, this isn't about what you can handle," Ranulf stated. "No gargoyle can take an angel one on one."

"So, this is just your usual 'there's an angel in town, pair up' procedure?" I asked.

"Yes," Atticus answered. Then he sent, *"It would also help put your Mate at ease."* An urge to grab me and run came through the link. The feeling was edged with bone deep fear. It took my breath away for a moment. That was so not fair.

"Alright. I'll buddy up," I agreed. The relief that came through the link left me weak kneed, how was Atticus not showing it at all? I guess I really didn't realize how much going off on my own bothered him.

"Thank you," he said. I met his eyes.

"No fair using the link like that," I sent. His lips twitched.

"Thanks for not fighting us on this," Ranulf said.

"I'm not completely unreasonable," I said before leaning forward. "So, what's the plan for taking it down?"

Atticus took a breath and let it out. "We're going to have to ignore the demons and hunt the angel."

I went still. "Wait, we can't do that. People will die."

"We don't like it but if we can cut off any more demons from coming through, then we can take them out," Ranulf explained.

"We only have two left," I pointed out. "If we leave with the sunrise, that should give us more than enough time to take them both out before they could hurt more people."

"One, actually. We got the Wish demon this afternoon," Atticus countered.

"She's got a point, boss," Ranulf said.

He looked at the coffee table, his eyes unfocused.

"The Wrath demon is still out there. Atticus, we can't let it

live much longer," I sent to him. *"The angel seems to have it under control now, but once it's free of that..."*

Atticus nodded, before lifting his head. "You're right. We can take care of the last one within a few hours."

"So, that's the plan?" Ranulf asked.

Atticus nodded. "Yes, we'll take the last demon out in the early morning, then start hunting the angel."

"Then I'm going back to my apartment," I announced. "I'm exhausted."

"Evelyn." Atticus's voice got my attention before I could stand up. "With an angel in the city, I would appreciate it if you stayed here."

"But I'm just across the hall," I pointed out. *"Were you not going to..."* The thought was sent before I realized it.

His eyes met mine. *"Of course I was. But with the others this close it's much safer. And it would help me sleep tonight."*

That's true. Through the link I could feel his energy, he was like a live wire right now. Besides, with their description of angels, safer sounded good to me. "Alright."

Ranulf looked between the two of us. "Okay, I expected a fight, or at the very least an argument. What's with you two?"

I turned to him and shrugged. "Angels are new to me and I don't know how to fight them or what magic would work." Ranulf seemed to accept that.

"Falk, take her to get some things from her apartment," Atticus ordered. Falk got to his feet and helped me to mine.

We left the males' apartment and crossed the hall to mine. I pulled an overnight bag out of my closet.

"Better get a bigger bag," Falk warned hoarsely.

"You think it will be that long?" I asked as I opened a drawer.

"Don't know," he rasped. I turned and walked over to

him. I held his throat and soothed the irritation. It took a few moments and I was back.

"Thanks," he said in a rough voice.

I winked at him as I got back to packing the duffle. "We'll be across the hall, I can make trips back if I need something."

"Good point," he admitted as he leaned in the bedroom doorway. I packed enough clothes for a few days, then went into the bathroom and grabbed my make-up bag and other things. When I was done, Falk picked up my duffle bag and headed for the door. I stopped by my bookshelf and picked out a couple of books then followed.

When I walked into their living room Falk was there with no sign of my bag. They were deep in discussion about notifying the Elder Council. Atticus was against it.

"Atticus?" I sent a tendril of thought through our link.

"First door on the left, Evelyn," he said absently, then went back to the conversation.

"Thanks." I went through that door and closed it behind me. There wasn't much in his bedroom. A queen-sized bed with a black comforter and gray sheets sat against the right wall. A small night stand on one side with a lamp. The closet was across from the bed, the small dresser on the other side of the closet.

On the bed was my bag. I set my keys and books on top of the dresser. I eyed my bag. I'll unpack in the morning. I pulled off my jeans and sweater leaving the cami on. After putting my clothes in the duffel, I set my bag on the floor by the dresser then picked up a book. I moved to the bed, pulled the blankets back and climbed in.

I was leaning against the wall, propped up by his two pillows, when he came in. Satisfaction vibrated down our link along with a sense of calming down. I looked up from my book to meet his eyes. He had an odd, tiny grin, barely a lift at the corner of his lips which he tried to hide as he went to the closet and took off his watch.

Acutely aware that I was in *his* bed, I watched him set it on the dresser and begin to unbutton his dress shirt. My body gave a hard throb at the sight of those tattoos. He looked over his shoulder and raised an eyebrow at me. I smiled but didn't bother to explain. His eyes ran over my body slowly, the warmth changing to concern.

"How are you feeling?" he asked.

"Alright, just banged up." I went back to my book because if he kept looking at me like that, bruised or not, I'd be pulling him in to bed and finishing my slow ride from the other morning. He took a long, steadying breath. Oh no. My face burned as I raised my eyes from the page, peeking up at him. He ran his hand through his hair and let out that deep breath. Oh, yeah. He heard that. I looked back down at the page and waited for my face to cool down. As he moved around the room, I kept my eyes on the book. It was the only safe thing to do with the others just past the door. He came to my side of the bed and touched my knee. Warmth ran over my skin as I looked up. He was only in those navy pajama bottoms again. But what caught my eye was the gash across his side; the blood was dry so it had happened earlier today.

"What the heck? Atticus?" I snapped, dropping my book on the bed and moving to the edge to inspect the damage.

He took my hand before I could touch his side. "It's fine. I'm more worried about your-"

"How didn't I see this?" I demanded, pulling my hand from his and examining the gash. The edges were clean, it'd be an easy heal.

"I changed my clothes before I came into the bathroom,"

he said, his hands trying to take mine from him. "Now, your bruises-"

"Forget my bruises," I warned as I smacked his hands away. I placed my hand over part of the wound and closed my eyes. It was only a few minutes before I opened them again.

"You didn't need to do that." His voice was strained as if he was trying not to yell at me. "You could have healed your bruises instead."

"You can't heal this many bruises. There are too many spread over too much space." I looked up at him. He had a small blue jar in in hands. "What's that?"

He sighed. "It's a bruise salve that Zahur makes." He knelt down in front of me as he opened the jar. He used his fingers to swipe some of it out of the jar then started rubbing it into the large bruise on my knee. I hissed at the cold, then relaxed as he gently rubbed it in. As it took effect I realized it was numbing the area.

"Okay, I need a tub of this," I announced, holding my hand out for it.

He shook his head. "You took care of me, now I'm taking care of you." He moved on to another bruise. I couldn't argue with that and I didn't really want to. He continued to move up my legs, his touch was soothing until he finished with the large bruise near my hip. He didn't hesitate, his hands moved to my knees and opened my legs to him. I caught my breath as heat built at my core. My eyes went to him, but he was focusing on the large, dark bruise high on the inside of my thigh. He started to carefully rub in the salve.

"You noticed that one too?" I muttered, trying to get my body to calm down.

"I notice everything about you," he said absently. My

heart warmed, I bet he didn't mean to say that. But he didn't seem to notice as he worked his way up my body, even making me pull up my camisole so he could cover my ribs in the goo. When he finished with my face his eyes met mine. "On your stomach."

I didn't even argue; his touch was relaxing. I pushed the covers down and scooted further onto the bed, then flipped to my stomach.

"Middle of the bed, luv," he told me, his accent slipping out. "We both know you'll end up there anyway."

I rolled my eyes as I scooted over. "Are you calling me a bed hog?"

The bed shifted as he climbed on, then straddled my legs. "You're not so much of a bed hog as a body-heat seeking koala that grabs on and won't let go."

I smiled into the mattress at the warmth in his voice. He pulled up the back of my cami and began to work the salve into those bruises.

"A koala, huh? So, I'm cute and cuddly?" I countered.

"And cling when you're dead asleep." His voice told me he was smiling.

I sighed dramatically. "Well, if you don't want me in your bed..." I acted like I was trying to get up. His hand immediately pressed between my shoulder blades and pinned me to the blankets.

"I didn't say that," he said quietly. I relaxed into the bed again as he went back to rubbing the ointment into my bruises.

"So, you don't mind the cute and cuddly, body-heat seeking koala?" I teased. He was silent for several minutes as he worked on my shoulders.

"'At times our own light goes out and is rekindled by a spark from another person. Each of us has cause to think with deep gratitude of those who have lighted the flame within us,'" he said quietly, quoting Albert Schweitzer. I grinned. He was saying that he didn't mind my bed hogging, that he actually enjoyed it. Before I could counter with my own quote he asked, "Are you going to unpack tonight?"

"I was going to leave it until the morning," I admitted, his hands pushing me towards sleep.

"That doesn't bother you?" he asked, surprised. I smiled.

"You're a neat freak, aren't you?"

"I prefer things put away," he hedged as he worked on my shoulders. My eyes rolled into the back of my head. I groaned as he hit a particularly good spot. All thought went out the window. When he was done he climbed off the bed, covered me with the blankets, then moved around the room. I floated in a state of relaxation

Eventually the bed shifted again and the light went out. Then his body heat was close to my skin. I relaxed but couldn't fall asleep. Finally his hand went to my unbruised hip and squeezed gently. Smiling to myself I dropped into a deep sleep.

20

DECEMBER 24

Atticus

I woke up with my hard cock pressing against my Mate's butt. As my head cleared I noticed the position we were in. I was spooning her, her body snug against me as if we were stuck together. I smiled. Definitely a heat seeking koala.

It was almost time to get up. I'd been getting up at 4:30 a.m. for so long it was automatic now. I took a deep breath of cherry blossoms. Maybe I could let her sleep a little longer. I laid there thinking about her. She was amazing, smart, resourceful, and forgiving. I was still angry with myself for hurting her so much when I was trying to keep her away. And her legs... Who would forgive someone for that? I ran my thumb over her belly, soaking in the feel and smell of her. That's when it hit me. I was in love with her. And I still haven't told her about Cyrus. I cursed myself. I should have told her days ago, but... I kissed her shoulder. I didn't want the way she looked at me to change. I was going to have to tell her soon.

She shifted in her sleep, rubbing herself against my groin. Heat shot through me, my dick already seeping against her. I thanked whatever God there was that gargoyles healed fast because her bruises were gone this morning. Desperately needing to touch her, I kissed the back of her neck softly, trailing to her ear. My arm slid up so I could cup the weight of her breast, my fingers caressing as I kissed her shoulder. Her breath hitched and I knew she was awake and aware of what I was doing. The feel of her silky skin was enough to drive me mad, I moved back to kissing her neck as I played with her nipple. She took a deep, shaky breath and I grinned against her skin. I slid my hand down her toned belly until I was in her panties, my fingers slipping through her wet body. She groaned as I stroked her gently.

"Atty..." she breathed in the same sultry voice she had used the other night. I focused on causing those small moans in the back of her throat that drove me crazy. I kept touching her slowly, softly, until she was grinding and soaking against my hand. I pulled my hand from her and tugged her panties down just enough to give me access. I pushed down my pants then slid against her once, making her gasp before sliding into her fully. I grunted, she gasped. She was hot silk wrapped around me like a vise. I groaned quietly against her skin, her muscles squeezing me until I could barely hold on. I gritted my teeth as I pulled nearly all the way out before sliding home again while stroking her. She gasped, her body bathing me in scalding honey. She felt so fucking perfect that I wanted to stay here all day. I continued stroking her as I slid home over and over. "God...Atty... close..." she gasped, then covered her mouth with her hand as I continued the slow pace. Her whole body trembled as she started to tighten around me. Lightning streaked up my body and down to my toes.

I kept my pace slow and easy. She shuddered, her other hand twisting in the sheets. She grabbed a pillow and covered her face to muffle the sound of her crying out my name as she came. Her body locked down on me and it was too much. I groaned against her skin as I exploded inside her, as deep as I could get, her body squeezing mine until I was empty. I wrapped her in my arms as I tried to catch my breath, making no move to leave her. She just felt so good.

"That was a nice way to wake up," she sent, satisfaction lacing her thought. I smiled against her skin.

"I might have to wake you up that way every morning," I sent as I kissed my way up her shoulder until I reached her ear. She smiled as she ran her fingers over my arms.

"I'm torn between asking you to roll over so I can kiss you, or staying inside you as long as possible," I admitted. Her face turned pink.

"I wouldn't mind a kiss," she said softly. I watched her carefully as I slid out of her, she shivered. She rolled over onto her back so I could look down at her. I couldn't believe how beautiful she was. I cupped her face and ran my thumb over her cheekbone, enjoying just touching her. Her big cognac eyes ran over my face making me wonder what she saw there. My fingertips ran down her cheek, over her throat and down between her breasts where her locket sat. It looked perfect there, like it was made to sit between her breasts and no one else's. I leaned down and kissed between them, right over her heart. That amazing heart that I couldn't believe might one day love me. If I didn't mess it up. Her fingers went to my face, her hands were so soft.

Her eyes were confused when they met mine. "Mess what up?"

That damn link. "I think we need to cancel everything and just stay naked in bed all day," I said instead. She giggled as I took her hand and kissed her palm. She didn't ask again.

"We need to get out of bed so we can leave with the sunrise," she reminded me. I sighed then let her go.

～

Evelyn

ATTICUS PULLED AWAY. Something was different about him this morning. He seemed comfortable with me, almost open. It was new. And a big part of me liked it. I pulled my panties back up and climbed out of bed.

As he went to pull on his pants, I went to my bag only to find it empty except for my toiletries. "Atty, where are my things?" I turned to find him making the bed. I raised an eyebrow.

"They're in the closet and drawers," he answered absently as he made hospital corners on the bed.

"You are a neat freak," I stated, going to the closet and opening it.

"Perhaps," he hedged again. I smiled as I found my armor and started looking for something to wear while I went to the bathroom.

Atticus stepped behind me and wrapped an arm around my waist. "What are you looking for?" He whispered before he kissed my neck.

"I need to use the bathroom." I said as I relaxed against him. He reached around me and into the closet. He handed me a soft blue robe. "Thank you."

He kissed my temple before letting go to finish dressing.

By the time I found all the clothes I needed Atticus was still getting dressed.

When I stepped out of the bedroom I found Falk and Zahur in the kitchen eating breakfast. Falk raised an eyebrow and smirked. My face warmed. We hadn't been as quiet as I thought. I decided to pretend that didn't happen. I closed the door behind me and walked into the bathroom as if I wasn't blushing at all.

I cleaned up and quickly got dressed then went to put my clothes in my duffle. Atticus opened the door as I reached for the handle. He stepped back to let me by. He waited by the door until I was finished putting my clothes away. Then we went to the kitchen together.

I poured coffee for myself and Atticus while he dished up two plates.

"Where's Ranulf?" Atticus asked.

"He took off last night, said he had something to take care of," Zahur said.

Atticus handed me a plate, I handed him his coffee. He was frowning when he turned to the others. The front door opened.

"Morning," Ranulf said as he came in through the door.

"Where did you go last night?" Atticus demanded. I winced, it was too early for this.

"Went to a pub," Ranulf said as he poured himself coffee. Atticus set his mug and plate down.

"You went patrolling, didn't you?" Atticus growled as he leaned against the kitchen side of the breakfast bar and crossed his arms over his chest.

"No, I went to a pub," Ranulf repeated as he made a plate. I glanced at Atticus's face, his jaw was clenched.

"Then why are you just getting back now?" Atticus asked. Ranulf's shoulders grew rigid.

It really was too early for this. I reached over and rested my hand on his firm stomach. His eyes snapped to mine.

"The sun hasn't even come up yet," I reminded him. "He's here on time, it doesn't matter if he's doing the walk of shame." His eyes softened.

"Alright," he muttered before turning back around to eat his breakfast.

Ranulf winked at me as he moved to the end of the counter.

"So, we have a Wrath demon to face this morning," Atticus announced.

"I've never gone up against one before," Ranulf admitted. "What are they like?"

"Huge," I stated, looking up from my plate. "They range from eight to ten feet tall and have armor over their skin that blades can't get through."

"It usually takes a platoon of us to take one down," Zahur added. I nodded in agreement.

"Then how are we going to take this one with just us?" Ranulf asked.

I smiled innocently at him. "Oh, first thing I'll do is blast that armor right off him." Ranulf and Falk smirked. "That'll make him vulnerable to your weapons." I took another bite of toast.

Ranulf chuckled, Zahur nodded, Falk smiled, Atticus... he looked concerned.

"Evelyn-"

"I'm essential on this one," I told him, "and you know it."

He struggled with it for several heartbeats before he sighed. "You're right. I know you are. That doesn't mean I have to like it."

"I'll stay back," I promised. His eyes met mine before he nodded.

The rest of breakfast was talking over strategy. I offered what I could do and when. But otherwise my job was to blow the armor and stay back.

After breakfast everyone geared up and got in the car.

The Wrath demon's crime scene was bloody. As in blood on the walls and soaking the carpet. I really didn't want to go into the apartment. This one had been the worst memory. Wrath demons liked to infect humans with anger until they were ready to kill. Then they let the human go. This man had killed his wife with their three-month-old baby girl in her crib in the next room. The woman had to have known something was wrong with her husband because she hadn't screamed. If she had, she probably would have woken up the baby, and then they both would have been dead. The man that the demon infected committed suicide when he realized what he had done. At least the mess was only in one corner of the living room. I scraped blood off the wall and dropped it into the flame in my hand as usual.

"Just show gargoyles who caused the death of this woman," I said unceremoniously. The apartment was getting to me. I dropped the flame onto the blood. Nothing happened. The ball of fire just sat there. I closed my eyes. There was a thick, armor-like spell that kept my tracking spell from touching the blood. It was being powered by the demon, I just couldn't see where the energy line was. I smiled. "Tricky, tricky, tricky. But not good enough." I closed my eyes and focused. My hand moved over the spell shielding the blood. Heat seared my hand; I hissed and pulled my hand away. I opened my eyes as Atticus took my hand and examined it.

"Zahur," Atticus growled.

I ignored them cleaning and bandaging my hand and looked down at the floor. I couldn't use touch, so I needed a new tactic. I pulled energy, my markings glowed. I was about to change an elemental part of my eyes, and that took a lot of power. I could blast through the demon's spell but then it'd know we were coming. Without knowing where it was hiding today, I couldn't risk it.

"Evelyn?"

"Let go of my hand," I instructed as I closed my eyes. They let me go. "Ignore any sound I make." It was the only warning I gave them. I sent energy to my eyes. In my mind I could see the structures of my eyes. The optic nerves, retina, everything. But it was the macula I was after, the small central area in the retina that contained light sensitive cells and allowed you to see fine details. That was what I wanted to change. I carefully filled them with energy, upping their sensitivity to the level I needed. My eyes burned and streamed as I worked.

I bit back any noise I might make but it probably didn't help. Through the link I could feel Atticus fighting not to grab me and stop me, his chest aching at the sight of tears on my face.

"Done," I announced.

"What did you do?" Atticus growled. Hands were on my face instantly, wiping the tears away.

I kept my eyes closed as my hands caught his so I could explain. "The spell uses a different energy level. I changed my eyes so I can trace it. I'm fine. It won't last long, so we need to hurry."

He helped me to my feet, not releasing my arm. I took a deep breath and opened my eyes. The room almost looked normal, except I could see through the walls to the electrical wires behind them. Okay, not so bad. I looked down at the floor. The spell indeed looked like it was armor, but this armor had a thick cable running from it. I smiled. "Gotcha.

It's nearby." I took Atticus's hand. "I won't be able to look around once we're outside, it'll be too bright."

Atticus squeezed my hand. "I've got you," he assured me. "But later we'll have a chat about altering your body with energy without talking to me first." I resisted the urge to roll my eyes as he walked me out of the apartment.

Soon we were hurrying down the sidewalk and following the line. It wasn't far. The line led to a department store. I kept my eyes on the floor as we followed it to a stairwell that led down. Oh, goody. Everyone else pulled a weapon while Atticus helped me down the stairs. We reached a locked door; Atticus broke it open with his foot. The basement was enormous, full of the store's storage crates. I stopped everyone at a large metal door, then I looked up. Through the door I could see the demon. It was pacing back and forth, chafing under the control of the angel. The energy wound around its ankle like a chain then disappeared through another wall. From what I could see I could tell the angel wasn't here.

I closed my eyes and let them go back to normal. It burned again. I leaned into a parchment scented chest and waited until the pain stopped. Atticus was mentally cursing me, though I doubt he realized I could hear it. When the pain finally passed I stepped back, wiped my face and turned to face the door.

"Here?"

I nodded. Atticus sent the others a look. Everyone got ready. I pulled energy to me as I stayed at the front of the group. Atticus and I would head in first, I'd blast the armor off the demon before he even turned to us, then I would move to the side so the others could get by.

I pulled energy until I was practically vibrating with it. I looked to the others. They all nodded.

Atticus opened the door. The demon began to turn. Black armor was melted onto its red skin. That was all I saw before I threw all the energy I had at the seam under its arm. The energy knocked the demon sideways as it slipped in through his skin and underneath the armor melted onto the first layer. "Boom," I stated. The energy exploded out from the demon, taking the armor and the top layer of skin with it. It screamed in pain.

I barely managed to move to the side before the guys were running past.

"Eve?"

"Fine," I assured him. The sound of fighting was loud. During the next two minutes there was cursing, crashes and walls breaking. The demon was bleeding, but not down. Atticus moved so quickly that I couldn't keep up with where he was. He tried to keep the demon's attention while the others slashed, dodged and tried to do as much damage as possible. Ranulf's battleaxe slashed a gaping wound in its side, but the big boy wasn't going down. Well, I could fix that.

I pulled energy to me and formed a shockwave that would knock it on its back. Its head turned, spotted me with its yellow eyes. It grabbed a large chunk of cement that had fallen from the wall. With the way clear in front of me my hand slapped the floor. The shockwave raced towards the demon, shattering cement as it went. I looked up in time to register that something was flying at me. I couldn't get a barrier up in time. It hit, I dropped to the ground. Pain tore through me, then everything went dark.

Atticus

I WATCHED Evelyn go down hard. The demon dropped to its stomach. I slashed at the demon again and reached for her.

"Eve? Luv?" I sent, my veins starting to boil. There was nothing, no response. "Zahur! Evelyn!" I ordered as my eyes went to the demon who hurt my Mate. It chuckled as everyone backed off the demon and Zahur moved to Evelyn's crumpled body.

"Oh, big mistake," Ranulf declared. I could barely hear him through the blood pounding in my ears. My control shattered. I moved around the beast, slicing the back of its knees to the bone. It was barely a fraction of a second later and my blade cut through its arm at the elbow, severing it. The demon dropped the rest of the way to the floor. Then I was at the other one, severing that one as well. The demon roared. I jerked the battleaxe off Ranulf's shoulder and was back at its legs. Two swift hits and I took them too. The demon roared at being helpless. I walked in front of it so it could see me. Then I drove the axe into the flesh of its shoulders. I proceeded to chop that fucker to pieces for hurting Evelyn. Time didn't matter, no one stopped me, I just kept working.

Eventually Zahur's voice got through to me. "We need to get her home, Atticus!" Then I finally took the head of the begging demon.

I stood over the demon and caught my breath. Ranulf came to me.

"Did ye hear the doc?" he shouted. It got me moving. I handed him his axe then went to Zahur and Evelyn.

She was on her back, blood covered half her face, her arm at a bad angle, clearly broken. Blood covered that arm as well. "Can we move her?" I growled.

"She has at least a concussion, possibly a skull fracture. Move her gently," Zahur warned. I knelt down then gathered my wife's limp body to me as carefully as possible. Zahur supported her head until I was standing and she was in a good spot. Then we started moving. Zahur and I left the clean-up to the others.

Several security people tried to stop us as we walked through the stores, but we ignored them.

By the time we got to the car, sirens could be heard in the distance. Zahur got in back and I laid her in his arms so I could get us out of here without the police following.

Evelyn

I woke up dizzy. I reached up and touched my head. There was a scar near my hairline, what...? It all came back to me. The basement, the Wrath demon, the fight... and that big chunk of cement that hit me before I could throw up a barrier. I groaned. Why didn't I already have a barrier up? Stupid move, Evelyn.

I opened my eyes to the dim light of Atticus's room. Zahur set down one of my books and hopped off the dresser.

"How are you feeling?" he asked in a soft voice. I took stock.

"Like I got hit with a big hunk of wall," I said dryly.

He shook his head then held up his finger and pulled out a pen light. "Follow my finger," he instructed.

"If I end up clucking like a chicken, I'm coming after you," I warned. He chuckled as he examined my eyes.

"Well, no chicken clucking, but I want you to take it easy

for a few more hours," he said, putting the pen light away. "You had a nasty hit to the head, probably a bad skull fracture and a broken arm."

I looked down at my left arm to find it still bandaged. "Did it heal?"

"Yeah, after I got it aligned properly it healed quickly," he said. "I just didn't want to wake you up to take off the bandages." He leaned over me and started taking them off. "By the way, could you call Atticus and tell him you're awake. He's being a dick while hunting the angel with the others right now."

I smiled. Then closed my eyes and reached for him. *"Atty, I'm awake and alright,"* I sent with warmth along our link.

The tremendous relief that radiated down the link left me breathless. *"You're okay? What about your arm? What did Zahur say about your head injuries?"* I winced as his emotions swamped me.

"Can't keep this up, call me," I sent. It was barely five seconds later before my phone rang on the nightstand. Zahur handed it to me.

"Hi," I answered.

"Are your injuries healed?" he demanded. I bent my arm and flexed my fingers. No numbness, everything felt fine.

"Yes, good as new," I reassured him. "How's the hunting going?"

"Don't change the subject. What did Zahur say?" he shot back.

I sighed. "He wants me to take it easy for a few more hours because of my head injuries. Otherwise, I'm good. Now, how's the angel hunt going?"

"We're having to go street by street right now and it's

slow going," he admitted. I thought of the chain of energy around the demon's ankle.

"To keep control of the Wrath demon, it had to be within a couple miles of the department store," I told him.

"We'll head back and see if it's still there." His voice turned gentle. "You scared the hell out of me, Eve." The warmth in his voice made my pulse jump.

"Well, next time I'll have a barrier up before I go in. I usually do, I don't know what happened this time." Then I grinned. "I think you distracted me. Yeah, I'm going with that."

He sighed. "That's your story?"

I smiled. "And I'm sticking to it."

He chuckled. "I've got to get back. Take it easy, alright?"

"No problem. The couch sounds perfect right now," I assured him.

"See you soon."

"Bye."

I hung up then looked at Zahur. "Can I get out of bed now?"

He sighed. "Yes, but if you get dizzy tell me."

I gave him a thumbs up before sitting up at the end of the bed. I paused to see how I felt. No dizziness. I got to my feet and moved to the dresser. I felt grotty and wanted a shower. It took me a moment before I realized I didn't have any pajama bottoms here. Oh well, I grabbed a pair of Atticus's, a white shirt and panties.

My shower was quick; I didn't want to risk getting dizzy and falling. Nothing would be more awkward than having to get help from Zahur. I put my wet hair back in a ponytail and went into the living room. Music was playing. I paused behind the sofa to listen. It sounded... like Christmas music, but not. It was an orchestra and an electric guitar? What?

"Zahur, what's playing?" I asked as I sat in the armchair Atticus usually took.

"Trans-Siberian Orchestra, it's Christmas music," he said. "Haven't you ever heard them before?"

I shook my head. "No, I don't really do Christmas music." But this... this music I liked. It wasn't traditional, I could listen to it.

"Oh, sorry." He went to turn it off.

"No, leave it on," I told him. "I actually like it." He sat back down. I looked around the males' apartment. There was a small Christmas tree in the corner on a table. It was cute. But the gifts under it bothered me. "You guys went shopping for me, didn't you?"

Zahur looked away, suddenly very interested in his book. "Maybe."

I sighed. It was Christmas Eve and I didn't have time to get anything for them. Then I thought of something. "Do you think you guys would be happy with cookies as presents this year?"

Zahur lifted his head at the word cookies. "Yes. Definitely yes."

I smiled. "Okay, what's everyone's favorite?" I went to the pantry and started pulling out ingredients.

We had everything we needed for all the cookies except Ranulf's and Atticus's. I looked up at Zahur. "Could you run down to the store really quickly? I need chocolate chips, icing, and raspberry jam for the shortbread cookies."

He was already shaking his head before I finished. "No, I like my head attached to my body."

"Come on, it'll take five minutes to go to the corner store," I pleaded. "I'll be good, I won't go anywhere. I'll just stay here and get the cookies ready to bake." When he was quiet I added. "I won't even turn on the oven until you get back."

He sighed. "Fine. But if Atticus finds out-"

"I will take all the responsibility," I promised. I gave him the list again, along with colors for Falk's sugar cookies. Then he was gone.

I went back to the kitchen and started Zahur's cookies. Oddly, he likes shortbread. For some reason he seemed like a chocolate chip kind of man.

I listened to the Christmas music and made Christmas cookies. It wasn't until I was balling the dough for the cookie tray that I realized I was actually enjoying this. I smiled to myself. I had a husband, a Mate. I was surrounded by gargoyles who were my friends. It was incredible. Yeah, there was an angel in the city pulling demons through the barriers, but barring that... the last week had been the best one I'd had in decades.

I was starting to wonder if Zahur had to go to a store further away when there was a knock at the door. His hands must be full. I put the dough down and answered. But it wasn't Zahur.

Matthew stood in the doorway, in the same wrinkled suit and mustard-stained tie. My shoulders straightened for the fight. Then he raised his head. His eyes were glowing red. It wasn't Matt. Stunned, his hand shot out and grabbed my neck then lifted me off my feet. I fought his hold.

"Here she is," he growled, the voice wasn't Matt's. It was deep and dark, it sent fear skittering down my spine. Demon. Not just demon. High demon.

"Abaddon," I greeted as I tried to breathe. He smiled and threw me. I flew into the apartment and hit the floor hard. Ignoring the pain, I rolled to my feet. He stepped inside casually, as if he'd been invited. My brain started working again. High demon in ex-boyfriend. Shit. *"Atticus! Abaddon is here!"* Rage shot down the link.

Matt's eyes snapped to me. "No, no, no, we'll have none of that." The link between Atticus and I went cold. He'd blocked it. How? Figure it out later, stay alive now. Where the hell were my weapons? His eyes met mine as he strolled into the kitchen. I moved to the living room area. "I've wanted to have a word with you for some time now"—he dipped his finger into the bowl and tasted the dough—. "but you're always surrounded by those males." He met my eyes. "It's difficult to get you alone."

"Oh. Darn," I said sarcastically.

His eyes shot daggers at me. "I'm here to offer you your life. I suggest you listen."

I raised an eyebrow. "My life isn't yours to offer."

His gaze never left mine. "Then perhaps a job offer is more accurate." He walked around the breakfast counter. I moved toward the door, keeping him as far from me as possible. Hell, running was an option. Not a great one, but if it meant staying alive I'd take it.

"I have a job," I stated.

He scoffed. "I meant one that will keep you alive," he countered as he stepped towards me. "You see, you've taken out a lot of demons. My handler would rather see you dead, but where he sees a threat I see an opportunity."

I smirked. "Your 'handler?' Don't you mean the angel who is holding your leash?"

His eyes flared. "Work for me and you'll live." He looked around the apartment. "Your friends are going to die either way." My temper sparked as he met my eyes again. "That doesn't mean you have to as well."

I smiled and pulled energy, my markings glowed blue, burning lines through my clothes. "I don't think so."

He smiled. "I do love it when you gargoyles fight-" I blasted him through the wall behind him. And the one after that. Drywall dropped to the floor, dust was flung into the air. I didn't wait, I turned to run. Carol of the Bells began to play.

A hand on the back of my neck jerked me away from the door. I grunted as the door came off its hinges. "You surprise me," he whispered into my ear. I drove my elbow into his stomach and stomped on his foot before blasting him back again. His hand took hair with it as he took out the wall between the living room and one of the bedrooms. He sat up among the debris and spit out blood.

"That's the bitch about a mortal body. You get to feel pain," I said dryly. He smiled, then moved. I went to dive behind the couch only to be slammed sideways into the brick wall. I cried out as something inside me broke. He was laughing as he held me a foot off the floor.

"Yeah, but I'm not as attached to mine," he taunted as he raised his other hand. Flame raced over it. Before I could counter he pressed that burning hand onto my chest. I screamed as I pulled energy. I just couldn't think through the agony to use it. His hands left me. I shook as I realized I was still pinned to the wall. Think, Evelyn, think! It was a holding field, had to be. I knew exactly how to counter that. Fury flooded my veins as I opened my hand and ice covered him. He cursed and cried out but I kept at it until he lost his concentration and dropped me to the floor. Now I had both hands free I kept up the stream of energy until I blasted him again. I wasn't thinking about running anymore. I was just going to hurt him as much as possible. I reached up, used my abilities to grab the ceiling and the roof beyond it. Just like the Raskasha, I slammed it down on to him as he was getting to his feet. He dropped. Snow fell into the apartment as I strode towards him, another blast forming in my fist. He burst through the debris, his face bleeding and a smile on his lips.

"Oh, I like you! So lively!" he cheered. I went to blast him again only for him to deflect it back at me. I sidestepped the blast which continued through the inner wall, through the hall and into my apartment. As I turned around he back-handed me, sending me flying into the fireplace. My breath rushed out of me, more pain along my back and ribs. As I struggled to get to my feet it gave him the opportunity he needed. He threw fire around me. My hair singed, my skin began to burn. Fury riding me hard, I looked up and met his eyes through the flames. I pulled the energy from the flames around me. They snuffed out. His smile dimmed. I blasted him again, only this time with lightning. He slammed into the kitchen cabinets, shattering them. I got to my feet and moved around the couches. He wanted to play with fire? Fine. I created a ball of fire in my hand and threw it. He dropped to the floor just before it hit. The cabinets immediately caught fire.

"Oh, what's wrong? Worried what the flame will feel like on that mortal body?" I taunted as I moved out of the living room. The only sound was the crackle of flames as snow fell through the destroyed roof. I began pulling energy, but not to me. Into the sky above.

I wasn't buying his silence. I missed, I know I did. I looked around the room, wondering what his game was. He stepped in front of me out of nowhere. I was hit in the side, something stung. Then I was swinging. I broke his nose, and went in for more. He slashed at me with a bloody blade. Blood? I held his eyes as I felt my side. Warm, sticky liquid coated my fingers. Before it fully registered he kicked me in the chest, knocking me back into the brick outer wall. Something in my back shattered as I hit then dropped. I tried to get up only I couldn't move my legs. Shit! Pain forked through my body as I tried to pull myself away from the wall.

Abaddon cackled as the wall slammed down on me. I cried out as I was pinned to the floor. Bricks covered me from shoulders to feet. I tried to pull myself out but my side and back screamed in agony. Black dots danced in front of my eyes. I needed to stop the bleeding. Focusing, I pulled energy and quickly began closing that. The music was still playing.

Abaddon came over and smiled. "Now you'll listen." I ignored him as he kept talking. "It won't take too long for you to bleed out, so you better make a choice soon." The wound closed, I opened my eyes to glare at him. The energy in the clouds was almost ready. Abaddon tossed a few fire-balls into what was left of the bedrooms. The apartment started to burn. He turned back to me. "Just to give you more incentive." He rubbed his hands together and paced in front of me. Atticus was coming...

"You see, I want your talents. And quite frankly I don't need you, per se, but your body," he explained. I started laughing.

"You just broke my back, you idiot," I told him, laughing through the pain.

"You know your abilities can fix that," he chided. "Since you're not willing, I'm going to take your body and use it to destroy the city." I peeked up at the sky. It was ready.

I met his eyes. "Good luck." I directed the energy from the clouds towards him. The first bolt of lightning hit. So did the next. He started backing away but they kept hitting him as I pushed him back to the kitchen. He couldn't possess me if he couldn't touch me. I left some energy in the clouds just in case. He got to his feet, his clothes singed, his hair sticking out from his head. If I wasn't in so much pain it would have been funny.

His eyes glowed red as he strode towards me. Oh shit. I tried to reach for the clouds, but before I could, something dove from the sky and plowed Abaddon through the remaining walls and into my apartment.

The sounds of fighting reached me. I dropped my head to the floor and tried to think. Falk; he was the fastest flyer. The others wouldn't be far. I tried to pull myself out but it was no good. The weight pressing down on my damaged spine and ribs was killing me. I closed my eyes and pulled energy. I sent it down my spine. I found the shattered pieces and quickly brought them back through the tissue to where they should have been. Then I began piecing it back together. I worked quickly but jigsaw puzzles were never my thing.

There was a huge crash as Falk was thrown back this way. Before he hit anything his wings popped out, flapped enough to slow him and set him down, then his wings were gone again. He was battered and bloody. I didn't know how much longer he could hold out.

Three others dropped through the ceiling. Zahur dropped a plastic shopping bag, Ranulf and Atticus landed in a crouch. Atticus's gaze ran over me then went to Abaddon. "Get her out of here," he ordered. Zahur headed for me, along with Falk. Ranulf and Atticus went after Abaddon.

"What's damaged?" Zahur demanded as they started moving bricks off me.

"Ribs, burn and a fucking shattered vertebra," I grunted.

"Working on that last one." I closed my eyes and focused again while they worked to get me free. It took a little time but I managed to get the pieces back together and lightly fused. It wouldn't survive another hard blow, but right now I just needed it stable and not causing more damage.

I opened my eyes and nodded to Zahur. They each grabbed one arm and pulled me out from under what was left of the bricks. My damaged vertebra strained and I cried out as fire shot down the nerves of my lower body. They stopped moving me.

"We need to go; this place is going to burn to the ground," Falk announced, his voice rough. He carefully moved me to my side then lifted me up into his arms. I screamed into his shoulder as torture racked my body.

"We're going now. Take her, I'll tell the others," Zahur announced.

"Tell them to get clear, the sky is going to tear the place apart," I warned, I didn't have the energy to direct it. Falk shifted me into a better spot. I sobbed in his arms.

"I'm sorry, I know it hurts, we'll fix it soon, Evie," he rasped down at me. I nodded that I heard him. His wings began to flap and we were off the ground. He was a smooth enough flyer that it didn't hurt.

Suddenly raw fury poured through me. I gasped as it hit me.

"*Atty...*" I sent without meaning to.

"*Here.*"

"He's run off, let's get her safe." Atticus's voice was harsh. A hand brushed over my hair, it felt good.

"Lightning is going to hit any minute," I warned.

"Falk, keep her just in case. Ranulf take point, I'll watch your backs. Go!" Atticus ordered.

We started flying, the Christmas music faded away. Then

the sky unleashed on the apartment building, lighting up the night in flashes.

I floated in pain as we flew away.

The sound of church bells began to ring. It was Christmas. I licked my lips.

"Merry Christmas, guys."

EPILOGUE

I don't know how long we flew through the snow, but eventually we landed somewhere. The others spoke, then I was somewhere warm. Falk set me down on something soft. I whimpered in pain.

"Zahur," Falk called. A bag opened somewhere as I opened my eyes. There was a ceiling; a plain, wood-beam ceiling. A needle went into my arm. Everything became kind of blurry.

Zahur came into my sight and started pulling my shirt up so he could see my side. "Looks like she had a stab wound but she healed it." He probed my ribs. I cried out. "Several broken ribs." He dropped my shirt and pulled down the neckline a bit. "And what looks like a third degree burn across her upper chest." He made me look at him. "You said vertebra, did you fix it?"

"A light fusion, won't take a hit but it'll hold until after I rest a bit," I explained. He nodded, then got to work.

"What do you need?" A man's voice asked. Zahur demanded several things.

I floated there, waiting. I looked around the room. Everyone else was here, where was he? I needed to tell him.

"Atty," I called.

"Here." Warmth filled my mind making me want to smile. I opened my eyes and looked again. I didn't see him.

"I can't find you," I sent, the thought laced with confusion. Why wasn't he here? I had to tell him.

"I'm circling back on our trail, making sure we weren't followed," he explained.

"Where am I?"

"Saint Patrick's Church. With the Templars. The others are there, you're safe," he answered gruffly.

Zahur began to rub his healing goop over the handprint burn on my chest. I bit back a curse.

"Why?" I sent through the pain, whimpering aloud.

"I'm sorry Evie, but you don't want this to scar," Zahur explained. I didn't need an explanation, I just needed my husband.

Another prick in the arm. The pain faded. Zahur went back to work on the burn. I floated.

"Evie? Can you hear me?" Zahur called. I nodded. He checked my eyes. "You're going to go to sleep, okay?"

"Atticus," I muttered. I needed to see him first. It was important.

Zahur gave me an understanding smile. "He's checking our trail-" A door slammed open. Zahur turned to look behind him.

The bed dipped on the other side. The scent of parchment filled my nose. I opened my eyes to see Atticus's worried face.

"Falk, check our trail out past two miles," Atticus barked over his shoulder. Then he was taking my hand in his. *"I'm here, luv."* His other hand gently cupped my face.

The world was fading... he was here...

"Love you," I barely told him before the world went dark.

AFTERWORD

To stay up to date visit blbrunnemer.com.
Or join our fan group on Facebook at https://www.facebook.com/groups/TheVeilDiaries/